D1173679

Towers crossed with Freud."

—*Daily Telegraph* (London)

: of the most brilliant and entertaining literary debuts
s year. The precision of his language and the care with
hich he delineates the characters and their environment
s nothing less than astounding." —*Pittsburgh Post-Gazette*

"A nicely turned satire on the notion that the path to spiritual contentment lies in a pristine set of polished wooden floorboards.... *Care of Wooden Floors* indicates that Wiles has an eye for beauty, but an even more impressive eye for ugliness. It's a novel full of impeccably stylish writing."

—*The Guardian* (London)

"This is a terrific first novel, written with a very engaging deadpan wit and an understated sense of the absurd."

—*The Times* (London)

"This novel feels like a blend of Thomas Pynchon's "Entropy,' John Cheever's "The Swimmer,' Edgar Allan Poe's "The Tell-Tale Heart,' and any of Robert Coover's stories that push the limits of realistic actions."

—North American Review

"This novel has everything 7
tences are a pleasure, page
and as a whole, the novel is
precisely cut plank snapping pe
funny, creepy, atmospheric, and
realize that's a lot of adjectives, but
you'll see." —Charles Yu, author of
                How to Live Safely in a Science F

"Funny, beguiling, and quietly profound . . . a wo
well-crafted debut."   —*Times Literary Supplement (*

"If, like me, you've ever thought that your productivi
and creativity would explode if only you could get organized, let this be a (morbidly funny) wake-up call. . . . A
precisely written debut from one who knows the value of
letting loose."   —*Minneapolis Star Tribune*

"Guffaw-out-loud moments . . . married to the horrified
recognition that provokes empathy. A very funny novel
provoking schadenfreude and belly laughs."
                          —*The Independent* (London)

"Highly idiosyncratic, well-written, with a vivid sense of
place—and weirdly compelling."
                     —Michael Frayn, author of *Skios* and *Headlong*

"One of the funniest and cleverest books of the year. . . .
Care of Wooden Floors reads like a farce directed by Al-
fred Hitchcock, and the novel's denouement will surprise
even the most jaded readers."
                    —*Washington Independent Review of Books*

"*Fawlty*

"On
th

THE WAY INN

ALSO BY WILL WILES

Care of Wooden Floors

THE WAY INN

A Novel

WILL WILES

HARPER PERENNIAL

NEW YORK • LONDON • TORONTO • SYDNEY • NEW DELHI • AUCKLAND

HARPER ⬤ PERENNIAL

First published in slightly different form in Great Britain in 2014 by
Fourth Estate.

HarperCollins books may be purchased for educational, business,
or sales promotional use. For information please e-mail the Special
Markets Department at SPsales@harpercollins.com.

FIRST U.S. EDITION

Designed by Fritz Metsch

Library of Congress Cataloging-in-Publication data
has been applied for.

ISBN 978-0-06-233610-1

14   15   16   17   18   OV/RRD   10   9   8   7   6   5   4   3   2   1

For Hazel and Guy,

with my love

The house is the same size as the world;
or rather, it is the world.

"THE HOUSE OF ASTERION"
Jorge Luis Borges

PART ONE

THE CONFERENCE

The bright red numbers on the radio-alarm clock beside my bed arranged themselves into the unfortunate shape of 6:12. Barely four hours since I went to sleep, I was abruptly awake. I remembered that I had been in the bar, and that I had seen the woman again.

Apart from the red digital display—6:13—the room was dark. And the preceding day was clear: I had seen her again, and I had spoken to her. Over the years I had come to believe that my memory was steadily enhancing this woman. Our first encounter was so out of the ordinary that it took on a completely unreal complexion in retrospect, and I suspected that I might be elaborating on it, on her, to make the whole bizarre incident more exotic. But there she was again, matching perfectly what I had assumed was an idealized vision. Her Amazonian height, and her pale skin and red hair—even in the flesh, there was something about her that didn't quite match up to reality, as if she was too high-definition. Just hours later our reunion had already taken on the qualities of a dream. One that had been interrupted before it was complete. Maurice. Maurice had ruined it.

A return to sleep seemed unlikely and unwise. It was less than an hour until the alarm would go off and I had no intention of oversleeping and being forced to head to the fair without a shower and breakfast.

The hotel room was well heated, the carpet soft and warm under my feet. It was quiet, almost silent, but the air conditioner hummed its low hum, and there was something else in the air—a kind of electromagnetic potential, a distorted echo beyond the audible range. Or nothing, just the membranes of the ear settling after being startled from sleep. Outside it would be cold. I opened the curtains but could see little. The sullen orange glow of the motorway to one side, an occluded sky untouched by dawn, and on the level of the horizon a shivering cluster of red lights that suggested, somehow, an oil refinery. Maybe the airport—radar towers, UHF antennae.

I switched on the room lights. Latte-colored carpet, a cuboid black armchair, a desk with a steel and wicker chair, a flat-screen TV on the wall and of course an insipid abstract painting. It was like every other hotel room I've stayed in: bland, familiar, noncommittal, unaligned to any style or culture. I once read that the color schemes in large chain hotels were selected for how they looked under artificial light, on the understanding that the businesspeople staying in the rooms would mostly be there outside daylight hours. And that principle must also apply to the art on the walls—and again I remembered the woman in the bar, what she had said about the paintings. The indistinct background hum seemed a little louder—it had to be the air-con, or the minibar under the desk. It was a benign sound, almost soothing, a suggestion that I was surrounded by advanced systems dedicated to keeping me comfortable.

•

Showering took the edge off my tiredness, and allowed me to ignore it. I put on a Way Inn bathrobe and returned to the bedroom, drying my hair with a Way Inn towel. The TV was on, but showed only the hotel screen that had greeted me on my arrival in the room last night.

WELCOME MR. DOUBLE

Above this was the corporate logo, a stylized *W* in the official red. A stock photo of a group of Way Inn staff, or models playing Way Inn staff, smiled up at me. Room service numbers and pay-TV options were listed underneath. Today's special in the restaurant was pan-seared salmon. The weather for today and tomorrow: fog and rain. Temperature scarce degrees above zero. I picked up the remote and found the BBC News.

The sky had lightened, but the view had not improved. The glass in the window was thick, presumably sound-proofed against the nearby airport, and it gave the landscape a sea-green tint. Mucoid mist shrouded nearly everything. My room was on the second floor of the hotel. Outside was a strip of car park bounded by a chain-link fence, then an empty plot on which a few stacks of orange traffic barriers and half a dozen white vans were slowly sinking into mud. To the extreme right there was a road flanked by a long artificial ridge of earth scabbed with weeds, over which the streetlights of the motorway could be seen. The lights could also be seen reflected in the water-filled ruts that vehicles had left in the scraped-back land; under the mud everything waited to be made over again, more streetlights, more car parking, more windows to look out of.

Many people, I imagine, would find this a depressing

scene. But not me. I love to wake in a hotel room. The anonymity, the fact the room could be anywhere—the features that fill others with gloom fill me with pleasure. I have loved hotels since the first time I set foot in one.

I dressed, half-listening to headlines coming from the TV. It was nothing, everything, all things I knew, had heard before. Events. People crushed against a wall, wailing women somewhere hot, an American ambulance boxy orange and white in that too-bright American style of TV footage, then more familiar video-texture from the UK, flowers zip-tied to a signpost beside a road, tears in camera flashes, an appeal for witnesses. The newsreader looked up from her screen and seemed, for a split second, to be surprised by the sight of cameras. World weather. A list of major cities with numbers beside them, little icons meaning sunshine and storms, a world reduced to a spreadsheet of data points. I flipped open my laptop and it came to life. Heavy black unread emails were heaped in my inbox. Invitations, press releases, mailing lists, flight and hotel bookings. More headlines refreshing in my readers. For a moment I was aware of everything, everything was in reach, and then the WiFi symbol flashed and stuttered. A bubble warned me that my connection was lost, and I snapped my laptop shut. The TV was still on—a palm tree jerked and writhed, thrashing back and forth as debris passed it horizontally and the camera went dead. Unseasonal. The newsreader looked up, saw me, and told me the number of dead. I plucked my keycard from its plastic niche on the wall, killing the room.

•

Myself, reflected to infinity, bending away into an unsee-able gray nothing on a twisted horizon.

The lift came to a smooth halt. My myriad reflections in its mirrored walls stopped looking at one another. The doors opened, revealing the bright lobby and a potbellied man with a moustache, who stared back at me as if astonished that I should be using his lift.

"Sorry," I mumbled, a social reflex, and stepped out.

Music had been playing in the lift, softly, as if it was not meant to be heard. If it was not meant to be heard, why play it at all? To prevent silence, perhaps, to insulate the traveller from isolation and reflection, just as the opposing mirrors provided an unending army of companions that was best admired alone. But I had heard the music, and had been trying to identify it. The answer had come when the doors opened: "Jumpin' Jack Flash," instrumental, in a zero-cal, easy-listening style.

Wet polymers hung in the air. The hotel was new, new, new, and the chemicals used to treat the upholstery and carpets perfumed the lobby. Box-fresh surfaces blazed under scores of LED bulbs. The lobby was a long, corridor-like space connecting the main entrance with one of the building's courtyards. These courtyards were made up to look like Japanese Zen meditation gardens, a hollow square of benches enclosing an expanse of raked gravel, a dull little pond and a couple of artfully placed boulders, slate-slippery with rain. I have stayed in twenty or thirty Way Inn hotels and I have never seen anyone use those spaces to meditate. They use them to smoke. But that's hotels, really—everything is designed for someone else. Meditation gardens you don't meditate in, chairs you don't sit in, drawers you don't fill containing Bibles you don't read. And I don't know who's using those shoe-cleaning machines.

Opposite the reception desk a line of trestle tables had been set up in the night, and were now staffed by public-relations blonds. Business-suited people and mild conversation filled the space between the PRs and the hotel staff, checking in, carrying bags in and out, picking up papers, shaking hands. Beyond a glazed wall, the restaurant was busy. A banner over the trestles read YOU CAN REGISTER HERE.

Very well then. I walked over; confident, unrecognized, at home. These moments, the first contact between myself and the target event, I treasure. They do not yet know who I am, what my role or meaning might be. But I know everything about them.

A blond woman smiled at me from the other side of the table, over a laptop computer and a spread of hundreds of identical folders. "Good morning," I said, holding out a business card. "Neil Double."

She took the card, studied it momentarily, and tapped at the keyboard of the laptop. Although I couldn't see her screen, I knew exactly what she was looking at—my photograph, the personal details that had been fed into the "*required" boxes of an online form six months ago, little else. "Mr. Double," she said, English tinged with a Spanish accent, her smile a few calories warmer than before. "Welcome to Meetex."

A tongue of white card spooled out of the printer connected to the woman's laptop. In a practiced, brisk move, she tore it off, slipped it into a clear plastic holder attached to a lanyard and handed it to me. "You'll need this to get in and out of the center," she said. I nodded, trying to convey the sense that I had done this before, that I had done it dozens of times this year alone, without being rude. But she pressed on, perhaps unable to change course, conditioned by repetition into reciting the script set for her, as powerless as the neat little printer in front of her. "Sure, sure," I said. Panic flickered in her eyes. "Just hang it around your neck—if you want to give your details to an exhibitor, they can scan the code here." A blocky QR code was printed next to my name and that of my deliciously inscrutable employer: NEIL DOUBLE. CONVEX.

"Right," I said.

"You can just hang it around your neck," she repeated, indicating the lanyard as if I might have missed it. In fact it was hard to ignore: a repellent egg-yolk yellow ribbon with the name of the conference center stitched into it over and over. METACENTER METACENTER METACENTER.

"Right," I said, stuffing the pass into my jacket pocket.

"Buses leave every ten or fifteen minutes. They stop right outside. And here's your welcome pack." She handed me one of the folders, smiling like an LED.

I smiled back. "Thanks so much," I said. And I was fairly sincere about it. It's a good idea to stay friendly with the staff at these conferences; I doubted I would see her again, but it was better to be on the safe side. Generally it was a waste of time trying to sleep with them, though—they often couldn't leave their post, and they were kept busy. She had already moved on from me, directing her smile over my shoulder to whoever stood behind me. I saw that she had access to scores of disgusting emergency-services-yellow tote bags from a box beside her, but she had not offered one to me. A shrewd move on her part; I was pleased by her reading of my level of MetaCenter-tote-desire, which was clearly broadcasting at just the right pitch.

Breakfast was served in the restaurant, separated from the lobby by a sliding glazed wall. Flexible space, ready for expansion or division into a large number of different configurations. A long buffet table was loaded with pastries, bread, sliced fruit and cereals. Shiny steel containers sweated like steam-age robot wombs. Flat-screen TVs with the news on mute, subtitles appearing word by word. Current affairs karaoke. I poured coffee into an ungenerous cup from a pot warming next to jugs of orange, grapefruit and tomato juice, and put an apricot Danish and a fistful of sugar sachets on a plate. Then I started my hunt for somewhere to sit. Perhaps half of the seats were taken—lively conversation surrounded me. When a hotel is filled with people all attending the same conference, breakfast can present all sorts of diplomatic hurdles. I am rarely gregarious, and at breakfast time I am at my least social, always preferring to sit alone. This was in no way unusual—the hubbub disguised the fact that many of the diners here were alone, studying phones or newspapers or laptops. The first morning of an event can be the least social, before people fall into two-day friendships and ad hoc social bubbles. But I still had to be careful not to blank anyone who had come to recognize me. At other conferences, I might run into the same people once or twice a year. This one was different. These people I see all the time, everywhere; I am getting to know some of them; far worse, they are getting to know me. My detachment is a crucial part of what I do—these people don't understand that. They love to think of themselves as a "community"; they thrive on "relationships." No "community" includes me. But try telling them that. Or rather, don't try. Try telling them nothing. Adam had been most specific: keep a low profile.

But as I scanned the room looking for the right spot I realized, with a twinge of embarrassment, that I was not only looking out for people to politely evade—I was also trying to find the red-haired woman. But without luck. She was not in the restaurant.

A good spot presented itself. It was in a rank of small tables connected by a long banquette upholstered in white leather—a flexible seating arrangement, designed to suit both groups and lone diners. Two people I recognized were already sitting at one of the tables, and the chemistry of our acquaintance had about the right pH level. Phil's company built the scanners that read bar codes and QR codes. We had talked at length before—it helps me to understand that sort of technology. His companion I knew less well—her name was Rosa or Rhoda, perhaps Rhonda, and she worked for a databasing service. I nodded to them as I sat, an acknowledgement carefully poised between amity and reserve. Let them make the first move. They smiled back, and their low-tempo conversation resumed. Were they sleeping together? Phil was at least fifteen years Rosa/Rhoda's senior, and the ring finger of his left hand had shaped itself to his wedding band, but that meant almost nothing. Industry conventions dissolved other conventions. These events were often the Mardi Gras of their fiscal years: intervals of misrule, free zones where the usual professional and social boundaries were made fluid. At their worst they resembled the procreative frenzies of repressed aquatic creatures blessed with only one burst of heat per lifetime, seething with promiscuity and pursuit. And then, bleary-eyed, the attendees sat quietly on their planes and trains home, and opened their wallets not to buy more drinks, order oysters on room service or pay for another private dance, but to turn around the photos of their kids so they once again face outward. What happened in Vegas, Milan, Shanghai, Luton, stayed there; it stayed where they had stayed, in Way Inn, Holiday Inn, Ibis, Sofitel, Hilton, where nonjudgmental, faceless workers changed their sheets. But the body language between Phil and his companion didn't support my hypothesis. Pretending to read the information pack I had been given, I watched them—I am of course adept at observing unobserved. There was no surreptitious touching, no encrypted smiles. They had the easy manner of friends, but they were talking business—data capture, facial recognition, RFID, retrieval technologies. Little of what they said conflicted with what I knew already.

Since I was staring at the conference program, pretending to read it, I decided that I could divert some attention its way and give some thought to the day ahead. A couple of sessions on the timetable had been flagged up by my clients as mandatory—routine fare such as "The Austerity Conference" and "Emerging Threats to the Meetings Industry"—but it was always good to attend a few extra to get a rounded view of an event. No one expected a comprehensive report from every session—there were three halls of different sizes at the MetaCenter, with talks going on simultaneously in each, and further fringe events in function rooms in the hotels. All I needed was a sample. "Trap or Treat: Venue Contract Pitfalls and How to Avoid Them." To avoid, I think. "China in Your Hands: Event

Management in the Far East." That could be worth attending. By which, I don't mean I expected to find it interesting—or that I did not. The things that interest me are not necessarily the things that will interest my clients. And these trade fair conferences are nearly always very boring. If they were not, I wouldn't have a job. The boring-ness is what fascinates me. I soak it up: boring hotels, boring breakfasts, boring people, boring fucks, boring fairs, the boring seminars and roundtables and product demos and presentations and launches and plenary sessions and Pecha Kuchas, and then I . . . report. These people, the people sitting around me, the people whose work involves organizing and planning the conferences I spend my life attending: if they knew what I was doing, and how I felt about what they did, they might not be pleased.

A tuft of polythene sprouted from a joint on the underside of my table. It had only just been unwrapped. That chemical smell rose from the white leather of the banquette, adulterated but not hidden by the breakfast aromas. Was it real leather or fake leather? Its softness under the fingertips, its overgenerous tactility, felt fake, designed to approximate the better qualities of leather rather than actually possessing them, but I had no way of telling for sure. New leather, certainly. Everything new for a new hotel. Scores of identical chairs and tables. Multiplied across scores of identical hotels. It's big business, making all those chairs and tables, "contract furniture" they call it, carpet bought and sold by the square mile—and I attended those trade fairs and conferences too. If the leather was real, equipping all the hundreds of Way Inn hotels would mean bovine megadeath. But I remembered what the woman had said about the paintings in the bar, and thought instead of a single vast hide from a single unending animal . . .

That was why she was in the bar: she had been photographing the paintings. It was late, past midnight already, and I wanted a quick nightcap before going to my room. One of the night staff served me my whisky and returned to the lobby, where he chatted quietly with a colleague at the reception desk. I had registered that I was not alone in the darkened bar, but no more than that. What made me look up was the flash of her camera. I kept looking because I knew at once that I had seen her before—and, too exhausted for subtlety, I let the meter run out on my chance to gaze undetected, and she raised her head from her camera's LCD display and saw me.

We had met before, I said—not met, exactly, but I had seen her before. She remembered the incident. How could she forget something like that? Naturally, as a mere spectator, I was not part of her memory of what had happened; I was just one of the background people. Her explanation of how she came to be there, in that state, made immediate, obvious sense, but left me embarrassed. To close the horrible chasm that had opened in the conversation, I asked why she was photographing the paintings.

A hobby, she said. The paintings were all over the hotel—in my room, here in the restaurant, out in the lobby, in the bar. And so it was in every Way Inn. They were all variations on an abstract theme: meshing coffee-colored curves and bulging shapes, spheres within spheres, arcs, tangents, all inscrutable, suggestive of nothing. I had never really examined them—they were not there for admiring, they were there simply to occupy space without distracting or upsetting. They were an approximation of what a painting might look like, a stand-in for actual art. They worked best if they decorated without being noticed. All they had to do was show that someone had thought about the walls so that you, the guest, didn't have to. An invitation not to be bothered. Now that she had drawn my attention to them, I could see that she was right—they were everywhere. How many in total? I felt uncomfortable even asking.

"Thousands," she had said, as if sharing a delicious secret. "Tens of thousands. More. Way Inn has more than five hundred locations worldwide. They never have fewer than one hundred rooms. Each room has at least one painting. Add communal spaces. Bars, restaurants, fitness centers, business suites, conference rooms, and of course the corridors . . . At least a hundred thousand paintings. I believe more."

I could see why this was a calculation she delighted in sharing with people—the implications of it were extraordinary. Where did all the paintings come from? Who was painting them? With chairs, tables, carpets, light fixtures, there were factories—big business. But works of art? They weren't prints; you could see the brush marks in the paint. It was thoroughly beyond a single artist.

"There is no painter," she said. "No one painter, anyway. It's an industrial process. There's a single vast canvas rolling out into a production line. Then it's cut up into pieces and framed."

As she said this, she showed me the other photos on her camera, the blip-blip-blip of her progress through the memory card keeping time in her conversation. She was tall, taller than my six foot, and leaned over me as she did this, red hair falling toward me—a curiously intimate stance. The paintings flicked past on the little screen, bright in the gloom. The same neutral tones. The same bland curves and formations. Sepia psychedelia. A giant painting rolling off the production line like a slab of pastry, ready to be stamped into neat rectangles and framed and hung on the wall of a chain hotel . . . there was something squalid about it.

"Why?" I asked. "Why collect something that's made like that? What's so interesting about them?"

"Nothing, individually, nothing at all," she said. "You have to see the bigger picture."

"Late night?"

A second passed before I realized that I had been addressed, by Phil. His conversation with Rosa (or Rhoda) had lapsed. She prodded at her phone. Not really reading, not really listening, I had slipped into standby mode and was staring into space.

I made an effort to brighten. "Quite late," I said. "I got here at midnight." And then I had talked to the woman—for how long?—until Maurice detained me even later. Hotel bars, windowless and with only a short walk to your bed, made it easy to lose track of time.

"I got here yesterday morning," Phil said. "We're exhibiting, so there was the usual last-minute panic . . . got to bed late myself. Slept well, though. Did you get a good room?"

"Yes," I said. In truth I was indifferent to it, precisely as the anonymous designers had intended. Indifferent was good. "It's a new hotel." The same faces, the same conversations. People like Phil—inoffensive, with few distinguishing characteristics and a name resonant with normality. The perfect name, in fact. Phil in the blanks. Once I put it to a Phil—not this Phil—that he had a default name, the name a child is left with after all the other names have been given out. He didn't take it well and retorted that the same could be said of my name, Neil. There was some truth to that.

Phil rolled his eyes. "Too new. Like one of those holiday-from-hell stories where the en suite is missing a wall and the fitness center is full of cement mixers."

The hotel looked fine to me—obviously new, but running smoothly, as if it had been open for months or years. "There's a fitness center?"

"No, no," Phil said. He stabbed a snot-green cube of melon with his fork, then thought better of it and left it on his plate. "I don't know. I'm talking about the skywalk. The hotel is finished, the conference center is finished, but the damn footbridge that's meant to link them together isn't done yet. So you have to take a bus to get to the fair." The melon was lofted once more, and this time completed its journey into Phil. He gave me a disappointed look as he chewed.

"I don't understand," I said, patting the information pack in front of me, a pack that contained a map of the conference facilities, lined up next to one another as neat as icons on a computer desktop. "The conference center is two minutes away, but you have to take a bus?"

"There's a bloody great motorway in the way," Phil said. "No way around it but to drive. We spent half of yesterday in a bus or waiting for a bus."

"What a bore," I said. So it was; I was ready to bask in it. It's part of the texture of an event, and if it gets too much there is always something to distract me. In this case it was Rhoda, Rosa, whatever her name was, still plucking and probing at her phone, although with visibly waning enthusiasm, like a bird of prey becoming disenchanted with a rodent's corpse. Cropped hair, cute up-turned nose—she was divertingly pretty and I remembered enjoying her company on previous occasions. If there was queuing and sitting in buses to be done, I would try to be near her while I was doing it. Sensing my attention, she looked up from her phone and smiled, a little warily.

Behind Rosa, a familiar figure was lurching toward the cereals. Maurice. It was a marvel he was up at all. The back of his beige jacket was a geological map of wrinkles from the hem to the armpits. Those were the same clothes he had been wearing last night, I realized in a moment of terror. I issued a silent prayer: please let him have show-ered. But maybe he wouldn't come over, maybe he would adhere to someone else today. He picked up a pastry, sniffed it and returned it to the pile. A cup of coffee and a plate were clasped together in his left hand, both tilting horribly. My appalled gaze drew the attention of Rosa, who turned to see what I was looking at—and at that moment Maurice raised his eyes from the buffet and saw us. We must have appeared welcoming. He whirled in the direction of our table like a gyre of litter propelled by a breeze. Despite his—our—late night, he glistened with energy, bonhomie, and sweat.

It pains me to admit it, but Maurice and I are in the same field. What we do is not similar. *We are not similar.* We simply inhabit the same ecosystem, in the way that a submarine containing Jacques Cousteau inhabits the same ecosystem as a sea slug. Maurice was a reporter for a trade magazine covering the conference industry, so I was forever finding myself sharing exhibition halls, lecture theaters, hotels, bars, restaurants, buses, trains and airports with him. And across this varied terrain, he was a continual, certain shambles, getting drunk, losing bags, forgetting passports, snoring on trains. But because we so often found ourselves proximal, Maurice had developed the impression that he and I were friends. He was monstrously mistaken on this point.

"Morning, morning all," he said to us, setting his coffee and Danish-heaped plate on the table and sitting down opposite me. I smiled at him; whatever my private feelings about Maurice, however devoutly I might wish that he leave me alone, I had no desire to be openly hostile to him. He was an irritant, for sure, but no threat.

"Glad to see you down here, old man," Maurice said to me, not allowing the outward flow of words to impede the inward flow of coffee and pastry. Crumbs flew. "I was concerned about you when we parted. You disappeared to bed double-quick. I thought you might pass in the night."

"I was very tired," I said, plainly.

"Or," Maurice said, leaning deep into my precious bubble of personal space, "maybe you were in a hurry to find that girl's room!" He started to laugh at his own joke, a phlegmy smoker's laugh.

"No, no," I said. I am not good at banter. What is the origin of the ability to participate in and enjoy this essentially meaningless wrestle-talk? No doubt it was incubated by attentive fathering and close-knit workplaces, and I had little experience of either of those. At the conferences, I was forever seeing reunions of men—coprofessionals, opposite numbers, former colleagues—who had not seen one another in months or years, and the small festivals of rib-prodding, backslapping, insult and innuendo that ensued.

"What's this?" Phil asked, clearly amused at my discomfort. Rosa/Rhoda's expression was harder to read; mild offense? Social awkwardness? Disappointment, or even sexual jealousy? I hoped the latter, pleased by the possibility alone.

"Neil made a friend last night," Maurice said. "I found him trying it on with this girl . . . " he paused, eyes closed, hands raised, before turning to Rosa: " . . . excuse me, this *woman* . . . in the bar."

"Jesus, Maurice," I said, and then turning to Rosa and Phil: "I ran into someone I know last night and was chatting with her when Maurice showed up. Obviously, at the sight of him, she excused herself and went to bed."

Maurice chuckled. "I don't know. You looked pretty smitten. Didn't mean to cock-block you."

"*Jesus*, Maurice."

"You're a dark horse, Neil," Phil said.

"Just a friend," I said, directing this remark mostly at Rosa/Rhoda.

"Of course, of course," she said. Then she stood, holding up her phone like a get-out-of-conversation-free card. "Excuse me."

"So, what's her name, then?" Maurice asked. "Your friend."

A sickening sense of disconnection rose in my throat. I didn't know her name. Against astonishing odds I had reencountered the one truly memorable stranger from the millions who pass through my sphere, and I had failed to ask her name or properly introduce myself. I had kept the contact temporary, disposable, when I could have done something to make it permanent. Maurice's arrival in the bar had broken the spell between us, the momentary intimacy generated by the coincidence, before I had been able to capitalize on it. And now I was failing to answer Maurice's question. He surely saw my hesitation and sense the blankness behind it.

"Because you could ask the organizers, leave a message for her. They might be able to find her."

"She's not here for the conference," I said, relieved that I could deviate from this line of questioning without lying.

"Not here for the conference?" Maurice said, now blinking exaggeratedly, pantomiming his surprise in case anyone missed it. All of Maurice's expressions were exaggerated for dramatic effect. When not hamming it up, in moments he believed himself unobserved, his expression was one of innocent, neutral dim-wittedness. "She must be the only person in this hotel who isn't! Good God, what else is there to do out here?"

"She works for Way Inn."

"Oh, right, chambermaid?" Maurice said, and Phil barked a laugh.

I smiled tolerantly. "She finds sites for new hotels—so I suppose she's checking out her handiwork."

"So she's to blame," Phil said. "Does she always opt for the middle of nowhere?"

"I think the conference center and the airport had a lot to do with it."

"Aha, yes," Maurice said. Without warning, he lunged under the table and began to root about in his satchel.

Then he reemerged, holding a creased magazine folded open to a page marked with a sticky note. The magazine was *Summit*, Maurice's employer, and the article was by him, about the MetaCenter. The headline was ANOTHER FINE MESSE.

"I came here while they were building it," Maurice said. He prodded the picture, an aerial view of the center, a white diamond surrounded by brown earth and the yellow lice of construction vehicles. "Hard-hat tour. It's huge. Big on the outside, bigger on the inside: 115,000 square meters of enclosed space, 15,000 more than the ExCel Center. Thousands of jobs, and a catalyst for thousands more. Regeneration, you know. Economic development."

I heard her voice: enterprise zone, growth corridor, opportunity gateway. That lulling rhythm. I wanted to be back in my room.

"Did you stay here?" Phil asked.

"Nah, flew in, flew out," Maurice said. "This place is brand-new. Opened a week or two ago, for this conference I'm told."

"So they say," I said, just to make conversation, since there appeared to be no escaping it for the time being. To make conversation, to keep the bland social product rolling off the line, word shapes in place of meaning. While Phil again explained the unfinished state of the pedestrian bridge and our tragic reliance on buses, I focused on demolishing my breakfast. Maurice took the news about the buses quite well—an impressive performance of huffing and eye-rolling that did not appear to lead to any lasting grievance. "The thing is," he said, as if communicating some cosmic truth, "where there's buses, there's *hanging around.*"

There was no need for me to hang around. My coffee was finished, my debt to civility paid.

"Excuse me," I said, and left the table.

Back in my room, housekeeping had not yet called, and the risen sun was doing little to cut through the atmospheric murk beyond the tinted windows. The unmade bed, the inert black slab of the television, the armchair with a shirt draped over it—these shapes seemed little more than sketched in the feeble light. Before dropping my keycard into the little wall-mounted slot, which would activate the lights and the rest of the room's electronic comforts, I walked over to the window to look out. It wasn't even possible to tell where the sun was. Shadowless damp sapped the color from the near and obliterated the distant. The thick glass did nothing to help; instead it gave me a frisson of claustrophobia, of being sealed in. I looked at its frame, at all the complicated interlayers and the seals and spacers holding the thick panes in place: high-performance glass, insulating against sound and temperature, allowing the hotel to set its own perfect microclimate in each room.

A last look as I recrossed the small space—the brightest point in the room was the red digital display of the radio-alarm on the bedside table. I slid the card in the slot and the room came alive. Bulbs in clever recesses and behind earth-toned shades. Stock tickers streamed across the TV screen. In the bathroom, the ascending whirr of a fan. I brushed my teeth, stepping away from the sink to look at the painting over the desk, the only example of the hotel's factory-made art in my room. The paintings in the bar had seemed so threatening last night—remembering the moment, the threat had come not from what lay within their frames but from the possibility of what lay outside them.

You have to look at the bigger picture, she said—and she meant it literally. If the paintings were simply scraps of a single giant canvas, they could be reassembled. And if they were reassembled, what picture formed? We were being fed, morsel by morsel, a grand design. "A representation of spatial relationships" was how she described it. Her work, she said, involved sensing patterns in space—finding sites that were special confluences of abstract qualities, where the curving lines of a variety of economic, geographic and demographic variables converged. A kind of modern geomancy, a matter of instinct as much as calculation. She had a particular gift for seeing these patterns, any patterns. And the paintings formed a pattern. She was certain.

After midnight and after whisky, the idea found some traction with me. But in the morning, with the lights on, it sounded absurd. The artwork before me was simply banal, and I could not see that multiplying it would do anything but compound its banality. A chocolate-colored mass filled the lower part of the frame, with an echoing, paler—let's say latte—band around it or behind it, and a smaller, mocha arc to the upper left. Assigning astral significance to such a mundane composition was, frankly, more than simply eccentric, it was deranged. She had spent too long looking for auspicious sites and meaningful intersections for hotels, and was applying her divination to areas where it did not apply. I tried to trace the lines of the painting beyond the frame, to imagine where they might go next, extrapolating from what I could see. Spheres. Conjoined spheres. Nothing more. Spatial relationships—what did that even mean?

Spit, rinse. Bag, credentials, keycard. The shadows returned and I closed the door on them.

Music while waiting for the lift: easy-listening "Brown Sugar." The lift doors were flanked by narrow full-length mirrors. Vanity mirrors, installed so people spend absent minutes checking their hair and don't become impatient before the lift arrives. Mirrors designed to eat up time— there was some dark artistry, it's true, but a decorators' trick, not a cabalistic conspiracy. A small sofa sat in the corridor near the lift, one of those baffling gestures toward domesticity made by hotels. It was not there to be sat in— it was there to make the corridor appear furnished, an insurance policy against bleakness and emptiness.

In fact, given that this was a new hotel, it was possible, even likely, that no one had ever sat in it. An urge to be the first gripped me, but the lift arrived. Several people were already in it, blocking my view of infinity.

The first time I saw a hotel lobby, it was empty. Not completely empty, in retrospect: there were three or four other people there, a few suited gentlemen reading newspapers and an elderly couple drinking tea. And the hotel staff, and my father and mother. But my overriding impression was plush emptiness. Tall, leather, wing-back armchairs, deep leather sofas riveted with buttons that turned their surfaces into bulging grids. Lamps like golden columns, ashtrays like geologic formations, a carpet so thick that we moved silently, like ghosts.

Who was this fine place for? Surely not for me, a boy of six or seven—it had been built and furnished for more important and older beings. But where were they? When did they all appear?

"Who stays in hotels?" I asked my father.

"Businessmen," my father said. "And travellers. Holidaymakers. People on honeymoon." He smiled at my mother, a complex smile broadcasting on grown-up frequencies I could detect but not yet decode. My mother did not smile back.

A waiter had appeared, without a sound. My father turned back to me, his smile once more plain and genial, eager to please his boy. "What would you like to drink?"

"What is there?"

"Anything you like."

"Coca Cola?" I said, unable to fully believe that such a cornucopia could exist, that I could order any drink at all and it would be delivered to me.

Mother straightened like a gate clanging shut. "We mustn't go off our heads with treats. How much will this cost?" The question went to the waiter but her eyes were on me and my father, warning.

"Darling, the company will pay."

"Will they? Do they know it's for him? Is that allowed?"

"They won't know, and if they did, they wouldn't mind. It's just expenses."

Expenses—another word freighted with adult mystery. Expenses, I knew, meant something for nothing, treats without consequences, the realm of my father; a sharp contrast to the world of home, which was all consequences. And expenses meant conflict, but not this time.

My father sold car parts, but he never called them car parts—they were always auto parts. Later, I learned specifics: he worked for a wholesaler and oversaw the supply of parts to distributors. This meant continual travel, touring retailers around the country. He was away from home three out of four nights, and at times for whole weeks. I yearned for the days he was home. We would go to the park, or go swimming—nothing I did not do with my mother, but the experience was transformed. He brought an anarchic air of possibility to the slightest excursion. A gleam in his eye was enough to fill me with mad joy. It was life as it could be lived, not as it was lived.

This was, in my father's words, "a proper hotel"—plush and slightly stuffy; English, not American; not part of a chain. It was in a seaside resort town, far enough from home for the company to pay for a room, but close enough for me and my mother to join him for a brief holiday, a desperate experiment in combining his peripatetic career with home and child-rearing. A fun and, much more important, *normal* time would be enjoyed by all—such was my mother's anxiety on these points that she successfully robbed herself of any enjoyment. The hotel was quiet because it was off-season. Winter coats were needed for walks along the gray beach; the paint was bright on the signs above the metal shutters, though the neon stayed unlit. The town was asleep, and we were intruders. In the hotel, we dined quietly among empty tables, an armory of cutlery glinting unused, table linen like snow undisturbed by footsteps. I roamed the corridors. The ballroom was deserted and smelled of floor polish. The banqueting hall was a forest of upturned chairs on tables. Everything was waiting for others to arrive, but who, and when? What happened here was of great importance and considerable splendor, but it happened at other times, and to unknown persons. Not to me.

Maybe my father moved in that world, where things were actually happening. There was a provisional air to him, as if he was conserving himself for other purposes. Even when he was physically present, he conducted himself in absences. He smoked in the garden and made and received telephone calls, speaking low. I would listen, taking care that he did not see me, trying to learn about the other world from what he said when he thought no one was listening. But he spoke in code: *magneto, camshaft, exhaust manifold, powertrain, clutch.* And rarer, another code: *yes, special, away, not until, weekend, she, her, she, she.*

I was missing something.

The other lift passengers and I debarked into a lobby that had filled with people: sitting on the couches, standing in groups, talking on or poking at phones. Normally these communal places—the lobbies, the foyers, the atria—are barely used, inhabited only fleetingly by people on their way elsewhere, checking in or out, perhaps alone on a sofa waiting for someone or something. To see the space at capacity, teeming with people, was curiously thrilling, like observing by chance a great natural migration. This was it: I was present for the main event, when the hotels were at capacity and the business centers hosted back-to-back videoconferences with head offices all over the planet. I could see it all for what it was and what it wasn't.

Because even when thronged with people, the lobby is still uninhabited—it cannot really be occupied, this space, or made home; it is a channel people sluice through. Those people sitting on the sofas don't make the furniture any more authentic than the maybe-virgin seat I had seen by the lift. The space isn't *for* anyone. My younger self might have been troubled by this thought, that even the main event could not give the space purpose—but now I had come to realize that the sensation was simple existential paranoia. I recognized the limits of authenticity.

Where there are buses, there is hanging around; Maurice's dictum was quite correct. The driveway outside the hotel was protected by a porte-cochere. Under this showy glass and steel canopy, three coaches idled while conference staff in high-visibility tabards pointed and bickered, and desultory clusters of dark-suited guests smoked and hunched against blasts of cold, wet wind. The buses were huge and shiny, gaudy in banana-skin livery; their doors were closed. Evidently a disagreement or communications breakdown was under way—the attendants listened with fraught attention to burbling walkie-talkies, staring at nothing, or shouted at and directed one another, or jogged about, or consulted clipboards, but nothing happened as a result of this pseudoactivity.

I was about to retreat behind the glass doors, back to the warmth and comfort of the lobby, when I spotted Rosa (or Rhoda) standing alone among the huddle waiting for the buses, cigarette in one hand, phone apparently fused to the other. She had put on a brightly colored quilted jacket and seemed unbothered by the cold and the icy raindrops that the wind pushed under the shelter.

"Hey," I said.

Rosa looked at me without obvious emotion, although her neutrality could be read as wariness. "Hey."

"What's going on?" I said, nodding in the direction of the buses, where frenzied stasis continued. She looked momentarily dejected, and shrugged. We would never know, of course. The cause of this sort of holdup was rarely made clear, it was just more nontime, nonlife, the texture of business travel. Hotel lobbies and airport lounges are built to contain these useless minutes and soothe them away with comfortable seats, agreeable lighting, soft music, mirrors and pot plants.

"I'm sorry we didn't get much of an opportunity to talk back there," I said. Rosa's edge of frostiness toward me, her shrugs and monosyllables, bothered me. I was certain we had got on well in the past, and she seemed an excellent candidate for some conference sex, if we could get past this *froideur*. My failure to capitalize on the coincidence in the bar last night had left a sour aftertaste. Some sex would dispel that; it would divert me, at least. If Rosa reciprocated.

"You seemed busy," she said.

"Nothing important."

"Who was that man who joined us?"

"Maurice? I thought you knew him. A reporter, for a trade magazine."

"I've seen him around."

"He's hard to miss."

"A friend of yours?"

"Not really."

"So this girl he mentioned . . . "

Sexual jealousy, was it? That was a promising sign.

"You shouldn't believe a word Maurice says," I said. "He was only trying to stir up trouble. I was having a drink with an acquaintance. You know how you keep running into the same people at these things. Which can be a very good thing."

"Yeah." I was rewarded with a shy smile. Pneumatics hissed—one of the buses was opening its doors at last.

I decided not to overplay my hand—there would be other opportunities. "Really good to see you again," I said. "Let's talk later."

"Sure," she said. "I'd like that." Her mobile phone, briefly removed from the social mix, reappeared like a fluttering fan.

Boarding the bus, I felt heartened by the encounter. It wouldn't be too difficult after all.

The bus filled quickly, but there was a further mysterious delay before it got moving. Still, it was warm and dry, and the throbbing engine was as soothing as the ocean. The air had a chemical bouquet—new, everything was new. I stared at the patterned moquette covering the seat in front of me. Blue-and-gray squares against another gray. Hidden messages, secret maps? No, just a computer-generated tessellation reiterating to infinity. People milling around outside. New tarmac. A woman sat in the seat next to mine; I appraised her with a half-glance and found little that interested me. She ignored me and thumbed her phone, her only resemblance to Rosa.

Movement. One of the organizers appeared at the front of the bus, craning her neck as if looking for someone among the passengers. The bus doors closed with a sigh;

the organizer sat down. The engine changed its pitch and we moved off.

We drove along an access road parallel to the motorway. The motorway itself was hidden from view by a low ridge engineered to deaden the howl of the high-speed traffic. The beneficiaries of this landscaping were a row of chain hotels: the Way Inn behind us, ahead a Novotel, a Park Plaza and a Radisson Blu, all in the later stages of construction, surrounded by hoardings promising completion by the end of the year. Here was the delayed skywalk: an elegant glass-and-steel tube describing most of an arch over the access road, the ridge and the unseen motorway, but missing a central section, the exposed ends sutured with hazard-colored plastic. On the Way Inn side of the road, the skywalk joined the beginnings of an enclosed pedestrian link between the hotels at the first-floor level. Eventually guests would be able to stroll to the Meta-Center in comfort, protected from the climate and the traffic, but only the Way Inn section was finished. Perhaps all this construction work was evidence of industry, investment, applied effort—but the scene was, as far as I could see, deserted. There were no other vehicles on the road.

Signs warned of an approaching junction and myriad available destinations. The bus circled the intersection, giving us a glimpse down on-ramps of the motorway beneath us, articulated lorries thundering through six lanes of filthy mist, and then of the old road, a petrol station's bright obelisk, sheds, used cars. We didn't take either of those routes. Instead the bus turned onto another access road, again parallel to the motorway, but on the opposite side. A vast object coalesced in the drizzle: eight immense white masts in two ranks of four suggesting the boundary of an area the size of a small town, high-tension steel crosshatching the air above. The MetaCenter. My first instinct was to laugh. For all its prodigious size and expense, and the giddying alignment of business and political interests it represented, there was something very basic about it. It was, in essence, a giant rectangular tent, with guy ropes strung from the masts supporting its roof, keeping the rain off the fair inside. Plus roads and parking. So there it was, the ace card for the economic planning of this whole region: a very big dry place that's easy to get to. And easy to see——the white masts, as well as holding up the immense space-frame roof, were a landmark to be noticed at speed from the motorway; while from a circling plane, the white slab would glare among the dull gray and brown of its hinterland.

The bus was off the access road now, onto the MetaCenter's own road network: bright yellow signs pointed to freight loading, exhibitors' entrances, bus and coach drop-off. Flower beds planted with immature shrubs were wrapped in shiny black plastic, a fetishist's garden. There, again, was the ascending loop and expressive steel and glass of the unfinished pedestrian bridge. A handshake the size of a basketball court dominated the white membrane of the façade, overwritten with the words WELCOME MEETEX: TOMORROW'S CONVENTIONS TO-DAY. This was accompanied by multistorey exhortations from a telepresence software company: JOIN EVERYONE EVERYWHERE.

A zigzag curb, coaches nosing up to it diagonally. We dropped out of the front door one by one in the stunned way common to bus passengers, however long their journey. But we recovered quickly——no one lingered in the half-rain—and we scurried toward the endless glass doors of the MetaCenter, past an inflatable credit card that shuddered and jerked against the ropes securing it to the concrete forecourt.

Hot air blasted me from above, a welcoming blessing from the center's environmental controls. Thinking about my hair, I ran a hand through it, a wholly involuntary action. Gray carpet flecked with yellow. Behind me, someone said, "Next year we're going to Tenerife, but I don't want it to be just a box-ticking exercise." Queues navigated ribboned routes to registration and information desks. Memory-jogged, I fished my credentials out of my jacket pocket and slipped the vile lanyard over my head. Door staff approved me with a flicker of their eyes.

A broad ramp poured people down into the main hall of the MetaCenter. Gravity-assisted, like components on a production line or animals in a slaughterhouse, we descended, enormous numbers of us—a whole landscape shaped to cope with insect quantities of people. Hundreds of miles of vile yellow lanyard had been woven, stitched with METACENTER METACENTER METACENTER thousands of times to be draped around thousands of necks now prickling in the bright light and outside-inside air of the hall. Ahead of us, and already around us, were the exhibitors, in their hundreds, waiting for all those eyes and credentials and job titles to sluice past them. There is the expectant first-day sense that business must be transacted, contacts must be forged, advantages must be gleaned, trends must be identified, value must be added, the whole enterprise must be made worthwhile. Everyone is at the point where investment has ceased and the benefits must accrue. A shared hunger, now within reach of the means of fulfillment. Like religion, but better; provable, practical, purposeful, profitable.

At another fair, in other company, these thoughts might have been mine alone. Not here. All those thousands of conferences, expos and trade fairs around the world, of which I have attended scores if not hundreds—their squadrons of organizers comprise, naturally enough, an industry in itself. And also naturally enough, this industry revels in get-togethers. It wants, it truly needs, its own conferences, meetings, summits and expos. Its people spend their lives selling face-to-face, handshake, eye contact, touch and feel, up close and personal, in the flesh, meet and greet. They believe their own pitch—of course they do. They actually think they are telling the truth, rather than just hawking a product. (*Our* pitch is very different.)

A conference of conference organizers. A meeting of the meetings industry. And they all knew the recursive nature of their gathering here—they all joked about it, essentially telling the same joke over and over, draining it of meaning until it is nothing more than a ritualized husk, but they laugh all the same. Just *a* conference of conference organizers, one among many—Meetex joins EIBTM, IMEX, ICOMEX, EMIF and Confex on the calendar, and all of those will include the same jokes and the same small talk, redundancy piled on redundancy, spread out across the globe. This repetition proliferating year after year was enough to bring on a headache. And indeed a headache had stirred since I left the hotel, accelerated perhaps by the stuffy bus and its throbbing engine, its boomerang route, the swinging 360-degree turn it had made around the motorway junction.

Hosting Meetex was a smart move by the Meta-Center—this space, which could swallow aircraft hangars whole, was in a way the biggest stall at the fair, advertising its services to the people who, captivated by its quality as a venue, would fill it with gatherings of other industries in the coming years. The airport! The motorway! The convenience! The state-of-the-art facilities! The thousands of enclosed square meters! A space without architecture, without nature, where everything outside is held at bay and there is no inside—no edges, the breezeblock walls too distant to see, a blankness above the steel frame supporting scores of lights. But inside this hall was a space with too much design. The fair, the exhibitors, all *exhibiting*. It was an assault on the eyes, a chaos of detail, several hundred simultaneous demands on your attention. And it was active, it came to you with bleached teeth and a tight T-shirt. Many stands were attended by attractive young women, brightly dressed and full of vim; there must be an inoffensive technical term for them, perhaps along the lines of "brand image enhancement agents," but they are mostly referred to as booth babes. They jump out at you, try to coax you to try a game or join a list, or they hand you a flier or a low-value freebie like a USB stick or a tote bag.

Combined, these multitudinous pleas—each an invitation to enter a different corporate mental universe and devote yourself to it; invitations that are the product of enormous investments of time and money and creativity—formed a barrage of imagery and information and signs and symbols that at first challenged the brain's ability to process its surroundings, becoming an undifferentiated blaze of visual abundance, overwhelming our monkey apparatus like lens flare. Which was precisely the point—it was in the interest of the organizers and the host to dazzle you, to leave the impression that there's not just enough on show, there's more than enough, far more than enough, a stupefying level of surplus. For a fair to imply that it might have limits is anathema—that's why they rain down the stats and the superlatives, the square meters and the daily footfall, the record numbers of this and that. What other industry stressed that its product was near-impossible to consume? No wonder my services were needed. Adam was a genius.

It wasn't impossible to see a whole show on this scale, but it was difficult. It took work. You had to be systematic, go aisle by aisle, moving up the hall in a zigzag, giving every stand some time but not so much time that it diminished the time given to others. That used to be my approach, but I found that route planning and time management occupied more of my thoughts than the content of the show itself. I was lost in the game of trying to see every stand, note every new product and expose myself to every scrap of stimuli—the show as a whole left only a shallow track on my memory. And my reports were similarly shallow. They were evenhanded but lacked any texture; they were mere aggregations of data. In being systematic, I saw only my own system. Completism was blindness: it yielded only a partial view.

After a year of trudging around fairs in this manner, I realized my reports were formulaic and stale, full of ritual phrases and repeated structures. And the entire point of the endeavor was to spare clients that endless repetition.

They employed me because they already knew the routine aspects of these fairs or didn't care to know them—what they wanted was something else. So I threw away my diligent systems and timetables and started to truly explore. Today was typical of my current method of not having a method—I would strike out into the center of the hall, ignoring all pleas and distractions, and from there walk without direction. I would try to drift, to allow myself to be carried by the current and eddies of the hall, thinking only in the moment, watching and following the people around me. Beyond that, I tried to think as little as possible about my overall aims and as much as possible about what was in front of me at any given time. I would give myself to the experience, keep my notes sparse, take a few photos. It's not easy to be purposefully random, but it pays. Once I started taking this approach, my reports became colorful and impressionistic. They were filled with telling details and quirky insights. The imperfection of memory became a strength.

It's only on the second and subsequent days of a fair that I seek out the specifics that clients have requested and conduct any inquiries they might have asked for. More detail accrues naturally, organically, around these small quests.

Surrounded by conference organizers, I am the only professional conference-goer. It's what I do; nothing else. And they—the people here, the exhibitors, the venues, the visitors, the whole meetings industry—have no idea.

The stands passed by, hawking bulk nametags, audiovisual equipment, seating systems, serviced office space. Not just office space—all kinds of space are packaged and marketed here, and places too. You can get a good deal, a great deal, on Vietnamese-made wholesale tote bags at Meetex, but what it and its competitors mostly trade in is locations. Excuse me, "destinations." Cities, regions, countries; all were ideal for your event, whether they were Wroclaw, Arizona or Sri Lanka, or Taipei, Oaxaca or Israel. All combined history and modernity. All were the accessible crossroads of their part of the world. All were gateways and hearts. All had state-of-the-art facilities that could be relied upon. All had luxurious yet affordable hotels. Most important, all of these hundreds of places across the world were distinctive, unique and outstanding. Consistently, uniformly so.

Those comfortable, cost-effective hotels and state-of-the-art facilities were also present at Meetex. Other conference centers promoted themselves, boasting of the inexhaustible square kilometers they had available on scores of city outskirts. Within a giant space, I was being coaxed to other giant spaces; a fractal shed-world, halls within halls within halls.

Another section was devoted to the chain hotels, and its promises of pampering and revitalization were hard to bear. Women wrapped in blinding white towels, cucumber slices over eyes. Men, ties AWOL, drinking beer in vibrant bars. Couples clinking capacious wineglasses over gourmet meals. Clean linen, gleaming bathrooms, spectacular views. These were highly seductive images for me. I wanted to be back at the hotel, reclining on the bed, taking a long shower, ordering a room service meal, perhaps with some wine thrown in.

It mattered little that the images were a total fiction—

posed by models, supplied by stock photo agencies, the gourmet food made of plastic, the views computer generated, the bar a stage set—the desire they generated was real. Meetex was dominated by these deceitful images, defined by them. The location on sale is immaterial. The picture, the money shot, is nearly identical everywhere: a gender-mixed, multicultural group unites around an arm-outstretched, gap-bridging handshake, glorying in it; game-show smiles all around, with an ancient monument or expressive work of modern architecture as the backdrop. Business! Being Done! The transcendent, holy moment when The Deal is Struck. Everyone profits! And in unique, iconic, spectacular surroundings, heaving with antiquities and avant-garde structures, the people bland and attractive, their skin tones a tolerant variety but all much alike, looking as if they have just agreed to the sale of the world's funniest and most tasteful joke while standing in the lobby of a Zaha Hadid museum.

If they only looked around. Business was done in places like the Way Inn, or in giant sheds like the MetaCenter. Properly homogenized environments, purged of real character like an operating theater is rid of germs. Clean, uncorrupt. That's where deals are struck—in the Gray Labyrinth. And that's where I headed, because I had business to attend to.

The Gray Labyrinth took up the rear third of the center's main hall. This space was set aside for meetings, negotiations and deal-making, subdivided into dozens of small rooms where people could talk in private. It was the opposite of the visual overload of the fair, a complex of gray fabric-covered partitions with no decoration and few signs. All sounds were muffled by the acoustic panels. The little numbered cubicles were the most basic space possible for business—a phone line, a conference table topped with a hard, white composite material, some office chairs. Sometimes they included a potted plant, or adverts for the sponsor company that had supplied the furnishings. Mass-produced bubbles of space, available by the half-hour, where visitors videoconferenced with their home office or did handshake deals. They loved to talk about the handshake, about eye contact, about the chairman's Mont Blanc on a paper contract—these anatomical cues you could get only from meeting face-to-face. They wanted primal authenticity, something that could be simulated but could never be equalled. But it all took place in a completely synthetic environment—four noise-deadening, view-screening modular panels, a table, some chairs, a phone line. Or, nowadays, a well-filled WiFi bath in place of the latter.

I had booked cubicle M-A2-54 for 10:30 a.m. It was empty when I arrived, four unoccupied office chairs around a small round table. A blank whiteboard on a gray board wall. No preparation was needed for the meeting and I sat quietly, drumming my fingers on the hard surface of the table, listening to the muted sounds that carried over the partitions.

The prospect was seven minutes late, but I didn't let my irritation show when he arrived, and greeted him with the warm smile and firm handshake I know his kind admire.

"Neil Double. Pleasure to meet you." False—I am indifferent about the experience. Foolish to place so much faith in a currency that is so easily counterfeited.

"Tom Graham. Likewise." Graham was an inch or two shorter than I was but much more substantial—a man who had been built for rugby but, in his forties, was letting that muscle turn to butter in the rugby club bar. His thick neck was red under the collar of his Thomas Pink shirt. Curly black hair, sprinkled with gray, over the confident features of a moderately successful man. We sat opposite each other.

"So, Tom, why are you here?"

He jutted his bottom lip out and made a display of considering the question.

"A friend told me about your service, and I wanted to find out more about it."

Word of mouth, of course—we don't advertise.

"I meant," I said, "why are you here at the conference? Aren't there places you would rather be? Back at the office, getting things done? At home with your family?"

"Aha," Tom said. "I see where you're going."

"Conferences and trade fairs are hugely costly," I said. "Tickets can cost more than two hundred pounds, and on top of that you've got travel and hotel expenses, and up to a week of your valuable time. And for what? When businesses have to watch every penny, is that really an appropriate use of your resources?"

"They can be very useful."

"Absolutely. But can you honestly say you enjoy them? The flights, the buses, the queues, the crowds, the bad food, the dull hotels?"

Tom didn't answer. His expression was curious—not interested so much as appraising. I had an unsettling feeling that I had seen him before.

I continued. "What if there was a way of getting the

useful parts of a conference—the vitamins, the nutritious tidbits of information that justify the whole experience—and stripping out all the bloat and the boredom?"

"Is there?"

"Yes. That's what my company does."

I am a conference surrogate. I go to these conferences and trade fairs so you don't have to. You can stay snug at home or in the office and when the conference is over you'll get a tailored report from me containing everything of value you might have derived from three days in a hinterland hotel. What these people crave is insight, the fresh or illu-minating perspective. Adam's research had shown that people needed to gather only one original insight per day to feel a conference had been worthwhile. These insights were thin gruel, such as "printer companies make their money selling ink, not printers" or "praise in public, criti-cize in private." But if Graham got back from a three-day conference with three or four of those ready to trot out in meetings, he'd feel the time had been well spent. That might sound like a very small return on investment, and it is, but these are the same people who will happily gnaw through cubic meters of an airport-bookshop management tome in order to glean the three rules of this and seven secrets of that. Above those eye-catching brain sparkles, a handful of tips, trends and rumors is all that sticks in the memory from these events, and they can get that from my report, plus any specific information they request. Want to know what a particular company is launching this year? Easy. Want a couple of colorful anecdotes that will give others the impression you were at the event? Done. Just want to be reassured that you didn't miss anything? My speciality.

And if you want to meet people at the conference, be there in person, look people in the eye and press the flesh—well, we can provide that as well. I'll go in your place. Companies use serviced office space on short lets, the exhibitors here have got models standing in for employees and they use stock photography to illustrate what they do. That pretty girl wearing the headset on the corporate website? Convex can provide the same professional service in personal-presence surrogacy. We can provide a physical, presentable avatar to represent you. Me. And I can represent dozens of clients at once for the price of one ticket and one hotel room, passing on the savings to the client.

Of course I still have to deal with the rigmarole of actual attendance, but the difference is that I love it. Permanent migration from fair to fair, conference to conference: this is the life I sought, the job I realized I had been born to do as soon as Adam explained his idea to me, at a conference, three years ago. It is not that I like conferences and trade fairs in themselves—they can be diverting, but often they are dreary. In their specifics, I can take them or leave them—indeed, I have to, when I am with machine-tools manufacturers one day and grocers the next. But I revel in their generalities—the hotels, the flights, the pervasive anonymity and the license that comes with that. I love to float in that world, unidentified, working to my own agenda. And out of all those generalities I love hotels the most: their discretion, their solicitude, their sense of insulation and isolation. The global hotel chains are the archipelago I call home. People say that they are lonely places, but for me that simply means that they are places where my needs only are important, and that my comfort is the highest achievement our technological civilization can aspire to. When surrounded by yammering nonentities, solitude is far from undesirable. Around me, tens of thousands are trooping through the concourses of the MetaCenter, and my cube of private space on the other side of the motorway has an obvious charm.

Tom Graham appeared to be intrigued by conference surrogacy, and asked a few detailed questions about procedures and fees, but it was hard to tell if he would become a client or not. And if he did sign up, I wouldn't necessarily know. Discretion was fundamental to Adam's vision for our young profession—clients' names were strictly controlled even within the company, as a courtesy to any executives who might prefer their colleagues not know that someone was doing their homework for them. Today, for instance, I knew that clients had requested I attend two sessions, one at 11:30 and one at 2:30, but I had no idea who or why. After the second session, my time would be my own—I could slip back to the hotel for a few hours of leisure before the party in the evening.

A few hours of leisure . . . The thought of my peaceful room, its well-tuned lighting, its television and radio, filled me with a sense of longing, the strength of which surprised me. It was almost a yearning. Right now, I imagined, a chambermaid would be arranging the sheets and replacing the towel and shower gel I had used. Smoothing and wiping. Emptying and refilling. Arranging and removing. Making ready.

Also, a return to the hotel would give me another chance to encounter the redheaded woman—a slim chance, but it was an encounter I was ever more keen to contrive. Her continual reappearance in my thoughts was curious to me, and almost troubling—a sensation similar to being unsure if I had locked my room door after I left. Her shtick about the paintings might have been a sign that she was a miniature or two short of a minibar, but it had only increased her mystique. She was unusual—of course, that had been obvious the first time I saw her, years ago. Beautiful too. And there was something about the rapture with which she described the potential of the motorway site, its existence at the nexus of intangible economic forces . . . she knew these places, she had some deeper understanding of them.

After I had said my good-byes to Tom and left the muffled solemnity of the Gray Labyrinth, the jangling noise and distraction of the fair were unwelcome, so I fled into the conference wing to find the first session. There, I found some peace. The seats were comfortable, the lighting was dimmed for the speaker's slides. It was straightforward stuff: business travel trends in the age of austerity. I jotted down a few of the facts and statistics that were thrown out. Tighter cash flow, fewer, shorter business trips and less risk-taking meant potential gains for the budget hotels. Michelin stars in the restaurant and the latest cross-trainers in the gym were much less important than reliable WiFi, easy check-in and a quiet room. Good times for Way Inn, and for me. It was reassuring, almost restful, stuff. For some of the session, I was able to come close to drowsing, letting my eyelids become heavy and enjoying being off my feet. The end of the talk was almost a disappointment. Applause was hearty.

I was beginning to feel that a peaceful routine had been restored—a sensation that was a surprise to me, because until that point I had not realized that my routine had been disrupted. Maybe I wasn't getting enough sleep. Maybe, instead of pursuing Rosa or the redheaded woman into the night, I should get to bed early, spend some quality time in the company of freshly laundered hotel linen.

But first, lunch. There were various places to eat in the MetaCenter, and like an airport or an out-of-town shopping center—anywhere with a captive audience, in fact—they were all likely to be overpriced and uninspiring. Rejecting branded coffee shops and burger joints, I headed for the main brasserie. In less image-conscious times, this would simply be called a canteen: big, bright and loud, serving batch-prepared food from stainless-steel basins under long meters of sneeze guard. A hot, wet tray taken from a spring-loaded pile and pushed along waist-height metal rails; a can of fizzy drink from a chiller, a cube of moussaka from a slab the size of a yoga mat; green salad in a transparent plastic blister. It might sound awful, but it was fine, really, just fine. I was eating alone and had no desire to linger—there was no need for me to be delighted by exotic or subtle flavors, and any attempt to pamper me would surely have been a delay and a provocation. It was good, simple, efficient, repeatable, forgettable. For entertainment, I sorted through some of the fliers and cards I had picked up from the fair. To carry these, I had brought my own tote bag, one from a fair last year which had unusually low-key branding. In my line of work, you never run short of totes.

In the MetaCenter's central hall, even within the perplexing grid of the fair, navigation was not too hard: giant signs suspended from the distant ceiling identified cardinal points, and if you somehow managed to really, truly lose your sense of where you were, you could simply walk toward the edge of the hall and work your way around from there. In the wings of the center, formidable buildings in themselves, a little more spatial awareness was needed. To find the venue of the second session on my schedule for the day, I had to consult one of the information boards that stood helpfully at junctions in the miles of passage and concourse. Before me, the conference wing was sliced into its three floors, splayed out like different cuts at the butcher's and gaily color-coded. I began to plot my course from the brasserie to the correct auditorium: Meta South, east concourse, S3 escalators . . .

This locative reverie was obliterated by a hard, flat blow between my shoulder blades, delivered with enough force to knock the strap of my tote bag from my shoulder. I wheeled around, part ready to launch a retaliatory punch even as I experienced sheer unalloyed bafflement that anybody could be so assailed in a public place, in daylight. What greeted me was a wobbly smile, wrinkled linen and strands of blond hair clinging to a pink brow.

"Afternoon, old chap. I say, I didn't take you off guard, did I?"

"Jesus, Maurice," I said. "What the hell do you think you're playing at?"

Maurice put up his hands. "Don't shoot, commandant!" He chuckled, a throaty, rasping gurgle. "Don't know my own strength sometimes, it's all the working out I do." Comic pause. "Working out if it's time for a drink!" The chuckle became a smoker's laugh, and he broke his hands-up pose to wave me away, as if I was being a priceless wag.

"You startled me," I said, stooping to pick up my bag.

"So what's in store next?" Maurice asked, leaning over me to examine the map. I became uncomfortably aware of the proximity of my head to his crotch. The crease on his trouser legs was vestigial, its full line only suggested by the short stretches of it that remained, like a Roman road. "You going to 'Emerging Threats'?"

"Yes," I said, straightening. I wanted to curse. Trapped! It would be impossible to avoid sitting next to Maurice, and there was no way to skip it: "Emerging Threats to the Meetings Industry" had, after all, been requested by a client. Sitting next to Maurice meant having to put up with his fidgeting, lip-smacking and sighing, and a playlist of either witless asides or snores. It had all happened before. And afterward he would ask what I was doing next and if I said I was going back to the hotel there was a very real risk he would think that a fine idea and decide to follow me, and we would have to wait for a bus together and sit on it together, or I would have to spend time devising an escape plan, inventing meetings and urgent phone calls . . . the amount of additional energy all this would consume was, it seemed to me, almost unbearable. I wanted to lock the door of my hotel room, lie on the bed and think about nothing.

"Bit of time, then," Maurice said, looking at his watch. "I'm glad I ran into you again actually, there's something I keep forgetting to ask you. Do you have a card?"

"Excuse me?"

"A card, a business card. I'm sure you gave me one ages ago but"—he rolled his eyes in such an exaggerated fashion that his whole head involved itself in the act—"of *course* I lost it."

For a moment I considered denying Maurice one of my cards—it would be perfectly easy to claim that I hadn't brought enough with me that morning and had already exhausted my supply—but I decided such a course was pointless. The cards were purposely inscrutable and were intended to be given out freely without concern. Just my name, the company name, an email address, a mailing address in the West End and the URL of our equally laconic website. I gave Maurice a card. He made a show of reading it.

"Neil Double, associate, Convex," Maurice recited in a deliberately grand voice. "Ta. What is it you do again?"

"Business information," I said. I am quite good at injecting a bored note into the answer, to suggest that nothing but a world of tedium lay beyond that description.

Maurice blinked like an owl. "What does that entail?" he asked. "I'm sure you've told me all this before, sorry to be so dense, but I don't think I've ever really got a firm handle on it. Strange, isn't it, how you can know someone for years and never be clear what their line of work is?"

I smiled. There was no risk. "Aggregating business data sector-by-sector for the purposes of bespoke analysis."

"Right, right . . . " Maurice said, his vague expression indicating I had successfully coated his curiosity with a layer of dust. "Great . . . Well, we had better get moving, I suppose. Aggregating to be done, eh?"

We started our trek toward the lecture hall. People streamed along the MetaCenter's broad concourses and up and down the banks of escalators, redistributing themselves between venues. Homing in on the right room, narrowing the range of possible destinations, finding the right level, the right sector, the right group of facilities, I felt a rush of that peculiar, delightful sensation that comes in airports sometimes: of being an exotic particle allowed to pass through layers of filters, becoming more refined. Except that Maurice, a lump of baser stuff, was tagging along after me. And all the way, he kept up a monologue—inane business gossip, his opinions of the MetaCenter, what else he had seen that day and what he thought about it.

The lecture hall was larger than the previous one, with ranks of black-upholstered seats fanning out from a modest stage, where chairs and a lectern were set up. Almost half the seats were taken when we arrived, well ahead of the starting time, and most of the remainder filled as we waited for the session to begin. There was an expectant babble of conversation, although I wondered if that might be more due to the fact that everyone had just eaten—or drunk—their lunch, rather than due to any treat in store. I took the schedule from the information pack in my bag and examined it again, to see if there was anything particularly alluring about the talk. The title, "Emerging Threats," was so ill-defined that it might have lent the event broad appeal. Next to the listing was the logo of Maurice's magazine, *Summit*—it was a sponsor. He hadn't mentioned that. I glanced at Maurice, who had seated himself next to me. He was staring into space, mouth slightly open, notebook and digital recorder on his lap.

Like me, apart from the open mouth. He was uncharacteristically quiet, even focused.

Electronic rustling and bumping rose from the audio system: the three speakers had arrived on the stage and were being fitted with radio microphones. I closed my eyes and wondered how much of the discussion I could pick up through a drowse if I let myself slip into one. A gray-haired man was introducing the speakers—the usual panel-fodder from think tanks and trade bodies; middle-aged, male and stuffy. One of whom was very familiar. It took me some moments to establish that I really was looking at the person I thought it was, and while I stared at him, he found my eyes in the audience and smiled at me. It was Tom Graham, hands interlaced in his lap, legs crossed, sleek with satisfaction.

"Last of all," the master of ceremonies said, reaching Tom, "a man who really needs no introduction—a fairs man through and through: Tom Laing, event director of Meetex."

Applause.

"Always the same old faces at these things."

"We must stop meeting like this."

"Small world."

"Groundhog day."

"Another day, another dollar."

"Are you here for the conference?"

"Why else?"

"All well?"

"Fuck, stop, just stop, I can't stand it."

Adam and I felt the same way about male small talk: we

hated it. He introduced me to the term "phatic utterance," words said purely as social ritual, not to convey any real meaning: when you're asked "how's it going?" and not expected to reply. Noise, he said, useless noise; a waste of human bandwidth. Trim out all the phatic utterances and interaction could be made a lot more efficient. That was the way he thought, and I loved it. Away with all that hopeless banter and rib-jabbing. But we had turned this shared belief into our own form of banter—a private game, where, on running into each other, we would try to keep up the dismal phatic chitchat for as long as possible, repeating the same old clichés and phrases and saying as little as possible that was new or interesting until one of us cracked and stopped and we could talk about things that actually mattered.

"That was quick."

"I can't take any more small talk. I've just come from a funeral. My father died."

"Oh. I'm so sorry."

"*Bzzzt.* Phatic."

"Damn! Checkmate, really. What else is there to say?"

"It's OK. I didn't know him very well, my parents divorced and he travelled a lot."

"And you thought: that's the life for me?"

I laughed. "Yeah, kind of."

When I met Adam, before he founded Convex, I worked for a firm of cost consultants in the construction industry. They specialized in "value engineering": professional corner-cutting, driving down the expense of projects by simplifying designs and substituting cheaper materials. When a building is completed and only barely resembles the promotional images revealed by the architects years before—more plain, more clunky, more drab; graceful curves turned into awkward corners; shining titanium and crystalline glass replaced with dull panels of indeterminate plasticky material—then my old firm, or one like it, has been wielding its shabby art.

Ugly work, literally. I preferred not to reflect on it, and I focused hard on my particular minor role, which was to scour trade fairs for those cheaper materials. What could stand in for stone, what would do in place of copper, what was the bargain-basement equivalent of hardwood? All my life I have been interested in what the world was truly made from; if not all my life, then at least from the very early age when—looking at the chipped edge of a table at home, a wood-grain veneer over a crumbling, splintery inner substance—I discovered that surfaces were often lies.

"Fake walnut interior," my father once said to someone over the phone, winking merrily to me as he did so, letting me in on a joke I did not understand. "Better than the real thing." It was years before I connected this remark to cars, years spent wondering why someone would fake the interior of a walnut, and how the results could possibly improve on an actual walnut. Years of imagining tiny fabulous jewelled sculptures in walnut shells, not inexpensive automobiles. Then years of suspicion in cars. Real or fake? Suspicion everywhere, which eventually gave way to fascination.

I trawled the fairs, learning the trade names of all the different kinds of composite panels, all of which looked alike and inscrutable—cheap façade materials having gone from fiction to encryption, no longer pretending to be something else and instead trying to be unidentifiable. At one of the fairs I met Adam. He worked for a trend-forecasting company, in the normal course of things a world away from builders' merchants and anodized zinc cladding. This company built meticulous indexes of every last shoe and shawl shown by every label at every fashion week, databases you could subscribe to and see exactly who had launched what and not have to sit through endless catwalk shows. The company had dreams—wild and hopeless dreams—of doing the same for construction materials, and Adam was part of the team building this library of Babel for uPVC drainpipes.

It was a tedious waste of time, and he knew it; but it had given him the idea for conference surrogacy. "One man representing thirty, forty executives—imagine the savings! All this sentimental bullshit that gets dished out about face-to-face, firm handshakes, eye to eye . . . all these body parts that are supposedly so important . . . it's all just so . . . " He reached for an insult. " . . . So fucking analog."

When he quit the trend analysts to set up Convex, I joined him. The thirty thousand pounds I inherited from my father, that joined, too, invested in the business. It was all I had and, with a value-engineered salary mostly paying for a one-bedroom flat, and none of the clubability that men like Laing have, it was all I had been likely to have, ever.

Once the discussion started, Laing stopped staring at me to join in. I was too distracted by his presence on the stage to listen to what was being said. Graham was a false name; Graham was Laing; and Laing was the man behind Meetex, the man who had found exhibitors for the fair and set the program for the conference. Why would he want to know about conference surrogacy? He had to be here; it was his gig. If anyone loved fairs and conferences, it was him. I knew where I had seen him before now: not from personal acquaintance, but in photographs—photographs in the welcome pack, photographs in *Summit*, photographs everywhere. Laing shaking hands, Laing cutting ribbons. He was a true believer, and I had told him about Convex. It was unnerving.

The panel were discussing intellectual property. Businesses in the Far East were sending people to trade fairs to photograph the products and fill wheelbarrows with brochures, so they could manufacture knockoff products based on the information. Furniture and consumer goods manufacturers were worried—could anything be done to protect them from the copycats? Laing had not made a contribution for a while. Then he leaned in and spoke.

"It's not just our exhibitors who should be concerned about piracy," he said. "We should as well. Conference pirates exist. They exist, and they're here now."

A murmur of uneasy amusement passed through the audience. Maurice flipped his notebook over to a fresh page.

"I'm quite serious," Laing said, addressing the hall. "Conference pirates. I met one earlier today." He had been scanning the audience, and as he said this his eyes fixed on me.

My first instinct was to laugh. Pirate—it was absurd. The modern meanings of the term—downloaders and desperate Somalians and Swedish political parties—were well known to me. But all the event director's invocation of it generated for me was a burst of kitsch imagery: peg legs, parrots, rum, *X* marks the spot. Not me at all.

"He works for a company called Convex," Laing continued. "They say they can give their customers the benefit of attending a conference without actually having to attend. They send someone in your place—a double, let's say. And it costs less than attending the conference because this . . . double . . . can represent several people. You get a report. Meanwhile we only sell one ticket where we might have sold ten or twenty—it's our customers being skimmed off. And they denigrate the conference industry, say that conferences are a waste of everyone's time, while selling a substandard product in our name."

All this time, Laing had stared me, and I began to fear that others in the hall might be figuring out who he was talking about. One other pair of eyes was certainly on me: Maurice was rapt.

Laing's attention flicked away from me. He was warming to his theme, wallowing in his own righteousness, letting his oration build to a courtroom climax. "Lawful or not," he said, high color apparent in his cheeks, "this practice, this so-called conference surrogacy, is piggybacking on the hard work of others in order to make a quick profit—which is on a natural moral level dubious, unhealthy, unethical and simply wrong!"

I was being prosecuted. Unable to respond, I wriggled in my seat and felt my own color rise to match Laing's. How dare he! Flinging slurs around without giving me a space to reply, naming our company in particular—it was unbearable. I imagined springing to my feet, challenging Laing, giving him the cold, hard, facts right between the eyes. We identified a need and we are supplying a service that fulfills it. That's the free market. If Laing's events were more interesting, more useful, less time-consuming and less expensive, there would be no need for us. Conferences and trade fairs are almost always tedious in the extreme. People would pay good money to avoid going to them. They do pay good money—to me. All this moral outrage was just a smoke screen for the basic failure of his product. The muscles in my legs primed themselves. I was ready.

"I've got to run," I whispered to Maurice. And with that I scuttled from the room. I have no idea if anyone other than Laing and Maurice even noticed.

From the lecture hall, I marched down one of the concourses of the MetaCenter conference wing, passing many people strolling between venues or talking in small groups, that damned yellow bag seemingly on every other shoulder. I felt extremely hot in the hands and face. I was moving without a destination clearly in mind, moving forward to keep the unsteadiness from stealing into my muscles. All I wanted was to clear the area of Emerging Threats before the hall emptied out; then, all I wanted was to be off the concourse, away from the other conference-goers, the sight of whom filled me with hatred. Laing had tricked me, and trapped me, and it was hard not to implicate everyone at Meetex in the deed.

When I saw the sign for some restrooms, I stopped. In the frosty fluorescent light of the toilets, I splashed cold water on my face, trying to get my surface temperature back down and gather myself together. A couple of other men were using the urinals and the other sinks—I ig-

nored them, trying to weaponize the normal mutual in-
visibility pact that pertains at urinals so that they would
literally disappear. There was no way they could have
been in the same hall as me, no way they could have seen
what just happened to me, but I still didn't want them
looking at me, the pirate gnawing away at their livelihoods. I looked at myself in the mirror above the sink,
pale though not red-faced as I had feared, skin wet, a drop
of water clinging to my chin. Tired, maybe. The tube
lights flickered and stuttered—an item on a contractor's
to-do list, one of the hundreds of glitches that infest new
buildings. Plasma rolled in the tubes. Sometimes it's new
buildings that have ghosts, not old ones; new buildings
are not yet obedient. New buildings are not yet ready for
us. I wanted to be back in my room at the Way Inn, and I
realized that it was already that time. Leaving now was
no kind of retreat; it was what I always planned to do.

In something like a trance I left the MetaCenter, its fire-
minded evacuation conduits directing me without fuss to
the departure point for the shuttle buses. Between the cano-
pied assembly area outside the conference center and the
bus, there was the briefest moment of weather, something
the planners of the site had made every effort to minimize
but which still had to be momentarily sampled. It came as
a shock after hours in the climate-controlled halls. The
dead white sky was marbled with ugly gray, and in the
coach the heater was running. Barely half a dozen other
passengers accompanied me; the late-afternoon rush back
to the hotels had yet to truly begin, and we got moving
almost immediately. I sat slumping in my seat as my

memories of what had just taken place flexed and froze. It was all malformed in my mind: instances running together with no clear impression of what had been said or what it meant. We passed through acres of empty car parks, like fields razed black after harvesting.

The sign for the Way Inn, a red neon roadside obelisk on an unplanted verge, was as welcome as the lights of a tavern on an ancient snow-covered mountainside. It was a breath of everywhere, offering the same uncomplicated rooms and bland carpet at similar rates in any one of hundreds of locations worldwide. On seeing it, I smiled, perhaps the first time I had smiled naturally all day. And then, as I tried to recall where I had stowed the keycard for my room, I realized that I had left my bag under the chair in the lecture hall. Nothing of great value was lost—my keycard, wallet, mobile phone and other significant personal possessions were all in my pockets. But the leaflets, press releases and advertising materials I had gathered, the price cards and fact sheets, and the Meetex information pack with its maps and timetables, were all gone. Would they be found and moved to a lost property office? Unlikely. Fliers and brochures look like litter in the slightest change of light. A day's work thrown away— the bag had contained my pages of notes too. I would have to cover much of the same ground again tomorrow. This was frustrating, even infuriating, but somehow it managed to refresh me. The debilitating tangle that had hobbled my thoughts was cut straight through by the loss, which felt somehow auspicious—a way of severing my connection to that catastrophe of a day and leaving it in the past. As I walked through the glass doors of the Way Inn, my mood was much restored.

The hotel lobby was almost empty. Flat-screens showed the news without sound. Behind their desk, the reception staff were chatting in lowered voices. Other than them and the handful of returning conference-goers—who drifted, unspeaking, toward the lifts and stairs—there were a couple of lone, suited men sitting in the blocky black leather-and-chrome armchairs, reading newspapers or studying laptops. No one sat at the Meetex registration table—the information packs, tote bags, lanyards and other bric-a-brac had been cleared away, and only the banner remained, now clearly false. You can no longer register here.

I took the stairs to the second floor, not wanting to find myself cooped up in a lift with any Meetex people. But when I reached my floor I became disoriented. It was not that the hallway was unfamiliar—on the contrary, it looked equally familiar in both directions, and I couldn't readily tell which way lay my room, number 219. For a moment I tried to figure it out from where the lift stood in relation to the stairs in the lobby, and where I stood now, but it was not possible. I was thrown by the stairs' dogleg between floors, the way they doubled back on themselves to end above where they began. And I could not be at all certain of my other calculations regarding the relationship between my room and the lift shaft— walking casually, following signs to the lift, it was quite possible to make a turn without thinking, and certainly without remembering it. Ahead, opposite the stairs, windows looked out onto a courtyard containing one of those neat little Japanese meditation gardens. Across the courtyard was a row of windows, tinted metallic blue and opaque to me. This was definitely the courtyard that was next to reception—where was that in relation to my room? Was there more than one courtyard?

I picked a direction almost at random, relying on a sliver of instinct, and was rewarded with a promising ascent of room numbers—210, 211, 212, 213. Between each door and the next hung an abstract painting, all from the same series—intersecting latte and mocha fields. The corridor took a right angle in one direction, and then in the opposite direction. Facing 220, beside a painting of a fudge-colored disc barging into a porridgy expanse scattered with swollen chocolate drops, was 219. I inserted my keycard in the slot on the door lock and nothing happened. The little red light above the door handle remained red. The door was still locked, the handle was unmoving. I withdrew the card and tried again. Nothing. A lead pellet of frustration dropped in my stomach. I flipped the card over and inserted it again. The red light glowed insolently, refusing to turn green. I tried a fourth time, this time jiggling, cajoling, exercising force of will. The world, or at least my immediate surroundings, remained spectacularly unchanged—the red light, the immobile handle, the sleeping doors of the other rooms, the paintings, the faint perfume of cleaning fluid, the soft background hum of the hotel's air conditioning, which to my ears now sounded a note of complacency, an indifference to the injustice of the world.

Irritated, I returned down the corridor to the stairs and descended to the lobby. The same suited men in the same armchairs, still reading the same newspapers. The staff at the front desk heard my purposeful approach and looked up, smiling benignly.

"I'm locked out of my room," I said, flashing a brief,

formal smile of my own. "My keycard doesn't seem to want to work. It's two-nineteen."

The man behind the desk beamed at me. He was young, no more than early twenties, and wore—like all his colleagues—a long-sleeved, red polo shirt with buttons at the collar and Way Inn embroidered in white over the breast. "This can happen sometimes," he said in accented English; Dutch, maybe. "Have you had your card in your pocket with perhaps your keys and your cell phone?" Keish, shelfon. "The card can lose its magnetism. Please, let me see it."

I gave the man the card. It disappeared from sight beneath the counter to be reenchanted. Seconds passed, and I took in the reception desk. Above it, Way Inn was spelled out in bold Perspex letters, lit red from behind. The desk was more a counter on my side, high enough that it required me to raise my elbows if I wanted to rest them on the dark, polished wood.

"OK then," the young man said. "That should work just fine now—let's go see." He stood, eagerly, my keycard still in his hand.

"That's really not necessary," I said. "I can let myself . . . "

But the helpful fellow was up and out from behind the desk, heading toward the rear of the lobby in a determined straight line. Watching the man's back, I noted with dismay that he was aimed at the elevators rather than the stairs. "Surely the stairs . . . " I began, again, but the man had pressed the button and smiled a prim little smile at me. We waited together, an awkward, chaste moment. I tried to look as if I was preoccupied with matters of grave importance; the staffer looked up, as if blessed with X-ray vision and able to see the lift approaching through layers of concrete and breezeblocks.

"Awful weather today," I said. I had to say something.

"Awful," the young man said, shaking his head at the horror of it all. "It barely even got light, did it? And it's already getting dark."

The lift arrived and we stepped in together. Moody light, mirrored walls and soft music, like a tiny nightclub. Out of the lift on the second floor, the staffer walked briskly down the corridor, throwing my bearings again—I had wanted to see where I was in relation to the stairs, but missed the chance. At the door to 219, the staffer inserted the keycard into the box above the handle and was rewarded with an immediate green light and satisfying clunk. The handle turned and the door opened.

"If you keep it away from your keys, your cell phone and your other cards, it should be just fine in future," the staffer said, handing back the card with one hand and holding the door open with the other.

"Thanks," I said, stepping into my room and sticking the card into its niche in the wall. The room lights turned on.

"No problem," said the young man with a little bow, hand behind his back and smiling broadly. And he turned sharply away, as if relishing the fact that this moment did not call for a tip. The front door closed.

While I had been at the center, the room had been cleaned. The bedspread was as creaseless and immaculate as the icing on a wedding cake. My few belongings had been organized and now looked absurd and tawdry in the pristine room. A newspaper I had bought yesterday had been neatly placed next to my laptop on the desk, looking filthy and out of date. I had left yesterday's clothes strewn across the bench at the foot of the bed—they were still there, but folded, their creases a source of shame. The shirt I had draped on the armchair had been placed on a lonely hanger in the wardrobe. On the bedside table, a small heap of crumpled scraps of paper and low-denomination coins was scrupulously untouched like an exhibit in a museum of low living. Everything about the scene suggested to me that the cleaner had been greatly dismayed by the poor quality of the clothes and possessions they had been forced to deal with, but had done their best.

This was paranoia, I knew, but it still needled me. I dropped the newspaper and some of the paper scraps into the bin, and stuffed the clothes back in the bag. Then I took off my tie and shoes. I opened my laptop; there was nothing of any importance in my email inbox—including nothing related to Meetex that could explain the incident with Laing at Emerging Threats. Just arrangements for coming trade shows and conferences—my life, my work, stretching out into the future in a reassuring manner, beyond this unfortunate professional hiccup. I snapped the laptop closed, took a beer from the minibar fridge and lay on the bed, back and head propped up with cushions. Eight cushions on this small double bed, along with the two pillows—serving no purpose beyond their role as visible invitations to be comfortable. This was presumably exactly the sort of moment a chain hotel imagined itself making a positive intervention—the weary guest comes in from a challenging day of combative capital-B Business and finds solace; a private cube of climate-controlled air; a cold beer; a yielding bed covered in well-stuffed cushions. The group intelligence of the operating corporation's marketing and public relations people, its designers and buyers, its choosers and describers had considered this moment, it had considered me. It was only a simulation of hospitality, of course, but still it provided some respite.

I sipped the beer straight from the can and listened to the quiet sounds of the hotel around me: the low vibration of its air systems, distant doors opening and closing. I closed my eyes, but sleep didn't seem likely or desirable. Instead, I mentally replayed the day, examining and twisting it like a Rubik's Cube, trying to line up its faces so it made sense. A man I had thought to be a prospective client was instead the event director of Meetex. I had given him a very detailed description of the service we offered, and in short order he had named me as a threat to the meetings industry. A threat to the meetings industry! How pompous, how vain of Laing to see himself as the guardian of a stronghold of civilization, an "industry" no less—though he would probably consider it a "community" and a "family" as well, the self-aggrandizing prick. It was a stunt, a bid to look important and concerned for his customers, but a splash that would ripple away quickly. What troubled me, as a matter of pride as much as any practical concern, was that my anonymity had been breached—certainly this afternoon many more people knew the nature of my work than did this morning. Adam had really labored the message that I had to be discreet on this particular job: he had told me so in every email relating to it, and in all our recent phone conversations. Perhaps he had had some premonition of what was in store, or had picked up on clues pointing to the ambush? If so, why hadn't he warned me? But I was getting too far ahead of myself.

Adam would have to know about all this—in time. For

a couple of minutes I considered emailing him right away, and I experimented with different wordings in my head. But I did not want to attach an air of emergency to the incident, and make it into a bigger problem than it really was. Sure, Laing knew who I was and what I did, but how many others? A couple of hundred people heard him—but were they listening, and did they care? A couple of hundred out of tens of thousands. There was Maurice to consider. He had gone to some effort to sit next to me. Maurice, early for a talk! He was a consummate latecomer, a man who no amount of tutting would deter from blundering past the knees of seated audience members to reach an empty seat in a middle row while a speaker was in midflow. It was, in retrospect, an incredible performance by him. If he had not found me after lunch (how long had he been looking?), I could be fairly sure that he would have lain in wait at the door of the lecture hall until I happened along. And now I remembered his request for a business card, our conversation about what I did. Cunning—far more cunning than I had imagined him to be—but, mysteriously, I once again found it hard to muster much anger toward the journalist. And for the first time in our acquaintance, I discovered I was looking ahead to the next possible moment I could contrive a meeting with him. I needed to know his view on what had happened, and minimize it in his eyes.

He would be at the party tonight, of course. The party. With so much looking back—dismantling, examining and reassembling the recent past—I had neglected to look forward. For a brief while I considered not going to the party. But that wouldn't do—hiding away, acting as if I had something to be ashamed of, was not the way to behave. It would be business as usual. And I would have an opportunity to prove to myself that I remained anonymous. And besides, I wanted to go: my ego had taken a knock, and a few drinks and some flirting would set that right. There would be girls there, for sure. Things had been going pretty well with Rosa—maybe something could happen there tonight, and I could hang the Do Not Disturb sign on my door. That would certainly restore the natural balance of my interior ecosystem. The aggressive energy generated by Laing's subterfuge had left me restless. I had obtained my day-long desire, to be back in my hotel room, and I was almost ready to leave it again.

After finishing the beer, I dozed on the bed, letting the painting on the wall in front of me focus and unfocus. An idea coalesced. My mobile phone was on the bedside table: I picked it up and used it to take a photograph of the painting on the wall. One more for the woman's collection—one she could not have seen, because it was in a guest's room, not a public area. If we did run into each other again, I would have something to say to her, a way to show interest in her pastime, and if she wanted the picture she would have to give me a mobile phone number or an email address. I would not lose contact with her again.

Around me, I could sense the hotel filling with life as people returned from the conference in greater numbers. Footsteps and fragments of muffled conversation sounded in the corridor. From the room next to mine, 217, I could hear music playing faintly through the wall, drifting in and out of the realm of perception in a way that was more distracting than if it came through loud and clear. I switched on the television. It had reset to the hotel welcome page, the smiling staff, the weather for tomorrow and the latest from the restaurant, which was "Closed for private party." I turned to a news channel and ordered a sandwich from room service. Forty-five minutes to an hour—they were busy. I half-watched the news, which was fretting over a lackluster economic statistic—a poker-faced little number representing the aggregate of thousands of individually bland decisions made in fabric-covered cubicles, all added together, up a fraction of a percent, down a fraction of a percent . . . while along the motorway, more and more boxes were built to accommodate those people and their nanoconsequential impulses and resolutions, their planning, their decisions.

As a child, I marvelled at office blocks—what could they possibly find to do in all that space? Office interiors were generally such anticlimaxes, just desks and filing cabinets and telephones. I saw men in suits on the street and elsewhere and they only ever seemed to be talking or reading, never really doing anything—not like people driving trains or building buildings. There were so many of them, men and women, doing impossible-to-tell jobs. This impression was particularly forceful in unfamiliar cities where, I was amazed to discover, life also went on as normal, wrapped up in this arcane charade of offices and paper and neckties. On the occasions he was available for questioning, I would quiz my father, the only representative of this world I had at hand. "But what do you *do*?" I would wheedle and insist. Sell auto parts, he would say.

But what do you *do*, I would repeat, meaning what actions does this involve, what is said and heard, how on earth can anyone fill days and weeks just doing that one thing, or any one thing? Maybe more detailed explanations were forthcoming but I don't remember them, so they can't have satisfied me. Or, depending on his mood, he would say that he put food on the table, and that was that. I asked my mother too. Her answer was "he travels," which was no answer at all. But I did not like to pursue inquiries about him with her; she became chilly before long, although it was some time before I realized that she was concealing her lack of knowledge, not a grand secret. Or perhaps that was the grand secret, that she knew so little about the man she'd married.

These questions—like my concerns about the actual substance of the world—at times bother me to this day. I can see from the world of trade fairs and conferences that every tiny thing has an industry behind it; all things from the grandest to the tiniest are backed by thousands of people in scores of competing companies resting their livelihoods on the rise or fall in sales of that thing, and having conferences and trade fairs devoted to the endeavors and future of their enterprise, which naturally they regard as central, pivotal and vital to the national interest. Conferences and trade fairs, for all their expansive rhetoric, were insular, introverted exercises in commercial navel-gazing and solipsism. So what did it mean to attend all of them?

My food arrived, a well-stuffed BLT. The paper napkin that accompanied it would also have its day, its market share and prospects earnestly discussed at Caterex and

Snackcon and Bulk Ply Paper Products Forum and Mouth Hygiene Expo. Once I had finished my sandwich, I showered, imagining many showers taking place in the hotel at that moment in the early evening, particulates from the MetaCenter and the motorway being washed from many bodies and swept into the drains beneath the Way Inn; all the new infrastructure that had so excited the redhead, the new connections being made and the exotic ridges and spikes of potential they generated on her maps and charts—development gateway, investment zone, emerging regional hub. As she said these phrases, these pert word couplings charged with promise and yet light on immediate meaning, a change had come over her. She had slipped from detachment into deep trancelike concentration. "Enterprise opportunity corridor . . . public-private gateway zone . . . motorway halo . . . " A new link, a new pathway through cheap land; octopus-like, journey-time diagrams flex and stretch out their tentacles, and the ground is sown with tax breaks and more infrastructure and superfast broadband and hey presto I'm taking a shower, eating BLTs and watching rolling news thirty feet above undistinguished frozen dirt.

My lift to the ground floor was shared with other party-goers. The doors, when they opened on my floor, burst a bubble of heavily perfumed air; three men in suits with slicked hair, two women in cocktail dresses, all doused in scent and aftershave. It looked crowded in the small compartment, and I indicated that I'd wait for another lift, but they laughed and huddled up together and coaxed me with homely quips like "Room for a small one!" and

"The more the merrier!" They held the doors and would not depart without me, so I had to board. When the doors slid closed on us, the cube rapidly filled with volatile hydrocarbons and laughter. A sequinned rear end was pressed, by obligation of the close quarters, against my right thigh. Was I here for the conference, the owner of the rear end asked me. Of course, I said.

"Of course he's here for the conference, Jan!" said one of the men. He was around my age and looked like "Hapless Dad" from an advert for cleaning products, but here he was on form, in his element and revelling in it. "You're going to the party, yeah?"

Yeah. The lift arrived in the lobby, the doors opening like a breach in a containment facility for hazardous materials under pressure. My companions in descent and I chatted as we joined the line of people filtering past clipboard-bearing PR brunettes into the party. They all worked together, naturally, in the kind of intimate environment that breeds in-jokes, so nothing more than a cryptic half-comment or a facial expression could set them all off laughing. Their purpose was to promote a provincial city, a "fast-emerging destination"—there was a stand in the MetaCenter, had I seen it? I said I had probably been by, which was probably true, and that I would look out for it tomorrow. Don't come by too early in the morning, they said, all laughing as one, before accusing one another of being intent on intoxicated mayhem, and of an inability to moderate their alcohol consumption.

Normally I would expect to hate these people. I would find their ease with one another and with me intolerable and I would want to be elsewhere. But at this time I appreciated their temporary inclusion of me in their group.

It was reassuring—there would be thousands of people here who were unaware of my "unmasking" earlier, and who in all likelihood would care little if they heard of it. And this sense I felt of no longer being anonymous, no longer having to guard myself, was tantalizing. Much as I like to be unknown, I was drawn toward candor as if the ground sloped that way. Our ideology, as a business, was after all to ease the flow of information.

The clipboards were closer now. My new friend from the provincial chamber of commerce asked me: "What brings you here?"

"I'm a pirate," I said.

He enjoyed that, immediately wading into what he imagined was a joke on my part. "Oh yeah? Where's your parrot, then?"

"Upstairs. Flat battery."

"Eye patch?"

"Don't need one. Laser eye surgery. It's transformed piracy."

He laughed. "What do you do then? Go around nicking other people's ideas, or what?"

"No, nothing like that. I'm a conference surrogate. If someone doesn't want to go to an event like this, they pay me to go instead. Some people consider that piracy."

Chamber of commerce digested this. "Doesn't make a difference to us, I shouldn't think."

"Yeah, that's what I thought."

"So you go to conferences? That's all? Nothing else?"

"Nothing else."

"Are there lots of conference surrogates?"

"As far as I know it's just me. But the company I work for wants to expand. Are you interested?"

"Not for me, mate," he said. Perhaps concerned that my feelings were hurt, he quickly clarified his remark. "I mean, we go to four or five of these things a year and they're always a great time"—he looked toward his colleagues, who had hurled themselves deep into the party, and who were already dancing together—"but they're a getaway, you know? Something different. Doing nothing else would do my head in, quite frankly."

I regarded him sympathetically. "I think it takes a particular kind of person," I said.

A rare kind of person. We were past the PRs, and I excused myself, telling chamber of commerce that there were people I should say hello to, releasing him to rejoin his colleagues. It occurred to me that the reason I found it hard to mix with the people I saw every day was that I didn't see much of myself in them.

For the party, the hotel restaurant and bar had been combined—a sliding partition was all that separated them, and it had been pushed back to make one large space. Not for the first time, I admired the careful design of the hotel: its adaptability, its multiple possible configurations and reconfigurations, its promiscuity as a venue. Features refined through hundreds of repetitions of the same basic form. I took a glass of champagne from a passing tray, drained it swiftly, and found another, which I preserved. With this prop, I made an unhurried circuit of the room. The person I really wanted to see was Maurice—strange, after so long trying to avoid him—but his uncanny ability to manifest himself whenever I had no desire to see him had, it seemed, an unfortunate corollary: when actually needed, he was absent, or at least not apparent. There was free booze to be had, and he was nowhere. It defied reason.

The party was hosted by the Way Inn group and the
promotional point was heavily made. WAY INN WELCOMES
MEETEX read a banner that ran the length of the glass wall
of the lobby. Fatty clusters of red balloons were suspended
from the ceiling, each adorned with the Way Inn logo. In
one corner a stand had been set up and a young woman sat
behind it handing out fliers, USB sticks and ballpoint pens
and other merch. I took a pen. A display related the history
of the chain: America in the 1950s, giant cars, ranch-style
motor courts, flamboyant neon-Aztec roadside signs, the
development of the interstate highways. Then, nothing
but growth, growth, growth—the end of the display, the
end of history, was a map of the world freckled with red
markers indicating Way Inn branches. Hundreds of markers on six continents, with coastal America and northwest-
ern Europe completely obscured. WAY INN EVERYWHERE,
read the closing caption.

It was approaching nine already—I had spent longer
lounging in my room than I had realized. The party had
been going more than an hour and the ice was well broken—the air pulsated with chatter, laughter and amplified music, as if this mutual sound was a medium in
which we all swam. In this buoyant scene, I could usually
pass unnoticed, and would be free to strike up promising
conversations with any women who caught my eye. But
more than once I suspected eyes were upon me, and, although I could not be certain, I felt I was not being regarded with favor. Finishing my second champagne, I
started toward the bar, and a heavyset man going the
other way blocked my path, forcing me to abruptly and
ungracefully change course to avoid colliding with him;
I could not help but believe that this was deliberate. The

bar was mobbed—other drinkers trying to place their orders did not give me an inch of spare room or extend the slightest courtesy; twice someone pushed ahead of me. All of these individual incidents were barely incidents at all, but they disturbed me.

Having at last secured a whisky from the bar—a treble, to delay my return to the scrum for as long as possible—I set out to look for Maurice once more. The venue had filled noticeably in the preceding half hour. When I arrived, I had been able to saunter up and down the length of the room unobstructed, so that it was notable when someone contrived to get in my way; now we were all almost shoulder to shoulder and movement amid the throng was slow, a question of navigating narrow channels between knots of people, seeing gaps between pairs of turned backs and squeezing through. More than once, I was jostled, bumps that I feared might not have been pure accidents. Every aspect of the party was taking on an ugly complexion, and the crowds, malign or not, were sapping my energy. I was increasingly ready to leave, to take my drink up to my room and enjoy it in peace, when someone tapped me sharply on my shoulder. I was primed for the worst.

But when I turned, I saw a friendly smile. Its owner was Rosa (or Rhoda—my memory was no less impaired). She was wearing a very simple, almost austere, gray dress which clung attractively to her petite frame. Her smile was enhanced by light pink lipstick, and she had a decorative burst of tinselly metal pinned in her short hair.

"Neil!" she said. "I thought it was you."

"Hi!" I said.

"Busy, isn't it?"

We pushed our way to one side of the space, near the

windows overlooking the car park, a lacuna in the mass that gave us enough room to face each other.

"Lots of people here," I said, uselessly.

"Nowhere else to go, right?" Rosa said, casting an eye to the window and the low brows of the cars beyond, streaked by rain and security lights. "Not much nightlife around here."

"I don't know," I said. "We could head down to the airport, there might be a Starbucks or an Irish pub there or something . . . "

She laughed. Her lips sparkled. Was it lipstick, or lip gloss? I am hazy on these crucial details. I wanted to kiss them, in any case. "Yeah, wild. We could hit the travel chemist and get wasted on antimalarial drugs. That stuff is mental."

"See, now you're getting into it," I said. Nonchalant: "Are you here with colleagues?"

"I was," she said, "but they've disappeared. You on your own?"

"Yes," I said. "Well, not entirely, no. I'm talking to you."

"Did you have a good day?"

"Not really," I said. A bit of vulnerability and candor would help me here, I calculated. "One of the sessions I attended turned out to be a premeditated attack on my business, and on me personally."

"What, an attack on conference surrogacy?"

My glass almost slipped from my hand. The ball bearing of anxiety that had been spinning at high speed in my abdomen broke apart, sending splinters ripping through my viscera. She knew? How? Was it common knowledge already?

"You know about that?"

"I can imagine it wouldn't go down too well here. It's also a novelty, I suppose, and that can disturb people."

"How did you hear about it?"

"Hear about what?"

"That I'm a conference surrogate. Who told you?"

"You told me," she said, narrowing her eyes. "You don't remember?"

I narrowed my eyes too, as if focusing the moment in my mind, which was in fact a total blank. I couldn't remember talking with Rosa at any length before, let alone telling her something like that. "No, no, sure," I said.

"It's like you said," Rosa continued. "Most of this business is just an exchange of information—sign-up information, name badges, business cards, publicity material, URLs. Names, addresses, job titles. It's nothing more than a big box for sorting information, the MetaCenter; they all know it, because they employ my company to harvest all that information, to build lists of names and email addresses and phone numbers, to rank and cross-reference and update. We already read bar codes and QR codes on name badges to access the data that you provided to Meetex when you signed up, so people know who's looking at their stand, and we collect and scan business cards, run them through text-recognition programs to strip out the data . . . soon enough everything will be chipped, we'll be reading the data automatically as you approach the stand. After that, who knows? Face recognition, iris recognition, gait recognition . . . " She had a very intent, thoughtful expression, still looking past me. It reminded me of the redhead, a coincidence that felt, nonsensically, like infidelity. "I don't think they object to you funnelling the information out of trade shows and conferences—what they hate is the fact that you're denying them information by allowing people to attend without being here. You're a black box."

"How much do they care, truly?"

"You'd be surprised," Rosa said. Her soliloquy on the magic of databasing had left her slightly flushed. "Personal data is currency. Treasure to be hoarded. You might as well be the scouting party for an advancing horde of barbarians, as far as they're concerned."

"I don't feel that barbarous," I said.

"You don't look at all barbarous to me," she said. Full eye contact, smile—all very promising.

"How was your day?"

"Tedious," she said. "Shall we skip this? I guess you don't want to talk business, and I don't want to either."

"True," I said.

"It's good to see you again too, you know," she said. "You told me you were pleased to see me again, and I just wanted you to know I feel the same way."

"That's good to hear," I said. I confess, I did not expect this to go so well. There was little danger in pushing on to the next stage, as far as I could see. The next stage was an invitation, one it seemed I had been invited to make. "From what I've heard, all the important business takes place in hotel rooms, anyway. We're wasting our time down here."

Something was wrong. Rosa frowned. "Yeah, so you say." She had shifted her attention from me to behind me. "I think your friend wants you."

I turned. Maurice was lurking behind my right shoulder.

"Sorry, chaps, chapess, I didn't quite know how to

approach—almost gave Neil here a heart attack earlier, sneaking up behind him, didn't want to finish the job." He had a beer in each hand. "Am I interrupting something?"

"Kind of," I said, biting back my usual instinct to tell him to get lost. I needed his goodwill. If he took the hint and gave me a bit of space now I could catch up with him later.

"Sure, sure," Maurice said, remaining solidly at my side. "Didn't mean to intrude. I don't think you introduced me to your friend earlier . . . ?"

"Right," I said. He was looking to me for the introduction, not Rosa. He wanted me to do it. Anger writhed inside me. All the old-fashioned rubbish he spouted, it was nothing but an affectation! No one still behaved like that, not outside of a golf-club bar! Ask her! Ask her her name! "Maurice, this is . . . "

It was time to guess. Rosa felt probable—I still suspected Rhoda or Rhonda, but who was called Rhoda or Rhonda nowadays? It had to be Rosa. She had detected my hesitation—for a moment I thought she might step in and introduce herself, but instead she fixed her gaze on me, awaiting my answer with undisguised sternness.

" . . . This is my friend Rosa."

"It's Lucy," she said. Lucy—I felt the word as if it had cut from my genitals to my throat. Of course it was Lucy, and remembering this brought a peal of other memories, memories which might in other circumstances have been pleasant, but which now only amplified my errors. Not one error—many.

Maurice had extended his hand to the furious woman, but she ignored him. "Fucking hell, Neil. I didn't have any illusions after last time, I didn't think it was more than it was, just something we both wanted at the same time. But I thought you might at least remember it, and not use the exact same line on me . . . " she broke off from this salvo, delivered in an emphatic, vicious hiss, overcome by her anger and the scale of my malfeasance. Looking away from me, her faced cracked into a terrible, bitter smile, and her next words came with a breath that could have been a laugh, but for its complete lack of mirth. ". . . And to not even remember my name!"

"Jesus, look, I'm sorry——"

She cut me off. "No, forget it." Savage it might have been, but her onslaught to this point had at least been discreet, surgically targeted at me. Now, however, her volume rose. "You don't give a shit about other people, you're completely wrapped up in your mystery-man fantasy. I can't believe I felt sorry for you." Her eyes widened in astonishment at her own credulity—gray eyes. Despite what she was saying, I was struck again by how pretty she was. "You're pathetic. You deserve everything that's coming to you. Fuck you."

A beat went by—she appeared at last to be at the end of what she had to say. I thought I might be able to reply, to begin atonement for my mistake, and redeem myself somehow. Although I had no idea what I could say—or even where to start—I knew I had to say something. But as I opened my mouth to begin, she lunged, and threw the contents of her wineglass in my face.

It didn't feel liquid—the impact had real firmness to it, and I thought for a moment that I had been slapped. But my face was running with wine, alcohol stung my sinuses, and wetness spread across the front of my shirt.

"Nice to meet you, Maurice," Lucy said. The journalist, his jaw hanging slack, found enough composure to bob a little bow in reply. Lucy, though, did not see—she had already turned her back to us, and was heading for the lobby.

I ran my hand across my mouth and flicked wine from my fingers. The shock of the assault had caused me to jump, and I had jolted icy whisky out of my glass and down my sleeve. My shirt clung wet and cold to my sternum. A few heads had turned toward us as Lucy's diatribe reached its climax, and those onlookers had all been rewarded with a good view of me getting the wine in the face. Some still looked in my direction, smirking or holding their hands up, feigning shock in order to conceal amusement. I wanted to leave, but it would look like a humiliating retreat. Nothing gives the appearance of running away like running away. Besides, Lucy might still be near, waiting for a lift, and I could not stand the thought of seeing her again. Not right now.

A puffy pink hand rested on my shoulder. "Mate . . . " Maurice said tenderly. He was obviously uneasy, most likely in the grip of the conflicting emotions of those who find themselves at the ringside of high emotional drama— childish excitement mixed with the overpowering knowledge that they must appear absolutely serious and concerned. "Are you OK?"

My tornado of feelings narrowed for an instant into rage at Maurice—once again, the harbinger of humiliation—but this failed to endure.

"No," I said. "That was my fault. I've got to get out of here."

"What was that all about?"

"Wasn't it obvious?"

"Forgetting the name of someone you've slept with," Maurice said in a philosophical tone, examining the situation from arm's length as if he was a disinterested expert. "Unpleasant."

I glared at him. "You had to ask."

"Well, old chap," Maurice said with chiding emphasis, "I thought you would know!"

"Fucking hell," I said—to myself, not to Maurice. It was true, he could hardly be held responsible.

"Pity she wasn't wearing her thingy," Maurice said thoughtfully. "Her name badge. They've helped me out of tight spots more than once."

"Look, Maurice, I've got to clean up," I said. Ridding myself of the stickiness creeping around my chest and neck had become top priority. "I'll see you later." I drained what was left of my whisky, a good slug of it. It froze and burned; my back teeth hurt. It felt good.

"I wanted to talk with you about what happened earlier," Maurice said. His demeanour had altered, and surprised me—he was all business. "At the conference."

I summoned myself. "I want to talk to you about that too, but this isn't the best time." Stickiness was developing between my fingers and under my chin. "Can we do it tomorrow?"

Maurice looked doubtful but didn't say anything right away. Instead, he took a pen and a card—my business card, I saw—from his inside jacket pocket. "What's your mobile number?"

Only hours ago it would have been inconceivable for me to give my number to Maurice. Circumstances had indeed changed. I told him, and he jotted it on the back of my card. "I'll give you a call," he said. "I want your side of the story."

"Right," I said. "I'll see you later, then, Maurice."

"Good show," said Maurice, his normal joviality returning. "Don't worry, the drinks will be on me!"

The keycard worked on the second try. The first time, the little red light on the door lock was enough to make me deliver a sharp kick to the bottom of the door and swear. After a deep breath, I tried again, and the light blinked green, the lock behind it opening with a satisfying click. No need to go down to the lobby, I could lock myself in and put the day behind me.

Inside, with the door closed, I took off my jacket and shirt and stuffed them into the red plastic sack provided by the hotel dry-cleaning service. I hadn't been wearing a tie. In the bathroom I filled the sink and washed my face with the warm water. There was wine on my neck, down my front, in my hair. Another shower? I had taken two already today; the notion of taking a third struck me as almost decadent, whatever the immediate need for it. But this was a hotel shower. Even though I spent most of my life in hotels, I still revered their showers: hot water at a pressure that scoured the skin; clean, dry washcloths and towel; no fungus or grime between the tiles; the bright white light of a NASA dust-free lab. Not to forget the little individual soaps and bottles of shampoo that so impress people unaccustomed to hotels, though those are just part of the greater truth of the hotel shower. The whole experience is like one of those little bottles. It is used only once or twice, then replaced. Every day the whole shower is reset by invisible staff, as if you had never been in it. In your shower at home, your repeated visits will eventually accumulate, and you must continually clean the unit. This, more than the dribbling water or the Swiss watchmaker precision needed to set the temperature between glacial and scalding, is the true disappointment of the home shower: you are constantly encountering yourself. What should be a fresh experience becomes a rendezvous with scum, mold and hair. But the hotel shower is permanently renewed.

And I needed renewal. My chances with Lucy were now zero. Probably less, a terrifying negative value a great distance from zero. I had flunked with women before—had come on too strong, or inadvertently insulted them, and they had cut me dead, called me a prick, stormed off, whatever. And it had been nothing: a ping-pong ball against a suit of armor. So why did I feel profoundly affected by the collapse of this passing and not long-sought flirtation? I had a sense of some distant and serious damage being done—the deep vibration though a ship's hull that says it has struck something and is taking on water, felt long before the decks begin to list and the passengers head to the lifeboats.

In previous times I could have contented myself with anonymity. When I was not known, my failures and foulups were not noted or remembered—I could simply disappear again. I was a meaningless part of the background. But Lucy remembered me, and I had been remembered at the fair. For the first time, I suspected I might have a reputation, and I suspected it was not a desirable one. My ability to live as I pleased, with no consequences, was compromised.

I dried myself and put on one of the dressing gowns that hung by the bathroom door. It was not too late to order something comforting from room service—perhaps a dessert—but the idea felt somehow effeminate, so I resisted it. I switched on my laptop, intending to write an email to Adam telling him what had happened today. But the room's WiFi signal was perilously weak. The computer would connect to the Internet and show a few tantalizing signs of loading up websites—then the progress icons would slow to a crawl and eventually stop altogether with an apologetic bubble-message stating that the connection had been lost. Once I had repeated these steps three or four times, there was no sign of improvement and I had little inclination to persist.

Instead, I took a half-bottle of red wine and a glass from the minibar and lay on the bed, sipping mindlessly through the television channels. Sitcoms and crime dramas gave way to telecasino operations, home shopping and sign-language repeats of documentaries. My surfing soon beached on a music channel, about the only source of brightness or novelty on the digital dial as the hour got later. I had seen the news many times over already, the same stories in their constant loop, a spectacle so excruciatingly tedious that I found myself yearning for a major disaster—a natural catastrophe somewhere with a high incidence of cameras per head, an ornate political scandal, an episode of histrionics on the financial markets. So I watched the music channel, sound low. Men and women, mostly women, strutted and thrusted and shimmied. I considered that perhaps my restlessness had an angle of unrelieved tension, and turned my mind to the hotel's on-demand "adult" television services, their promise of rapid gratification in return for a discreetly worded but substantial addition to your room bill. The menu was reached via the welcome screen, and I passed again the hotel's personalized greeting, its forecast for tomorrow's weather and its helpful hints about how to book a business suite. Once I found the adult pay-TV options, past the feature films and the kids' programs, the titles did nothing but stir my self-loathing, and I returned to the less penetrative displays of secondary sexual characteristics in the music videos.

The half-bottle of wine seemed very parsimonious, disappearing in less than two glasses, and it made way for two whisky miniatures. I thought that after a drink I might begin to be ready for sleep. But although the day had taxed me greatly, it did not seem to have tired me. There was, I believed, no original thought left to have about my various confrontations, but still they turned over and over in my mind, certain phrases bubbling back up, certain moments replaying in a loop. I formulated snappy and witty rebuttals, unanswerable comebacks; I scripted and rehearsed future encounters. And this ceaseless, futile mental activity disgusted me even as I felt myself unable to stop indulging in it. The alcohol had done some valuable work, dissolving the worst of my embarrassment and regret. Consequences mattered less now. But rather than giving me peace, instead I felt a rising anger: anger at the event director for his ruse, anger with Lucy for making an unnecessary scene and for not giving me an opportunity to apologize, anger at Maurice for his thick-headed insouciance in the face of everything, for blundering into the wrong moment again and again and for generally being Maurice. It was extraordinary that anyone so shambolic could thwart me so effectively and consistently. But more than anyone I was angry at myself.

Meanwhile, the party downstairs and the other functions around the hotel were breaking up. Guests returned noisily to their rooms, bumping along the corridor and slamming doors. Some travelled in pairs and groups, intent on sex or combined raids on minibars, or simply stretching out the joy of boozy togetherness to the ultimate possible second, before they reached their doors and had to part. Maybe they were using their mobile phones, too, drunkenly texting wives and girlfriends, or husbands and boyfriends, and setting plans for tomorrow with colleagues and lovers—I guessed this, because the clock radio by my bed began to trill with interference, burbling and bleating along to some imperceptible traffic in the air around it. I braced for my mobile phone to ring or receive a text, but nothing came and the noise continued. Muting the TV, I leaned over to see if the radio had a volume control or standby button I could use to shut it up. Between its electronic yelps and growls, there was a velvety purr of static—so low it could barely be heard—with silvery variation. I ceased my fiddling with the controls to focus on this background layer. It suggested the faintest trace of music or speech coming from the speakers, even with the radio turned off. Was that possible? I had heard speakers pick up taxi radios before, delivering a short burst of dispatch communications, but that was when they were turned on—could the same happen when the radio was turned off? Was it truly off? It was plugged into the mains, to power its bright red display. Every time I felt I was getting close to the subliminal pattern, almost identifying a tune or a voice, another bout of loud static chatter broke in and I lost it. Frustrated, I reached under the bedside table and yanked the plug from the wall.

Nothing happened. The clock showed the same time as before, and continued to natter and whisper. How was that possible? A backup battery, perhaps, to keep the alarm set through any power outages—shrewd design, but was it plausible? How long could it stay on? The muttering had developed a sinister, repellent aspect. It dredged up a memory—I had heard it before, that morning. It had woken me, intruding into a dream, and dissolving before I could grasp it.

Uneasiness grew in me. I unmuted the television and watched, trying to enthral myself with the seedy commercial pop videos, and ignore the treacherous, whispering device beside me. But their appeal was waning. The drink had made me woozy, but still not sleepy. Perhaps if I turned off the TV and lights and got under the covers, sleep would come. A formless, visceral distaste adhered to that idea—I didn't want to go to sleep, I had to cancel my sense of being a victim with some kind of action. I wanted to do something—anything—with an urge that felt almost animal. Returning to the bar was out of the question—it would probably be closed now, while the staff arranged the restaurant in preparation for breakfast tomorrow. If by some miracle it was open, there would be stragglers from the party down there, and I had no intention of amusing them with a ghostly reappearance. Still, I had to get out—this room, which had beckoned so hospitably through the day, was tightening around me. While it had been so pristine on my return from the conference, I had now sullied it with my presence—clothes scattered abou t, condensation in the bathroom, a clutter of empty miniatures and cans on the bedside table. And the squalls of static from the clock radio continued to trouble me, with their suggestion of a pervasive disquiet in the invisible spectra, and their indifference to mains power.

Some actions could be taken. In a burst of energy, I rose from the bed, gathered up the empty bottles and cans and dropped them in the room's bin. I hung up the towel I had used, wrung out the flannel and folded away my clothes. I opened the room door and left the dry-cleaning bag in the hall for collection, along with the tray and plate that had carried my room-service sandwich.

The corridor was empty. There was no sound from the direction of the lifts. Perhaps everyone had already decided what bed they were going to spend the night in and had taken to it. Other trays and other bags were left outside other rooms.

Faced with the gathering quiet of the hotel, sleep spreading through it, conquering room after room, I would normally have wanted to succumb, to spend my last waking moments revelling in the thought that I was one among many solitary sleepers, all subject to the same gentle lullaby from the air conditioning, recycling our slowing, deepening breath. Tonight, agitated and unready to rest, I wanted to participate in that shared experience in another way: by being out in it, awake and alert, moving and thinking amid general still oblivion. I thought of the urban fox, busy in slumbering streets, an outsider but blissfully independent. I dressed quickly, just a shirt and trousers. Now was also the hour of the redheaded woman—or it had been yesterday, at least. Was that only yesterday? It seemed so much longer ago; again she was receding from reality to an afterimage.

Her hour. The first time I saw her, that shining memory, she had been sleepwalking. It had been a recurring problem, she told me last night, particularly in unfamiliar surroundings like hotels. But she had overcome it. Way Inn hotels were now so familiar to her that her night-time expeditions had ceased. Maybe she retained some affection for the night, when the corridors were quiet and the paintings could be found and photographed in peace, and that was what had drawn her down to the bar yesterday, and might lead her to be out tonight. Grasping at straws, yes, I knew that—the chances of just happening upon her in the corridor were a million to one against, especially past 1 a.m. Still, however infinitesimal the odds, they were better than zero. And all I wanted to do was walk.

I stepped into the corridor and let the door of my room close behind me, a task it completed with a certain grace, slowing as it narrowed the distance to the jamb, braked by a hidden mechanism. They would not slam by themselves, these doors; left to its own devices the hotel was quiet, considerate, unobtrusive. Normally, on leaving my room, I would turn left to go to the lifts and stairs—in fact, I would do that in all circumstances, like most guests. I never had any reason to turn the other way. There was nothing down there, only other rooms, other doors. But I turned right.

The black doors I passed—one on my left, then one on my right, then one on my left—gave my pace a satisfying rhythm, and I turned my saunter into a brisk stride. Ahead, the corridor terminated in a fire door, which I pushed through. It opened directly onto a T-junction, obliging me to choose a direction again. From what I knew of the hotel's geography, a left turn would make me complete half a circuit around the Zen courtyard—if I followed it with another left, then another left, I would arrive at the lifts and stairs. So I turned right again; the other, unexpected direction.

The corridor turned to the left, and I with it. I tried to picture the hotel in my head, as a model or a wireframe graphic I could manipulate and manage—it was, from the portion I saw from the outside, a long rectangle in plan, its shorter edge facing the motorway and the service road, its bulk stretching back into the dreary fields. The courtyards were essential to bring light into its inner rooms—but how many courtyards were there? Two, I thought, making the whole layout a figure-of-eight. But already the hotel seemed a little larger than I anticipated—there could be three courtyards, arranged in a line or a triangle pointed at the road.

No one else was about, but I was not alone. Most of the doors I passed were silent, but from behind some came the sound of conversation or laughter, or a television with the volume higher than it should be at this time of night; in at least one room avid, gasping intercourse was taking place. It was, relative to the dead quiet of hotels at other times, a fairly lively night—I fancied it would have been possible to guess that a party had taken place even if I had not known about it. Many rooms had trays and dirty crockery left outside, evidence of earlier meals or midnight snacks; in some, elaborate feasts had been consumed, their remains piled on trolleys. DO NOT DISTURB signs hung from many door handles. Many people had clearly had a much better day than I had had. Bitterness welled inside me.

Another fire door; beyond it a bank of windows overlooking a second courtyard, deeper in the building. Weedy security lights only hinted at the artfully arranged stones and boulders, aided by the low gleam from the wet surfaces. The lights' reflection in the black of the pond danced and scattered, broken by the falling rain. Not even die-hard smokers out at this hour. The hotel above this sodden yard was no more than a grim implication of bulk, its tinted windows patches of thorough blackness in a dark that otherwise would have appeared total.

I kept moving, left, right, right again, trying to randomize my route as I did at the fair, to defy any logical path and experience the building naturally, like a forest, without desire, without rational choices. More inscrutable black doors, continuous indirect lighting, halogen spots on the omni-similar abstract art, painting after painting. Thank God there was no single artist shouldering the job of supplying wall candy for Way Inn. Just this one hotel would ruin his wrist and his eyesight; many more hotels would open while physiotherapy restored him to health. A new Way Inn in Hefei, in Curitiba, in Sharjah, all needing his inimitably imitable visions in shades from chocolate to eggshell. Again his fingers would have to twist around the ragged brush. But the redhead had said they had found a way to industrialize the process, to collectivize it—of course. Looking at the hotel, seeing its size, it quickly became clear how mistaken the impression of a single artist was. No one man or woman could supply the hotel.

Big hotel, really big hotel. I kept my pace up, moving powerfully, covering distance, and still I felt I was in new territory. A big container for people, forever waiting to be filled. This was only the start, the motorway axis was meant to grow, grow, grow—more flights into the airport, more vehicles on the roads, more visitors at the Meta-Center. Even in hard times, a global corporation like Way Inn knew that growth could always be found somewhere. That was what the redheaded woman was employed to find: places to grow. Business leaving other areas had to go somewhere . . . people sloshing around the world, needing a vessel for their night hours. At any given time, five hundred thousand people are in the air, in planes. Five hundred thousand. At all times. Half a million. A city. This population is stable, distributed globally. How many people in hotels, worldwide, at any one time? Many more: a super-city, a megalopolis, its doors always open, its lights always on; twenty-four-hour room service, check in at all times; people sifting through without end. Its population peaks with the passage of night—an empire on which the sun forever sets. These cities are only invisible because most of their inhabitants stay for just a short time, a night or two. They never really stopped to think of their presence in this invisible city. You had to stay longer for that.

Right now, however, I was aware of the guest population thinning around me as I struck toward the hotel's rear. There were fewer trays outside doors, fewer televisions, fewer shouts of laughter or ecstasy. Only the gentle noise of the air conditioning and my own footsteps could be heard. I passed a stairwell and, shortly after, another courtyard. Empty, of course, and as lonely and distant behind the tinted glass as video beamed from a robot probe on the surface of another planet. If there was a moon in the sky, it was thoroughly obscured by the mile-deep shroud of freezing moisture that was the autumn atmosphere.

When I tried to move farther, I found my body resisting me. Not far beyond the third light well, I had to stop. I was out of breath, choked by an acid dryness. Black lightning exploded behind my eyes, surrounded by random, fleeing points of light. Anaerobic pain turned the inner fibers of my legs caustic. Almost without realizing it, without thinking at all, I had been running; I had drained my body's resources before I knew I was making a demand on them. Furthermore, there was nowhere else to go. The corridor ended in a fire door—unlike the others I had gone through, this one was adorned with warning signs. THIS DOOR IS ALARMED. USE ONLY IN EMERGENCY.

No more. I slumped to the floor, sitting under one of the abstract paintings. The muscles in my legs ticked and pinged. For a couple of seconds I wondered if I was likely to pass out, but then my tether to consciousness drew in its slack. Late at night, several whiskies, a long day—I had meant at least to wear myself out, so, mission accomplished. It was time to retire. In front of me was a room door. The number on it was 281. Only 281? Surely I had travelled farther? But that meant sixty doors between here and my room, and that was enough.

My strength had returned, and my little dizzy spell now felt like an embarrassing aberration. The whole day felt like an embarrassing aberration. Once I had retraced my steps back to the last turning I took, I glanced at a room number to check my progress.

288.

Not right. The numbers should be descending toward 219, not climbing. Had I somehow completed a circuit or doubled back on myself? The chicanes and doglegs in the hotel's layout had forced me to take many turns, but I was sure that I had been maintaining one overall direction; toward the rear of the building, away from reception. However, one misplaced turn and I would have been heading in the wrong direction; if I had missed two turns out of my calculations, I could have reversed my course without knowing it. I had been moving without thinking, almost willing myself to get lost, after all.

Just like that, my mental model of the hotel melted away. I no longer had a conception of my place within its walls. Inspecting my current location had little use—of course this T-junction looked like one I had seen before; they all did. A sign pointed to rooms 290 to 299—were there more above 299? 2100, 201a? It seemed unlikely that a hotel would have exactly 99 rooms to a floor, but why was that number less plausible than 90 or 105? Even the corridor I had just walked down seemed tinged with doubt—had I really come that way? I tried to picture my former self a few minutes ago, coming down one of these corridors like a ghost walking the same path, but couldn't do it—my former self was everywhere, walking in every direction with equal certainty. There was door 281—had I sat under that painting? And a little farther along was door 280. The numbers were infallible—all I had to do was follow them back down to 219 and bed.

So I proceeded, watching the numbers decline through the 270s. Before long, I came across a light well, a promising sign—it had to be the one I had seen earlier, before I had been obliged to take my break. It was followed by a flight of stairs. I approached these and leaned over the banister—no one else was about. I moved on.

The corridors and junctions I passed were identical to the ones I passed on my outward journey, but that did not mean they were the same. I considered the problem of how to know if they were the same corridors and junctions passed in reverse by my former self. I wished I had done something to better remember where I was as I sped through earlier—not marking my path with string or a trail of bread crumbs, but somehow making a mental note of my surroundings. How? Remembering which doors had Do Not Disturb signs on them? A study of the paintings? The redheaded woman had said as much—that she believed the paintings were a way of encoding spatial information, which sounded to me like a map. This might be mumbo jumbo, but the paintings were the most variable feature in the otherwise completely unchanging corridor environment. But how could I tell them apart? One arrangement of curves and blocks in sober colors looked much like another. They were as indistinct as the corridors they decorated. The surface interest they added to the walls was an illusion—just another layer of banality textured to resemble something more interesting. It was maddening—and at the same time I had to remind myself that I was not lost; that the numbers could not lie.

Ahead, though, something was different. I had become accustomed to the low, warm, nighttime lighting of the corridors; against the rain-soaked blackness outside, it was cheerful and welcome. But more brilliant light now intruded, making the corridors I had seen so far appear dim by comparison. In front of me, the passage took a left turn. From beyond this corner spilled a rhombus of radiance.

An emergency light of some sort. A glitch in the environmental controls, a faulty rheostat turning the ambient luminaires to their maximum output. A fault, quite normal, to be expected anywhere, not least in a new hotel with a newly installed plant and electronics. Still, it held me to my spot. For long minutes—though perhaps they were no more than seconds—I could not move. The persistent sameness of the hotel had lulled me; this interruption to it was fundamentally disturbing. And something about the quality of the light was quite wrong.

Without hurry, I walked to the corner and looked around it—*looked* around it; I did not step around it, I wanted to see the source of this luminosity before proceeding.

The light was not coming from the luminaires or halogen spots in the corridor. They were switched off. The light was coming from outside, through a bank of windows overlooking a courtyard.

I approached the windows, briefly concerned that even this short distance would be too much for me, given the sudden weakness in my legs. After two steps I had to hold up my arm to shield my eyes against the sun, reflected in the mirrored glass of the windows on the far side of the courtyard. The same sun inscribed every detail of the Zen meditation garden two storeys down, driving shadows back into the deepest recesses between the gray pebbles; spawning a twin in the unmoving, crystal water of the pond; and finding seams of copper and ruby in the red hair of the woman sitting upon the flat boulder. The woman from the bar—the sleepwalker—cross-legged, hands resting upturned on her knees, back straight, eyes closed. She was meditating. No clouds interrupted the blue sky above her.

Had I passed out? What time was it? My watch and mobile phone were in my room—I had dressed rapidly in my sudden enthusiasm for a stroll and had not thoroughly reequipped myself. My keycard was the only thing in my pocket. Could it be morning already? Past morning, in fact, as the sun was high above us. And it *was* the sun, unmistakably, not security lights or anything else. The stones in the garden were dry; indeed, they looked baked, and I could feel the heat being held back by the air conditioning. There were no blushes of damp between the stones or puddles waiting in shadows. The woman was wearing clothes suitable for the gym, not a bitter autumn—leggings, running shoes without socks, a sweatshirt. A Way Inn sweatshirt.

The woman. Her long neck, framed by the sloppy collar of the sweatshirt, was porcelain pale; no wonder she appeared to exult in the sunshine. By her pallor this might have been the first time she had seen the sun in years. She would be able to explain, she would know the answer to this conundrum. I beat the flat of my hands against the window, feeling the pane barely vibrate under my blows, and shouted "Hey! Hey!" But she didn't move, not a flinch or twitch—if she heard me, she did a fine job of concealing the fact. It was night, I remembered, suddenly overcome with regret at causing such a noise when people were sleeping. How could it be night, though, with the sun in the sky? I needed to reach the woman, I needed to draw her attention—and I realized it was useless to try that from here; even if she heard me she would not be able to see me through the one-way glass. There would be a stairwell nearby, or a lift shaft—light well, stairwell, they went together, that much had been a consistent feature of the hotel's otherwise unhelpful internal scheme. And the stairwell would be easy to find; all I needed to do was follow the emergency exit signs—the little green man heading for the door with the backlit arrow was everywhere, by law.

I found one, and followed it; it led to another, which led to a corner. Around the corner was a fire door.

FIRE EXIT. THIS DOOR IS ALARMED. USE ONLY IN EMERGENCY.

My hands hovered above the bar that opened the door; I let them rest on the metal, feeling its coolness in the hinge of my palm. On the other side of the door would be a staircase, a utilitarian concrete affair or a galvanized steel structure fixed to the outer shell of the hotel. But it would lead down to her; I could get to the garden and talk with her again. How serious was the alarm? Was it a true nuclear-strike-warning din that would wake everyone in the hotel, or one that would wake everyone in the corridor, or would it alert only the night staff, who would come up to investigate? If the sun was up, would it be the night staff or the day staff? Maybe the sign was all for show, and this was just a door, not attached to any grander system. But there were regulations, serious life-or-death regulations. There would be CCTV. I took my hands off the bar.

Perhaps one of the windows overlooking the courtyard opened. That didn't seem so unlikely. I retraced my steps, passing the little green emergency men fleeing in the opposite direction. She would still be down there.

There was no light from the light well. I had to cup my hands against the window like a visor to see anything at all against the minimal reflections from the nighttime, dim hall lighting on the glass. Low-power security lights suggested the features of the Zen garden—the boulders, the pond—but it was deserted. Drizzle flecked the glass. I closed my eyes, pinched the bridge of my nose—again, the black lightning crackled, and the corridor carpet heaved under me. No sun, no light, no woman. It was more than twenty hours since I had woken in my Way Inn room, and that was after barely four hours of sleep—it was too much, I was exhausted, it had been an emotional day, delusions like this could be understood, all I needed was some sleep.

A nearby room number: 233. That was comforting. My door was only a couple of turns away, and I found it without drama. But the door, having been found, declined to open. The keycard, pushed into its slot, produced not the green light of admission but its evil red twin.

I inspected the door, wondering at the composition of the black wood—not hardwood, for sure; a good quality composite of some kind, fireproof and noise-resisting and pleasingly solid-sounding when it shut, covered in stained wood-grain veneer. The metal numbers screwed to the door continued their obstinate insistence that this was room 219, and taking it at its word I tried the keycard again, and again was shown the red light. Not really a red light, I saw—it was more an orange light, perhaps out of deference to the infallibility of the Way Inn customer. A truly red light would be too brusque; the orange light regretted the inconvenience and accepted that the guest probably did deserve access to this room but, unfortunately, access was impossible to arrange while the data held on the card failed to match the code stored in the lock's tiny memory. This made me only more tired and angry, because regardless of the geniality of the LED color choice, the overall result was identical: I could not enter my room. Why not? The keycard had been the only thing in my pocket, without any exposure to the supposedly memory-addling rays of my mobile phone or keys or anything else. Fury and tired acceptance of circumstance battled within me, and acceptance won. After one last try—orange light—there was no option left but to go to reception.

What time was it now? Approaching three in the morning, I guessed, perhaps later if I truly had zoned out during my trek. It took far longer than I expected to find my way back to the lifts, and in their recursive mirrors, I was treated to the sight of a greatly reduced man, not improved by his multiplication. An army of slouches, open collars, dark rings forming under the eyes, shadows at the jaw.

There was no clock in the lobby, but dawn was not visible through the main entrance, just the orange undawn of the motorway. To the credit of the Way Inn corporation, not one fiber in the appearance of the young man on the front desk betrayed the slightest surprise or distaste at my demeanor. On hearing my complaint he accepted my card with a sympathetic smile, fed it into his reader, blinked a couple of times at a screen I could not see and handed it back to me with another smile of greater magnitude than the first.

"It should work fine now, sir," he said. "Would you like me to come up and make sure?"

"No, thank you," I said quickly. "That won't be necessary." Fortunately he did not need convincing to stay put.

"I'll be right here if you do need anything, sir," he said.

"Thanks, good night," I said.

This time, I got the green light. To enter I had to step over my room-service tray and the plastic bag containing my wine-soaked shirt and jacket, which I had left in the corridor for collection. Even through the fatigue that dogged my last waking moments as I kicked off my shoes and stripped off my clothes, the tray and the bag stayed in my mind like moths beating at a lightbulb. They, not the apparition of the woman in the sun-filled courtyard, were the last thing I thought of before sleep came. Because when I consulted my memory of arriving back at my room after my midnight stroll, and getting the orange light, the bag and the tray formed no part of that memory. There had been nothing outside the door—that other door, that other room 219. I would have sworn to it. Another room 219.

PART TWO

THE HOTEL

"Housekeeping."

Words in space, like the monolith hanging above Jupiter at the end of *2001*. Obviously filled with meaning, but beyond meaning.

A modest knock. "Housekeeping."

"Yes." This was me.

A mechanism worked, metal moving neat against metal. The door unlocked and opened.

"No, wait." I moved sideways quickly, out of the bed, planting feet on warm carpet. The Way Inn-branded dressing gown was hanging on the corner of the bathroom door—I put it on and stepped nimbly to the room door, which had opened wide enough to admit a head and a shoulder garbed in industrial pink.

"Oh, sorry," the woman, the chambermaid, said in accented English. "Clean room?"

"No, thank you, not now, later," I said.

She seemed chagrined by my reply, as if cleaning my room was a much-delayed treat. "Later?" she said. I couldn't place the accent.

"Later, later," I said. "It's OK, it's not important." I was in a bind—on the one hand I didn't want her hanging around, waiting to clean my room; on the other, I didn't want to dismiss her, to tell her or even imply that no cleaning was needed today. A clean room would be a pleasant thing to return to later.

"Later," she said, giving me a serious but not unfriendly look. Did I mean it, this promise to her?

"Later," I said, organizing part of my face into a smile, hoping it was the correct part.

The chambermaid receded and the door closed behind her with the softest click.

My purpose in sending the chambermaid away had been to return to bed. I had not set an alarm for myself. By no means did I intend to go downstairs and present myself at the breakfast buffet, or join the queues waiting for buses at the peak hour. Let the rush pass, then I would make my way to the MetaCenter in my own time, under fewer eyes. But the time on the clock-radio digital display was 11:22. My lie-in was over already; I had slept through it. Breakfast finished at ten. The day was advancing without me. This realization left me feeling cheated: I had been denied the pleasure of knowing I was skipping breakfast and starting late, the sensation of being able to go down and join in but instead choosing not to. The day had started in a state of alertness, not leisure. Rather than lounge and wait with a cup of coffee, I needed to go straight to work. There were conference sessions to be attended in the afternoon, and two days' work to be completed at the fair.

I washed and dressed. With me I had two suits, both unremarkable but well-made business numbers, one marginally smarter than the other. Lucy had sauced the smarter jacket, leaving me its humbler sibling. This was fine—no more parties, not this time. I thought of Lucy lensing rage at me; her remarks (that I was pathetic, that I deserved any future misfortune), though they stung when I recalled them, felt like only a preface to a more fundamental condemnation that, when she arrived at it, she could not put in words and had instead stated with pinot grigio. How could I express in words my sorrow at what had happened if her anger had exceeded words? Nothing I could formulate seemed up to the job. And only part of me wanted to express any sorrow or remorse—I also felt a strong impulse to simply forget the incident. In the past, this would have been my overriding sentiment: to hell with it, a fugitive moment with a single woman among thousands. But there was a persistent sense of the event persisting—that a permanent record of my actions existed somewhere, updated in indelible ink; that I was leaving a psychic trail.

These thoughts kept with me as I buttoned my shirt and fastened my belt. As I tied my tie, I went to the window to move my mind along; to address the day I was facing, not the day that had passed. The only credit that could be given to the weather was that it was an improvement on yesterday. A pale blot in the muesli-milk clouds betrayed the approximate position of the sun. Puddles wrinkled in the wind, but were not presently accepting new drops of rain. The streetlights were off. As I completed the knot at my neck, a plane descended into view, heavy and close and slow, easing itself into the airport. Only the faintest vibration sounded through the glass.

I was stalling—I knew it. I did not want to return to the MetaCenter, where the witnesses to my humiliation yesterday were all boxed up together. But I had to do my job. Just two more days, then this toxic concentration of people who knew me would be safely diffused into a more palatable, homeopathic solution. Until then, there were stands to visit, there was information to gather. It was a shame about the lost bag, and the duplication of effort it entailed, but at least I had a spare tote, from another conference last year, and I would not have to pick up one of the nauseating yellow MetaCenter bags.

When I left my room, I hung the "Do Not Disturb" sign on the door handle, turned to the "Please Clean My Room" side. The chambermaid was busy in another room; I did not see her, just the open door onto a stranger's disordered sheets, her multistorey hygiene pantechnicon out in the hall, stacked with soaps and toilet rolls, a mobile fetish-altar for a religion based on cleanliness and making the past invisible. Complex, nonionic, surfactant scents rose from it like incense. The glimpse of another room, resembling mine but occupied by someone else, felt at once intrusive and utterly discreet, like seeing the open cavity of a body undergoing surgery, their face covered by green cloth. A vacuum cleaner was running, bumping against furniture. Power cords trailed along the floor. The lift, when I entered it, smelled of air freshener. The world was being made over. It raised my spirits. Everything that had happened yesterday—the event director's trap, the disaster with Lucy, my distressed nighttime excursion—had all taken place in an earlier, prototypical universe, one that had been superseded by this latest, improved model.

Way Inn red had replaced MetaCenter yellow as the dominant color in the lobby. It was an improvement. The chain was taking maximum advantage of its captive audience and had set up a promotional stand where the registration desk had been yesterday. And it had clearly spent more on the effort than the conference center: there were wide-screen plasma TVs, freestanding displays, a cornucopia of merchandise and a couple of brand-enhancement agents in tight white T-shirts and red hot pants and base-ball caps. With the morning mêlée long gone, these brand agent, booth babes, whatever, were underemployed, and one bounced toward me as I walked toward the exit.

"Attending Meetex, sir?"

"Yes," I said. Of course, what else?

She thrust a flier into my hand. Big smile. "Way to go!"

"Thanks," I said. The flier was hook-shaped so it could hang from a door handle, like the "Do Not Disturb" sign, but printed with details of the convention facilities available at Way Inn hotels: "THE PERFECT ENVIRONMENT FOR BUSINESS." It folded out into a grid showing the different formats of space that the chain offered, and their availability and capacity at nearby locations: meeting room, theater, parliament, boardroom, U-shape, classroom, cabaret, reception, dinner, dinner-dance. A thesaurus of human congregation. The range of different configurations was so comprehensive, so varied, it was curiously deadening. It stamped on alternatives: this was all that was possible to achieve in a room. Another column gave the distance from each location to the nearest airport. "Way Inn, any way you want."

The restaurant was being set up for lunch already, and the bar had opened with early trade from a few coffee-drinkers. Every trace of the party was gone, and the space it had occupied had been repartitioned and repurposed.

Outside, under the undulating glass canopy, a coach was waiting, door open to the curb. The sallow daylight carried no warmth and I hunched against the biting air. A short sit in a bus with its heaters on was a prospect I found unexpectedly pleasant. I hopped aboard nimbly and turned to find a seat, but was halted by the voice of the driver behind me.

"Excuse me!"

I turned. The driver was leaning out of his seat, craning around to see me, looking me up and down expectantly.

"Yes?" I said.

"D'you have your pass?"

I did—it was in my jacket pocket. I found it and handed it over. The driver scrutinized it with a level of care it had not been subjected to before. Then he took a gray plastic handheld device from a pocket in the door on his side of the bus and positioned it over the QR code on the pass.

Bip, said the device. *Bee-baw*.

The driver tried again. *Bip. Bee-baw*.

"This pass is voided, sir, I can't let you travel."

"What?"

"Your pass," the driver said, louder and slower, disdain now clear in his eyes, "is voided. It's been voided. You can't come on board."

"Voided?" I said. I couldn't get a grasp on the word. It meant nothing to me.

"Voided. It's void. You'll have to get off the bus." The driver's expression blended boredom and implacability. His eyes were lidded. I felt the edge of coercion, the implicit possibility of force.

"I don't understand," I said. "It was fine yesterday, now you're saying it's invalid?"

"Voided, yeah," the driver said.

"But it was fine yesterday," I said.

"Yeah, well, since then it's been voided."

"This has to be a mistake," I said. While we had been having this exchange, another conference-goer had arrived at the step of the bus and was waiting to board. I was blocking his way, and his patience was visibly diminishing. He clasped his credentials, bit his lip, looked tautly between the driver and me. I felt other eyes on me, from the seated passengers waiting for the shuttle to depart.

"This has to be a mistake," I repeated. "I've paid for the whole three days."

"Look," the driver said, "all I know is I can't let any voids on. You'll have to get off. Go to registration, if it's a mistake they'll be able to sort it out."

"How am I expected to get to registration if you won't let me travel?" I said.

"That's not my problem," the driver said, the professional, customer-facing tone of synthetic respect gone from his voice, which was now pure civilian scorn. My invalid pass was clearly, as far as he was concerned, damning evidence of my degenerate character. "Please, get off the bus."

"What about people who just arrived?" I asked, scenting a loophole. "They can't register at the hotel, how are they expected to get to the show?"

"Preregistration guests can travel without a pass," the driver said. "Courtesy service."

"So that's fine!" I said. "I'm going to reregister."

"You can't register. You've got a pass already," the driver said, holding the laminated square up.

I snatched my pass from the driver and stuffed it into my pocket, catching a finger on its rough, unexpectedly sharp edge. "There! It's gone. I don't have a pass. I'm going to register."

"Sir," the driver said, his eyelids descending still farther, more dangerous blandness seeping into his voice, "you have a pass. I can't let you travel with a voided pass." Under their lids, his eyes dropped to my pocket. "I can see the ribbon."

"But someone without a pass can travel?"

"Sir, if you're going to get aggressive . . . "

I pulled myself in and spoke evenly. "I'm not getting aggressive, I just don't know why I can't come on this bus to get this . . . mistake fixed if you let everyone else travel."

"Everyone else has a pass, or they don't have a pass."

"I have a pass!"

"Your pass has been voided."

"This is crazy!"

"Sir—"

"I know, I know, I'm not getting aggressive," I said, closing my eyes and rubbing my face.

"Excuse me!" The man waiting to board the bus broke in. The driver beckoned him on, paying only the slightest attention to his pass. Another passenger followed. They squeezed past me without much consideration.

"I'm not starting the bus with you on board," the driver said. I heard an exaggerated sigh behind me, and a loud tut.

"So what do I do?" I knew I had lost.

"Call the organizers, I suppose," the driver said, his expression making it plain he didn't care if I lived or died.

"Right," I said.

The doors hissed and quivered closed as soon as I stepped back onto the curb. I watched the coach's swollen rear maneuver around the Way Inn's drive and onto the service road. Its departure left me alone. Even the smokers were gone. Again, the freezing air took me by surprise after the stuffy warmth of the bus. I pulled up the lapels of my jacket but did not go back inside.

A mistake. That had to be it. This was a mistake, not malice; not a personalized strike against me. A glitch. It was impossible to believe the alternatives. No one could be so petty. Could Laing really be so insecure? Just weighing the possibility made me furious and ready to lash out. But as quickly as this thirst for vengeance arose, it subsided, weighted down by my realization that readmittance was more important than retaliation. There were sessions I had to attend, material and impressions I had to gather for clients. Contracts, turnover, repeat business; all depended on me getting back into the fair.

In the minute or two I spent brooding on my options, nothing passed on the access road—not a single car or van, and certainly no pedestrians. The motorway, sunk behind its embankment, produced a steady hoarse roar, a Niagara of activity that balanced the stillness but did not dispel it. I only appreciated how empty the road had been when a vehicle finally appeared: a canary-yellow bus, another of the conference shuttles on a return leg. A different bus with a different driver.

Before the new driver saw me waiting, I ducked through the sliding doors of the hotel. This new bus would not have many customers—not only was there no one outside, the half-dozen men and women scattered around the Way Inn lobby didn't look as if they were in a hurry to get to the conference center. The bus would linger a few minutes before again crossing the divide.

The booth babes were standing to attention by the Way Inn promo stand. One hopped on tiptoes in a caffeinated manner.

"Can I have one of those baseball caps?" I asked the closest babe.

"Sure!" she said, brandishing a form. "But you have to sign up for our conference services e-newsletter."

"I'm a member of the My Way program," I said, taking my wallet from my back pocket and producing the red membership card. "You have all my details. Can I have a hat?"

The babe smiled uncomfortably and again offered the form. "Sorry, it's for the conference services—"

"—E-newsletter, got it," I said, taking the form. "No problem. Can I have a pen?"

The form didn't take more than a couple of minutes to complete. I considered giving fake information, but the creativity involved would take more effort than simply telling the truth. I had a "fake" email address which I handed out freely, and gave my "real" email to almost no one. But I had to check the "fake" account, on the possibility that important leads were going there, and to supplement research. Because it got more traffic, I had to check it more often than my pristine, quiet "real" account. Consequently, Adam now wrote to that account knowing that I would see his messages sooner there. I had to wonder which was really the fake account. And trying to go incognito seemed to be a source of bad luck for me at present. Still, the necessity of offering up more personal details to the world brought out a mischievous streak in me. Under "Nature of job" I put "disgraced back channel." Under "What Way Inn services would you like to know more about?" I wrote "Satanic art conspiracies."

Information. Everyone just wants more information from everyone else, that's what Lucy had said. Your personal details aren't the new currency, but they are the new price of admission. I recalled her face, that delicate face twisted with hurt and anger, after she ran out of insults but before she threw her drink at me. A situation caused by information that had been improperly stored and proved impossible to retrieve. A databasing specialist should have been able to appreciate the problem. Or perhaps not.

In return for this latest dribble of data into the corporate networks, I got a hat—a red baseball cap, and a good one too; cloth, not synthetic foam with that horrible plastic netting at the back. Way Inn embroidered in white thread at the front. Quality merch.

The view through the glass doors was still eclipsed by the flank of the bus. I exited the hotel, putting on the cap and pulling the brim low over my eyes, flashing my pass casually, holding it so my index and middle finger "accidentally" obscured much of my mug shot.

"Wait, wait," the driver called to me as I hurried past her. I froze.

"Yes?" I said, half-turning, showing her no more than part of my face in profile.

"I need to see your pass," she said. "We're checking passes."

I handed over my pass, resigned to the inevitable.

Bip. Bee-baw.

"I'm sorry, sir—"

"Voided, right?"

"Yes."

"I had a feeling." And I did have a feeling: a rising fountain of stomach acid, a bubbling horror summed up by the words *not a mistake*.

The bus was empty. I glanced wistfully at its tidy ranks of paired seats before I descended the steps back to the forecourt.

Fretful that others in the lobby might have noticed my repeated failure to board a bus, and my erratic peregrinations in general, I walked to an armchair with exaggerated ease and sat in it. The air I wanted to project was one of total purpose, as if all my movements that morning were part of a grand plan developed some time ago and proceeding better than anticipated. No one, in fact, took the slightest interest in me, but still I felt myself surrounded by animus and censure. There was decreasing reason to doubt that the sudden scrutiny the drivers were applying to delegates' credentials had nothing to do with any al-Qaeda threat and a lot to do with me personally. I had drastically underestimated the event director's vindictiveness. He wanted me to know that he had the ability to stop me doing my job, and that he wanted to stop me. The drivers would have been looking for me alone.

Laing, then, was proving to be an officious swine. And I had a job to do. Clients had requested that I attend three sessions today—two presentations by experts and a panel discussion. A full afternoon, and the first of these scheduled entertainments started in about two hours. I had never missed an event scheduled by a client, until yesterday anyway. I had never taken a sick day or missed a flight. Did Convex even have a procedure for a situation in which its surrogate could not attend what he had agreed to attend? There must be some arse-covering clause in the contract invoking *force majeure* and exceptional circumstances. But how would Adam react? He worked out of a tiny, subterranean office in the Business Design Center in Islington, growing his company client by client through late nights and personal recommendations. His whole pitch was based on reliability, on being in the right place at the right time regardless of circumstances, of being present when the client was absent. And this setback was, I had to admit, at least in part my own fault—I had failed to keep a low enough profile. Adam would not be pleased.

I returned to room 219, looked up the Meetex customer service line in the booking documents and called it. As soon as I pressed the call button on my mobile, a cacophony of barking and gibbering interference rose from the clock radio, and did not subside. When the call was answered by an efficient female voice, I could barely make it out. As well as the robotic stuttering and deranged kazoo-chorus from the radio, there was a deep boiling rush on the mobile connection itself, UHF rapids around transmitter-tower reeds.

Preferring not to shout and repeat myself, I ended the call without saying a word. The radio was intolerable, it would have to go. The noise would be bad enough at the best of times, and in my present unhappy state it was an aggravation too far. What's more, there was a quality about it, a deeper tone in the general din, that I found detestable. It had a foul edge.

But first things first. I dialled Meetex on room 219's landline phone—possibly an exploitative addition to the bill, but I was beyond caring.

"Meetex, this is Fran."

"Hello, Fran," I said. Normally I find it creepy when people use the first names of service staff in this way, but I was hopeful it would generate an iota of extra goodwill. "I'm a ticketed Meetex delegate and I've just been prevented from boarding one of the shuttle buses at the hotel. The driver said that my pass had been voided. I don't know what that means. Could you find out what the problem is please?"

"Yes, sir, I'll check that for you," Fran said. "Your name and booking reference, please."

I supplied the information. There was a pause—not silence, but the sounds of keys being pressed and a few scattered mouse clicks. In the background, a colleague of Fran's was unpicking a billing dispute of some kind: "Yes . . . yes . . . I can't override the charges now, but if you . . . "

"Sir?"

"Hello."

"Yes, I'm afraid your guest pass has been voided." Fran's voice had been efficient before, and so it remained, but the edge of service-industry solicitude had gone. She was all business. And as this expression came to mind, it stalled me. All business? Surely she was all business earlier? I wasn't an old friend ringing to reminisce about old times. What had changed was not the disappearance of actual geniality from her voice, but the cessation of simulated geniality. Deriving any comfort from the simulation was as pointless as warming my hands on a photograph of a log fire. But if that generated the impression of warmth, what was the true difference between the placebo and the real thing?

"Voided."

"Voided, yes, rescinded."

"I paid for all three days."

"Yes, sir, and there's an instruction here to refund you if requested. Should I go ahead and action that?"

"Yes. No!" That was to accept the verdict. And Adam might see the refund and would wonder what was going on. "Does it say why it's been voided?"

"Conduct contrary to Meetex's terms and conditions."

"What? How?"

"It doesn't say, sir." I could infer from Fran's Arctic tone that she was busily imagining the worst—a full-frontal nude streak down the main axis of the MetaCenter, a fist-fight during a health and safety roundtable, an all-comers orgy in the Gray Labyrinth. "You endorsed the terms and conditions as part of the billing process."

"What can I do to get my pass restored?" I said. "I have a job to do, I need to get back to the conference."

"It's not something I can action over the phone, sir. We can refund your remaining days, and you can write or email . . . "

"You know that'll never get seen in time," I said. This was charitable: I was entirely certain they would just ig-nore any letter or email from me. "Is there any way I can get it sorted out right now?"

"Sir, I can't do that, not over the phone," Fran said.

"But if I was there in person, at the MetaCenter, you might be able to do something?"

"We're not based at the MetaCenter, sir . . . "

"Then who do I talk to?"

"If you send an email . . . "

I felt, as a very distinct physical sensation, a burst of

foul language form in my throat and soft palate—and I stifled it. There would be no aggressive behavior. I would calmly and assertively make my reasonable case.

"Can I speak with Tom Laing, please?"

"Excuse me?"

"I'd like to speak to Tom Laing. The event director. Could you put me through to him, please?"

"I can't reach him from here, sir . . . If you email . . . "

I gritted my teeth. "It's fine. I understand. He's still at the MetaCenter, right? I'll go there myself and get this dealt with. Thank you so much for your help, you have completely transformed the situation for me."

"Sir—"

I put the phone down on Fran's closing remarks. She was useless to me. No doubt she wasn't even directly employed by Meetex, but by a customer-relations contractor, defying time zones in a shed off another motorway, maybe in Europe, maybe in Hyderabad or Chennai. She might as well have been a push-button answer tree. In five or ten years those jobs will be replaced by voice-recognition algorithms. Dealing with her wasn't going to get me anywhere, and it wasn't her fault. She was there to deflect awkward customers away from the company itself, not to deal with them. It was all an illusion; doors painted onto a solid façade. No central exchange, just a labyrinth of dead ends in which my complaint would be left to expire. I had to find the event director and address this directly.

In the bathroom, I poured a glass of water, drank it, and poured another. The second was properly cold, cold enough to hurt my teeth. Pipes in frozen earth. In the mirror above the sink, I saw with a shock that I was still wearing the

Way Inn baseball cap. My mind had been elsewhere. I took it off, threw it on the bed, and left the room.

"Good afternoon, sir," the young man at reception said. He was another twentysomething, similar to the one who had followed me back to my room the first time my keycard failed to work. His name badge said John-Paul.

Afternoon already—time was getting on. "Good afternoon," I said. "Neil Double, room 219. There seems to be a problem with the clock radio in my room—it keeps making strange noises, picking up interference from somewhere."

"I'm sorry to hear that, sir, we'll send someone up to take a look at it," John-Paul said, with perhaps the faintest touch of a French accent. He referred to his screen, tapping at the keyboard. "Room 219 . . . Right, no problem."

"Thanks," I said. I hesitated. "There's just one room 219, isn't there?"

"Excuse me, sir?"

"Is there more than one room 219? Last night, I must have been confused by the layout upstairs, because I got the impression there was more than one room 219."

John-Paul smiled sympathetically. "Oh no, sir, there's just the one room 219—it really would be too confusing if we started doubling up room numbers." His eyes darted back to his screen, which must have been a valuable source of intelligence on the man—me—who had raised this unusual issue. I hoped my years of loyal patronage of the Way Inn group, my My Way member status and superb credit record balanced out the impression that I was a street-corner ranter. "Apparently you had trouble with your keycard last night—it was reencoded a couple of minutes after half three in the morning. You see, sometimes the keycards . . . "

"Yes, yes, you explained this to me yesterday. Your colleague did."

"Ah, yes! Well, that should account for it, yes? You had the right room, but your card had lost its, its . . . "

"Mojo," I supplied.

"Mojo, precisely." John-Paul seemed very pleased with this whole exchange. "Is there anything else I can help you with today?"

"Uh, yes," I said. I threw a glance to the main entrance—there was no bus waiting there. I didn't want to imply that I might have been barred from the conference. It made me feel so disreputable, and I resented being made to feel that way. "How do I walk to the MetaCenter?"

"There's a free shuttle-bus to the MetaCenter, sir, it leaves from right outside the main entrance every ten or twenty minutes."

"I know, but I'd like to walk instead."

This seemed to perturb John-Paul far more profoundly than my hypothesis about the existence of a duplicate room 219.

"The trouble is that they haven't finished building the skywalk yet, I'm afraid, so there is no direct pedestrian link to the MetaCenter."

I smiled confidently, hoping to dispel any hint that I was deterred by this, and was instead relishing the prospect of a bracing stroll. "Yes, I know, but there must be an indirect route, yes? At ground level? Along the same roads as the bus drives?"

In the course of this exchange, John-Paul's front desk

colleague had turned to eavesdrop. He now turned to her and they shared a look of concern. She shrugged and shook her head, combined tiny actions that resembled a shudder at the thought of traversing the terrain around the Way Inn on foot, an articulate but wordless answer to an unspoken question. John-Paul returned his attention to me, a quite distressing lost look in his eyes, a man who had been forced beyond the bounds of anticipated and role-played customer-service routines.

"Most people come by car," he said. "Or the airport shuttle. Or taxi."

"Fine, taxi, right," I said. I didn't believe that it was so unthinkable to walk to the MetaCenter, but I could put that aside for the time being. "Could you call me a taxi?"

"Certainly, Mr. Double," John-Paul said, patently pleased to be back on familiar territory. "Where to?"

"The MetaCenter."

"The Met—right." He picked up his phone receiver and stretched out his free hand to indicate the expanse of sofas and armchairs behind me. "Please, take a seat, I'll let you know when it gets here." And he gave me an immense smile, as if intending to use it as a kind of firehose of sunshine that would propel me away from the desk and into a chair.

I didn't need the encouragement. I relished these little periods of enforced relaxation. The time was approaching half twelve. A client (or multiple clients) had asked for a summary of a presentation which started at 2 p.m. There would be a multitude of taxis in the area—the airport was a guarantee of that. So there was time enough to have a reasonable conversation with the event director and get my pass restored. And the fact that I was travelling to the

MetaCenter independently, circumventing their petty bus-ban, gave me great satisfaction. Did Laing expect me to simply accept defeat and go home, or sulk in my hotel room until it was time to go to the next conference? He had underestimated my determination. I was not dependent on their transport; I was in command of my situation, and I was going to calmly assert my rights. This ban was a monstrous overreaction and it would surely be reversed.

The wait was also high-grade hotel time, an opportunity to really enjoy the lobby, which was after all designed for this purpose. It felt good to be performing the appropriate rite in the appropriate venue, especially an underrated venue like a hotel reception. True, it was a space to be passed through, not a space to really *be* in, to inhabit or somehow make significant. Not a place to labor or decide or worship or build or fall in love, or whatever acts we are supposed to perform in other, more authentic, places. But what made those other places so special? So here I was, waiting for a taxi in the lobby of a chain hotel on a motorway. Daily newspapers were laid out for my appreciation, and I appreciated the courtesy without feeling the need to pick any of them up. I might, if time permitted, order a coffee, brewed—with pride, according to a sign—by a global franchise. I was not carving a turkey on Christmas day or writing a sonnet or casting a bowl on a potter's wheel—and while those activities might be more enjoyable and memorable than my present occupation, were they really any more authentic? This ranking of places baffled me. I was still human, still engaged in a task. I do not know if I possess such a thing as a soul, but if I do, I do not imagine that it deserts me when I arrive at the business hotel, the convention center, the airport terminal. So these places were bland, all alike and un-memorable. There was value to deliberately forgettable environments. They were efficient, spiritually thrifty, requiring little heed and little mindfulness. They were hygienic in that way, aseptic. Nothing from them would linger with you.

Besides, I believed it possible that I had fallen in love while in a hotel lobby. It was in the lobby of the Way Inn in Doha, Qatar, where I had first seen the red-haired woman. We had not spoken then—there was no way we could have—but something had happened to establish her in my mind. Not falling in love, but something; a moment of alchemy, the recognition—instant, spontaneous, total recognition—that she stood apart from the thousands of people I saw in a year, even from those I took to bed, even those (a smaller set still) I actually liked.

From where I sat—the stiff leather creaking in the new chair—the Way Inn promotional stand was in my eyeline, its pair of perky brand agents accosting passersby with door-hangers and a glossy corporate video repeating itself on the two large flat-screen TVs mounted on a framework behind the table. An Asian woman takes a sip from a crystalline glass of water—sunshine lens-flare through the glass—and kicks off her high-heel shoes to sit mermaid-style on a bed. A patrician gray-haired gentleman checks out with nothing more than a flash of his My Way card; staff beam in joy at his benediction and he boards a waiting taxi as a plane passes low over the white hotel behind him. A flash of fire from a wok and a blond woman is delighted by the grilled king prawns that are placed on her plate on a skewer. A Germanic man on a bar stool takes off his steel-framed glasses and laughs with suited colleagues over bottled Mexican beer. A black man in shirt sleeves points to an animated graph projected onto a screen and his colleagues around a boardroom table lean back and converse with obvious satisfaction. Night-lit fountains, Eiffel Tower behind them, are reflected in a sliding glass door as a young couple enter a hotel, hand in hand. We zoom out from a gray-and-white globe being steadily covered in a rash of red markers. The hotel's corporate logo, that coiled *W*, fills the screen before receding to form part of the words WAY INN EVERYWHERE.

I must have watched the same loop of images ten or fifteen times. And here I was, living the promo dream, enjoying the facilities of a Way Inn, so the video pleased me. It seemed like a celebration that I could share in. But after the tenth or fifteenth viewing, I saw that in each clip in the sequence, one of the hotel's abstract paintings appeared. On the subsequent couple of repeats of the film, I watched for that detail in particular. My initial suspicion proved correct—it wasn't just a painting in each scene, it was the same painting in each scene, two fields of different shades of umber separated by a serpentine boundary, with a oval patch of a paler loamy color in a lower corner. Was this on purpose? It was hard to tell which possibility was more difficult to believe: that the same painting had recurred by accident, or that care had been taken to use the same one each time. Perhaps the video was shot on a series of purpose-built sets in the same location, and the set dressers had only the one painting to use. Or were the paintings more alike than I had imagined? The red-haired woman had said they were all unique—deranged she might be, but I was ready to state with confidence that on this subject her derangement made her an authority whose word could be trusted.

Once seen, this quirk in the video could not be unseen. I shifted in my seat in an effort to exclude the screens from my field of vision, then moved to another armchair so I had my back to them. Still, I turned the apparent coincidence over in my mind, feeling its weight and the questions attached to it. Its defiance of easy answers made me want to simply turn away from it, as I had turned away from the screens. Just as I wanted to do with the obstinate memory of the woman meditating in a sunlit courtyard at 3 a.m. This—how to even describe it?—this vision had been very real to me and my recollection of it was rich in detail when so many other aspects of the previous evening were smudged in retrospect. It had all the qualities of a lucid dream—not that I was familiar with lucid dreams, but this had been lucid, and it must have been a dream, so those were the most important points covered. I had exhausted myself running through the hotel and had slipped briefly into oblivion. My subconscious had obligingly furnished me with a bit of wish fulfillment, the wish being my devout longing to see the red-haired woman again. At some point I regained my wits and returned to my room. The neutral corridors of the hotel had proven ideal for masking the edge of sleep, making it possible to cross the boundary between reality and unreality without noticing. In her sleepwalking, she herself had shown this to be possible. This was the rational palisade I built around what I had seen in the courtyard.

"Mr. Double?" It was John-Paul, calling across the lobby.

"Yes?" I answered him from the chair, then stood to approach him at the front desk.

Perplexity was written across his face. "There's a problem with the taxi, Mr. Double."

"Oh?"

"Yes. They can't find the hotel."

"What? How come?"

"They can't find it. On sat nav. It's not showing up."

I frowned. "How can that be?"

"Well, this is a new hotel—in fact this whole area is new, the street, the motorway spur, everything. And sat nav hasn't caught up yet, the software hasn't been updated. The access roads from the motorway junction do appear, but they all share a postal code, so they appear as a single road, not two parallel roads."

"So what?" I said. "He can still get here, can't he?"

John-Paul swallowed. I think my face was already set in a cast of thunderous disbelief, and he seemed apprehensive.

"As I say, the sat nav considers the access road serving the hotels and the access road serving the MetaCenter to be the same road. And apparently that means they can't put the route into the sat nav, because it sees the point of departure and the destination as being the same place, a journey of zero miles, which they can't log for fare purposes."

"I don't care." I kept my tone as level as possible. I was going to be confident and assertive and remain in control, and not let my anger rule me. "Where is the driver now? We can direct him by phone. Cash in hand for a three-minute drive. He can tell his bosses anything he likes."

"I'm sorry, sir, he never set out—they said a journey that short wasn't worth their time." John-Paul was clearly in real distress at the whole affair, or doing a very convincing impression of being distraught. My own feelings were complex but not uncommon: I felt the visceral frustration and uselessness of a person confronting a bureaucratic obstacle, the same feeling that had afflicted me while speaking with "Fran" from Meetex customer services. It was a feeling analogous to discovering that the open road ahead is not in fact an open road at all but a hyperreal photograph of an open road printed on a satiny smooth, completely impervious surface—a prospect utterly closed, without any hope of appeal, but presenting a mocking mirage of free access. This was rage; towering, futile, empty rage. John-Paul's distress was perhaps related to his innocence in the matter. If it was Way Inn that was placing the senseless barrier in my path, I was sure he would be more placid and satisfied. That is the way of the corporate wall.

"OK," I said. I felt curiously short of breath, as if the air had been forced out of me by the fury within.

"I know," John-Paul said, grimacing. "It's frustrating."

The front desk no longer seemed able to assist me—the services it offered were now startlingly irrelevant. But I did not move from my spot. There had to be a way of arranging transport to the center. This defeat seemed premature. John-Paul was looking at me as if he had just been told by his parents that the family dog's increasing senility meant it would have to be put to sleep, and I was the dog.

"I have an idea," he said.

"Yes?" I said, hoping I didn't look too pathetic in my eagerness to hear what he had to say. "Go on."

"We could call a taxi for a round trip—pickup here, go to the airport, then to the MetaCenter. It'll cost more—"

"Brilliant," I said, slapping my fingers on the desk surface, uninterested in the cost. "Do it. Please."

John-Paul smiled—and this, I believed, was a real smile, not a service smile. It was an outward sign of true pleasure in cracking the problem. "Certainly, sir. I'll call you when it gets here."

"Excellent, John-Paul, excellent. Thank you. I'm going to get an espresso—I'll be in the bar."

The thought of a taxi—my taxi—heading toward the hotel lifted my spirits. Taxis were a personal service of a kind I adored. Even though they were a routine part of my working life, they still felt wickedly decadent and grown-up, a wild and daring prodigality. They were the realm of my father and his expenses. And my few childhood memories of taxis are also memories of my father. My mother, when she was present in the back of the cab, could not have been more out of place. Every drawn line on her face and tensed muscle screamed of a desire to be elsewhere. She would watch the progress of the meter as if its every accumulating flicker was an insult.

That stare of my mother's: I remember it so clearly, her severity in the face of the slightest expenditure, the icy laser with which she strafed supermarket shelves. Even today, tearing a piece of clothing makes me fearful; a memory of her exhausted anger if I damaged one of the few items in my wardrobe. All-new outfits still have an almost mystical significance for me. Her watchfulness for extravagance and hypervigilant conservation of every last dull copper in the household budget was essential, of course. We had very little. Expenses were the problem—my father's expenses. His basic salary was never large, his employers preferring to reward him with a generous travelling budget as compensation for having to spend the bulk of his life away from home and loved ones. But this left the marriage unbalanced. While he ate in restaurants and slept in comfortable hotel rooms, my mother was stretching postage stamps of cling film over half-cans of baked beans and resisting turning on the central heating until past the first frost. We were not poor—not in any sense that keeps the word meaningful—but my childhood was one of constant secondhand and second-best. What made this unbearable for me was its obvious necessity. There was no parental illogic or arbitrariness or double standard to rage against, just blunt, gray, unarguable household facts, picked over at length during the continual acrimony that accompanied my father's sojourns in the family home. All the tawdry details of budgets and economies and pleasures downgraded or deferred were paraded in front of me at the dinner table as my parents growled and hissed at each other. To my gravest embarrassment, I was dragooned as an ally by my mother: my involuntary sacrifices, my diminished experience of life, exhibited as the result of my father's choices and unwillingness to change course. I suspected that to be obliged to spend one's life travelling, away from the hearth and family life, might not be such a sacrifice. The dreams I fostered in these dreary circumstances were modest indeed: taxis, hotels, to buy something as small as a drink and think nothing of it.

Then the arguments stopped: the marriage was over, a few weeks before I reached my teens. Although the paperwork wasn't formalized for two or three years, my father never set foot in that small house again. The privation did not stop, of course; my mother went out to work and strained every particle to ensure that my conditions did not worsen. But my father's permanent, engulfing absence was a new and unbearable, inconceivable impoverishment. Unlike the others, I saw it as one my mother had chosen, one she had deliberately and unnecessarily brought down upon us. And resentment took root.

Coffee was the primary scent in the air of the Way Inn bar, backed with a hint of a chemist's approximation of a pine forest. I ordered an espresso—consciously thinking nothing of it—and scanned for somewhere to sit.

She was there. The redheaded woman. She was neglecting a cappuccino, hunched over a sprawl of papers covered in excitable doodles. Her hair was tied back, and everything about her pose said deep thought. It was as if the designs in front of her had just unexpectedly danced on the page, and she was waiting to see if they would repeat the trick.

I hesitated. I wanted to approach her very much, but I was wary, after what had happened with Lucy, of making another blunder. This was the second time I had seen this woman in this hotel—not counting my vision of her sun-worshipping in the light well—and we were almost acquaintances. Almost, but not. We were still in the default interpersonal mode: strangers. The best kind of strangers, maybe—old, close strangers—but strangers. And the protocol for one stranger to approach another in a public place is delicate and fraught with risk, especially if one stranger is male and the other is female. I did not want to be a pest, not with her. But while my frontal cortex measured the situation, my instinct, and what felt like every other part of me, howled its eagerness to *go on, go ahead, talk to her; this is what you want, the thing you want most, she's sitting right in front of you, what are you waiting for? How many other chances are you going to get? Do it however you want, but do it, don't delay!* In the past I would never have waited long before yielding to that more base voice, confident that the embarrassment of a rebuff would be short-lived and I would soon be on to other places, other hotels, other women. But my purpose here wasn't a quick liaison; I was seeking a lasting connection.

"Can I help?"

She had seen me prevaricating and intervened, solving my immediate problem. But her expression was not kindly and her inquiry seemed intended to move me along rather than inviting me to linger.

"I'm sorry," I said. "We spoke the other night. About the paintings."

"I remember," she said, not exactly smiling, but no longer frowning.

The barman appeared with my espresso. "Are you sitting here, sir?"

"Do you mind if I join you?" I asked, trying to keep it light. "Only for a moment, I'm waiting for a taxi." I hoped this lessened the sense of intrusion—I wouldn't be around for long.

"Sure," she said. And this time I did get a smile—or part of a smile, a limited half-mouth lip-twitch, which might have been a smirk at my puppy-dog deference. Somewhere in this social fog were boundaries separating the pathetic from the winning, and friendliness from creepiness. Their location was hard to pinpoint.

I sat, and the barman arranged the tiny coffee cup, a nanojug of milk and a thimble containing misshapen brown sugar lumps in front of me. A slip of paper was proffered—I signed next to my room number. The barman receded.

"I didn't mean to interrupt you . . . " I said, indicating the sheets of graph paper she had been working on. They were covered in columns of numbers and interlocking circles.

"It's nothing," she said, swiftly squaring the sheets together, folding them twice and stuffing them into the front pocket of the sweatshirt she was wearing. She was dressed for the gym. When her eyes returned to me, they were piercing and interrogatory. "But you clearly did intend to interrupt me, didn't you? Let's not gloss it. That's what you wanted, yes? It's not a problem, I just want to be clear about that."

"I was considering the etiquette of a situation like this," I said. "A public place, someone you've met before, but you don't really know them . . . "

"What did you conclude?"

"I didn't conclude anything, you interrupted me."

"Right," she said. "My fault. I didn't mean to. If I had known that I was intruding on vital work in the field of social anthropology . . . " It was hard to read her mood. She was not wearing makeup. Her eyebrows matched the cinnamon dust at the rim of her coffee cup and her lips had a ghostly suggestion of arterial blue about them.

"I'm sure I would have concluded by saying hello," I said. "You know, when you're in a hotel, unlikely to see a person ever again, where's the harm?"

"Yeah, I've noticed guys are less inhibited about striking up conversation in a hotel bar. Guys in general. In hotels in general. I've always assumed there was some slow-witted male equation at work. Unaccompanied woman in hotel bar equals prostitute. Or slut, anyway."

This remark didn't seem to be pointed at me, so I smiled in response. "Could be. For some men."

She shrugged. "It's a building that also contains beds. Maybe that confuses them. They think, well, this woman is already sleeping somewhere in this building, surely it won't make much difference to her what bed she's in or who's in there with her."

"I think it might be related to my anthropological conclusions," I said. "Where's the harm? There's less danger of lasting social embarrassment from saying hello to a stranger in a hotel bar, because if it turns out badly you can go and hide in your room and the next day you both check out and that's that. It's a completely disposable moment. And prostitution promises a similar deal, in its way—it's completely disposable sex, no lasting traces, no aftermath."

"For the man, anyway," she said with a grimace. "Apart from a nice STD, maybe. And, I should hope, a hell of guilt."

"Well, as I said, that's the *promise* of prostitution, not the reality." It was time to steer the topic away from the street corner. "Not that I would know, of course."

"Of course." She said this with a completely straight face. "As a matter of fact, I think you're right. The hotel generates a bubble of exceptionality."

"How is your research going?" I asked, with a slight nod toward the baggy pocket into which the notes had disappeared. The pocket was troubling me for reasons I could not discern. A red pocket in a red sweatshirt, a sweatshirt that had WAY INN written across the front in official lettering above said pocket. Not an unusual piece of clothing at all.

"Fine." She shifted uncomfortably in her seat. I had looked too long at the words WAY INN, though it was the sweatshirt that had my total attention, not the physique beneath it.

"Were you up last night?"

"Excuse me?" She was scowling now.

"Last night," I said, "I think I saw you—you were in one of the courtyards, those little pebble-gardens, meditating. You were wearing that sweatshirt. It was about 3 a.m., but somehow you looked as if you were in daylight . . . "

Her expression was hard to read, but it certainly wasn't approving.

"Impossible," she said.

"I know, I don't understand it," I said. "But you were wearing that sweatshirt—I've never seen you wearing that before, and if it was a dream, how come I dreamed you in an item I had no idea you owned? One you're wearing right now, the morning after?"

She took a moment to think before answering. "You might not remember it at all. Your subconscious might be retrospectively adding it to a half-remembered dream. That's what sleep does, what dreams do—iron out the inconsistencies in our experience, reconcile tattered bits of memory . . . "

"But it wasn't a memory because I had never seen it before, and it certainly isn't half-remembered. It was as real as this conversation is now."

We had, in the course of this exchange, leaned in closer to each other—me so the other bar patrons wouldn't hear my talk of dreams and visions; her mirroring me, adopting a conspiratorial hiss. But now she leaned back, puffed her cheeks out and widened her eyes.

"You call this a real conversation?"

"OK, fine, granted," I said. "Fair point. But I haven't heard you actually deny being in the courtyard last night."

She wasn't looking at me anymore—her focus had shifted behind me. A sickening jolt of déjà vu hit me. Again? How could the same lousy luck strike the same guy three times in three days—twice in the same place with the same woman? I turned, my lips already pressed together to form the *M* of Maurice, to see John-Paul standing at the threshold of the bar. Behind him was a short, dark man in blue jeans and a leather jacket.

"Mr. Double? Your taxi is here."

"Thanks," I blurted. I had forgotten about the taxi. "I'll just be a minute—can you ask him to hang on?"

"Sure." John-Paul turned with a smile to talk to the man in the leather jacket.

"Where are you going?" the woman asked.

"The center," I said.

"Ah," she said. "Aren't we all." She wasn't scowling at me anymore, perhaps because she knew that my disappearance was imminent and probably permanent. But this was my precious second—third—chance with her, surely my final opportunity to make a lasting connection, and there was no way I could let this moment pass by without playing every card in my hand.

"Look," I said, investing my words with the smallest portion of the urgency I felt, which was still enough to make me sound thoroughly panicked. "I know I haven't made the best, the, er, sanest, impression, but I'd like, if you'd let me, to see you again."

She raised her eyebrows.

"You see," I continued at speed, not giving her an opportunity to decline me before I had fully made my case, however desperate it might sound, "I'm sure that the fact that we keep seeing each other, keep running into each other, means something, maybe something important, and I don't want to lose the chance to find out what that might be. I'm not crazy, or even superstitious, but I do believe that sometimes the universe tries to tell us things, and when that happens we should try to listen. And I think the universe might be trying to tell me something about you."

I found I had run out of rhetorical road much sooner than I expected. Was that it? Was that the sum of the case I had to make to this woman? Was there nothing more to say?

To her credit, she didn't laugh at me or terminate the conversation. Instead she seemed very still and very serious.

"Maybe it's the hotel trying to tell you something."

"Hotel, universe, fate, whatever you want to call it."

"So what is it you want from me?"

"Maybe your mobile phone number?" Mention of mobile phones jogged my memory. "In fact I have something for you—I took a picture of the painting in my room. Maybe I could send it to you? For your collection."

"May I see it?"

"Sure." I took my phone from my pocket, summoned the picture to its screen and handed it across the table.

"Very nice," she said.

I stood. The taxi driver was still in the same spot, staring at me with bored animosity. "So, if you give me your number, I can send it to you. And maybe we can meet for a drink some time?"

"Well, maybe," she said, also standing. A curious change had come over her—she seemed suddenly irresolute, possibly nervous. Her eyes darted between the screen of my phone and the lobby at my rear. "We're not going to fuck, you know."

For precious seconds I was sure I had misheard her. "Excuse me?"

"We are not going to fuck, you and I," she repeated. To emphasise her point she raised my phone and showed it to me, as if she were a teacher, I was a schoolboy and the phone was a contraband packet of cigarettes.

"I didn't—"

"That isn't where this is going."

I was awash with futility. If that was how she saw my attentions, then she was already decided and I could say nothing to change her mind. Inevitably, my denials would sound insincere and tactical. Was she wrong at all? It was generally sex I wanted, even if a woman made for pleasant or stimulating company on the way there. But how true was that with the redhead? She was different, in every way she was different, though I could not place or define that difference. Was that love? Was love the total certainty that someone was unlike all the others, and total mystification as to the nature of that difference? The hotel generates a bubble of exceptionality, she said, and whatever that meant, she was certainly exceptional.

"Honestly, that's not what I thought," I said. "I just . . .

all I wanted was to find out where this is going. You seem to be a very interesting person and I would like to get to know you better." Inwardly I cringed at the *interesting* and cursed the generations of male liars—my brothers, my comrades!—who had used those words as a euphemism for *I would like to get you into bed*; I had been free with those words in that meaning myself, and now that I needed them for their original sense I found them tainted.

She did not appear to take my clunky line the wrong way. Her eyes sparkling, she smiled down at me—not a pleasant smile, I realized, but before I could parse it, she had hooked her right hand behind my neck and kissed me on the lips. A small, closed, experimental kiss. She pulled back.

I stared at her. I felt I might never be able to speak again. Her eyes blazed with energy and delight. With mischief.

"You'll have to catch me."

And she ran.

Her long legs had carried her out of the bar before I fully grasped what had happened. As she sprinted through the lobby, conversations stopped and heads turned. The desk staff stared, John-Paul's mouth a perfect O.

She had my phone.

"Fuck!" I said, just a useless ejaculation. "Hey, stop!" She had reached the stairwell. My body was filled with misdirected energy, firing everywhere but where it was needed; my limbs suddenly seemed to require an elaborate start-up procedure I had forgotten. The barman and his patrons were looking toward me. I stared back at them, helpless.

Energy redirected. I ran, out of the bar, through the

lobby and past the taxi driver, who raised his hands in exasperation as I passed. Behind me, someone called out, maybe John-Paul, but I ignored them.

As I approached the stairwell, I heard the echo of the woman's pounding feet. At the bottom of the stairs I looked up, thinking I might somehow be able to tell which floor she had run to—and I was rewarded with the sight of her face, looking down at me from three storeys up. The instant she saw I had seen her, she dodged from view and I heard a fire door bang.

Had I not seen her, I might have given up on that spot, at the bottom of the stairs. If she was simply attempting to escape me, then she would already have an insurmountable advantage. Not only did she have the lead generated by surprise and my subsequent paralysis, she was dressed for running and I was not. And I suspected that even if the playing field was levelled, she would still be able to outrun me; she had inches on me and was clearly in superb shape. But she had waited for me—she didn't want to disappear. Perhaps she was goading me; perhaps this was her way of flirting. For my part, I just wanted my phone back. I *needed* my phone back.

So I hit the stairs, two at a time. Six flights to the third floor, and by the sixth my knees pulsed with pain. I was less fit than I thought. The corridor beyond the fire door was empty, but instinct told me which way to turn— deeper into the hotel.

A left, a right, a left, and a long stretch of corridor opened up. At its end a fire door was slowly swinging shut on its pneumatic closer. I sprinted, paintings blurring together, reaching the door as it completed its slow passage back to its frame. Shouldering the door violently aside, I saw a tall figure silhouetted in the autumn light penetrating a bank of courtyard windows. Then she darted away.

Appearing suddenly in the fire door, I must have looked fairly frightful. I could feel the sweat on my brow and back, and greasing the inside of my collar. My lungs burned and my legs were acid-scoured from the uneven, unexpected effort. Running again, I tried to set a more sustainable pace, and tugged my tie from my neck. She had gone left; the next corner took us right, and I glimpsed the woman at the far end of the next stretch of corridor powering along as gracefully as an athlete warming up on a track.

"Stop!" I shouted. "Please!" But she had already rounded the next corner.

I plodded after her, conscious that the pursuit was coming to an end. Soon, very soon, I would have to stop. And soon enough we would run out of hotel—she would already be near that point, and would have to either double back, returning along the corridors on the far side, or go to another floor. Or stop there and wait for me—for what? Would she jump me, and either clobber me or screw me? Or do nothing more than laugh? In other circumstances I might have been aroused or afraid or a tingly combination of the two—but I was worn out, sticky with sweat, a collection of unready, sore joints. I didn't want to negotiate this now—the waiting taxi was a monstrous cloud over me, like a running bath or a pan on a stove in another room, an unforgettable, cumbersome obligation that insisted on my return.

A noise. At first I thought it was the product of the blood ringing in my ears from an oxygen-starved brain. It was a high-pitched whine—the highest pitch, with, for

sure, further upper frequencies I could not hear—that
within a few strides became a sustained one-note shriek.
Its source was a fire door at the next junction, one bearing
the stern warning THIS DOOR IS ALARMED. It certainly was
alarmed, maintaining its banshee whistle until it had finished closing, a slow, sedate occlusion on its air-filled pis-
ton. Once it was fully closed, the metal bar that opened it
clunked sharply back into place and the alarm ceased.

The door was between us—as far as I knew she was
just beyond it, waiting for me. The alarm had been triggered once already and what had happened? No sprinklers
doused the hall, no panicked guests surged into the corridors, no extinguisher-wielding staff appeared. If the
alarm was triggered again, what would be the cost?

I pushed down on the metal bar. The alarm was like a
knitting needle shoved violently into each of my ears. It
had physical strength, surely; an impact that sparked a
kind of convulsion in the wet matter under my skull. For
a moment I sensed the edge of the void and feared a seizure. Black lightning, again, obscured my sight. I released
the bar to put my hands to my ears. They did nothing to
stop the alarm. It scythed through flesh and bone to dis-
rupt my essential electricity, violating the millivolts of
power that crackled in synapses and neurons, the interference that thought it was me. The corridor had receded—I
was nowhere, amid a bubbling, seething mass of spheres,
and a mouthless scream.

Clunk. The bar had reset. Carpet under my hands. I
was kneeling, reduced to an almost fetal position. Silence.
Not silence—a distant television, the murmur of the aircon. There was no pain, no ringing in my ears, no dizziness. Only a disquiet in the pit of my stomach—the sole

sensation left over from what had just happened. I was fine. My shirt front was cool on my chest as sweat evaporated from it.

Alarm? It was more like an antipersonnel weapon, a Pentagon blacklist toy seriously misapplied on civvy street. But they couldn't claim I wasn't warned. THIS DOOR IS ALARMED. It wasn't the only one.

That was enough. If this was a game of hers, I was losing, or at least not playing well. Maybe refusing to play would bring her back. Was she a mere thief? Of course not—she wanted the picture, or some hold on me, not the phone. I would get it back. The staff had seen everything; they would be able to help. John-Paul would help. They would know her room, they would have her name and address in their files. This could be dealt with. Later. I had a cab waiting. I turned back the way I came.

The lobby, again. After the run, my limbs had acquired a strange sense of springiness—a sudden surfeit of energy where there had minutes earlier been a fatal deficit. I almost bounced into the reception, scanning the landscape of armchairs, pot plants and flat-screens for the taxi driver. An apology, a bit of masculine bridge-mending, was on my lips, ready for deployment. But he could not be seen. Instead John-Paul rose sharply from his seat behind the reception desk.

"Mr. Double," he called, "the taxi, he just left—"

His urgency, his quick gesture toward the hotel entrance, suggested to me that it might not be too late. Once more I lunged into a run, drawing glances as I traversed the lobby at speed, passing through the sliding glass doors toward the smokers' realm beyond. But nothing was parked under the glass canopy. My eyes found the taxi as its brake lights and indicator went dark at the end of the Way Inn's drive and it pulled onto the slip road. Stopping heavily in the roadway, feet buzzing, acridity seeping up my throat from my lungs, I watched the taxi accelerate away.

I cursed and turned back toward the hotel. A pair of smokers watched me, one neutral, the other amused. Adjusting my gait to seem unconcerned, I passed back through the sliding doors.

"No luck?" John-Paul's expression was tense, an encouraging half-smile around the mouth and sympathy, or maybe pity, in the eyes. My failure was blatant and undeniable.

"No," I said, striving to appear calm. It wasn't John-Paul's fault—he had tried to help. There was a list of things that had to be done and I had to move on to the next item. It was past one o'clock already. I was late and I did not want to be much later. "The woman—you saw the woman I was talking with, just now?"

"Yes."

She existed, at least—that was a start. Her talent for eluding me had made me worry that there might be something intangible about her—that she might be nothing more than an idea of mine. But she was real.

"Who is she?"

John-Paul looked at me blankly. "I don't know, sir. Don't you know?"

"No," I said. "She's a guest in the hotel. We just met. Can you give me her room number? Or can I leave a message for her?"

"I'm not sure she is a guest in the hotel, to be honest with you, Mr. Double."

"No. No, there's no doubt." I wasn't going to be deterred. Those smooth, hard walls of business courtesy would slide back. "She's staying here. She works for the company. She has a keycard. She was wearing"—without meaning to, I let my voice rise, always an error in this kind of situation—"a Way Inn sweatshirt!"

John-Paul looked gray and worried. All at once I saw myself as he saw me: deeply unstable and unpredictable, full of unprecedented and impossible complaints and requests, apparently incapable of satisfaction, perhaps operating on another medical or pharmacological plane. A customer relations nightmare. How close was I to being ejected from the hotel? Barred from the conference, expelled from the Way Inn—that really would be the end, the end of this job, of everything I had worked for. Which was what, exactly? The My Way card? I had to reel it back in, master myself.

"I'm sorry, I don't mean to shout," I said, smiling modestly, not a nutter—a good man having a bad day. "She took my phone . . . A joke, I think. I wanted to show her a picture, and perhaps she thought I was giving her . . . Anyway." I lay my palms flat on the reception desk, fingers splayed. "Anyway, I really need that phone back. What with everything else, this problem at the conference . . . " I gestured toward the glass doors, and John-Paul frowned sympathetically. "I really need that phone back. Now, I know that this woman works for Way Inn—she could be staying here as an employee. Maybe one of your colleagues knows her or checked her in. Perhaps you could make some inquiries? It's really vital that I speak to her again."

"Yes, sir," John-Paul said. The other member of staff behind the desk, a young Asian woman, had been looking in my direction since I let my voice rise. I turned to smile at her too, including her in my request. She acknowledged this with a flicker of movement from the eyes and a barely perceptible nod. As soon as I left the scene, she and John-Paul would discuss me, I knew.

"What should I tell her?" John-Paul asked.

"That I need to speak to her," I said. "That I need my phone back. Give her my room number, email, pho—Just make sure she knows."

"Yes, sir." John-Paul was quiet, cooperative, clearly aware that I was about to go away and relieved at the prospect.

"Great, thank you," I said, trying to pump a few hundred candelas of extra brightness into my smile. The clock above the reception desk was pushing one thirty. "I have to get to the conference center."

"You're going to walk?"

"Yes."

John-Paul looked as if he was about to say something, but visibly choked back this urge.

"Have a nice day, sir."

Above the access road was the kind of autumn sun that you could look at quite safely. An opaline layer of cloud sapped it of all potency, leaving it a bleak disc in the sky. Wind with a wet, icy texture sliced straight through my wool suit jacket. Only one side of the access road had a pavement, and that was basic black tarmac, much marked by the muddy treads of construction vehicles. Across the road was the motorway embankment, doing all it could to deaden the permanent yell of traffic. Its spiky coat of saplings in white plastic sheaths vibrated in the wind.

The feeble, unfamiliar sun and the provisional feel of the surface beneath me—a recent and tenuous bulwark against an ocean of mud, an ocean that stood ready to reclaim this hinterland at any moment—gave me the sense of being on an alien world subjected to still-fragile terraforming. Gains were being made, the environment was being made safe for habitation and for business, but it remained basically hostile. All around was the infrastructure that was taming this place—not a wild place, just a regular, unresolved, semiurban waste, a ragged place being steadily stitched up. Above me was the steel-and-glass tube of the skywalk, which would help complete the picture. It would, when finished, link the hotels via new lobbies at the first-floor level, not involving itself with the squalor of the pavement—the earth—at all. For now, only the Way Inn section was complete, and the motorway bridge lacked that crucial central section, so it merely underscored the isolation of the hotel; an island of espresso-availability and pan-seared salmon and cotton sheets in a barren world, surrounded by mocking gaps.

Anger rose up in me again, trailing boredom and frustration behind it—boredom and frustration with my own rage, recurring like heartburn. What good did it do, getting angry? Everyone I dealt with—the conference, the hotel, the woman—was impervious to my anger. No, not quite—the hotel cared. John-Paul's face, his desperate but helpless concern, formed in my mind's eye and helped calm me. The hotel wanted to do the right thing. I thought of my My Way loyalty card, a comforting presence in my wallet. Minutes after leaving the Way Inn's lobby I was already longing to return to it—the wind was whipping over the embankment, rattling the saplings, reddening my cheeks and stirring darker clouds into the sky.

The empty plot next to the Way Inn was surrounded by hoardings faced in glossy plastic and printed with advertisements for the hotel that was intended for the site. Stock photo people went from hotel checkout to airport check-in in a single giant business-class leap. All the usual handshakes and halogen smiles, but the opening date was weeks away and the view from my window had shown that nothing was happening behind the fence. Not so much as a foundation had been dug. A financial spasm—loans cancelled, profit warnings issued—meant the absence of a building where a building should stand. A lack of alchemy; base materials remaining base. As I passed the vacant lot and reached the other hotels in the row, it appeared to me that they might not be doing a whole lot better. Their gray steel frames were up, and one had most of its cladding in place. The cladding came in the form of prefabricated panels of an indeterminate smooth modern material. Most of these panels were a dull blue, but some were other colors—paler blue, lilac, teal, red—distributed on the façade apparently at random. How was this nonpattern decided? Did a frustrated colorist with an arts degree painstakingly choose blue, blue, blue, lilac, blue, blue, red? Or was the effect generated instantly, at the click of a mouse, by an algorithm buried in a specification program? These programs exist—I knew those conferences and fairs, for the cladding manufacturers, design-and-build contractors, specifiers and cost consultants. To try to derive meaning from the pattern was senseless, just as it was senseless to try to discern a grander design in the paintings in the Way Inn. If they were mass-produced, as the woman had said, then their patterns might easily be generated by a machine.

Here, the pattern wasn't even complete. The top floor and much of the floor beneath it were missing their panels. The interrupted matrix resembled a pixelated image frozen mid-download, and like a stalled download, the unfinished façade prompted mild anxiety. Was it stopped for good, or merely paused? There was no evidence of activity on the site, no workmen or noise or moving machinery. Strips of safety tape and Tyvek stirred on the frame in the wind, and metal rattled against metal. With its competitors halted, the Way Inn must have been printing money as the only hotel within easy reach of the Meta-Center. Presumably, the redhead had contributed to this coup by selecting the site at the most auspicious moment, allowing the Way Inn to churn out profit where the others were still wading in loss. If, that is, she had been telling me the truth about what she did for a living. And whatever her skill as a geomancer, I was disinclined to put much store in many of the things she said. She was clearly unstable—why would she just snatch my phone like that? What was she playing at? It *was* play, I was convinced. I could see her face looking back at me, waiting for me to close the gap between us. When she could have evaded me easily, she kept me in sight. She wasn't trying to be caught, but she wasn't trying to be lost either. She was trying to lead me to something.

Great distances separated everything around me, an impression heightened by the fierce headwind, which carried with it stray drops of rain, hard as hail. The

unfinished hotels passed as slow as glaciers. My
unexpected run through the Way Inn had poured glue
into the muscles of my legs. As the motorway junction
approached, I felt a hundred years old. In the buses, this
terrain had taken minutes to cross. But they, with wheels
and engines, were the genus of life this environment had
been designed to accommodate, not me.

The motorway junction itself presented new problems.
The access roads serving the hotels and the MetaCenter
met the old road in a giant landscaped roundabout, perhaps a hundred meters across. Beneath this ring passed
the shrieking motorway, and the two were connected by
generous ramps. A narrow pavement ran around the
roundabout, so grudging a concession to foot traffic that I
wondered if its deterrent effect on strollers was deliberate,
or if it was even intended as a pavement at all. Cars and
lorries circuited the junction unceasingly, and after the
deserted access road their up close presence, banking like
chariots in the hippodrome, was profoundly threatening.
To reach the MetaCenter, I would have to cross the access
road, then cross the path of an off-ramp which was spew-
ing traffic into the junction. After traversing one of the
bridges that carried the roundabout over the motorway, I
would have to cross an on-ramp. Only then would I be
within reach of the MetaCenter.

The off-ramp wasn't as difficult as it first appeared. I
could see straight down it, onto the mechanized torrent of
the motorway itself. I could see cars separate into the exit
lane and start climbing the ramp, toward me. As they
climbed, they slowed, ready to merge into the traffic already circling the roundabout. How did I look to them? A
man hovering at the edge of the road, tie writhing in the

wind, suit crumpled, hands empty, staring down the ramp. It seemed unlikely that I would look like someone who knew what he was doing, someone with a sense of purpose. No, I would look lost, perhaps even a potential suicide. When I saw someone in the wrong place on the motorways, trudging sadly along the hard shoulder, trying to cross far from any crossing, my first instinct was to look away. They were the breakdowns—vehicle, mental, social. Best not to look. Behind the glass of the windscreens of the cars that rose up the ramp, the eyes of the drivers were always focused ahead, on the junction, never on me.

It was easy to get a sense of the timing of the cars: if a car passed me, leaving the ramp, and no other car was yet on the ramp, I would have at least a couple of seconds. I waited, three cars passed, the ramp was empty, and I jogged across. Even at walking pace, I would have been fine.

The bridge was a nightmare of noise. Channelled by those carefully sculpted embankments, the motorway was a sound cannon pointed straight at me. Added to that were the cars and lorries on the bridge itself and, above, the shriek of a jet lifting itself out of the airport. Engines on three levels. I could feel the noise coming up through my feet, the tarmac vibrating, a deep sense of it in my diaphragm. Between this and the petulant, snatching wind, made more turbulent by the thundering passage of canvas-sided juggernauts, for a moment I feared it possible that I could be swept off the bridge altogether. I looked to the crash barrier for reassurance. Small notices were attached to it at regular intervals: each bore the number for a suicide prevention hotline. Over the edge was a sharp drop onto a hard surface, into the path of motorists treating the speed limit as a minimum rather than a maximum. That would do it. That would certainly do it. Of course, there was the risk of causing an accident, taking a few strangers out with me—maybe more than a few. Hence the numerous signs—whatever you do, don't do it here. The paths must remain open, the traffic must flow, investment will follow. The signs were new, their screws shiny—new like the motorway, like the hotels, like everything. Had anyone jumped yet? Or were the official pleas preemptive? Who measured the need for them? Were there guidelines? A bridge so high and so wide at such a height over an eight-lane motorway—crash barriers tested to such-and-such standard will be needed, with don't-top-yourself notices every twelve feet. In time I was sure I would find myself at a trade fair for infrastructure specialists or civil engineers. When I did, I must remember to ask one of them.

Only the on-ramp remained to be crossed, but it presented the biggest challenge. I could not see the cars approaching—they came at an angle, hurtling around the roundabout, and it was seldom clear if they were going to keep on circling or peel off and pelt down the ramp. If they were heading for the on-ramp, they tended to be accelerating, anticipating communion with the glorious rush of the motorway. The distance I had to cover seemed, now, vast. Each vehicle that passed was like a door slammed in my face. They would never slow down, flash their lights and let me cross, not in a million years. I doubted the drivers even saw me, and if they did it was as a troubling glimpse, not as an overture to communication and courtesy. By the time I figured in their mind, they would be down the ramp, and I would be a forgettable memory already. Walking it and challenging them was a suicide as sure as jumping off the bridge— no time to see, no time to brake, no way to evade. It would have to be a dash.

I went for it. A burst of energy. The rough concrete surface felt loose and gritty under the pounding soles of my shoes, and my only thought was *I shouldn't be here, I don't belong here, this is not a place to be.* All through today I had been compelled to run, and how often did I run in normal circumstances? And as soon as the fact that I was running and had to continue running had properly regis- tered, it went from being a natural reflex to being a vastly complex feat of conscious coordination, and I thought how easy it would be to trip and fall and die on the on-ramp, roadkill smashed by tire-treads and ground into the sur- face. My legs abruptly felt a couple of inches shorter than they were meant to be. I turned my head to see a pair of cars vectoring out of the orbit of the roundabout, acceler- ating into an escape velocity, aiming for me. Their head- lights were on—the weak, alien sun was gone. The lead car sounded its horn as I hit the stony shore on the far side of the ramp and the furious blaring note Dopplered away behind me, ricocheting off the precisely formed flanks of the embankment. This was it—the far side, my destina- tion, safety. Part of me wanted to sink to my knees in thanksgiving, but the ground—not pavement, just left- over dirt verge—was muddy and sown with litter and debris from the road. Cracked hubcaps and crisp packets; a coiled item of clothing, blackened and pressed into the dirt by the rain. Clothes abandoned by the road always had a sinister air, suggesting sex crime or self-destruction, arising from the question of how they got there and who they had left unclothed. After a few moments to regain my breath, I trudged on.

The permanent rush of traffic could not obscure the death of the old road. Fresh concrete gave way to potholes and smashed paving stones. Still I was the only pedestrian. On the far side of the road was a wide two-storey office building, with TO LET and a telephone number spelled out in big fluorescent characters in the windows all along its upper level. A secondhand car dealership farther along the road was winding down toward closure. Its lot was half-empty and the glass walls of the showroom displayed only red and black posters proclaiming EVERYTHING MUST GO and FINAL REDUCTIONS. A Suzuki Jimny dangled from a cherry picker by the roadside—a carnival tactic to grab the attention of passing trade in better times that now resembled a corpse on a gibbet. The microboom that the motorway, the MetaCenter and the hotel were supposed to unleash clearly had yet to arrive. Hundreds of millions in public and private investment. Gateway. Hub.

The MetaCenter was on my side of the road. Not the building itself, merely the edge of its immense site, an edge marked by a landscaped ridge of bare flower beds topped by the word METACENTER spelled out in big white blocks like children's toys. A billboard on a mast advertised Meetex. The great white bulk of the center was down an access road that was the parallel twin of the road to the hotels. Before reaching it, a succession of huge, empty car parks had to be passed, each separated from the next by another low earthen ridge planted with saplings in their plastic surgical braces. Only sections E and F had cars parked in them. The first living souls appeared: smokers clustered under the canopy shielding the main entrance. One of the main entrances: Entrance A1. The skywalk passed overhead nearby, a gangway connecting to a sparkling ocean liner. But they never built any ocean liners this size. A man in a foam rubber mobile phone outfit was handing out leaflets, face showing through a hole in place of one of the app icons.

Inside, past the puffing smokers and the dejected mobile phone, the air had a little more purpose. I too had a little more purpose—I had a job to do. The first session was pretty much a write-off—they would be halfway through already. But the rest of the afternoon could be salvaged, and there was all of tomorrow. A short queue preceded me at the registration desk. I did not let it rankle me. The walk here had been unpleasant, an outrageous imposition in fact, but it had also been cathartic. And the rain had held off for me—events were tilting in my favor. The motorway junction had been a mighty obstacle placed in my path, one that nobody expected me to be able to overcome. They had expected me to simply give up. But here I was, and any further barriers would surely prove as ready to fall. I smoothed my shirt and jacket and tidied my tie. In front of me, a woman was asking if she could get a refund on the last day because she had to leave earlier than expected. She wanted to stay but had to go. I considered giving her one of my business cards and telling her there was a way to get the benefit of the last day without actually attending. But it was probably better to keep a low profile.

A desk opened up. Behind it was a woman in her late thirties, with dark blond hair tied in a bun, a silk scarf around her neck and slightly too much makeup. MANDY, said the nametag on her dark blue blazer.

"Hi. My name is Neil Double. My conference pass has been revoked and I'd like to find out how to get it reinstated."

Mandy gave me an appraising look, one that led me to wonder how often passes were revoked, and for what sins. In Mandy's eyes, I was clearly capable of unfathomable deviancy.

"May I see your pass?"

I took the laminated card from my jacket pocket and gave it to her. She passed it over a device on her desk. *Bip. Bee-baw.*

"Yes, this pass has been voided," Mandy said.

This wasn't a surprise—what was a surprise was finding that the swollen knuckle of frustration in my chest had not been evaporated by the walk, but was bigger and heavier than ever.

"I know," I said. "How do I get it unvoided?"

"We can't do that," Mandy said. "I can't void a voiding. That's not possible." She sounded mildly impatient, as if other, unvoided customers needed her attention and a void was asking her nonsensical questions about painting the sky another color.

I needed to be calm. "Why was it voided?"

"Any breach of the terms and conditions would render the pass void. This is all quite clear in the terms and conditions. You read and accepted the terms and conditions when you applied for a pass."

"I might have accepted the terms and conditions, but I didn't read them. Nobody ever does."

"You stated on the form that you had."

"I ticked a box. And it wasn't even me, it was my office. Maybe they read the terms and conditions, I don't know. I could call them and ask?" No mobile phone. The woman had it. A pang of loss. "It's not important—can you just tell me why the pass was voided? What part of the terms and conditions did I breach?" I forced a smile, and it felt like twisting a coat hanger into the shape.

"I'm afraid I can't give you that information."

"Aha! So there is information to give? Why can't you give it to me?"

Mandy's eyes flicked to her screen for a fraction of a second before returning to me. "It's Meetex policy not to share customer information with third parties."

"But this is information about me! I'm the customer! There is no third party!"

"This information pertains to a customer. You are no longer a Meetex customer. It's data protection."

"But it's my data! I'm the same person!"

"You are not a Meetex customer. If you were, you wouldn't want your private information shared with a stranger, would you?"

"I'm not a stranger! I'm the same person!"

While this exchange had been going on, the queue behind me had lengthened, and I became aware of increasing numbers of eyes on me. Worse, one of the black-jacketed security men had drifted away from his post by the entrance to the hall and was now watching me from a discreet distance.

"It's OK," I said, quietly and reasonably. "I understand. But I need to sort this out. I would like to speak to Tom Laing. Would you call him for me?"

"I'm not sure he's available."

"Find out, would you? Tell him Neil Double would like to talk with him. The least he can do is talk to me in person. Tell him he owes me that."

Mandy stared at me, lips an over-painted line, an implacable outer surface betraying nothing of the professional algebra within. A server box analyzing my query. Without answering or taking her eyes off me, she reached for her phone and punched in four numbers.

"Abi? Is Tom Laing available?" She turned away from the desk and hunched over, presenting me with a blazered back, and I could not make out the exchange that followed. In less than a minute, though, she turned back and passed the phone handset to me.

"Mr. Double?" It was Laing.

"Mr. Laing. Not Mr. Graham?"

"I'm a busy man, Mr. Double."

"Thank you for speaking with me. I am being denied entry to your conference and, as a paying customer, I would like to know why."

A sigh. "I should have thought the answer to that was obvious."

Mandy was shooing me to one side, pulling the coiled flex of the phone over her computer monitor so she could deal with the man queuing behind me. This man—older, haughty, also blazer-wearing—stepped forward, glaring at me.

"Terms and conditions," I said.

"Yeah, we'll find something in there," Laing said. "It's all boilerplate legal stuff, there'll be something that means what we want it to mean: inappropriate conduct, activities contrary to our commercial interests, abuse of intellectual property . . . to be honest with you, I haven't read them. But you know why we can't let you in. It's your business. Conference surrogacy. We have to put a stop to that."

"There's demand for it," I said. "Huge demand. We serve a useful purpose."

The event director laughed, a condescending saloon bar laugh. "Oh, I'm sure there's demand for it—I bet there's more demand than you imagine. Being able to get the value out of the conference without being there? It's brilliant. A brilliant proposition. I don't believe it, but many will, possibly enough to eat into our client base, and in the present environment . . . You're a tapeworm, son, and we've got to flush you out before you're ten foot long and we're starving to death."

Son? Laing was, what, maybe ten years older than I was? His use of that word stalled me, and meant his description of me as a bowel-dwelling parasite took longer to sink in than it should have.

"I don't blame you for being scared when your whole industry is based on a lie," I said. "This idea that you have to be somewhere in person, that you have to meet people face-to-face . . . it's crap. You make people feel as if they're missing out on something, and their only option is to spend one hundred fifty pounds a day half-asleep in a seminar. And people fall for it because they don't have much choice. Until now."

"You don't sound like a man asking nicely to be readmitted to one of my events."

"I am inevitable. That's what I'm saying. It was inevitable that someone would come up with an alternative to hanging round in sheds on the motorway, and now someone has. Give it ten years and there'll be conference-going robots, telepresence drones. All this fucking flesh-pressing will look as antiquated as semaphore. You'll be sucking up to conference surrogates because we'll be the warm, human alternative to wasp-sized camera-microphones. You need to get used to me."

"Here's the thing," Laing said, a harder edge to his voice, "I don't think you are inevitable, not at all. I think you will prove pretty easy to squash, mate. You're banned. You'll never again attend a conference or a trade fair organized by my company. And we'll be working with the industry's representative bodies to build a blacklist. Your name will be top of that list, son. We should be able to get you banned from every event in Western Europe. You're finished."

"We'll use other names. My identity is unimportant. That's the whole idea."

"I assumed you were using a fake name anyway. Mr. Double? Please. Next time you assume an identity try not to make it so obvious. It's one of the things that made us suspicious in the first place. And it won't work. Our databases are getting better and better. We can put a block on your company address and on the card it uses to pay. A new address and a new card for every event? That should slow you down. The next step is face-recognition software. It's almost there, improving every day. You will be stopped."

I opened my mouth, but no sound emerged. I had the sense of a threshold being crossed—of moving out from under a shelter I had never even imagined existed into an exposed and wild place. No privacy. Known.

"Still there?" the event director asked. "We understand each other? I think it goes without saying that your request for readmittance is denied. Kindly do not waste any more of my time or my staff's time. Right?"

I didn't respond. Instead I handed the phone back over the desk. My ear was hot and sore—the handset had been pressed against it hard. Mandy was dealing with another conference attendee and did not see me proffering the phone. I let it drop from my fingers and it clattered against her keyboard and the surface of the desk before falling from view, onto the floor. Mandy and the woman she was dealing with stared at me, mouths open, censure written across their faces. And I meant to say something, maybe an apology or an excuse, but I had nothing, so I walked away, toward the exit.

Outside, the rain was falling again. Wherever it had been all morning, it had returned reinforced and chilled. Umbrellas were on sale in the MetaCenter lobby: £10, hazard yellow, covered in Meetex logos and the emblems of sponsor organizations and trade bodies. Precisely the confederacy the event director intended to raise against me. Just no, no way.

By the time I reached section C of the MetaCenter car park, the rain had evenly saturated my jacket and the shirt underneath. I did not believe that I could get any more wet, but each additional step proved me wrong. At the height of the afternoon it was darker than dusk. A shuttle bus, passing me on its way to the hotel, seemed full of glowing smoke—its windows misted by its interior warmth, diffusing its interior light. At least the condensation made me invisible to its passengers. The new asphalt of the access road ran with water, as if even the puddles were fleeing for cover. Perhaps this was it, the end, and all the naked dirt landscaping would wash away, the tarmac would split and wear thin, and all the shiny new boxes would be swept into the channel of the motorway, draining toward the sea. Planes would circle like gulls above submerged runways.

I remember little of the walk back to the hotel. Waiting for the right moment to cross the on-ramp, blinking water from my eyes as headlights swept by, I realized that a suicidal person might accidentally kill themselves trying to get to the bridge to do the job properly. Did that still count as a suicide? What was on the other end of that phone number on the notices on the bridge? A reassuring voice, one who would tell you that everything was all right? That was a pleasing thought, and tempting, until it struck me that even if I wanted to call the number, I couldn't. The woman still had my phone.

The glowing red sign of the Way Inn, bright and blur-edged against the gloomy sky and through veils of rain, was my only source of comfort. The hotel was warm and dry. The hotel valued my custom and loyalty. The hotel wanted me.

A hotel shower, so hot my scalp crawled, the skin on my shoulders tingled and I felt a band tightening across my forehead, just under my hairline.

My jacket and shirt were soaked through—the jacket so much that its lowest edges were swollen and shining, laden with moisture. I put them both on hangers, but these were hookless, theft-proof, hotel hangers, so there was nowhere to hang them but in the wardrobe, where I feared lack of air might slow down their drying and leave them smelling moldy. After some prevarication, I left the door open. Steam from the shower and the hanging wet clothes made the room feel muggy and used. Lived in. The extractor fan in the bathroom whirred. The room had been cleaned in my absence, but there were too many of my possessions in it now for it to feel *truly* clean. A red baseball cap had been neatly placed on the plumped pillow of the bed. It took me a moment to figure out what it was and where it had come from—I had picked it up in the lobby when attempting to slip past the bus driver. That was three hours ago. It could have been months ago. The cap must have been left on the bed, found by the chambermaid and carefully relocated. Thought had gone into where to place it. And now I casually tossed it onto the armchair where some of my clothes were draped, and lay on the bed in my boxer shorts.

The scent of my underarm deodorant reached my nose. I had rolled it on after the shower without thinking too much about it, just routine. Why? For whom? Who was I going to see this afternoon?

Finished. I was finished. The event director's word. Banned. Blacklisted. Finished. But I was alive. My job was finished, maybe Adam's whole enterprise was finished—and with it my investment, destroying my one substantial asset—but I would go on.

No. It didn't seem possible. I knew it to be true, that my life would continue—no motorway bridge for me. But I couldn't picture it. Another job. A return to my flat in Docklands, a CV . . . What made it so hard to consider was that this near-future version of me, a very near-future version of me, was not doing *this* job. This job was ideally tailored to me. I would not have called it a good job, but it was the perfect job. And it was gone. Finished.

Into this bleak reverie, the clock radio injected a sudden chorus of modem burping and yelping and hissing—leakage from dying stars, planes of sense grinding against one another, mystery spectra made audible. My phone, I thought, and I tensed for the ringtone or the chime of a new message before recalling that it was gone, and feeling its loss all over again. I am told that grief works that way—the bereaved forget that someone is missing from their life, and a place or a joke or a book reminds them, and it's a new death all over again. And this continual forgetting and remembering is first suffered daily, perhaps even several times a day, their loss not a single blow against them but many blows; a volley of death, lasting for years, until remembering covers the forgetting.

So I am told, anyway. I had lost few people close to me—a couple of grandparents while too young to understand, an aunt and an uncle since, neither of whom I knew at all well, and whose passing necessitated dull trips to distant cities. The mountainous exception to this rule was the death of my father, and it had not matched up to that experience of forgetting and remembering. Our relationship was a varied catalogue of absences.

The worst of these was while he was still alive, after the end with my mother and before I left home. He was alive, somewhere, but I was obliged to behave as if he was not, as if in fact he had never existed. He was invoked only as a form of original sin, the basis of our family's fallen state. If he had visitation rights, they were not exercised. As my A-levels progressed and my departure from home to go to university approached, I insisted on a talk about his whereabouts and status. When it came, this talk was brief and unpleasant. I was told, not asked, not to communicate with him. There was no argument: just an immediate, silent resolution on my part to contact him as soon as I had the opportunity, and to keep the fact secret.

University gave me the cover I needed. At last I was beyond the bounds of home. After a modicum of amateur sleuthing—phone calls to employers—I had an email address, which I wrote to, incandescent with excitement. I forget what exactly it was I wanted, and it's possible I didn't know at the time, but I remember how desperately I wanted it. The want was pure and physical, almost painful. I yearned to have a complete, cohesive view of the man, something I had glimpsed only in fragments, and to have time with him; time enough, not snippets cut short. In place of trailers and clippings, I wanted the whole film.

Instead, I got more fragments. We exchanged emails that were basic in form and elusive in detail. Mine were little more than the outlines of the long, eloquent, moving messages I meant to send—I would fill three short paragraphs with news about my studies and then find it hard to expand on those. His replies, rather than supplying his own news, would offer acknowledgements of mine: Good to hear from you, son, that's great about the course, proud of you. He had settled in a distant, unfamiliar city, one where we had no family connections or history. A couple of times he came to visit me—we drank pints and ate a bland Sunday roast out of a freezer in a large, echoey pub near the railway station. It had remnants of a past glory—high ceilings and ornate glass, brass and moldings—but had been absorbed by a national brewery company that was part of an agribusiness multinational. English heritage by way of a Canadian-Swiss pesticide giant.

"Never drink in the pub nearest the railway station," my father said. "I suppose that's the kind of advice I should have been giving you all along."

Our conversations were monosyllabic, elliptic, phatic. Even when I was out of university, earning a living for myself, doing the kind of work I thought he would understand and respect, the signal passing between us faltered and carried little.

He absconded for good when I was in my late twenties, an ultimate absence.

The electronic gurgling and percussion from the clock radio showed no sign of abating. Hadn't I asked the front desk to fix or replace it? And still it chattered in that sickening, impossible way. My listlessness was abruptly supplanted by a furious energy. I swung off the bed, knelt down on my bare knees, and reached under the bedside table for the clock's plug.

The plug was not in the wall socket. It was lying on the floor beside it. I held it dumbly in my hand, as it dangled on its flex like a head on a broken neck. The radio buzzed and made coughing birdcall sounds—staticky tinfoil-feathered birds raised in wire-wool nests found in electricity substations. Power was clearly flowing within it—the clock face read 3:33, but the red glowing numbers pulsed on a slow beat, implying the device had lost power at some point and had reset to midnight. Was it half past three? That was quite plausible—my instinct was to check my phone, and I felt another incision of loss. Instead I turned on the TV.

WELCOME MR. DOUBLE

An angry black cloud shedding three blue drops of rain was the icon indicating today's weather. No kidding. It was the same for tomorrow, and for the "Weekend Prospect." Tonight's special in the restaurant was spaghetti carbonara and the soup of the day was French onion. The time was 3:51. Close, then: Had the hotel staff been in to fix or replace it, thereby stopping the advance of the clock for twenty-two minutes? Or had it been left undisturbed since I unplugged it last night? If there was a hidden backup battery, as I had suspected earlier, it was a good one.

I picked up the clock to inspect it more closely and it squealed in response—the kind of noise a theremin might make if you gave it a nasty fright—before degenerating into a low growl.

WOWWwwwrrr . . .

This startled me and I almost dropped the clock. It was vibrating very slightly, a shiver I found innately distasteful and sinister. There was a removable panel on its underside but it was fastened with small screws. For a moment I was gripped by an urge to fling the clock across the room, to smash it and hear the noise it made then. Its continual gibbering was annoying enough, and the more time I spent with it, the more it perplexed and annoyed me. And there was another angle to my puzzlement, one I thought absurd, but one which nevertheless heightened my wish to be rid of the device: the undeniable note of fear I felt rising within myself.

I put the troubling object down, picked up the phone and called reception. A woman answered and I complained that my clock radio was still malfunctioning. She said someone would be right up.

Someone would be right up. Boxer shorts would not be appropriate. I put on my last full change of clothes, casual gear meant for travel and downtime: chinos, a blue shirt, a gray jumper. No knock at the door. I glanced at the clock radio, to see how much time had elapsed since I had made the call. The display still read 3:33.

Not possible. At least a minute had passed—and more like five or ten. 3:33. I stared at the screen. It was, I realized, not 3:33 that burned against the black plastic but 3 33, without a dot or a colon separating the hours and the minutes. By looking closely, I could make out the ghost recesses of the unlit elements in the display, and there were darkened dots between the hours and the minutes. Perhaps 3 33 wasn't a time at all, but a warning of a fault, like ERR on a calculator. A fault that could be guessed at and easily corrected. I knelt again and plugged the clock back in.

The warbling and whining ceased immediately. I came to my feet and looked again at the clock. Blinking before me was the time 12:00, a silent, obedient default. No need to set the time—one of the hotel staff would be up shortly, after all.

I was still staring at the radio when it emitted a loud, piercing electronic peal, causing me to jump. What now? Was this the alarm? I thought of the alarmed doors in the corridors, a whole hotel stitched together by twitching nerves and sensitive tendons. The woman's face behind safety glass, daring me to follow her.

The peal repeated. It wasn't the clock radio at all—it was the phone. I answered it.

"Mr. Double?" An unfamiliar voice, not John-Paul or the young things at the front desk—older, precise, mid-Atlantic.

"Yes?"

"I'm pleased to have caught you," the voice said. "My name is Mr. Hilbert. I'm with the hotel. I wonder if you would be able to join me in the Gallery Room for a brief chat."

"Excuse me?"

"The Gallery Room is part of the conference facilities available at this Way Inn. You will find it on the first floor, in the business suite. This will take no more than a few minutes of your time, I'm sure you must be busy."

This last remark pained me like an insult. No, not busy, not busy at all. Nothing to do, in fact. Across the motorway the fair and conference would be going on without me. Was that the reason for this call? Adam knew what had happened and had cut short my stay at the Way Inn—my prepaid room was cancelled and I would have to leave, go home, go through the postmortem of my career in something like disgrace. Could my life unravel so completely so quickly? Was there so little to it?

"What is this concerning?" I asked. I realized that the very last thing I wanted to do was to leave the hotel. That would be the ultimate humiliation. Even if matters could not be patched up with the event director, I could not bear the idea of cutting short my stay. I wanted to enjoy this existence awhile longer if I could.

"We like to meet with our most loyal guests from time to time, to make sure we are doing everything we can for you," the voice, Hilbert, said. "And you are a most loyal guest."

I was weary. The day had drained me. "Is this necessary? I've never had a meeting like this before—it has been a very trying day, I would prefer—"

"Just a few minutes of your time," Hilbert said, his clipped tone making the interruption with patrician assurance, as if he believed himself to be constitutionally incapable of rudeness. "I think you will be pleasantly surprised by the number of ways in which the hotel can come to your assistance and improve your stay. Ways you might not expect. Gallery Room, first floor. I'm there now."

I was ready to reply, to defer and delay, but the line was dead.

Several large rooms comprised the business suite, all alike, with names that conveyed their very slight differences. The Vista Room, the largest, overlooked the motorway and the MetaCenter. The Garden Room overlooked one of the hotel courtyards. The Sunrise Room faced east. Each room could be configured in a vast variety of ways, depending on whether one wanted to hold a seminar, negotiate around a table, give a presentation, conduct a stockholders' meeting or any number of other corporate activities. Some of the rooms could be combined or subdivided, all to reflect the spatial desires of guest companies. Flexibility. A fully serviced environment. The options were all laid out in the welcome pack in each bedroom; a menu of different interactions—breakout session, AGM, Q&A, summit—that foreclosed on the possibility of any form of activity beyond those catered for.

The Gallery Room was one of the smallest in the suite. It was a rectangular space with a door at one end and a couple of windows looking onto the courtyard at the other. Hanging on the longer walls were a total of eight of the hotel's abstract paintings. In the middle of the room was a large oval table, seating eight.

When I arrived, the door was propped open. Hilbert—I could safely assume it was Hilbert—was at the far end, a black streak against the gray light from the window. He was looking out over the courtyard and I could not be sure that he had heard me enter.

"Mr. Hilbert?"

The dark figure turned and smiled at me. Hilbert was a tall man, perhaps six foot two or three, and his height was given emphasis by his skeletal thinness. His suit, an obviously expensive black pinstripe, hung on him as if from a wire coat hanger. The blackness of the suit was matched by his railing-black hair, swept over to one side and glistening with old-school barber product. This was an uncomfortable contrast with his pale skin which, like the suit, hung somewhat loosely off the frame beneath. Could the hair be a wig?

Hilbert's smile was enduring, his teeth long and plentiful. "Mr. Double. Thank you so much for coming. Please, close the door and make yourself comfortable. Can I offer you a drink? Coffee?" He extended a slender white hand toward a small table in the corner that bore mugs and glasses, jugs of water and a Nespresso coffee machine.

"No, no thank you," I said, shutting the door. Whatever Hilbert had said on the phone, I remained intensely suspicious of this meeting. It had all the hallmarks of "About your bill . . . " or "Unusual activity on your account . . . "

I chose a seat at the side of the oval table, near the door. Hilbert sat opposite me. My eyes flickered to his hair and probed its edges. Wig? Not a wig? It was hard to tell—the front of a wig is always the most convincing part; the back, where the join is obvious, gives it away.

"Now, then," Hilbert said. "Thanks again for coming down. And thank you for your custom over the years. We really do value your loyalty."

"It's nothing," I said. "My work involves a great deal of travel."

"Yes. You're here for the conference, I take it?"

"Yes," I said. Why else would I be here? Then it occurred to me that this was no longer true. I was no longer here for the conference. Why was I here? What was I doing?

Hilbert laid a black leather document folder on the table and unzipped it. "Our records show you have stayed in forty-one different Way Inn hotels in thirteen countries since becoming a My Way loyalty cardholder in 2006," he said, reading from the papers before him.

This felt uncomfortably like an interrogation. I feared somehow incriminating myself. "That sounds plausible. I've stayed in a hot of Hiltons and Novotels and Holiday Inns too. That's the kind of work I do."

"Nevertheless," Hilbert said, lips withdrawing over those long, straight teeth, "we are truly grateful for your business. For instance, I see sixteen stays at Way Inn Royal Docks in London."

"It's right by the ExCel Center," I said. "There are a lot of conferences at the ExCel Center."

"Of course," Hilbert said. "Your home address is in Westferry, London E14?"

A chill. "Yes."

"That's not far from the ExCel Center. And yet you choose to stay at Way Inn rather than at home."

I didn't say anything. There was an implication there, for sure, and I didn't much like it.

"We really do place a premium on that kind of superlative loyalty," Hilbert said. "It's one thing when a customer chooses us over our competitors but quite another when he chooses us over his own home, his own bed . . . "

"May I ask what this is about?" I said sharply. There was always the chance that there was no hostile agenda behind Hilbert's remarks, and that he really had invited me here solely in order to kiss my arse. Another time, I might have enjoyed a bit of corporate sucking-up, but today it felt like an intrusion and a waste of time. "I don't mean to be rude, but I'm having rather a bad day."

Hilbert's mouth turned down at the corners with mime-artist sadness. "I'm most sorry to hear that, Mr. Double. Not a problem with the hotel, I trust?"

"No, not at all."

"Is it perhaps something we could assist with?"

"I don't see how."

"The hotel is able to assist its most loyal customers in a surprising number of ways," Hilbert said. "Try us."

I shifted in my chair. It was a heavy modern thing like the one in my room, with a woven seat and back supported by a tubular chrome frame, and it did not shift with me.

"You're busy," Hilbert said, holding up his hands respectfully. As he moved his limbs, the razor-fine white pinstripes on his suit bled into one another and tricked the eye unpleasantly, like a pattern glitching on an old television. I dropped my eyes to the folder on the table. What else was in there? "Forgive my circumlocution. I will proceed to the heart of the matter. Our mutual interest. You asked the hotel for assistance. You wanted to contact a certain woman."

Hilbert's eyes glinted like coal. When he saw that he had my complete attention, he smiled. "As luck would have it, our interests coincide. This is so often the case. What do you know about her?"

There wasn't the slightest doubt he was talking about the same woman, the woman who had filled my thoughts for two days. Could it be that she was in trouble, not me? That would explain this inquisition, and if she had been running around pinching guests' mobile phones and setting off alarms, it didn't seem unlikely.

"I don't know much," I said. A narrow path had to be trod—I had no desire to accuse or incriminate the woman, but I wanted to get my phone back, and perhaps see her again. "I know she works for the hotel. I believe she's staying here as well. Beyond that, very little."

"How do you know her?"

The memory caused me to smile. "We met . . . We didn't actually meet until the day before yesterday. But I had seen her before. Years ago. It was at the Way Inn in Doha, Qatar."

"There are now three Way Inn branches in Qatar," Hilbert said. "Please go on."

"Right. I was at a conference, and I was waiting for a shuttle bus in the lobby. Where there are buses, there is waiting around. She walked in and . . . Well, she wasn't wearing anything. She just stood there, completely na-ked, eyes wide, like she was standing to attention. She didn't say a word at first, but within about ten or twenty seconds everyone in that lobby was looking at her. Total silence. I have never heard anything like it. And then the staff at the front desk went crazy. They started shouting at her, running about, trying to find something to cover her up. Obviously Qatar's an Islamic country, very conservative—I mean, there would have been a commotion anywhere, but there . . . They had cushions, towels, all kinds of things, to cover her up. When the shouting began she didn't move, but she looked less composed, more frightened and, still staring into space, she mouthed something. Then they reached her and grabbed her, carrying all these towels and jackets, and she screamed, terrible repeated screams, each one tearing all the air out of her lungs. I've never heard anything like it. Before, she had seemed strong, serene, and then it was as if all her muscles failed at once. She just slumped to the floor, screaming."

"And then?" Hilbert said after I fell quiet.

"I don't know. The bus arrived. We were shooed away. It seemed intrusive to stand and watch. I thought I would never see her again. And then I did, the night before last. I had to speak to her. I'd dreamed about her since."

This was too much information, and I didn't know why I volunteered the contents of my dreams. For all his elaborate courtesies, Hilbert had an air of authority. But the quietude of the room, its soothing paintings and designer chairs and little touches of hospitality, also gave me the sense that it was a place for candor.

"What did she say?" Hilbert asked.

"She was very polite, given the circumstances. Of course she didn't remember me, but we talked—"

"No. The first time. In Doha. You said she mouthed something."

This momentarily stumped me. It addressed a mystery that had been twisting at the back of my mind since that day. "Well, there's no way to be sure—by that time all the staff were in uproar, and I was standing near her, but not right beside her. And anyway, she was sleepwalking. It was a fragment, something dredged up from the subconscious, no context . . . "

"Indulge me," Hilbert said, sweeping away my caveats with a wave of those slender fingers, a porcelain blade.

"'It goes on.' That's what I think it was. 'It goes on.'"

"What do you suppose she meant by that?"

I frowned. "Nothing, I expect. Like I say, it was probably nonsense."

"Without a doubt," Hilbert said, his bluish lips turning into a smile again. "When you met her here, what did you talk about?"

This prompt movement from one line of inquiry to another increased my impression that this was more interrogation than friendly chat. I resolved to be a little more sparing with the details.

"Not much. Her work for the hotel. The art."

"The art? In the hotel?"

"Yes, the paintings," I said, gesturing at the examples around us.

"What did she tell you about the paintings?"

"'Tell' you? There was something to tell about the paintings? Hilbert was clearly interested. He had inclined forward slightly, and his question had a note of urgency to it.

"She really likes the paintings," I said. "Why can't you

ask her these things yourself? You both work for Way Inn; you know how to get in touch with her, which is certainly more than I know . . . "

Hilbert leaned back, which set off the moiré effect on his pinstripes so that his form became one large migraine blind spot, a void that was both sickening to the eyes and thoroughly compelling to them.

"She works for Way Inn, yes," he said. "Her talent, her ability to identify providential sites for hotel expansion, is unique and immensely valuable. But she has never been wholly reliable, and in recent months . . . What was your impression of her?"

"A bit of a flake?"

" 'A bit of a flake,' indeed, *yes*," Hilbert said, bringing his hands together in a clap of pleasure. "Well put. She has become steadily more erratic. Her work remains exceptional, of course, but I am concerned that her other activities might run counter to the hotel's best interests."

"She stole my phone," I said.

"I know. I have the query you logged with our front desk staff earlier today. It's what brought you to my attention. All I want is to talk to her, to ensure that she is not exposing Way Inn to any kind of harm or embarrassment. But while we work for the same superior, she goes to great pains to elude me, and ignores my efforts to communicate with her. Corporate politics, Mr. Double, all very tiresome but the way this world works. So I wonder if you would be prepared to act on my behalf. If you would be my stand-in, in fact. That is, after all, your business, is it not?"

It was my business, until today. But it was now finished.

Remembering that sombre state of affairs made this talk with Hilbert seem like a sinister sideshow—a murky distraction from more important matters. But what were those matters really? Going home and updating my CV? I nodded my answer to Hilbert's question.

"Of course the hotel would be at your disposal—you're with us another two nights, I take it? We can extend that; more than that, we'll upgrade your My Way cardholder status to include unlimited free nights."

"*Unlimited* free nights?" I was certain I had misheard. "Just for setting up a meeting?"

"A very important meeting. The highest possible priority."

"Wait," I said. "Aren't we getting ahead of ourselves? How am I supposed to set any of this up? I know nothing about this woman. Really. I don't know where she is, I don't know how to get in touch with her. I don't even know her name."

"Her name is Dee. And you have a phone number for her."

"I do?"

"She has your phone, doesn't she?"

This was true. I was embarrassed I had not thought of it before.

"Tell her you want your phone back," Hilbert said. "You do, don't you? If that doesn't work . . . "

He flipped over a couple of sheets of paper in the folder in front of him, eventually turning up a small piece of plastic tucked in with the documents. It was a Way Inn keycard, but the trademark looped *W* on it was black, not red.

"May I have your room key?" Hilbert asked.

I put the key on the table between us.

"This one," Hilbert said, holding up the black *W*, "is programmed for your room, but also has executive access to the business suite, including this room. Your friend likes the paintings—this room has a particularly fine selection, and I'm sure she'll be interested to see them. She will listen to you."

Four paintings hung on the wall behind Hilbert, and they appeared to be nothing more than typical examples of the art found throughout the hotel; the same swirling earth-toned patterns, the same lack of content, that same essential sameness. What made these "particularly fine" was hard to say. Then I saw that they connected. The curving lines of the pattern on one continued to the next; the outer edge of an umber sphere, which scraped into the frame of the leftmost painting, rose through the middle pair to fill the rightmost frame, by which time its interior had erupted with new arcs and bubbles.

"You see it?" Hilbert said. He had been watching my eyes. "A congeries of spheres. A whole sequence. Your friend will enjoy that."

"And what then?"

"The hotel's security systems log all keycard use. I am tracking this card. I will know when it has been used to open this room, and I will be with you forthwith."

"And then?"

"Then nothing. You will have done your part."

"And you want to talk with her? That's all?"

Hilbert smiled and held up his hands, a nothing-to-hide gesture, but the distortion of the bleeding stripes on his suit drove my gaze away. "Just to talk."

These reassurances were not doing much to reassure me. It was hard to summon up any trust for Hilbert—hard, in fact, to summon up any human fellow-feeling at all. Where had he come from? I assumed he emanated from the hotel's higher management, rather than the staff of this branch. If he had travelled from a regional headquarters for this meeting, that would make this business more important than he was letting on. It was hard even to tell his age— between the possible rug and the smooth, pale skin that hung a little loose, he could have been anywhere from thirty-five to seventy. His offer had its flaws, too: even if I was able to reestablish a connection with the woman, doing so on behalf of a man who might well be her professional foe didn't seem like a way to make a good impression. I wanted more than just to get my phone back.

"I don't know," I said. "It doesn't feel right to involve myself in Way Inn's office politics."

Hilbert narrowed his eyes. "I see. Well, this ethical concern does you credit. Do you always apply this test to potential clients?"

I didn't immediately respond. No, of course not—in general I had no idea who my clients were, let alone their motives. But all the discretion and secrecy, the skulking around not telling people what I do—did—seemed like a disappeared world now.

"To be honest, I'm not sure I'm even in that line of work anymore," I said at last.

"Yes, of course," Hilbert said. "This unpleasantness with the people at Meetex."

"How did you know about that?"

"This morning," Hilbert said, referring to another sheet from his folder, "you were trying to arrange transport to the MetaCenter, and you told the front desk your conference pass had been cancelled."

"Did I? I'm not sure I did tell them that."

"Well, it must have been easy to infer. And I made my own inquiries . . . it's really not important. What is important is that we can help you fix it."

"How?"

"You have time. You have executive use of the business suite. Book a meeting with the Meetex people in one of our rooms. I'm sure you'll get the result you want. Way Inn is the perfect environment for business." A sales-pitch smile was alloyed into the words, a sign they had been repeated many times. "And, of course, this is a modern, flexible building—many of these spaces can be reconfigured to your requirements. You need only ask."

It couldn't hurt. At least, it would have to be an improvement on me, exhausted and furious, spitting into a phone in the lobby of the MetaCenter. If, that is, I could get Laing into the room—I doubted he would even speak to me on the phone.

I reached out and took the black keycard. It was a little thicker and heavier than the regular one. More substantial. That extra weight was superficially pleasing—it signalled quality. Maybe those details made a difference. Like this room: the coordinated art, the tubular steel chairs; the palm in one corner and the Nespresso machine in the other; the brand-new projector on the ceiling and the teleconference hub on the table; the almost imperceptible sound of the air conditioning holding the temperature within half a degree of the chosen level; all these small touches that made it *the perfect environment for business*. So those people, the businesspeople, having gorged on stock photos and promo videos in which pretty actors smile and shake hands in places like this, enter a place like this and their conditioning kicks in. They smile and shake hands. Deals are done, agreements are forged, consensus is achieved. Business. And here I am, pocketing the black card and rising from my chair as Hilbert rises from his, agreement reached, deal done. I had little to lose from Hilbert's proposal, I calculated, and the alternative was simply to return to my room and the total lack of options that waited there.

At the end of the table, by the door, Hilbert and I came face-to-face, the closest we had been to each other. I was tending toward the conclusion that his hair was real but had been subjected to an extreme and retro treatment to give it an ageless veneer of artificiality. His suit fritzed and strobed over the jumbled angles of his limbs.

"I'm so pleased you're able to assist me in this matter, and I hope we are able to assist you. A pleasure to meet you, Mr. Double."

It was handshake time. Hilbert's smooth skin was icy.

My father's funeral. Another train journey in my black suit to an unfamiliar town, though this time on my own, without my mother. Hard seats in a modern brick crematorium in the suburbs. A reading from Psalm 39: "You have made my days a mere handbreadth; the span of my years is as nothing before you. Everyone is but a breath, even those who seem secure." Triangular sandwiches in a function room in a small hotel that had once been in the countryside, but which was now surrounded by dual carriageways and DIY superstores. Strangers in suits, men I had never seen before and would never see again, told me how good it was I had come. Who were they? Where did they come from? What did they do? What purpose did they fulfill in the world? What was their connection to my father? To them *I* was the absence. Small talk of the smallest and least meaningful kind. I could think only of the fact that my mother was not present. She had not wanted me to be there. Her injunction, that I was not to contact "him," had wounded me deeply. I resented the need to conceal my resumed communication with my father from my mother; I resented the fact that she wanted to deny me my father, and that my failure to conform was a betrayal to her. The end of their marriage was a rupture that drove all three of us apart.

A woman was there—middle-aged; short, curly, blond hair, visibly subsiding under bereavement. She was supported by a young boy about twelve years old—about the age I was when my father left.

I fled before speaking to them. I had nothing to say. Two weeks later, a lawyer's letter informed me I had inherited £20,000. I decided at once to join Adam in his conference surrogacy venture.

Psalm 39: "I dwell with you as a foreigner, a stranger, as all my ancestors were."

Somewhere in the hotel, in those hundreds of rooms, my mobile phone was switched on and ringing. It rang seven times—that doubled electronic purr of a connection repeated seven times—before there was a break in the pattern, a space for hope to erupt . . . and it went to voice mail.

What did I expect? Why would she answer? However

much I might want to believe she had stolen my phone as a flirty prank, she had still stolen it. I could be the police calling her to get a fix on her location. Within a second, I realized how stupid that thought was—as if the police would launch an elaborate operation to recover a stolen phone, anxious men in headphones watching red lines bouncing around maps as bloodhound software tracked cellular scent across satellites and transmitter towers, at last zooming in on an aerial view of . . . this hotel, presumably. As if she were a kidnapper or a secret agent.

The phone was still switched on, though. There was that. Even if it was in a wheelie bin.

My next call was more successful. I swallowed my indignation and adopted a contrite tone with Laing, the event director. The ban had come as a terrible shock, I said, and coupled with my ordeal crossing the wastes to the MetaCenter, well, I spoke crudely, and I was sorry about that. Laing's ruse, posing as a prospective client, had also upset me.

"You can hardly complain about that," Laing said. "Isn't that standard procedure for you? Pretending to be someone else?"

I felt my fingers tighten around the beige plastic of the phone receiver—hotels are the last redoubt of the beige plastic phone—and I wondered how much pressure it would take to crush it.

"Well, quite," I said. "What I mean is, we should meet properly, in person, and I'm sure we can put this dispute behind us."

"Meet properly?" Laing said. He sounded amused. "Face-to-face, you mean? In the flesh?"

The handset creaked in my grip.

"Ha, yes. You of all people must acknowledge the value of that kind of personal encounter. I can see that value myself."

"I most certainly do," Laing said, suddenly full of bumptious rugby-club bonhomie. "And I'm curious to hear what you have to say. It must be good. I'm having a breakfast meeting at your hotel tomorrow; I could give you ten minutes before that. Eight thirty?"

"That's great," I said. I wanted it to be sooner— today—but I wasn't about to push my luck. "Eight thirty. Come to the Gallery Room in the business suite at the Way Inn."

The call ended. For all Laing's mocking tone, his obviously low expectations, I was pleased. It was something: the smallest handhold in a situation where previously there had been naught but an impregnable barrier. I was not finished.

With some of my confidence restored, I called my mobile again. And again it went to voice mail. But the transfer to voice mail—that pregnant, stagey pause—chopped into the middle of the fifth ring. It hadn't done that before, I was sure.

I called again. Two rings then to voice mail. Not only was the phone switched on, someone was holding it and refusing my calls. She still had the phone. This hint of interaction with her, however slight, was enough to fill me with joy. Maybe I could still reach her. I decided to leave a message.

"Hi, it's Neil," I said after the beep. "You took this phone from me this morning. I don't know why, maybe as a joke. I really need it back I'm afraid, it's a real pain being without it, so maybe we could meet? It would be great to see you again, we barely got a chance to talk last time and there's a lot I'd like to talk to you about. I'm in room

219; you can call through the switchboard or leave a message. I'll be around, the rest of my day is, uh, pretty clear. OK. Hoping to see you soon. Bye, then."

As soon as I put the receiver down, I began to appraise my performance. How had I done? A bit needy? This concern itself concerned me. I had never feared coming across as needy in the past. I needed no one particular woman because there were plenty of other women and they were all basically interchangeable. And seeing them that way didn't make me even slightly guilty, because I am sure they saw me in a similar way.

Except Lucy. She had not seen me that way. She had, in fact, *seen* me—seen an individual, and remembered him. And too late, I had seen her, and remembered her.

This other woman, Dee—she wasn't interchangeable either. She was unique. My chronically tenuous connection to her was becoming too much to bear. Yet I could not stand the idea of her regarding me as some desperate hanger-on or stalker.

What was happening to me? I was no longer the anonymous blur I wanted to be. There was a person here, and there were people out there.

And I had made a serious mistake. After all that discussion with Hilbert, I had not used the voice mail message to play the strongest card in my hand—the black keycard. The bait I was given specifically for this job. It was too good to not use. Hilbert's name would have to be omitted, in case there was bad feeling between them—but that didn't matter.

I called my mobile number again. It went to voice mail after three rings.

"Hi, Neil again," I said, hoping for a casual air. "I forgot to mention, I've been using the business center for work and there are a couple of rooms there filled with paintings. Good ones, too, full consecutive sequences. You can really see the broader pattern. Anyway, I still have access to the rooms if you wanted to take a peek."

I hesitated. There would be no further messages after this. Two was desperate enough, if she even listened to them. I had to make the sale.

"Ever since you told me about the paintings—about how they join up—I've been fascinated by them. I see it too. There's some kind of meaning there, you're right. Lately, since I saw you in the bar the other night, I've been feeling that everything is connected somehow, that it all lines up like the paintings. You, me, the hotel, all aligned together. I really want to see you again and find out more."

There was nothing else to say. It was already possible that I had said too much. I hung up. The message was wherever it was, suspended in the air, in limbo, in a hard drive in a distant, anonymous shed, perhaps to remain there for ever. I was suspended, too; without tasks, without reason to leave the room. No business to do—but business would be wrapping up for the day in any case. There was no party in the bar tonight, but it would be filling up with conference-goers anyway, and I would not be showing my face.

Another night in the hotel. The minibar had been restocked, but for the time being I didn't feel like drinking. My smart suit, the one drenched by Lucy, had come back from the cleaners while I was meeting Hilbert, and had been left hanging in the wardrobe in a red plastic condom. Silence. Had the alarm clock been repaired or replaced? If I had been given a new one, it was identical to the old one. New or old, it was quiet now, and that's what mattered. The only sound in the room was the gentle hum of the air-handling units.

My thoughts scrambled and cohered like a radio finding a signal. At first I imagined that I had woken myself—maybe it was the pounding of my heart that roused me, but what unremembered terror had so roused my heart? I listened to it thumping in my ears. I had been prey for something in the passages of my own subconscious, something lean and athirst that cohered from the corners. No light in the room, no hint of dawn at the hems of the curtains. The alarm clock said 12:33. The night had barely begun.

A knock at the door—three knocks in fact, three sharp blows separated by deliberate, heavy gaps; a repeat of the pattern that woke me. Housekeeping? At half past midnight? Impossible. Someone else was out there.

"Just a minute. I'm coming."

Could it be her, perhaps? I had left her my room number in my voice mail. A nocturnal visit. My mind filled with tawdry, soft-focus clichés; the bottle of champagne and two glasses, a negligee under a dressing gown, "I couldn't sleep . . . " The word *tryst*. Some people, educated by rented DVDs consumed with cheap wine, do behave this way. Some drop unsubtle hints that they would welcome this kind of visit. I had seen it—I had done it. I had been to *those* conferences.

But not her, surely not her. *That isn't where this is going*, she had said. She was wise to the way hotels put sex on the brain, posing themselves as convenient selection boxes of beds and genitals. She would never pull a tacky insom-nympho stunt. *That isn't where this is going.*

As these thoughts ran, I was throwing on a Way Inn dressing gown and going to the door, repeating: "I'm coming, I'm coming."

There was no one there. Disappointment, then anger. Was this a moronic joke by a drunken guest, a bit of mis-chief on the way back from a heavy session in the bar? But there was no muffled laughter, no retreating footsteps. The evening's parties were over, the function rooms would be dark by now. I had been fully awake, without a doubt, when whoever it was knocked for the second time; it was not an intrusion from a dream. I blinked, rubbed my eyes, and looked down at my bare feet.

On the carpet outside the door of my room was a mobile phone. My mobile phone. It had been her at the door, but she had not lingered. She was just making a delivery.

I bent to pick up the phone, cursing my slowness. Once again I had missed my chance. But if she had wanted to see me she would have waited. This was exactly the way she wanted this to work out—to give me back my phone without talking to me. Whatever relief I felt at being re-united with my phone was thoroughly soured by the real-ization that it would not serve to reunite me with her. It had been a meager thread connecting us, but its breaking was a shattering breach. In regaining something that had been lost, I had lost something far more important.

Closing the door on the corridor, I turned on the room lights. The depressing sight of a room-service tray, dirty plates and a crumpled napkin greeted me. Earlier I had dined alone in the room, unwilling to face the restaurant, and had gone to bed before ten. Not so long ago, but long enough to slip into a deep sleep. Now I feared sleep would be elusive, at least until I had calmed myself.

That isn't where this is going. She had given me no time to weigh those words. This—whatever "this" is—was not going toward her bed. But it was going somewhere. A route for "this" had been left open. *You'll have to catch me.* The possibility was there, almost an invitation. It was not a dead end, it was a door, closed, but leading somewhere.

I woke the phone and thumbed through the familiar options and menus; perhaps there was a clue there. No new numbers in the phone book, no new text messages, nothing in the sent folder. I had a few fresh emails, but all routine, and nothing sent from there either. No voice mail—the messages I had left had been picked up. The call log showed a call to voice mail hours ago. She had listened to my messages earlier in the evening and then waited. Trying to figure out her next move? Waiting for me to go to bed?

The last thing to check was the camera. Nothing new here. My last picture, of the painting, taken from the same spot on the bed where I sat now, was still there. If she had copied it, she had not done so by texting it to herself. I put the phone on the bedside table. It wasn't going to help me.

Hilbert would be disappointed, of course. With no further means of contacting the woman, I had no way of fixing up the meeting he wanted. Would he be angry? It was his idea that had come to naught, not mine, so it was hard to see how he could infer failure or ineptitude on my part. A long shot had fallen short, that was all. But the thought of explaining what had happened filled me with concern. I strongly disliked the prospect of going back to him empty-handed. He had not so much as hinted at the existence of the mildest penalty for failure, and his demeanor had been consistently pleasant, if formal. Even so, I was powerfully disinclined to bring him bad news. I did not want to displease him. The realization stole up on me, and when it came I found it quite unshocking, as if I had known it from the start: I was afraid of Hilbert.

A chorus of buzzing and staticky chirruping burst from the radio-alarm, causing me to jump. Again, the same problem! Still not fixed! But before I had a chance to get properly annoyed, a new sound broke in: the trill of my mobile phone. All day I had been listening to the electromagnetic chattering of the radio and hearing the herald of a phone call that never came. And now the other shoe had dropped; the phone was ringing.

Unknown number. "Hello?"

"Hello?" A woman's voice. Her voice.

"Hi!" A squeak.

"Neil, yes?"

"Who else?"

"You have your phone back. Evidently."

"Yes, thank you."

"You know who this is?"

I wanted to say, you're Dee, but she had never given me her name—Hilbert had. "Yes," I said. "You're the art collector. With a sideline in phone collecting."

This was meant to be an icebreaker, but nothing came over the air in response. Which is not to say the spectra around me were empty—a rising and falling galvanic gale was emitting from the radio-alarm, punctuated by episodes of sharp ethereal percussion.

"What's that noise?" the woman said.

"It's interference from the clock radio, some kind of re-curring fault—they were meant to fix it, but it's worse than ever—"

As I spoke, I was yanking the radio's plug from its socket, which again failed to dim or quieten it, but turned its display back to 3 33. Or was it already showing 3 33? I had not checked. I wrapped the flex around the radio, which vibrated on a high frequency in my hand, and stuffed it under the duvet of the bed.

"There, that should be a bit better. It won't shut up even when it's unplugged. Really annoying."

"It makes that noise when it's unplugged?"

"Yeah. It must have some kind of emergency reserve power system, or something."

"An emergency reserve power system?" There was a teasing tone to her voice. "What do you think it is? A nuclear submarine? An incubator in a children's hospital? It's a cheap alarm clock in a hotel room. They buy them by the thousand. The *thousand*."

Underneath the duvet, the radio-alarm was continuing its frantic tittering monologue. I eyed the folds of cotton concealing it, as if expecting movement from below.

"What are you saying?"

"Nothing. You said you wanted to talk to me. Go ahead."

I froze, openmouthed. True, I wanted to speak with this woman, but most of all I wanted her to speak, to unpack the nested mysteries she represented. Somehow she had to be prompted, but I had no idea what questions to ask.

"As long as I can remember," I said, "I've believed ho-tels to be special places, important places. That they have power. In a hotel, you become a different person. Still you, but with new avenues of possibility open to you, new potential. And I sought out careers that would entail as much time in hotels as possible, so I could spend my life as that enhanced, unburdened hotel-person. It's how I ended up in my present job, which is perfect . . . "

"That's great," she said, cutting in. "You've found your niche. What does it have to do with me?"

"I'm coming to that. This world I've been living in—it's like an immense city populated solely by people who are just passing through, staying for a few days and then returning home. This city, this world, is my home. I'm not passing through. I live here. My flat is nothing to me in comparison—it's where my bank statements are posted, that's all. And when I met you, I realized that you were another permanent resident of this world, and that you had a unique affinity with it. So it was natural that I should want to reach out to you."

Nothing came in response. Even the radio-alarm had slipped into a lull.

"Since I ran into you in the bar a couple of nights ago, things have been going wrong for me, and at the same time I keep seeing you, at times when it's not possible, at 3 a.m. in daylight . . . Earlier today you said that maybe the hotel was trying to tell me something, and I admit I was pretty sceptical when you told me about the paintings, but now I think I see what you mean. Everything is joined together in ways we can't always see, and somehow the hotel is at the center of it."

Another silence. I had been rambling, saying almost anything, and there was nothing else. On top of my incoherence over coffee and my desperate voice mails, a clear picture must have built up, and I did not like to imagine how it looked.

"I've been here awhile," she said at last. "Since the first time you saw me, years ago. Not quite a permanent resident yet, but close, too close. And it matters that you saw me then and that you have now returned; it's more than a coincidence. You don't understand yet, but you will."

"Understand what?" I said.

"Can you leave your room? I want to show you something."

"Sure," I said. I would have to dress in a hurry, but I wouldn't have declined her invitation if I was stark naked.

Following directions from Dee over the phone, I left my room and turned right—away from the lobby, into the hotel. At each turning and junction in the corridor, she told me which way to go. In between these instructions, as I padded over the hardwearing carpet, she mostly stayed silent. When she spoke, it was in arcane aphorisms, not invitations to conversation.

"People form habits quickly in hotels. They nurture new routines. You go out of your room, you turn toward the lift or the stairs, and you repeat that same turn every time. There's no reason to turn the other way. What is there? More room doors, closed and locked. A fire escape. The rest of the hotel might as well not exist."

I walked. Tonight was midconference quiet, with none of the raucous behavior of last night. The air was thick with sleep.

"No room has its own key anymore. All are opened by keycards. These are programd centrally, told which room they open. You could have a locked room with no key. Your key could also open another room, and you would never know because you would never think to try. Rooms, locks and keys. It's all just data."

What if this was a joke? Was she mocking me, again? Leading me to a dead end for the satisfaction of her inscrutable sense of humor? Flattering her in order to keep our fragile connection alive was all very well, but not so long ago I was convinced she was deranged. Had she given me any reason to believe otherwise? Not to my knowledge. So why was I putting more of my faith in her? Maybe I was a little crazier now, and finding fixed reality more mutable to her version of it.

"The plans of the hotels, their internal layouts, are off the peg. I choose the site, recommend the number of rooms, and the design comes from a selection of fixed templates. A few minor concessions are made to locality in signage, reg compliance, façade treatment. But the plan is generic, universal."

My route was, I believed, roughly the same as the one I had taken on my unplanned jog the previous night. I passed one light well, then another. Outside it was drizzling.

"What I look for in a Way Inn site is a special unspecial quality. Every day there are more of these places. These places that are not places."

A third light well. A fire door. THIS DOOR IS ALARMED. It could have been the same dead end I came up against last night.

"Go through it," she said.

"It's alarmed," I said. "It's late. People are sleeping."

"It's OK," she said. "Trust me."

I pushed the metal bar. A shriek, maybe not loud but at a high, sustained pitch unknown in nature; a sharp chisel driven into my brain through each ear.

"Just push through," she said, nurse calm.

The shriek clawed at the partitions between consciousness and oblivion. Black lightning crackled. My eyes were closed. Distortion throbbed across the phone signal and my fingers weakened on the plastic.

I was through. The alarm died as the door swung shut. Nothing stirred beyond the doors of the bedrooms around me. Bedrooms, a corridor. The same as the other side of the door. No fire escape.

"Keep going."

In due course, a fourth light well. My mental sketch layout of the hotel warped again. I had passed lift shafts and stairwells. And how many rooms? The numbers were rising through the 250s. But I knew I had passed more than thirty doors since 219. More than fifty. More than a hundred. There had to be more than one room 219, perhaps more than two of them. My phone whistled in my ear, and I looked at it to check its battery. Only a sliver of power remained.

"How much farther?" I asked.

"How much farther do you want to go?" she said.

A fifth light well. How many were there, in total? I had not been proceeding in a straight line. Were there eight, ten, twelve? Three hundred rooms per floor, five hundred? That would make more than a thousand rooms in total— there were skyscraper hotels with that many, and sprawling resort complexes, with vast reception areas and hundreds of desk staff. How many people could be seated in the restaurant, or the bar, here? Fewer than a hundred. And what an exhausting walk the guests in this section would have before they were able to eat or drink or leave. It didn't make sense.

The light coming from the courtyard was curious. I was drawn toward it. It was not the brilliant sunshine of last night's illusion, but an animated bluish glow. Interference cascaded past the window.

Not interference. Snow. It was snowing. Outside. The Zen meditation garden was whited out. Foamy chunks of accumulated crystals clung to the slightest purchase on the walls of the hotel.

"It's snowing," I said. "I didn't think it was cold enough."

When it snows in the night, you wake to that special sparkling brightness, so that even before you open the curtains you can sense the world has been transformed. Snow magnifies and clarifies the morning light. It was not yet 2 a.m. I considered the possibility of airport floodlights, or a major nighttime event at the MetaCenter that I was somehow unaware of. No: that reflective, brilliant dawn light is unmistakable, and this was it.

"How can it be dawn already?" I said.

"It always is somewhere," she said.

An insistent beep in my ear. The phone's battery was near its end.

"My phone is dying," I said. "How much farther do I have to go?"

"How much farther do you want to go?" she said.

"You asked that already," I said. "I don't know. Not much farther. We're running out of time."

"Keep going. Left at the next turn, then right, then through the fire door."

Another fire door, another blast of that terrible alarm, its nauseating frequency tuned to slacken joints and take a buzz saw to the chains of reason. And another urgent whistle from my phone once I was on the other side.

A long corridor stretched ahead. Doors and paintings facing one another, maybe a dozen on either side, maybe more. It was a wearying sight. More of the same. Absurdly so. She was no genius. This was a mistake. A hotel this size, on this marginal site, was a staggering miscalculation. It could never be viable; it would never be filled, never.

Time to be assertive. "I can't go any farther. We're out of time."

"I'm surprised it has taken you this long," she said. "How far do you think you've come?"

"I don't know," I said. "I knew the hotel was big, but I had no idea it was this big."

"More than a mile."

"That's insane. That's like an airport terminal or something."

"Actually only the longest buildings in the biggest airports are anything like that long."

"How much more is there?"

There was a noise on her side of the call—an exhalation, a sigh. "You still don't see? I show you and you still don't see."

"It's more of the same. It just goes on and on."

"That's exactly—"

She was cut off by three sharp reports from the phone. Then silence. The phone was inert in my hand.

More than a mile. And more than a mile back. How

did I let her lure me all the way out here? A mile to walk back through the same numbing corridors. But I didn't know there was a "here" to be lured to; I would never have expected that the hotel went on like this. Who did? She had said as much, maybe as a warning, though I had not heard it as such. The hotel guest turns one way, always, and never the other. Thousands of people leaving their rooms and heading straight for the nearest lift, never imagining that, the other way, that same corridor went on and on . . .

"It goes on," I said to myself.

Not a single corridor, a corridor with branches. My mental map flexed once more, and panned out to reveal fractal continuation and tessellation. The paintings joined at the edges.

It goes on.

I looked down the corridor. At its end, far enough away to be hard to see, was a painting marking a turning or a junction. Then, as I watched, this ending shifted—not a painting, a door? Not a door, an angling of sight, like an effect produced by two mirrors, both shifting, and a longer vista appearing . . .

She was there, in the emerging distance. Behind her, the corridor continued impossibly, until perspective shrank it to an unseeable singularity. But before that point, there was the faintest hint of a curve, a horizon.

She was there, walking toward me, smiling. Behind her, the hotel went on.

It goes on.

The hotel went on forever.

PART THREE

THE INNER HOTEL

All hotels are an interface between the known and the unknown. You inhabit one room on one floor. What does the rest matter to you? You are in an unfamiliar place surrounded by strangers, and the hotel must make you feel comfortable and in place. They are structured illusions. Sculpted psychoactive environments. Mirages."

After we met in the impossible corridor, the woman and I walked a short distance and down a flight of stairs to the hotel bar. A hotel bar. The bar of a Way Inn in a Canadian city, where it was snowing and the sun had not long set. Some early diners were in the restaurant. Men and women came in from outdoors in bulky jackets, stamping slush off their boots. They all looked hearty, red-cheeked and wholesome. I was not dressed for snow but I was not cold. The lobby was the same temperate climate as all the other Way Inn lobbies across the world, neither too hot nor too cold. And why not—they were all the same building.

She was explaining, or trying to explain. A divergent pseudostructure. A non-Euclidean manifold. A prism projecting a hypersurface onto our space-time from a point . . . a point *outside*. It flowed past me. She clearly did not come close to understanding it herself. Her explanation mixed in generous measures of hypothesis and speculation. She was throwing concepts at the wall, seeing what stuck.

"There aren't five hundred branches of Way Inn. Well,

there are, but they're branches in the literal sense, sharing a single trunk, the inner hotel. One hotel, going on forever. And new branches all the time. New promontories."

"It's not possible."

"It's evidently possible. I just showed you. You see, I had to show you. If I did nothing more than told you, you wouldn't believe me. You'd say 'it's not possible,' but you'd look all smug and certain while you said it. Now you've got that cute wide-eyed expression. That's what I was going for. You've *seen* it."

There was some mockery in her words, but it was the friendly kind. She was more relaxed and pleasant than I had ever seen her. A great mass had been lifted from her, it seemed. And laid on me. I felt obliged to rebuild the world of fact around me, carefully verifying every detail. The measure of whisky in my hand, the hardwood floor under my feet, the existence of the woman in front of me.

"Canada. This is Canada?"

"Right. Want to go outside and make sure? It's minus five or something." She smirked. "We could go back. We could go somewhere warmer. The sun never sets on Way Inn."

My whisky, so far untouched, went down in a single gulp. Heat rushed down my throat, flared in my stomach. It was welcome, very welcome.

"Somewhere warmer. Show me."

We walked and I watched, wanting to register and remember every detail, every turn taken, every door passed. I wanted to see the seams. Stairs, corridors, fire doors. The migraine-fuel alarms of the latter didn't seem to have any effect on my companion—perhaps she was used to them. I felt their influence on me weakening.

She led the way, now and then glancing at a tablet computer she had taken from her black shoulder bag. I glimpsed the screen—a gallery of the abstract paintings, but in constant motion, shuffling and rearranging, grouping and regrouping into new sequences.

"I don't see how it's possible," I said. "People would notice. It wouldn't stay secret."

"People do notice," she said. "I noticed, and so did you. Although you took a lot of prodding. That's why people don't see. People will work overtime, perform all sorts of mental gymnastics, to smooth the utterly incongruous into their rational, seamless, clockwork universe."

I marvelled at the pile of the carpet, the accent lighting on the paintings, the grain of the dark wood of the room doors; that was it, the *grain* of the place, the cosmos of tiny details that made up everyplace mundanity. Triggers to ignoring and forgetting, a sedative microarchitecture. Seeing it, questioning it, made it all stand out in freakish obviousness. The red plastic cube of a fire alarm seemed to address me from the far side of an unimaginable mental gulf, like a Neolithic flint spearhead.

"This is going to take all night if you stand and stare at everything like that. You look pretty backward right now."

"This place should be swarming with scientists."

"Maybe it is. It's an infinite structure. There's plenty of room." She pursed her lips and for a second looked deeply downcast. "I can't be the only one who wants to understand and explain. Who looks and sees. Not like the others."

"The other guests?"

"The others."

After no more than ten minutes, we reached another atrium, glass-fronted and triple-height, singularly dazzling after the indirect lighting of the corridors. Once we stopped in that brilliance, she looked at me expectantly, waiting for something. The morning beyond the tinted glass was desert bright and the staff behind the reception desk had their hair modestly covered. I had been here before, and so had she.

"Doha," I said. "Qatar." She smiled at the answer. This was where I had seen her first—this precise spot. Seeing her returned to this context, I could not help but remember her as she had been then, and trace the contours of her naked body under her clothes. So striking, so statuesque in the astonishing glare of the Middle Eastern sun; when I later pictured her dressed, it was always in ballgowns or business suits. Instead, in actuality, she seemed consistently ready for the gym or a weekend around the house. Today she was wearing a black leather jacket slashed diagonally with a silver zip, a Dangermouse T-shirt, jogging bottoms and trainers. It still struck me as perfection. She was real.

"I think I told you about the sleepwalking," she said, looking around at the lobby of the Doha Way Inn as if seeing it for the first time. Maybe she was. As she spoke, we drifted toward one of the sofas and sat. Guests were heading to the restaurant for breakfast. "It explains a lot. About the nakedness. But other things as well. I was working for another hotel chain, studying Way Inn, trying to figure out how Way Inn selected sites for new hotels."

"In the Middle East?"

She laughed. "No, in Belgium. I was in a Way Inn near Antwerp. That's where I went to bed. I woke up a couple of hours later, here. I've been an occasional sleepwalker since I was a little girl, but while I was on the Way Inn project my sleep was particularly terrible, very disturbed."

Her eyes lost contact with mine and she fell into a thoughtful silence. "I haven't walked in my sleep since that day, mind. Not since I went to work for Way Inn."

"That's how you found out about . . . this," I said. My stupor was retreating, but it was still hard to assemble sentences that described my new knowledge and did not sound barking mad. The words were there: hotel, corridor, connected; distorted, curved, infinite. But putting them together—it didn't work. I was frightened of what I might say, of articulating something I would never have wanted to believe. The whisky in my system was helping in some ways, and not helping in others.

"Yeah. I was distraught. What you saw was only the start of it. The staff here didn't know anything about it, of course, and couldn't process what I was telling them. Trying to tell them. Go to sleep in Belgium, wake up on the Persian Gulf . . . I didn't know. I was incoherent. They got as far as establishing that I was not registered as a guest at the Doha Way Inn. Then I gave them the slip, and headed back into the hotel."

"Why?"

"I just wanted to be back in my room. And I didn't know how I could get there, but to go back the way I had come. They meant well, the staff, but I had suffered this extraordinary psychic trauma and they were interrogating me—I couldn't face it. I wanted to be elsewhere, to go back. And I did. The hotel opened up for me. It revealed itself, welcomed me. I found my way back to my room in Antwerp. After that I spent days, maybe weeks, exploring. Six continents on foot. Totally AWOL. It ended my job with the other chain. But that didn't matter. I didn't want that job any more. I was approached by others . . . representatives . . . from Way Inn. They knew all about me. What I did for a living, what I was doing in the hotel. And they offered me a new job, finding sites for new Way Inn branches. Unlimited hospitality in return for my talent and my discretion."

"Sounds like a good deal," I said. A robotic reflex, an obsolete one. In the past, very recently in fact, such a deal would have been the consummation of my dearest wish. That wish now seemed fundamentally tainted.

"Tempting, isn't it?" she said. "The hotel has so much to offer. Room and board is the least of it. It can influence people . . . And its innermost circle, they get special rewards. Have any of them approached you?"

"No, no," I said. "Not that I know of." The lie was prompt and deft, and it was a lie, I knew. Hilbert must be part of that innermost circle—this was among my most basic, primal certainties. Hilbert, with his wavering outer form and perfumed talk of quid pro quo and satisfactory arrangements. This innermost circle was new to me, yet there was not a moment of consideration or a whiff of doubt—Hilbert was part of it.

"You would know if you had," she said, eyes narrowing. Did she suspect me? But if she suspected me of any kind of collusion, why would she expose herself like this? "They get . . . benefits. But those benefits are contingent—they are bound to the hotel. When I started working for Way Inn,

they approached over and over, they made their pitch . . .
The rewards for the longest, most loyal service . . . "

She trailed off, her expression unfocused, bleak. What
had she seen?

"You said no."

"Never yes, never no. I have tried to maintain a semi-
detached position. Freelance, if you like."

The nested absurdity of my position struck me again, a
relapse of my first wave of disbelief and horror, which I
thought had gone into remittance. It was the middle of
the night, and I was thousands of miles away from my
bed. And a far greater distance away from any reasonable
explanation. Way Inn's interconnection, its defiance of
distance, its infinite interior: however I looked at the hotel, it looked back with a face of frank impossibility. Logical outrage stacked upon logical outrage. The ghostly
implications stretched out like those endless corridors.

"Who changes all the lightbulbs?" I asked.

"Lightbulbs?"

"Down corridors that go on for ever. Trillions of lightbulbs. Who changes them? The number that need chang-
ing every day must exceed all the resources of the
universe. There isn't that much glass and metal, anywhere, let alone that many people, that many staff . . . "

"I once read that it takes three power stations to light
all the emergency exit signs in the USA," she said. "That's
a lot of exits. Who paints all the paintings? It was the first
question I asked, the simple arithmetic was enough to
give me nightmares. My academic background is maths—
geometry, topology. I went into corporate real estate on
the theoretical side."

"Estate agents have a theoretical side?"

"Yes! As property has become more a financial instrument than a way of keeping the rain off, it has become quite profitable to study it in abstract terms, and all the smart propcos have a few pet topologists or exotic mathematicians. I've been staying in Way Inn for four years, and before that I was studying it for a rival. I know more about it than most, and I'm not qualified to answer your question. I don't know who is, or who might be. Physicists, string theorists, the gang at CERN. Philosophers. Theologians. Maybe nobody is.

"My best guess," she continued, "is that our reality provides a kind of template for the hotel, and the inner hotel is an extrusion from that template. There might only be a finity of lightbulbs or paintings, and our monkey cortexes"—she stabbed two fingers at her temple in a sudden gesture of frustration or contempt at her, our, limitations—"just fill in what we expect to see, in the way that our brain sketches over the visual blind spot. There's an objective physical reality to it, but aspects of our perception are . . . only subjective. Or perhaps a kind of objective delusion. Shadows on the cave wall. Ontology really isn't my field at all."

Under my hand, the silver covering of the arm of the armchair. Leather or synthetic? It was so hard to tell.

"You look a little lost," she said with a suggestion of underlying kindness.

"It's late," I said, glancing toward the morning sun. "This is a lot to take in. Too much."

"Drink might help. No chance of that here, first thing in the morning in a dry country." She produced her tablet again and stroked at its screen. "Premium drinking time in New Orleans, though. Coming up to nine in the evening."

"OK," I said, and we rose from our seats. Flitting back to the Americas for the second time tonight: it didn't seem any more likely or possible, but I knew it would happen.

Doha again. How strange to be back here, even divested of the more paranormal aspects of my journey. Where we both began, she on her path, and me toward her; two curves, separating then converging.

"I still don't know your name." A lie, another lie. She was at last talking to me, really talking, no riddles, no games, and I was lying and lying. It stung.

"Dee," she said, holding out her hand. "Pleased to meet you, at last."

The bar of the Way Inn near the New Orleans Convention Center was two-thirds full and noisy, dominated by a couple of large, raucous groups. Previously Dee had abstained from drink, but now she joined me in a double whisky. I needed spirits for the quicker effect, the better to punish those elements of my conscious mind that no longer matched up. A jigsaw with too many pieces; pieces doubled up, pieces that spread far over the edges of the frame, and too many were left over when I believed a picture was forming.

Suited men wearing credentials for a commercial kitchen equipment trade fair joked and laughed and bragged in southern accents. The money crossing the bar was green, the beer was Coors and Miller and Pabst. But it was a Way Inn bar, in a Way Inn hotel, very similar to all the others, and for that matter very similar to the bars of all the other chain hotels. One of these men, who had had a good day buying or selling stainless steel extraction hoods, would have a bit too much to drink, go upstairs, fumble his way into room 219 and go to sleep. And down the hall I would also be asleep in room 219, and so would the occupants of hundreds of other room 219s.

The barman was busy; levering bottles open, throwing ice, leaning forward to listen to orders, raising and lowering metal-tipped liquor bottles as he poured measures, teasing out the stream of liquid as far as he dared. Dee and I had said little since our arrival. I wondered if Vasco da Gama or Neil Armstrong had felt the way I felt—that a crucial mental boundary had been violated and would stay violated, and astonishment that this moment had been reached by the same human body and the same human mind that had done all the other humble and unremarkable things in their life. I had almost circumnavigated the earth, on foot, in a couple of hours. It was not the immensity of this feat that dumbfounded me—it was the fact that everything continued as normal around me. In Calgary dinner plates were placed in front of diners, in Doha the day's first arrivals were being checked in, and here the barman smiled and rattled the silver cocktail shaker.

Dee was quiet too, sipping her drink.

"Do the staff know?" I asked. I was still watching the barman. "This guy, the people at front desk, the chambermaids?"

"Room attendants."

"Sorry?"

"Room attendants, not chambermaids," Dee said. "'Chambermaids' is archaic and sexist. This isn't *Upstairs, Downstairs*. Room attendants."

"OK, room attendants. Do they know?"

"No. None of them. No need. Turnover among the customer-facing staff is typical for a large service-industry chain, which is to say high. Even within the corporate structure there are very few people who know. Board members and nonexecutive directors and department managers come and go, like any other company, without really knowing anything about the structure they serve." She fished a stray eyelash from the corner of her eye with her little finger and studied it intently. "Corporate apparatchiks are not naturally inquisitive creatures."

"I don't understand," I said, and immediately felt the pathetic scale of the understatement. "There are a lot of things I don't understand about all this, but right now I mostly don't understand how it could be kept secret."

"Do you want to tell someone? We could tell him," she said, jutting her chin toward a man alone on the far side of the bar reading a newspaper and drinking a beer. "Or one of the staff at the front desk? They don't look too busy. Or we could call CNN."

She was waiting for my answer, sarcastic expectation writ plain in her shining eyes. I didn't say anything. Her point was already clear enough.

"Telling is useless," she said. "You have to show. And the hotel has to want to be seen. Sometimes a fire door is just a fire door, and you're left in a concrete stairwell that leads down to where they keep the bins. The hotel must angle itself toward you, and it can easily untether itself from a branch if necessary. As a defense mechanism— against fire, against discovery."

"You talk about the hotel as if it's a living thing," I said. "Wanting things, defending itself."

"Yes. Maybe it is. Not alive in the sense we know. But

it wants, certainly, and it tells, it speaks, it shows, it reveals. It has whims. Maybe it has a purpose. Spend time with it and you sense . . . a mind. The inner staff, the hotel servants I told you about, believe themselves to be the sole expression of the hotel's will, but they are zealots. Zealots confuse their own fears and lusts with the interests of the cause they serve. Their judgement is clouded."

Did she mean Hilbert, and his concerns about her? That he was paranoid, and simply wrong about Dee posing a threat to the hotel? I could picture him as a kind of Travelodge Torquemada, a grand inquisitor entrusted with a great dark secret and taking it on himself to root out any threats to that trust, real or imagined. I had no desire, I realized, to facilitate a meeting between him and Dee. I would have to find a way out.

More troubling than the machinations of Hilbert was the question of what the hotel might want from me. If it had a purpose, then what was my role? The anomalies it had generated around me, its matchmaking—maybe the hotel is trying to tell you something, Dee had said. What, then?

"What does the hotel want?" I said. "Broadly, I mean, in general."

Dee shrugged. She looked tired. If this was how she lived every night, every day, her body clock must be shot to pieces. "What any organism wants, I imagine. To persist. To grow. To open new branches, increase its presence in our world. Every day more of our reality is its reality." Her weariness could have been depression. Perhaps she was disenchanted with her own role in Way Inn's expansion—perhaps that was the erratic element Hilbert feared.

Or perhaps he sensed that she was ready to tell others about the secret nature of the hotel.

"I think the hotel wanted us to talk," I said. "To get to know each other. It assisted that." Partly via Hilbert, I did not add.

"Yes," Dee said. "Although that's not why I called you."

"Why, then?"

"Don't flatter yourself," she said with a chiding smile. "Not because of any particular allure on your part. You might think there was something charming about your persistence. There really wasn't. Although it was amusing to watch the wheels coming off a character like you."

"What kind of character is that?"

"Fairly good-looking, fairly beguiling manner, obviously a master craftsman when it comes to the one-night stand. You've slept with a lot of women, yes?"

She arched her eyebrows with the query. I made no reply. This was a dismaying turn for the conversation—her candor up to this point had made me feel as if we were growing friendly.

"OK, a lot. If you weren't confident about it you probably would have blurted out some awful lie or euphemism or bit of self-deprecation by now. Listen, your success to date might not be due to your good looks or delightful personality but because of your sheer forgettability. You'll do."

She had been drinking. So had I. I felt myself heat up. "Vulnerable, are we? You're worried that you've exposed yourself, so now you lash out in case I get too close?"

"Oh wow, bravo," Dee said, pantomiming applause.

"First-rate, airport bookshop psychology, vintage stuff. I should have known better than to try anything like that, you're clearly a connoisseur of loneliness."

"You're not the only one capable of detecting patterns."

"That's the stage we're at now? 'Takes one to know one'?"

"You think I'm being childish? Well, you started it."

We lapsed into silence, out of place in the warm, beery good cheer of the New Orleans Way Inn. I felt cheated by this abrupt change in tone on Dee's part, and frustrated that I should have been so quickly relegated from her trust. The world had changed for me in the past couple of hours, completely and perhaps forever, and I now discovered that my one ally in this transfigured reality thought I was an arsehole.

She hadn't really denied what I said about her, though, just as I had been unable to truly contradict what she said about me. Which was presumably why we had reached an impasse. Our silence was inward, and shared.

"It hasn't been working that well lately," I said. I calculated that some openness, some humility, might end the standoff. Three in the morning is no time to fight. "The charm, all that. I've pissed people off. People I should have behaved better toward. Yeah, I was forgettable. I was treating forgettability like a superpower. But people remember."

"Do you want another drink?"

I did. Minutes before, floundering in the revelation of the inner hotel, I would have considered sleep impossible. Now the idea of it was growing unstoppable. My walk across continents and the day's other excursions were seeping from my joints as soreness, a deep bone-ache. The high tiredness that comes after high emotion; fuck tired, breakup tired. Dee was at the bar, black leather back to me, a couple of inches taller than the men on each side of her. The trainers and the jogging bottoms made sense. She spent most of her life on foot, in the corridor, long strides down those inexhaustible avenues, looking for the middle of the maze.

"No ice, right?" she said on her return.

"Right." The same as hers.

"The reason I called you," she said, holding her glass as a barrister would hold the piece of evidence her case rested upon, "was I suspected that you were very close to figuring out the hotel on your own. You had clearly seen the inner hotel; it had been revealed to you, but you didn't know what you were seeing. It, this, the conversation we're having here, was a big risk for me, but I wanted to get to you before they did. Before the inner staff."

No ice, but a chill nonetheless.

"Given the path you were on, I figured it was inevitable they would contact you. So I intervened."

"Am I in danger?"

She leaned forward, eyes wide, serious and alert. "Don't sit down with them. Don't talk with them. Don't deal with them. Just don't. They will be pleasant and plausible. Their lies are like the hotel: unending, and you can lose yourself in them, never find a way out. They will offer you exactly what you want and you must turn your back."

Too late. Too late. Too late. I had sat down with Hilbert, dealt with him, accepted his offer. I felt a spasm of panic. What had I done? What had I undertaken to do? Could I extricate myself? Surely the encounter couldn't entail the mortal hazard that Dee's severity implied.

"Maybe it does take one to know one," she continued after I failed to reply. What was the outer manifestation of my inner turmoil? Did I look pensive? Serious? Concerned? Sweat had broken across my brow, despite the perfect global equilibrium assured by Way Inn's untiring air-handling units. "Permanent residents of the passing city. Hotel people. Isn't that what you said? The others flow around us, we remain."

"You've been out here four years now. In here. Four years in Way Inn. Is that right?"

Dee nodded, lips tight.

"Family?"

"Not really," she said. "No one close. Why do you ask?"

"Constantly travelling, being away—it's not family-friendly."

"I'm not away. I don't have anything to be away from. No rent, no bills, four years' salary straight in the bank, untouched."

"My father was a salesman. He was away more often than not, in hotels around the country. It was hard on my mother. On us both."

"That didn't stop you following in his footsteps, though."

"Hardly in his footsteps," I said. "I told you, I didn't care for it. It was a means to an end."

"To be the better person, the hotel person."

"Yes."

"Free from encumbrances. Limitations. Floating. Weightless."

"Yes."

"Like a different state of matter. A higher state of matter."

"Yes."

"That's what I figured." She drained her glass. "I just like not having to tidy up. That goes a long way. I never really imagined that daily housekeeping would be my price for pledging service to an indifferent and possibly hostile entity with unimaginable power and unknowable goals, but in retrospect it makes perfect sense." She examined the traces of liquor clinging to the sides and bottom of her glass. "I really fucking hate making the bed. Fuck that shit."

It was hard to tell if she was joking or not. Her whole style was one of misdirection and sleight of hand—an edge like a stealth bomber, to disappear, to not be seen. Everything she said could be taken as a way of not saying something else. This could apply, I realized, to the barrage of revelations about the hotel she had let slip earlier. It could simply be a blind for another course of inquiry—about her, perhaps. But I was three doubles down and fighting a rising tide of exhaustion.

"Speaking of bed," I said, "I'm going to have to get into mine pretty soon. Maybe we should be getting back?"

Back across the Atlantic; the ocean was elsewhere, unrelated to the structure we walked through. From the bar in New Orleans we took the stairs up to the second floor. We had done all our walking on the second floor, the same floor as my room. And perhaps hers?

"Why the second floor?" I asked. "Is your room here?"

"No," she said. "The hotels don't connect on the ground

floor. That seems to be a necessary part of preserving the illusion they are discrete buildings. We're using the second because that's where your room is. And it's a good floor. Mostly just guest rooms, little extraneous junk like fitness centers and business suites."

The business suite. "I was going to show you those paintings in the Gallery Room. Eight of them, in a sequence."

She stopped, and I stumbled to a halt with her. We had been in a corridor, of course; her long, limber pace had consumed the carpeted kilometers with ease and obliged me to half-trot to keep up. Moving at that speed, it was not hard to see the hotel as a limitless maze, as doors and paintings and turns and light wells went by without the opportunity of consideration. Standing unmoving in a generic stretch of the hotel—uncertain where on earth we might be, if we were on earth—was a cue to again realize that this was a hotel. A real hotel, not a stage-set illusion. One of the subdued uplighters had a minor fault and was gently stuttering. The nearest doorknob had a DO NOT DISTURB sign. In all likelihood there was a sleeping businessman or woman behind the door, unaware of the man and woman outside, unaware of where they had come from or where they were going. Tiny mysteries were common in hotels at night. The sudden sound of feet running past the door. A fraught, whispered conversation. A stranger trying their keycard in your lock, turning the handle. Screams, sobs, and mirthless, maniacal laughter. These abnormalities were normal. I ascribed them to drink and the diversity of humankind, and turned over, and went back to sleep. Would they be so easy to disregard now? I feared not.

However tired I might be, it was possible my freshly laundered hotel pillow would never again be so comfortable, and the tiny chocolate it supported would never again be so sweet.

"I try to avoid the business centers," she said.

This struck me as odd, given her obsessive-compulsive, completist traits elsewhere. "Why?"

She didn't answer.

"It's the middle of the night," I said. "There'll be no one there. Everyone is asleep. We won't be disturbed. We'll be quick." It was perfect, in fact: I could tell Hilbert I had taken Dee to the Gallery Room, fulfilling my side of the deal we had made, and it was his tough luck that the visit had taken place at such an unexpected hour, and had taken no more than a minute.

We resumed our walk.

"So which floor are you on?"

A scowl was tossed over her shoulder at me. "Three, actually. Not that you have any business knowing."

Once Hilbert was off my back, I figured I would be able to tell Dee that the inner staff had approached me and had been rebuffed. I could fudge the chronology of events. Then she might begin to trust me. "I was wondering how we would stay in touch. I feel like we've only scratched the surface of what's going on here. Perhaps I can help you."

"We've only scratched the surface, yeah," she said after a snort that could have been derision or assent. "That's all any of us do, scratch the surface—useless . . . "

"So we could meet again?"

This time she stopped dead, and I almost ran into the back of her. The look on her face was grim.

"Do you remember our little talk? About fucking? About how it's not going to happen?"

"Listen—"

"That is not where this is going. My problems"—she widened her eyes at the thought of those problems, and I wondered what they could be—"are not going to be solved by your penis. Just back off."

"Listen." I was riled. It was frustrating to be continually dumped back at square one. But more frustrating was Dee's obsolete view of my motives. "I am not trying to get you into bed. I'm sure, if we did do that, it would be memorable. Really bad or really good. Memorable, anyway. What I'm looking for . . . What I want . . . You have shown me something pretty *freaking* incredible, yeah? It's not sitting all that easily with me. I remember when you discovered the same fact, you were reduced to a screaming heap in a hotel lobby, and in fairness I think I'm handling it pretty well. But I want an ally. A friend. Someone I know, who knows about"—I raised my hands at the Way Inn corridor—*"this."*

Her severe countenance barely altered, but I believed I saw within it a rapid succession of reactions.

"As well as not being your fuck buddy," she said, "I'm not your therapist or your babysitter. Your peace of mind is not my concern. You had all this explained to you over stiff drinks, wide awake. Having your hand held by someone with, I might add, considerable patience. I was woken from the nightmare of all-time by strangers in a strange country. Naked." She looked down at the ground and chewed air. "Also, don't imagine this is easy for me. I've been on my own for four years. Don't crowd me."

"OK, fine. I'm not pushing."

"OK. I've got your number. I'll use it."

As we talked, our voices low but pitched with emotion, she had hunched over. Now she sucked in her breath and reared up again, back straight.

"There's more," she said.

She did not elaborate. Navigating by the restless screen of her tablet, Dee led me deep into the hotel again, a different climate and time of day appearing in each light well, but between them the same monotonous corridors. Then came a stretch where there were no windows, just an unending corridor, pushing out to the far curve of the horizon.

"I don't like doing this," Dee said. "It draws attention."

"There's no one here," I said. We hadn't seen another soul for more than half an hour. I had the sense of being deep, very deep, in the inner maze. "Where are we, anyway?"

"Where do you want to be?"

"I thought we were going to the business suite."

"OK then." She swiped the screen of the tablet, then pointed at the wall. "Do me a favor, would you? Keep an eye on that painting."

I stared at the painting she indicated. There was nothing special about it. A dough orb settling on a field of billowing mahogany arcs. The air conditioning picked up, sending cool breath across the back of my neck.

"Do you find hotels disorienting?" Dee asked.

"Yes, sometimes," I said, keeping my eyes fixed on the painting, expecting a trick to reveal itself, a hidden pattern or submerged representation. "What you said about always turning one way out of hotel rooms, never the other; that's mostly true, but sometimes it's impossible to go the right way. You keep making the wrong turn, your brain can't correct itself."

"Fire doors. Going through a doorway causes forgetting. All doorways, not just here. That's why you sometimes enter a room and can't recall what you wanted there. Or if you go through a couple of fire doors to find your hotel room, you can't remember the route you took. Buildings are mental as well as physical. Way Inn exploits psychoactive effects found everywhere. It is in a constant state of inner flux, and that flux can be, well, steered. OK, we're done."

"I didn't see anything."

"No? That's a pity." She gave me a smug little smile and stepped out of sight, behind me.

I turned and found myself in an intersection, looking down a corridor that had not been there seconds before. At the far end was a glass door frosted with the words BUSINESS CENTER and an icon of peg-like figures sitting around a table.

"Coming?" Dee asked. She was almost at the door.

I didn't move. Had I missed something—a door, a sliding section of wall? There had been nothing but paintings and bedroom doors behind me, not this.

"It's quite safe," Dee said. "I just made us a short cut. Minor spatial kinesis. It'll close up by itself in a minute, so don't dawdle unless you want to get trapped on your own."

That didn't sound appealing, so I followed Dee. "How did you do that?"

"Maths and meditation. But I don't like to do it. The inner staff can detect all but the slightest rearrangement, and they're on you like hounds. It's best to keep a low profile."

"Very wise," I said. A fresh breeze from the air conditioning brushed my cheek, and I turned to see what I already knew—the way I had come had gone, replaced by the lift shafts, light wells and corridors of the MetaCenter Way Inn.

No one had been in the business suite for hours, and its lights, detecting no movement, had switched to a near-dark power-saving mode. As we arrived they blinked up to full brightness, the corridors coming alive around us. But in one corner the lights had not slept. Beyond the Gallery Room, in the direction of the Vista Room and its scenic overlook, was a pool of light and a rhythmic rustling.

Without a word passing between us, we ignored our destination and moved instead toward this activity. The spectral presence sharing the space with us was plastic tape, put in place by contractors to block off a stretch of corridor, which had come loose and was coiling and uncoiling in a draft like deep-sea tentacles. Behind it, a lobby area like a scaled-down version of the one on the ground floor, ghostly in construction-site temporary light, some glass and steel surfaces wrapped in anti-scratch coating, a few leftover tools and dust sheets in a corner.

"The skywalk," I said. "They're still building it."

"Look at this, even the potted palms are ready to go," Dee said. "All the other hotels are way off schedule. You hear of the same plots being refinanced three, four times."

"Not Way Inn."

She smiled, a spontaneous eruption of the professional pride that had been just detectable as she looked at the skywalk lobby. "Way Inn has certain advantages."

I opened the Gallery Room and dropped the black key-card into the slotted box on the wall inside. The lights came on—a ring above the table, a spot for each painting. Since my meeting here earlier, the room had been used. "Design as a driver of user-centered innovation" was written on a flip chart.

Moments later Dee joined me. She had taken a camera from her shoulder bag—nothing special, a compact digital point-and-shoot. I had half-expected her to be in a Ghostbusters costume, testing the air for ectoplasm. Without fuss or preamble she started to photograph the paintings.

The Nespresso machine in the corner glinted with the promise of uniform, repeatable, predictable cups of coffee of acceptable quality. Perfect for chain hotels, of course. I even have one at home, in my little-used flat.

"So why don't you like the meeting rooms?" I asked.

"I like to stay in control," she said. Snap. She peered at the screen of her camera, checking the picture she had just taken, and moved on. Snap.

"I noticed that," I said. "But that doesn't really answer my question."

"The hotel wields spatial influence." A shot was lined up. Snap. "Its inner spaces are, let's say, suggestive." Snap. With all the paintings on one wall photographed, Dee crossed the room to photograph them together in a single shot. "All the decisions and agreements reached in Way Inn's meeting rooms end up benefiting Way Inn. Directly, indirectly, short term, long term, in the end they always benefit Way Inn."

"What? How?"

"Way Inn wants to reproduce, to grow, to open new branches and turn more of our space into its space. For that it needs certain conditions. It needs suitable sites in which it can operate. I identify these sites and, let me tell you, there's never any shortage of them. Suitable places near suitable numbers of suits, and the suits come and meet in these suites . . . How fortunate for Way Inn."

"What are you saying? What is the hotel doing to us?"

But she wasn't saying anything, not now. She had completed her circuit of the room, bringing her back to the door. There she was staring at something on the wall. Not a painting. The slot containing my keycard.

"Where did you get this card?" she asked, her voice quiet and oddly flat.

I froze. The black keycard. Telling the truth would be a disaster, that much was instantly obvious, but no plausible lies stood ready to take its place. The black keycard was its own fatal truth, out in the open between us, and denying it was impossible.

Given a couple more seconds, maybe I could have formulated something. But Dee didn't give me those seconds. She whirled around and advanced toward me, face taut, closer to profound grief than anger.

"Where did you get that?" Her voice had risen to a shout, shrill with panic.

"I gave it to him."

Hilbert slipped sideways into the room, smoothly and quietly, shutting the door gently like a man arriving late at a meeting and trying not to disturb the others present. Had the door been open? A sliver, but that was enough. He had spilled in like ink into water. The shining hair and strobing suit were an active blackness that conducted a pale face and pale hands like the dangling light of an angler fish.

Dee shrank back from him, toward me. In the corner, I had nowhere to retreat. My hip bumped the table carrying the Nespresso machine and the neat pile of cups beside it moved fractionally. Even without being at all clear what manner of threat Hilbert represented, my primal brain, the deepest crux of survival instinct, was not ambivalent. It screamed *Flight! Flight! Flight!*

"I'm sorry," I said, to Dee. "I'm sorry. I didn't realize . . . "

"There's really no cause for concern," Hilbert said, opening his arms, palms out, conciliatory. "I just want to talk. We three have so much in common, and we can prosper together. Please, take a seat."

"Fine." Dee straightened, put her camera in her shoulder bag and pulled one of the steel tube chairs out from under the table. She stood behind it, hands on either side of the chair back, knuckles white, stiff and expressionless as a statue. The rooms had power, she had said—was this it in action, reducing her to an automaton?

Hilbert smiled, a dreadful act of blue lips and angled teeth. "I'm so pleased . . . "

Dee swung the chair out from under the table, lofted it above her head and brought it down on Hilbert with the sum of her strength. The blow was sickening, and was followed by an almighty crash as the chair, still in Dee's hands, hit the table. How Hilbert remained on his feet, I don't know. The weight of the metal frame wielded with Dee's considerable muscle would surely have put any man on the floor with a fractured skull or a broken neck. He buckled and bent over, arms rising to shield himself, and emitted an animal roar—shock and anger, not fear or pain.

Not hesitating, breathing fast in rough but even gasps, Dee brought the chair around like a scythe, smashing into Hilbert's side. What could have been ribs cracking could also have been my teeth clamping together as I winced at the strike. Hilbert reared up, eyes closed tight, and I must have been made dizzy by the adrenalin because the room itself seemed to widen around him, and painted shapes swirled. But Dee had wasted no time, swinging the chair back behind her right shoulder and whirling around like a shot-putter for a third blow, aimed high. This connected cleanly with Hilbert's head, continuing with a spray of blood to strike one of the paintings. Dee let the chair fall to the floor, and the painting fell with it, its frame cracking. Hilbert fell too, straight down, like a suit of clothes suddenly vacated by its wearer. Blood ran freely from his mouth and a fissure on his brow, trickling into his hair, giving it a new kind of blackness. An arc of scarlet drops was spread across the wall and the paintings. It ran off the shining chrome of the tumbled chair. Spots turned into lines.

"You killed him."

"No such luck. If only."

"I'm serious, you must have killed him."

"He's alive." Dee turned toward me. "I trusted you. I trusted you and you lied. You led me to him."

"I'm sorry," I said. "I didn't know, I didn't understand the danger . . . " And I still didn't—I was inferring it from her preparedness to maim—to kill—before Hilbert said a meaningful word to her. "I didn't know you . . . "

"The hotel doesn't want us together," she said. "It

wants you two together, you and him, and his kind. You're perfect for them." She zipped up her jacket, hoisted the shoulder bag and stepped over the crumpled form of Hilbert. She looked down at him as she passed, then back at me.

"Stay away from me." Calmly, without hurry, she left the room, as if we had done nothing more than conclude a meeting without success. I was left alone with the man she had tried to murder. And it was attempted murder—an assault that savage was most definitely attempted murder, whatever Dee's breezy assessment of Hilbert's chances of survival.

With a nauseating wrench, I felt myself return to the very present of the room. Before, I had felt like a distant witness, as if watching events on a screen from a remote location. But I was there, at the scene, within feet of a man who might very well be dead or dying. I had responsibilities.

I approached Hilbert, who was a jumble of many-angled limbs. His head was turned sideways to his body, outward, toward me, eyes open but insensate. One was glazed with blood. My instinct was to rearrange him into a more natural, comfortable position, but if he had suffered a neck or spinal injury moving him could cause paralysis. So instead I knelt beside him and examined his face for evidence of life. Blood covered his features and had pooled on the floor, dark and thick. Hilbert's bruise-colored lips were open. I leaned in to see if I could detect breath. A blood drop had formed above the aperture of the mouth; it shivered in time. He was breathing, just.

How serious was the head wound? It looked bad, bad

indeed—a six-inch tear starting level with the left eye and proceeding up past the hairline. Its edges were a mess of clots and matted hair. Late, I thought I should do something to stop the bleeding. But as I wondered what I could apply to the gash, I saw that there was no bleeding. Far from it. The wound was already drying.

Hilbert blinked. His lips moved, smearing the blood drop I had watched earlier into a lipstick stain. A stomach-turning grind of bone on bone issued from the vicinity of his shoulder. His arm shifted.

I sprang to my feet. Hilbert's eyes were not yet focused, but they had activity behind them. His whole body, which a moment previously had been a heap of rags and junk, now seemed animate.

My sense of responsibility abruptly expired. Hilbert was not only alive, he was more alive with each passing second. He was far too alive, quickened by something more than life, something beyond human mortality. The room pulsed with whatever this galvanizing force was, and the light seemed suddenly thickened, physical; had the air conditioning always roared like that, a low rush of sound from deep in the fabric of the building?

I knew, at a level more profound than opinion or established fact, that I did not want to be near Hilbert when he had fully revived. I fled the Gallery Room, pausing only to extract my keycard from its slot on the wall. The room did not die, as it should have. Motion sensors tripped and the corridor brightened.

At the stairwell, I stopped, torn. Up to my room on the second floor, or down to the lobby, to the staff there—

normal staff, *outer* staff, who might need to know about the grisly crisis in the Gallery Room? Something told me that Hilbert would not be going to the authorities about what had happened to him. It seemed increasingly mistaken to think of that assemblage of capabilities and terrible potential called "Hilbert" as a *him* at all. The higher power he would seek would not be police or paramedics: Hilbert had everything he needed from his "employer." But the authorities, the actual authorities in the outer world, might offer some reinforcement or comfort to me.

The lobby was deserted and the bar was closed. The Way Inn promotional stand had been stripped to the trestle and banners, its flat-screens dark. No one was at the front desk, but a blue flicker of television irradiated the back office. I called and the night porter appeared, the same young man who had helped me with my keycard the previous night. Was that really only the previous night? Only twenty-four hours had passed—almost to the minute—but it felt more like a month. And recognition registered on the night porter's face, too—he must deal with very few people in the small hours, making a repeat customer all the more memorable. I did not like what my re-apparition implied—to be so regularly out of my room at an hour like this must have an odor of alcoholism or loneliness or desperation to the staff. Whisky would tell on my breath, and high exertion in my eyes; who knew what ghastly hints could be drawn from looking in my eyes. But I was beyond truly caring about such questions of appearance. They occurred as a kind of memory—the itch of a departed concern, a phantom limb.

"I couldn't sleep so I was looking for the fitness center," I said. This man wasn't a police officer—a little lie to insulate myself from events would not harm me. "I thought half an hour on the treadmill might do the trick. Anyway, I was in the business suite and I thought I heard a noise coming from one of the rooms. A crash. Might be worth checking out."

He agreed. Together, we returned to the first floor. The lights in the corridors were still on.

Hilbert was gone from the Gallery Room. Also missing was the damaged painting, leaving a gap in the sequence on one wall. Four carpet tiles had been taken up from where Hilbert's body had lain, and with them the pool of blood. But not every trace of the conflict had been removed. A line of dribbling blood drips, dried to a less gory brown, remained beside the position of the missing painting. Only I saw them because I knew to look, just as only I saw the blood that still streaked the curved metal frame of one of the chairs, now lined up neatly at the table with the others.

"Are you sure it was this room, sir?"

"Yes. Absolutely sure."

"No one here."

"I must have been mistaken."

The night porter smiled at me, an impatient GP with a waiting room full of sick people placating a hypochondriac. "Things go bump in the night."

"They do. Sorry to have troubled you."

"No trouble, sir. Sleep well."

Tomorrow—today, in fact, later today—I would check out, leave the Way Inn, go home and never return. I had to meet with Laing in the morning, a meeting too important, too hard-won, to relocate or defer. But however that turned out, my next move was to the airport. And I would make it a condition of travel planning from now on: no Way Inn. Never again.

Interrupted sleep poisoned the air in room 219. When I dropped the treacherous black keycard into its slot, only a couple of lights came on, by the bed and by the door. The sheets were pushed aside, the pillow crushed. It was a scene oddly frozen in lost time, as if another version of me had left hours before and would never return.

I straightened the duvet, ready to get back into bed, and found the clock radio wrapped in its folds, where I had stuffed it while talking on the phone to Dee. I wasn't sure of the time—it would have been useful to know, but the digital display read 3:33.

As I looked at it, it changed to 3:34. The plug still lay on the floor, away from the wall. Error message, or the actual time? It could easily be half past three, but the coincidence seemed too much to stand. Any synchronicity now seemed frightful. The hotel generates a bubble of exceptionality, Dee had said. I saw it now, perfectly. It was a concealed confluence, where corridors but also people and lives joined together in unforeseen ways. How many branches were there around the world today, each one a tendril feeding hungrily on the potential of our warm, clamorous, coincidental world? I returned the clock radio to the bedside table and then, after a moment spent staring at it with considerable hatred, wrapped its own flex around it and stuffed it into the drawer with the Gideon Bible. It could not be trusted. Instead, I plugged in my phone and set its alarm.

It was 3:35. The time I set on the alarm was 7:30. Less than four hours, but that would do. Though sleep seemed a wild ambition, the idea of no sleep was an obvious impossibility. Sleep, then.

The last time I saw my father alive was during a conference and trade fair for the manufacturers of door systems. Not doors, although doors did play their small part: door systems. Pneumatic closers, heavy-duty hinges, push plates, kick plates, magnetic locks, fire sealant strips, all the different bits and bobs that get attached to doors in workplaces and hotels, all of which have their manufacturers. And all those manufacturers need to get together a couple of times a year to talk about aluminium prices and the pros and cons of setting up factories in Vietnam. And to slap one another on the back and have regrettable sex. That year, Ingress Solutions Expo had taken over a Radisson (or it might have been a Hilton) in the city my father had settled in. He came to the hotel and we had a drink in the bar.

"Brand-new, this hotel," he said, looking out of the picture windows at the filled canal beyond. "Came here before a few times. All used to be warehouses. Allied Tungsten—made brake lights—was here, shipped them down the canal to Coventry. They got bought by, let's see, Philips, or was it Toyota? Gone now, anyway. All these hotels and flats here instead."

Often I prompted my father to reminisce about his days on the road. Now that I travelled on behalf of the value engineers, I imagined that I had common ground with him, and I hoped—a fairly desperate hope—that I might at last be able to regain in some form whatever it was that I had lost in his absence. But his stories were mostly useless, revolving around disappeared companies serving a dead industry. The country he had roamed was mostly gone.

I pushed him. Didn't he appreciate the serendipity of us having gone into similar jobs? Did he have any advice he might be able to pass on? Father to son?

He rotated his pint of bitter and avoided my eye. "How's your mother?"

It had been a while since I had seen her. Unhappy, that was how she was. No real time to visit, I said, what with work. Surely he would understand. Of all people.

"You should visit your mother," my father said.

It's not easy, I said.

"You want advice? Father to son? You should visit your mother."

I didn't say anything. I watched a jogger pounding along the restored towpath, white flex of her iPod jumping like an electrocardiogram, wraparound shades, sweatshirt announcing membership of the netball team of a huge firm of accountants, the only human soul I had seen pass that way in a while.

"Were you with your mother when she came to the hotel?" my father asked. "That time? The last time?"

Yes, I said.

"She said you were downstairs. Did she tell you what happened?"

No, I said.

He weighed this information, mesmerized by the laminated bar snacks menu.

"You were always your mother's boy. There's much more of her in you than me. It's uncanny, just looking at you I see her. That way you have of . . . watching. Always thinking. That's her."

This was not what I wanted. It was useless trying to connect with this man.

"No one can stay angry for ever, Neil. People can change."

The alarm woke me. Tiredness came as a form of pain, an atom-level stress in every part of my body. So tired. Three days in a hotel, not leaving a half-mile radius, but I was rowing-alone-across-the-Atlantic tired—tiredness was frozen into me, as basic to my body's composition as water. This was the result of hauling my pampered, gym-estranged form up and down corridors and across roads. But I wondered if on some elemental level my physical being knew where it had truly been; that it had crisscrossed continents, and was somehow making deductions on that account. I yearned to linger in bed awhile longer, but matters of importance awaited. And as more of the events of the previous day and night filtered back into my mind, the more the bed, the room, the hotel, seemed unreliable and deceptive.

But the shower—the shower was still faithful. The hot, powerful hotel shower was a dispenser of innocence. When I reflected on my father's habits in hotels, I thought of how he must have valued the shower, with its permanent supply of fresh starts and its destruction of evidence.

My suit was hanging in the closet, still cocooned in its dry-cleaner's plastic. Having finished my shower and shave, I tore into the red wrapper, pleased that Lucy had done what she did, pleased it meant a crisp, clean outfit on this last day rather than the days-old, suitcase-wrinkled, conference-end garb everyone else would be wearing.

Bright blackness flickered through the torn wrapper. A burst of moiré effect—an unseeable, unthinkable conflict of lines—caused me to blink and refocus.

I kept tearing at the plastic, pulling it down over the suit until it lay fizzing and crackling on the floor, tremoring with tiny, obscene movements like a deep-sea invertebrate dying on a beach. Its staticky, chemical reek was on my hands and in my sinuses.

Before me, on the hanger, was Hilbert's pinstripe suit.

This was no error. Even allowing for the hotel's talent at perverting chance, a mix-up was impossible to imagine. This had to be deliberate. What, then, was its deliberate purpose? A taunt? A warning? A reminder that a score remained to be settled?

But of course it was not Hilbert's suit—at least, it was not the suit Hilbert had been wearing a few hours earlier, when Dee assaulted him. At that moment, this suit was already in my closet, or so I believed—so this was another suit, identical to Hilbert's, sent instead of my own between my first meeting with him and the violent second encounter. Sent while he believed me to be working for him.

It repulsed me. Not the fabric of the thing: the linen was soft and heavy, perhaps hand-stitched. The tricks the close-placed stripes played on my eyes, the way they swarmed at me in my peripheral sight, sickened me inwardly, not least because I found my gaze compelled to return to them, like a migraine bruise throbbing in my visual cortex I could not help but press again and again. But mostly the idea of it sickened me. I was being manipulated. To further dispel any illusion of chance, under the jacket was my white shirt, which Lucy had also soaked and which I had also included in the dry cleaning. More evidence of calculation.

I checked my other suit, the one drenched during my walk back from the MetaCenter yesterday. It was no good. Damp still clung to it, in the armpits and the crotch; it was wrinkled and faintly marshy. There was my leisure gear and the comfortable clothes I travelled in—would a casual look offend Laing, could it make any difference to the outcome of the meeting? He struck me as a stickler, the kind of man who wore shirts under jumpers at the weekend. Maybe, in the pub on a Sunday afternoon, he would opt for a neatly pressed rugby shirt or a Ralph Lauren short-sleeved number.

Sitting on the bed in a Way Inn dressing gown, I looked at the suit hanging in the open wardrobe. Its optical-illusion properties aside, it was just a smart suit, evidently expensive and well made. What made it sinister to me was that it was an outpost of Hilbert in my room; what made Hilbert terrible was, in part, the sharpness of his curiously anachronistic suit.

My room? Not my room—Way Inn's room. I had to remember that everything around me was supplied by Way Inn—the walls, the furniture, the dressing gown I was wearing, even the conditioned air. Keeping that in mind, and exercising all possible caution, would surely be crucial to my continued health and well-being as I navigated this last couple of hours. I didn't mean any harm to the hotel—all I needed was to conclude my business and leave.

To get to my smart, clean, dry, white shirt I had to take the suit hanger off the rack—being a theft-proof hotel hanger, it could not be hung anywhere else—and take the jacket off the hanger. As I put on the shirt in front of the full-length mirror on the bathroom door, my eyes repeatedly revisited the jacket and trousers, which were now laid flat on the bed, and with each visit my mind went back to the events in the Gallery Room. The incident had been a decisive rupture—almost certainly the end of my deal with Hilbert and also the end of whatever I had with Dee. She had been clear: I had betrayed her. As far as she was concerned, I was with Hilbert and his kind. I sensed the first falling flakes of the great snowdrift of sadness that I knew would come to bury my memories of her, that I would have to dig through with freezing fingers and stinging eyes if I ever wanted to find anything good beneath. We had had so little time together. But there had been the possibility of more, and that possibility was now quashed.

There would be time to mourn later. Hilbert, however—Hilbert was alive, at large and presumably none too pleased. He remained a possibility, a glowering and horrible one. In twenty minutes, I would do precisely what summoned him earlier—open the Gallery Room with the black keycard. If he were to reappear, desiring vengeance, perhaps it would be best to pretend that nothing had happened, that I was proceeding with our arrangement along the lines we had agreed, that all was well? I had, after all, played my part according to his terms. Dee's behavior was hardly my fault. If Hilbert was to be appeased in these last hours, my wearing the suit could be taken as a gesture of cooperation.

I tried it on. It fit perfectly—the trouser cuffs sat in the ideal place on the laces of my shoes, and the set of the jacket on the shoulders and across the back could not be improved. I had assumed the fit would be awkward. Hilbert was taller and leaner than I was, and he had seemed less substantial beneath the suit, a mere hanger himself. But this suit couldn't have been more tailored to my more average frame. Two suits, outwardly very similar but very different: one blood-soaked and wrapped around an insane hotel employee, the other fit to me.

Exactly fitted to me. Made for me. In the bathroom mirror, under color-stripping fluorescent light, a Hilbert-like figure looked back at me—better fed, better hair, but of the type. *You're perfect for them*, Dee had said—she had been enraged and panicked when she said it, and I had heard it as an attempt to wound, like Lucy's thrown drink. But how much truth was in it? Was Hilbert's approach, his deal with me, merely the prelude to an offer of a more permanent arrangement? Unlimited free nights suggested permanence, a perk of employment. I believed I could see the meaning in the suit—it was an overture, an invitation. It was not the suit that fit me; I fit the suit. I fit in here.

Well, they had missed their opportunity. Once I was out of the hotel, the suit was going to the charity shop. Let it exude sinister magnificence among the tweed jackets and creased shoes of the deceased. I was finished.

Keycard out, lights off, room dead.

"Nice suit." Laing was early, which felt like a play against me. An effort that undermined my own early arrival and seemed designed to get me apologizing. I bristled, but remembered: apologizing was what I was there to do.

"Thanks. Shall we?"

Once we entered the Gallery Room, my hand hovered over the wall-slot. So this was what I was reduced to—Dee and Hilbert had messed with my head to the extent that I now attributed mystic power to a quite mundane use of a perfectly normal keycard. My hand was stayed as if it was about to complete a dire voodoo rite. After a flash of anger and resentment, I inserted the card. The room lights went on, obliterating the pallid autumnal dawn.

The carpet tiles were back in place—not the same tiles, I suspected, but replacements from a hidden store. Flexible, interchangeable, low maintenance. The shark's multiple rows of teeth. One of the paintings was still missing from the wall, but the wall itself and the chair frame had been wiped clean. A parabola of brown drops could be made out on an adjacent painting, well camouflaged by its rusty color scheme; blood cast off by Dee's assault forming an energetic addition to a constellation of fawn and treacle spheres.

"Do you think we could get started? I don't have much time."

"Ah, yes, of course," I said, sitting opposite Laing.

"Are you OK?" Laing said. "You look a bit off-color."

"I'm fine," I said. "I had a slightly disturbed night."

I was not fine. The enormity of what Dee had revealed to me—both its size and its catastrophic implications—had been dulled by sleep. Rest had placed it in the background, out of proper perspective. Rest, which knits together irreconcilable truths, and enamels inconvenient memories. Rest in one of Way Inn's rooms. The hotel had revealed itself to me on three successive nights, each time when I would normally have been asleep; each night it had torn the surface of my world a little more, then stitched it back up. It was normalizing itself in my eyes, making itself just part of the scenery, as ubiquitous and permanent as the weather. Dee had been right about this, as she had been right about everything else: falling to the floor screaming was absolutely the correct response to Way Inn. Anything else was aberrant. How deep was its influence in my room, where it handled the air, and the invisible electromagnetic spectrum pulsated with malignity?

"Are you sure you're OK?" Laing said. He seemed genuinely sympathetic. "You don't look at all well."

I forced a smile. "I'm fine," I repeated. "Thanks for agreeing to meet, I appreciate it. I truly feel that there's no difference between us that can't be resolved."

"Me too," Laing said. "And I don't want to be causing you sleepless nights or whatever. I don't take any pleasure in trying to destroy a man's livelihood. We just needed to be sure that you didn't pose a threat to *our* livelihoods."

"Misunderstandings on both sides," I said, and I held up my hands in a conciliatory gesture. Then I remembered that I had seen Hilbert making the same gesture. Those long, white fingers, stalks of fungus in a mile-deep cave. A shiver passed up my spine and my hands closed, without a thought, into fists. "I was angry—you called me a parasite . . . "

"Yes, I'm sorry about that . . . "

"No, don't apologize—what I wanted to say was, the most successful parasites don't harm their hosts. Naturally we don't want to damage the meetings industry. But we can provide a service at the margins, for people who are unable to attend your shows."

"And you'll tone down the sales pitch? Nothing more

about how everyone secretly hates trade fairs and conferences, and no one in their right mind would go if there was any alternative?"

"Sure, that won't be a problem. And you won't ban me?"

"No, there'll be no need for anything like that," Laing said, beaming, the chunky knot on his silk tie shining with satisfaction. "You see, here we are talking this over together like men, eye to eye—isn't this an improvement on the phone or email or communicating through lackeys? I've been in this game a few years and I've often found . . . "

He was away, giving the full spiel on the merits of the flesh, looking me in the eye in order to communicate his authority, but hardly seeing me at all. How much of him was really in the room and how much of me? To what extent did he believe his patter? It barely mattered; we might both be sitting here, but we were both simply avatars of different formations of money, trying to find ways those formations could continue to grow without coming into conflict—representing arrayed abstractions, conflicting and cooperating configurations of capital and interest. Like the actors in the stock photos, playing roles, representing messages, making empty images for empty communication. I thought about what I had just said, about parasites and hosts, and symbiosis, like the organisms in the gut that aid digestion. Like the hotel. The hotel behaves like an organism. It depends on all the people staying within it, working for it, meeting within its walls.

We were helping the hotel. Laing and I, right here, right now. We had met in a meeting room and come to a

conclusion that benefited us both, but which also benefited Way Inn. Adam and I would be able to continue
sending people out to conferences and the "meetings industry" could grow unmolested. More meat for Way Inn's
myriad upon myriad rooms. Laing was talking about the
MetaCenter, about expansion, about growth and vitality.
Another MetaCenter planned for another city; more conferences, more fairs, more regeneration. More business
suits for business suites, as Dee had said; how fortunate
for Way Inn. The perfect environment for business. It was
working on us now, this environment, this endless fiction
woven around us. And I saw it so perfectly, the aggregate
of hundreds of thousands of meetings like this one; they
led to more hinterlands, more motorways, more out-of-
town convention centers and investment hubs, more office
parks and redevelopment areas, all of which led to more
places for Way Inn. Leaving the hotel wasn't enough. The
hotel wasn't just reproducing itself. It was making more
places where it could appear, more of these anonymous
locales. The hotel was turning more and more of the
world into its world.

"I'm serious: you don't look well," Laing said. He
might have been quiet for a while before saying this,
observing me as I stared into the interlocking orbs of the
paintings on the wall opposite. I could imagine how I
looked. I could feel the cold sweat on my top lip and on
the back of my hands, and my head throbbed—possibly
a psychosomatic reaction as I strained to detect physio-
logical evidence of the hotel's influence. What I expected
to feel, I don't know—a tingle, a pulse, a spreading seda-
tion? But it was working on me somehow, working on us

all. Remaking me, remaking us, remaking everything. Sucking out the color, as the suit was bleeding the color from my complexion.

"Under the weather, that's all," I said. "Maybe a dose of convention flu. I need a break, I think."

"Don't we all," Laing said, chuckling merrily. "Setting up a new show—it's a roller-coaster ride, nothing quite like it. I'll be pleased when I can look back on it."

You fool, you're just doing what it wants, and what it wants is no past, no future. You're nothing more than an algorithm wearing rugby-club cuff-links. "I don't want to take up too much of your time, you must be busy. Thanks for agreeing to see me."

"It's been good to straighten things out with you. I'm glad we can move along."

"Yes. Thanks again. This has been really constructive." More than anything, I wanted to complete this meeting and be gone. This was, I supposed, a far easier and more thorough success than I had anticipated. But it served the hotel first and the hotel above anyone, and its very ease made me fearful of how deep the hotel's influence ran through us. I could not enjoy my success. What I felt was failure, a serious moral and practical failure. A failure as a human.

"Sure, excellent," Laing said. He stood and I stood with him. Social codes. An action occurred to me, Dee lifting the chair and bringing it down on Hilbert; it occurred to me as a physicality in the room, a shape in the air, as if the muscles employed had left trails for others to follow. If I tried to kill Laing, what then? Would the hotel preserve him as it had preserved Hilbert? Would it preserve them all?

We shook hands. I held the door for him. Left alone in the Gallery Room, I poured myself a glass of water from one of the bottles provided for my convenience. I drank. I had to get out. Killing Laing had not been a senseless atavistic impulse. The action had existed, ready in the space between us, loaded up in my musculature like an app. Yet I simultaneously felt enfeebled; I doubted I could even get one of those heavy chairs over my head. I had to get out.

But here I was. Lingering in the Gallery Room, staring into space—this potent, subversive space—when I could be far away.

As I turned to the door, it opened. Pure fear skewered me. Hilbert, again Hilbert.

"Neil!" Maurice said as he stepped into the room. "What a pleasant surprise. Sorry, did I give you a fright? You look like you've seen a ghost."

"Maurice." I could feel myself grinning, an entirely involuntary reflex, sheer relief. "How nice to see you."

Maurice smiled back. We both knew I did not smile at him often, and he was enjoying it, cheeks shiny with appreciation. He was normal—immensely, joyously, reassuringly normal. His pinkness and paunchiness, which I had despised, now seemed signs of abundant life. "Are you using this room? I booked it, but I think I'm early."

"No, no," I said. I realized I was still holding a glass and I put it down on the table. "I'm finished. It's all yours."

"Good good." Maurice had been hanging awkwardly in the doorway; now he moved into the room, dropped his large, shapeless satchel noisily onto the table and started to remove items from its depths. "I'm wrapping up here myself," he said. "Doing one or two interviews, then heading off in a couple of hours. Are you doing the last day?"

"Ah, no, I'm off too."

"Well, see you on the road then. Straight on to the next show for me. I was looking for you yesterday. I wanted to catch up. All that craziness with young Rhian, Rita, Robyn ... "

"Lucy."

"Yeah. I kept an eye out but I didn't see you around."

"I wasn't at the conference yesterday. I had some stuff to sort out."

"Not there yesterday, not there today," Maurice said, shaking his head happily. "You need someone who'll go in your place!" He gaped at me, delighted with his own joke.

"That's what I was sorting out, actually."

"With Tom Laing? Saw him in the hall. Interviewing him later."

"Yes," I said. "I was patching things up. He was going to ban me. Now he isn't."

"Good. Ban you? Seems a bit excessive. You're not doing anyone any harm. I knew what your work involved. Not hard to put it together. For all your cloaky-daggery stuff, you're not that discreet. The big mistake is being all cloaky-daggery. Makes people think you've got something to hide. Probably what got Laing so wound up."

"Right. I'll try to keep that in mind." It was possible that Maurice was lying, pretending to have known what he did not know, but maybe I had been underestimating him. Genial bumbling was a fine camouflage for guile.

"Sounded like a good idea to me," Maurice said. "A way to get out of going to conferences. Tough on you, though. What do you get out of it?"

"I like hotels." My usual answer. It didn't feel true anymore. Maybe it was time to retire it. Maybe I was the one who should be doing the retiring. Or at least finding another career. "What do you get out of it?"

Maurice had been arranging equipment on the table: notebook, push-button pencils, digital recorder, pens, a little digital camera on a little tripod, a couple of copies of his magazine. He stopped and looked at me, mouth open, entire face open in fact, lost midthought. Puffy features unshaped, a ball of spare Plasticine. Then they resolved into a smile. "I like meeting people. People are amazing. Every one different. Every one interesting. When you talk to them. Get to know them. When you listen." He looked down at his various tools, adjusted a pencil. "Don't care too much for hotels, to be honest with you. They're all the same."

"Have you ever been approached by anyone from Way Inn? Offering a job?" I asked, but I already knew the answer would be no. Maurice wasn't the right material. Clearly. It was clear to me now.

"Nope, not me. Why? You? Thinking of leaving the caravanserai?"

"Yes. Not to do that, though." I was transfixed by the tools Maurice had laid out—tools of journalism, of recording, of reporting, of telling stories to a wider world. "Maurice, Way Inn isn't hundreds of different hotels, it's all the same giant hotel, a hotel that goes on forever. There are people who live in it. The hotel can warp the reality within it. It changes people. I'm worried it's eating the world."

Maurice chuckled. "Yeah, I feel that way sometimes too. Sounds like you need a holiday. Any plans for Christmas?"

Of course. You couldn't tell, you had to show. "Can you spare twenty minutes? Half an hour? I'd like to show you something."

"Not really, old chap," Maurice said, baring his teeth in consternation. "I've got people due . . . Another time, yeah? We'll have a beer."

"Another time, then."

"Nice suit, by the way. Give my regards to Al Capone."

I passed the first of Maurice's interview subjects on my way out of the room. Nothing more than a bloke in a suit, but then I was nothing more than a bloke in a suit. Seeing Maurice had somehow stabilized me, made me feel less as if the ground beneath me was tilting and the walls were mere figments. But it had not subtracted anything from the fear I felt or my resolution to leave the hotel immediately. The fact that Maurice was unaffected—would never be affected—did not mean I was safe. They already knew me. The hotel had enfolded me in its designs. Even if the nature of the threat was unclear, I did not fancy remaining in place to see it come into focus.

It took very little time to clear all trace of myself from room 219. My possessions went into my bag, the few scraps of rubbish I had produced went into the bin. I returned the pinstripe suit to its hanger and changed into the casual clothes I had worn yesterday. Where was my suit, the one the pinstripe had displaced? Still with the cleaner? Held hostage? Voided? I could always buy another suit. When I passed reception I would ask about it, but my next stop would be the front door. It struck me that I didn't have to stop at reception at all—I could check out and pay my bill from my room, through the TV, and do away with any possible bureaucratic holdups or ambushes at the front desk.

Bag packed, I switched on the room TV. WELCOME MR. DOUBLE. Good-bye, Mr. Double. The same stock photo of smiling Way Inn staff. Today's special in the restaurant: Thai green curry. Weather outlook: clouds and rain, the same symbol repeating into the future. No more. Maurice was right, I did need a holiday. I would go somewhere without a Way Inn, wherever that was. Katmandu, Timbuktu, a nameless corner of the world.

Using the remote control, I selected "hotel services" and "quick checkout." An account of my room extras appeared: drinks from the minibar, phone calls, room service meals, dry cleaning. Do you accept? Yes. Charge my card. Proceed to checkout. A crude progress wheel appeared under the words PLEASE WAIT. Under the wheel: TRANSACTION INCOMPLETE. DO NOT NAVIGATE AWAY FROM THIS PAGE. Never reassuring, the progress wheel—unlike the progress bar, it doesn't progress, it just goes around and around. Its purpose is, I assume, merely to imply that something, somewhere, is working; that servers in sheds somewhere are talking to other servers in sheds elsewhere. But so often the wheels keep spinning over a completely stuck machine, like the wheel of an overturned car in a ditch beside the road.

"What are you doing?"

I jumped hard enough to provoke a squeak from the box mattress of the bed I was sitting on, and looked toward the door to see who had spoken. But there was no one there. A soft dry rattling came from the air-conditioning vent. There was movement on the screen—

not the inane rotation of the wheel but, beside it, where the staff of the Way Inn flashed their shining smiles at me, radiating welcome and readiness to serve. Actors, maybe. The movement seemed to have come from the photo, from among the ranks of the staff—and as I looked, one of their number turned, edged sideways and stepped out of the immobile group. It was Hilbert, a small televised Hilbert, strolling across the red-and-white backing of the screen as if it were a stage.

"Bunch of stiffs," tele-Hilbert said, looking back at the photo from which he had emerged. "Superficially pleasant, but lacking the human touch. So often the case nowadays. That's the difference between good service and great service, don't you agree, Mr. Double? The human touch."

I mashed buttons on the remote, but nothing happened. Moiré patterns flared and blazed on Hilbert's suit as he walked slowly forward—toward what? Through what? There was no camera, this was a menu; toward the screen, then, toward me.

"Nowadays the hotel business is all about making an emotional connection—making the business traveller feel their soul is being taken care of as well as their body. Or faking it, anyway. Hence the quote from Michel de Montaigne on the cover of the service directory, hence the ostentatious environmental concern about towels, hence the email on your birthday. 'We are delighted to look after your coats while you are enjoying our hospitality.' *Delighted*. Healthy living, too, the photo of the sliced kiwi fruit on the room service menu, the spa and fitness center. *Mens sana in corpore sano*, yes? A healthy mind in a healthy body. We all want to live forever."

As he spoke he advanced on me. Blocky digital distortion, aliasing breakdowns, compression fragments, ragged swatches of acidic machine-green and machine-blue, inexpressible noncolors smearing red-black and purple-black, boiled at the crisp edge of his approaching form. He could not be resolved, not by the display technology, not by perceived reality. The pixel froth stirred up by his progress was the screen's rejection of him. But I was transfixed.

"Does the outer hotel care? It cares about appearing to care. It cares enough to make me sick, anyway. It wants your business, it wants your approval. But it doesn't know you the way the inner hotel knows you. Transaction incomplete, Mr. Double. Transaction incomplete."

Hilbert's face filled the screen, pallid skin splitting with horizontal bars of bruise-colored digital interference. Distortion streamed from the open wound on his brow, where Dee had struck him with the chair. He was bleeding noise and chaos.

I overcame my paralysis and lunged for the off button on the TV itself; Hilbert turned as if able to see my arm—and the screen blinked to black.

"No," I said, suspecting I could be heard even if there was no one there to listen. "I'm finished. Leaving. Transaction complete."

They, whoever they were really, could keep the suit. They could keep Dee. I took my bag and left the room in a hurry.

The watered-down Stones tune playing by the lifts was "Sympathy for the Devil." I hit the down button and a set of doors opened immediately. I hit G for Ground, for Go, for Get out. The doors shut. Maximum occupancy six persons. In the event of fire do not use lift. A photocopied sheet of paper in a frame tells me that the weather outlook is uniformly cloudy and rainy and today's special is Thai green curry. Beside this is a framed advert for the hotel's conference facilities. Way Inn and Way Inn Metro branches. Registered trademark.

My reflection, in opposed mirrors. Me, my back, me, my back, and so on, the line of us curving away as the tiny difference in angle between mirrors increased with each repetition. The slight curvature in the line of Doubles obscured the vanishing point—when I try to look round me to see infinity, the other mes are always bending to stay in the way. A mercy, perhaps. Who first placed two mirrors opposite each other? Was there a moment of vertigo when they saw the hole they had made in finite space? Were they afraid? I hoped they felt fear. Fear would have been an entirely appropriate reaction. It often is. I was afraid. Terribly afraid.

Mirrors eliminate the experience of waiting. We preen and this reduces the aggravation of forced inactivity. Like parakeets distracted from their prison. The mirror swallows time. My appearance was not good. Dark rings had appeared under my eyes. I looked rattled, haunted. How much time had been swallowed? Was the lift even moving?

One of my multiple reflections leaned out of line. Just one. I hadn't moved, only the reflection had moved. Then it stepped from its column, leaving a gap. It was four or five repetitions deep. The pinstripes of the reflection's suit were reddened toward the collar, but its pale skin was clean. He turned toward me. We stared at each other, mirror-Hilbert and I. Hilbert did not look angry—more terrible than that, he looked pleased and knowing. Then he broke eye contact and leaned to one side, looking around and behind me.

I turned. In the opposite mirror, all the reflections were Hilbert. Those that had their pinstriped back to me all turned as one to join the others in facing me. They stared at me, still with that freezing smile.

In panic, I don't know if I jumped toward the lift doors or fell toward them, my body not waiting for impetus from the incapacitated mind but making its own decision, cobbling together an ad hoc reaction from the few responsive muscle groups it could raise. But my desperate fingers found the button that opened the doors, and the doors slid apart as I slumped against them, leaving the lift in a couple of heavy, seasick steps, almost collapsing. I leaned back into the lift to snatch up my bag, not looking at the mirrors, at the impossibility they were showing me.

The lift doors closed. This was not the ground floor. It was the second. Signs told me to go right for rooms 201 to 240 and left for rooms 241 to 280. I had not moved at all.

Stairs. But the fire door to the stairwell was not there. If I could only believe that my memory deceived me and the door was in fact elsewhere. How I yearned to remember that it was around the corner or down the corridor. If only. But I knew that it had been here as fixedly as I knew that it was now gone. In its place was a white wall and a painting.

A soft *ping* issued from the lift and its doors rumbled apart. Hilbert stepped into the second-floor corridor. The expression on his face conveyed no sorrow or anger, nor anything that suggested he was dealing with another human being, or had ever been one himself. He shimmered with distortion. I tensed, but there was no preparation for the blow he delivered, without preamble, with the flat of his right hand to my left temple.

The room died.

Waking for the second time today, I experienced pain as a kind of tiredness. That one blow had knocked all the power from me as surely as it had deprived me of reason. My head was clouded as if from deep sleep. Within it, my brain felt just a little too small, and seemed to shift with the slightest movement, sliding and bumping in its cushioning gravy.

I was sitting at a table, slumped over, head resting on my left arm. My left arm felt good, and I did not want to move. I could see my right arm, and behind that was a glass of water.

My left arm had gone to sleep. I tried to move it, to get some feeling back in the hand, and was rewarded with an igniting match of new pain in the arch above my left eye. A small exclamation of complaint escaped my lips: "Ah!" The table was hard and white, a durable artificial substance, surely trademarked.

"Mr. Double."

I lifted my head to see where the voice had come from, though I already knew who had spoken. Hilbert sat at the other end of the conference table. For a moment I thought I was back in the Gallery Room—same size room, the same table in the middle. But this room was sparse, the light utilitarian, the door behind Hilbert plain, not dark wood. The walls were white-painted breezeblocks, and only one painting hung on them—one with a broken frame and a liberal dash of Hilbert's blood. I had the sense of being underground. Air conditioning whirred loudly.

"Have some water, Mr. Double. I'm afraid you hit your head quite hard on the floor on your way down."

Hilbert sat with his hands clasped in front of him. Blood had soaked his shirt around the collar and stained his suit. But he had cleaned it from his poached-egg skin. The wound on his brow was half-covered by shining black hair.

On my way down. You sent me down, you bastard. I took a sip of water and tasted iron—blood in my mouth. Probing for its source, I found I had bitten my tongue: a neat notch on its right side which started to hurt as soon as I discovered it. So Hilbert was prepared to be violent, prepared to strike and injure and imprison on behalf of the hotel. My fear in his presence was, for the moment, drowned out by anger. He had assaulted me and I wanted to assault him back, or to hit at the hotel itself—to injure it, or at least scare it, in some way. How, though, do you threaten a hotel?

"TripAdvisor is going to hear about this," I said. "Just you wait. This place is going to get some serious one-star reviews."

Hilbert smiled. "I apologize for the direct nature of my approach. I hope we can put it behind us and move into more productive areas of discussion."

"On balance, I think I'm done discussing with you," I said. "I did everything you asked. Brought her to the conference room. I'm not responsible for what happened. She's your problem now. I'm useless to you. I've got no way of getting in touch with her and even if I had, she'll never trust me again. Thanks to you."

"Precisely," Hilbert said. "She could never be relied upon—you see that now as well as I do. That woman has burned her last bridge with me. And you should understand that she has nothing to offer you. She is increasingly temperamental and secretive. Unstable. Perhaps dangerous."

"Yes," I said. As he talked about Dee, Hilbert's tone had turned sour, and this made my bruised jaw ache with pleasure. "How is your head?"

Hilbert's arm flinched at the elbow as he overcame an obvious impulse to put his fingers to his brow and feel the broken edges of his skin. His hands remained tightly clasped in front of him.

"Fine, thank you. Healing very nicely. How is yours?"

My pleasure dissipated. Scoring points against Hilbert could never be more than momentarily entertaining. Whatever brief satisfaction it brought was followed by a powerful sense of futility.

"I don't know why you need me at all," I said, a complaint that towed a great tiredness behind it. I wanted to be done, to go home. "You're obviously a very powerful man, so how has she been able to elude you?"

Hilbert widened his eyes in a look of bafflement and shrugged, an incongruously human, even vulnerable, act. "It's something of a mystery to me as well, Mr. Double. She is not without abilities herself, and has been able to shield her location. The hotel will be aware of her, of course, but its interventions in our business are oblique at best. That's why it needs employees with initiative and zeal—employees who can take a more direct approach. Which brings us smartly to the next item on the agenda: my offer to you. I'm afraid I need to push you for a commitment."

"Offer? What offer? We're done here. I did my part, you did yours. Thank you. Now it's time for me to go."

"It's not nearly time for you to go," Hilbert said sharply, rearing up suddenly in his seat, eyes flashing like geodes. "Not until you see the bigger picture. The keycard, the suit—these items are not given lightly, Mr. Double! We had a deal!"

"You can keep them," I said, but with care; Hilbert's temper was clearly up and I didn't like the way he seemed to flare with visual noise as his ire rose, a representation straining and breaking down. I didn't want to peer behind that representation at whatever once-human remnant was there. He was more agitated than I had seen him, even when under direct attack. "You're most kind, but this is a mistake. This isn't me."

Hilbert smacked the table with the palm of his hand, hard enough to make me jump in my seat and to set the water in my glass seesawing from side to side. "You don't understand what you're rejecting! It's not just a suit and a card; the potential of the hotel far exceeds anything you can imagine! You have the use of an infinite structure. Do you see? An infinite structure, one reflecting human desire—no boundaries, no limits. An unending supply of transient visitors, too. Ones that won't be missed. You can take whomever you wish into the inner hotel, take whatever pleasure you wish . . . and they're gone, lost, forever. Such fun times we've had down the more remote corridors, far beyond any hearing or caring from the limited, outer world."

The rise of his rhetoric had lifted him out of his chair, and he leaned over the table, tongue working behind teeth, a trail of blood again trickling from his head wound. "It's no world at all, the outer world, not really, not like our world . . . But you know that already, don't you? You're already in the undergrowth of our world, and you can see the woods beckoning, sense the freedom there . . . "

Freedom, yes; I had sensed it, known that it was out there, this freedom that Hilbert offered. Not out there—*in* there, within the hotel, within my ringing head. And looking at Hilbert, into those red-edge, blade-shine eyes, I saw the meaning and the price of that freedom, what manner of liberation it truly was. Hilbert was quite unfettered. He was far beyond the restraints of sanity. Whatever his compact with the hotel, however he had chosen to enjoy it, it had driven him mad.

"How long have you been serving the hotel, Hilbert?" I asked, working in a note of pastoral concern.

"Yes!" Hilbert said. He appeared delighted at my query. "I knew you sensed it. I knew it. Precisely the question. How long? That is what we are offering, Mr. Double. Time. Life, life unlimited. Eternal life. Time in the inner hotel is not time spent. It is not deducted. No sickness, no growing old, no death! Don't you see, Mr. Double? There's the promise!"

I started to consider escape. Whatever hopes I had of reasoning with Hilbert had to be discarded. And I did not intend to find out what pleasures he sought and found in the chambers of the inner hotel, willingly or unwillingly. The only door I could see was on the far side of the room, behind Hilbert—I would have to pass him to reach it. Letting him rant on, I turned slowly to look over my shoulder, trying to make the act as subtle and relaxed as possible.

There wasn't a door or window behind me; but what there was gave me a jab of surprise. Heaped up against the rear wall of the room, as far as the ceiling, was a mighty landslip of clock radios. All were identical to the one in my room—possibly the original radio from my room was somewhere in this mass—but most were damaged, their screens smashed or their casings cracked. It was impossible to tell where the rear wall actually was, so deep and high was this pile, which trailed power cords like the exposed roots of a wind-felled tree. Hundreds, maybe thousands, of clock radios—the kind of thing you'd see at a factory liquidation or tumbling from a spilled shipping container on a dockside—all in this hotel basement. Maybe there was no rear wall, and the radios went on forever. I was ready to accept almost anything as fact.

"How about you give me some time to think about it?" I said.

"Why would you need more time to think?" Hilbert said. "The decision is, surely, already made. It's the offer of a lifetime, quite literally. Your life has led you here. You are prepared. If you do not want this, then there is nothing you do want. And if you seek nothingness rather than fulfillment, well, that can also be arranged."

"Recently I've been considering making some changes in my life," I said. "I think maybe you've come to me at the wrong time."

"Nonsense. The advantages of what I am offering are plain. Immortality, liberty and luxury. An infinite world, at your disposal."

"A finite world. Nothing but hotel. Hotel all the way down."

The trail of blood from the gash on Hilbert's forehead had progressed down the side of his nose, a neat red pin-stripe, and reached his hairless top lip. The tip of his tongue appeared, tasting it, as if he had only just noticed it. "You have the manner of a man about to make a fatal mistake."

"You could let me leave now and I'll never return. Gladly. No one would ever hear about this, you have my word."

"But I have a very simple way of making sure that no one ever hears about this. Why should I reject that option for the uncertainty of letting you go?"

We were clearly coming to the crux of the matter, the inescapable collision of our respective trajectories, and I had to be ready for action. Dee might not have killed Hilbert, but she had incapacitated him long enough to escape him, and that was all I needed. The chair I was sitting on was a plastic folding affair, not nearly as heavy as the ones in the Gallery Room, but it might serve. But my body was not at all ready. My legs felt like badly packed supermarket carrier bags. Nowhere in me lay the blueprints and resources for sudden, inspired violence of the kind that Dee had meted out. And more than anything, she had the element of surprise, and I did not.

"You don't really want to kill me, Hilbert. That isn't the way to go."

"Whoever said anything about killing you?" Hilbert said, amused. "Killing you is quite superfluous. We are in a labyrinth. I know the way out and you do not. That's all it comes down to. You would be living out your time in the hotel one way or another. And it's not a question of what I want—it's a question of what the hotel wants."

"You're crazy."

"Not a very original line to take, Mr. Double. And you know what they say about glass houses. You've spent three days in the midst of a paranoid fantasy about mystery women and infinite mazes. And now imaginary murder plots. Having isolated yourself from your fellow man you find yourself facing the possibility of losing your job and your savings, and you lose your mind in a hotel room. Hearing things, seeing things. A breakdown, a psychotic episode. We get suicides all the time. People often choose a hotel room as the place to end their life. Did you know that? It's a consideration in the design of the light fittings, and some of the other aspects of the room, although not one we'd admit to. Maybe they do it because they know the body will be found; it won't rot undiscovered in a one-bedroom Docklands flat. So the hotel becomes an antechamber of the morgue. Sounds plausible, in your case, doesn't it? It's something to consider. A way out."

A deep, cold sickness swirled within me as Hilbert spoke. He meant to screw with me, to push me into a corner in which I felt helpless, unable to do anything but agree to join with him in his little room-service cult—I knew all this, I could see the tactics, but nevertheless what he was saying hurt me, it twisted me around until I wasn't sure of myself, wasn't sure of the fact of Hilbert and those walls and this hard white conference table in front of me, its composite surface cool and smooth under my hands, a benign surface maybe; it was a real object, not a figment or an illusion, the only real thing I was feeling apart from pain and loss. I blinked several times, saliva flowing freely in my mouth—was I nauseated? Or was this a concussion? The looseness in my skull was giving way to a swimming sense of dizziness, a resumed bout of black lightning above the top of my spine. The air around me was thickening, charged with energy, frothing with inaudible, invisible frequencies and messages. I was not in the world, the world I used to believe was the only world—I was in the hotel, in its inner place, the place it was making for us and within us, where I could be destroyed by mere forgetfulness. My life was, as Hilbert had said, already lost to it. The choice before me was already largely made. But it was not my extinction that I found myself thinking of. I was not thinking of myself at all.

"What will happen to Dee?"

Hilbert did not answer. He appeared to be listening closely, but gave no sign of having heard my question. Indeed, he no longer appeared to register my presence in the room. His head was bent over slightly and his brow knotted in concentration, as if trying to remember an elusive melody or straining to hear a distant noise.

"What is going to happen to Dee?" I repeated. "What are you going to do to her?" Though it filled me with fear, the question also gave me a sense of control. I could try to make sure that Dee was safe, that she was beyond Hilbert's grasp. Even if she had no need of my help, she had reached out to me, and I had failed. Going on made sense if its purpose was to make good on that allegiance to Dee. It was a reason to fight, to aid her, to misdirect her enemies. If I could hold on to that promise to myself, part of me would be held back from Way Inn. A locked room within myself, reserved for me. Hilbert might get to me, but not to her.

Whatever it was that had distracted Hilbert still had his total attention. He appeared almost catatonic—only

small movements made by his eyes suggested his continued cognition. Tension was etched into the angle of his
body and the hunch of his shoulders. At one point he
mouthed a word, a small word, perhaps "Yes." I began to
wonder if it might be possible to simply slip past him to
the door while he was in this diverted state. As he had
retreated into himself he had lost most of the menace that
had held me in my seat, and I felt a normal level of control
and animation returning to my fear-frozen limbs. But before I could reach a conclusion, he rejoined me, as sprightly
and pleasant as an old business buddy making small talk
before renewing a long-standing contract.

"Right," he said, straightening. "Good. I'm going to
step out for a moment so you can consider the offer. Do
excuse me, back shortly." And he smoothed down his suit
jacket, which oozed unlikely spectra under his palms.
Blood ran freely from his head injury, but he did not appear to care.

The door shut softly behind him. I was alone. Why? To
"consider the offer"? I wasn't going to do very much of
that. Even the vague outline of Hilbert's luxurious little
hotel cult appalled me, and I was sure its details would be
unspeakable. What really amplified my revulsion at the
idea of pledging myself to the hotel and to Hilbert's kind,
however, was my knowledge that had I been asked a couple of days ago I might have readily agreed, and without
much thought. What had changed in that time?

I had changed. And I had met Dee. She might have
saved my life—or if not my life, some other vital aspect
of me, which had been past ripe but not yet rotten. Hilbert
seemed to have cashed in a significant part of himself—
not just his sanity but also a base element of his being,

opening himself to a corruption that an eternity in fitness centers and hot showers could not expunge. And he made this forfeit to serve this monstrosity, this unthinkable warren, an unlimited appetite on a limited planet.

Refusing meant what, though? Death? Abandonment in a labyrinth without exit, as Hilbert had suggested? Could the hotel eliminate guests itself, driving them to despair, withdrawing their oxygen? I realized with a thrust of fright that I was in a sealed, windowless room. The air-handling units still hummed, but were they still handling unadulterated air? I sniffed for any diminishing of the atmosphere. Nothing seemed amiss.

Sacrifice one way, sacrifice the other. Neither was my style. I walked over to the door and hesitated beside it a moment, wondering if Hilbert might be waiting on the other side. Then I tried the handle. It was locked. There was a key slot above the handle and I tried it with my black card, but was given the orange-red light. Another two tries produced the same result.

I was stopped from further pursuing this futile repetition by a noise from behind me. It was a percussive burst of interference from one of the clock radios, like the herald of a mobile phone call. As this first *blat-blat-blat* of sound receded into a softer chattering and fizzing, another radio struck up, and then another, and steadily more joined together in a deafening chorus of seething, yelping electronic ululation. I turned toward the great mound of damaged devices to see light flickering on their clock faces, little red digital fragments dancing and guttering in time with the mindless tune of the cackling speakers. Quickly alight with anger, I picked one up, causing a couple of others to slide down the pile like scree, and examined it. White plastic. Made in China. Normal. Its normality was a taunt. I hurled the radio against the breezeblock wall. Its casing burst and its inner mechanism separated into three parts, still tenuously connected by wires. The din rose to fill the room, the radios joined by a rising roar from the air conditioning and by a buzzing in the air itself. I had the sense of standing in a gale, in the presence of forces that could tear me apart if I were subjected to more than a fraction of their slightest influence. Buffeted by the onslaught of potency blizzarding through the room, I felt my mind yaw and pitch. There was no sensory apparatus that could cope with this fury, and my body was desperately lying to itself when it interpreted the storm as heat or light or pressure, my struggling mind serving up its own analogies to plaster over the splintering impossibilities being revealed. I laughed, a high-pitched, agitated laugh which merged perfectly with the maniacal piping of the interference from the hundreds of radios.

The room died—the impression of it collapsed, replaced with an immense arena of space choked with endless congeries of interlocking spheres, their edges fizzing like fractals down to infinite detail. Black lightning arced in the spaces between the spheres and in my inner space, where it blazed through and scorched away any last coherent thought.

Later. Time had elapsed, but in the unchanging, blatant light of the room in which Hilbert held me, I had no way of telling how much time. I was sitting on the floor, back against the wall by the door. Without that wall supporting me, I would have been lying on the ground. Had it always been there, or had it gone and returned while I had been . . . wherever I had been? And the floor? Both felt solid and real, which was comforting if not comfortable. At the other end of the room was the mountain of radio-alarm clocks. They were real too, and inert. Could they be tampering with the air, lacing it with hallucinogens? Aerosolized LSD, subsonic frequencies? Why? My memory of what I had seen was fragmentary, just a series of glimpses and unwholesome impressions. This, I believed, was a mercy.

I pushed myself onto my feet, the synthetic fibers of the carpet rough under my fingers. Real—real synthetic, any-way. The clock radios were mute, their trailing plugs advertising their powerlessness. I stumbled toward them, unsteady on stiff, numb legs. Separate from the main heap was the radio I had smashed against the wall, a dead crab on a beach. I thought of smashing lobsters in seafood restaurants. Those shellfish experiences aren't for me. They're for couples, for families. They're not good for lone dining. That's why you rarely see them in a hotel.

I like hotels. Because you can leave.

Behind me, the metal sound of a latch working.

The door was open. I could leave.

No Hilbert in the corridor. And it was a corridor, not a bare underground utility passage—I wasn't in a basement at all. A routine hotel corridor, dark wood doors, careful lighting, cream carpets and regular abstract paintings.

Such was my surprise that I let the door from which I had emerged close before I thought that it might be better to keep it open. But it closed—a dark wood door, indistinguishable from the others. The number on it was 219.

I tried the black keycard in the slot. Red light. Another room 219. I put my fingers against the number 2. It was hard, cold, real. Where my finger had rested, a little halo of fog was left on the metal. This trace of the warmth of my hand disappeared within seconds. But it had been there.

The corridor, the same, of course. Always the same, everywhere the same, forever.

Where to go? My options were, I supposed, unlimited—six continents, and an untold universe within these walls. But it was six continents of airport sprawl and peripheral highways, business parks and enterprise zones. The outer realm of Way Inn, where it could blend in, get comfortable, be unnoticed. What about inward? Not just into the hotel, into myself—into that objective delusion Dee had talked about, that she had in fact visited. I had glimpsed it—the inconceivable gulfs between screeching geometric thunderheads, falling into a gas giant composed of ever-denser intersections, those monstrous spheres that the paintings hinted at, though even en masse, even when the edgeless jigsaw was reassembled, still the paintings could only hint. But I thought I saw how it was done—not in the frames but in the zones of potential between them. When Dee had discovered the hotel's secret—when it had discovered her—she had spent weeks exploring. I was not her, though. I didn't have her intrepid spirit. I didn't even have my bag—it had been with me in the lift and was not with me now. And I was a hunted man. The hotel had presented me with an exit, out of that other room 219, and I had to assume it was a limited offer—an act of clemency, a stay of execution—and that Hilbert's distraction would be only temporary. Leave then, go, get out. Find Dee.

The bag was nothing: disposable, replaceable, just clothes and toiletries and a work laptop used only to read work emails. I stumbled back toward the lifts. Whatever had happened in that room—a blow to the head, a seizure, a fainting spell with added visuals—had left me giddy and confused. The route from room 219 to the lifts was different. It wasn't "my" room 219, I had to remember. I felt the floor tilt under me, a fresh bout of dizziness, and I slumped against the wall, knocking a painting askew. My own little realignment of space. I laughed at this thought as my legs continued to buckle under me. Then fear settled gray across my mind again. Get out. Could someone help? The door nearest me was 211. I hammered my palms against it.

"Is anyone in there? Help. I need help."

Silence within. Of course. If the hotel truly was infinite, and the number of guests remained finite, the chance of coming across an occupied room would be infinitesimally small. Especially here, wherever *here* was.

Room 211—lower than 219. Counting down might lead me out. Night rain was falling in the nearest light well. Manchester? Manaus? Manila? It didn't matter, I had found the gray metal doors of the lifts, their vanity mirrors, their potted palms and unused sofas. I pressed the call button and immediately realized my mistake. The lift was nothing more than a trap—if Hilbert had found me there last time, he could find me there again.

I looked for the stairwell, but couldn't find it. Perhaps that was all it was: I just couldn't find it. But I suspected it would be more accurate to say it wasn't there to be found. It had been edited away. Only the hotel's corridors, branching out for ever. No way down, no way out.

Everything curved back. In front of me, again, was the door of room 219. The route I had taken from the lifts was the same route I took every time; the same route I had taken on the first day, carrying my bag, after checking in. Outside, in the courtyard, the autumn daylight was already beginning its retreat. And it was drizzling—as expected. The usual route was impossible. It could not exist in the same space as the route I had taken from the other room 219, where Hilbert had tried to inter me. The structure had rearranged itself, or my perception of it was being changed. It was useless to try to thwart the hotel. You cannot escape a labyrinth that can reconfigure itself. I could go only where it wanted me to go to, and that was back to room 219.

The card worked in the lock, the light turned green and the door opened. It was gloomy inside, and I moved the card to the wall slot to bring on the lights. No hesitation—I could hardly prevent Hilbert or the hotel doing as they pleased, so let them come.

Housekeeping had been. The bed was made, the bin had been emptied. On the bed was my bag, neatly aligned on the ostentatiously smooth and tight-cornered sheets. The television facing the bed had come on with the lights; on the screen was the default hotel menu. WELCOME MR. DOUBLE. It was as if I had just checked in, as if my bags had been brought up for me and all I had to do was unpack and make myself comfortable. To put my toothbrush in the bathroom and eat the complimentary chocolate. To explore the minibar and browse the pay-per-view movies. As if nothing had happened.

I went to the phone and punched zero, for reception. A single ring and the call was answered.

"I'm in room 219," I said. "I want to check out, immediately."

"So soon?" It was Hilbert. His voice purred with concern and the sibilant electromagnetic breath of the phone line agreed. "Your account has not been settled, Mr. Double. Services have been rendered and the hotel has not been compensated. There are numerous extras on your bill. Way Inn takes a dim view of guests reneging on their commitments."

The subsidence in my stomach deepened as I watched exits disappear. But as I slid down into dread and my options dwindled, I felt the return of something I thought lost for good: fury. The final fury of the cornered animal, perhaps, but still a motivating fire. Had Hilbert been in the room with me, I would have smashed the phone into his face with the purest pleasure. Denied this, I was reduced to snarling at him: "How about I set this fucking room on fire? How would that affect my account, huh?"

"I think we both know you are not going to do that."

Damn him, he was right—it was little more than an empty threat, and we could both see it. I had no matches or lighter with me, and the days when they could be found in any hotel room are long gone. Was there some way to make a spark by smashing a bulb or damaging one of the appliances? I could plug in the clock radio and chuck it into a full bath—but what would that achieve, really? Would it start a fire? More likely it would only blow a fuse and I might electrocute myself in the attempt. Hilbert's words about suicide returned to me, how the act had been considered by the hotel designers. Recessed light fittings, nowhere to attach a ligature, a jumpy fuse box, windows that don't open. These measures protected the desperate from themselves, but also protected the hotel from the desperate. Desperate men like me, unable even to make fire, reduced to a lower level than our Neolithic ancestors.

I did not speak.

"Please wait," Hilbert said. "Someone will be with you shortly."

There was a click, and silence—not true, natural silence, but the detectable electronic non-sound that indicated I was listening to a machine. Then, music: an instrumental, sambafied version of "Paint It Black."

I was on hold. He had put me on hold. It was hard to believe, and hard to imagine a greater insult. No, I wasn't going to calmly stand by for his arrival, and I certainly wasn't going to spend that time in Muzak limbo. No more waiting around, no more fatalism. The fury flowed through my viscera and brought heat to my neck and jowls. In a sharp movement, I yanked the handset away from the phone, meaning to detach it or pull the jack from the wall. Instead the phone fell to the floor, from where I kicked it against the wall with precisely targeted power. Its beige plastic casing fractured. The handset, still in my hand, erupted with a synthetic siren noise, a designed note of agony, the sound of warranties being voided and consumer rights being forfeited. Taking the coiled flex in both hands, I pulled on it like I was starting a motorboat. The complaints from the handset ceased with its separation from the phone.

It felt good to attack the hotel, to physically damage

part of it, no matter how minuscule the blemish I made on its face. I wanted more. Maybe I was a condemned man wrecking his cell, but wreck it I would. And I knew what to strike next—all I needed was a tool.

Nothing could be found in the bathroom, only tiny soaps and doll's-house bottles of shampoo. A sewing kit came as part of this little collection of courtesy objects, but was hopeless. If I smashed the mirror it might yield a deadly shard or two, but I feared it would prove deadly first and only to me. The wardrobe in the bedroom offered only featherweight slippers, a hair dryer and a shoehorn. Hilbert's suit was gone—a symbol of the offer Hilbert had made to the vile, sightless part of me I had let grow in my inward darkness over the years. The part that had been so close to taking me entirely, and which was well suited to Way Inn, well suited indeed. But the suit had disappeared, maybe reclaimed with my rejection of that offer.

The hanger that supported the suit was topped with a flat-ended spike, rather than a hook, that slotted into an irremovable ring on the rail. That spike, though utterly blunt, might just work. I took one of the hangers and felt it in my hand—yes, it could work. The painting in my room was like all the others, a treacle wave lifting over a caramel field and retreating nutmeg spheres. I raised the hanger like a hand ax and brought it down on the center of the canvas. Despite its flat head, the spike went clean through. Pulling the hanger down, it was easy to rip a long gash into the canvas, down to the bottom edge of the wooden frame. Again. Again. I made three long downward tears in the painting, the second and third on either side of the first. Then I tried to slash across it, before hacking randomly at the disintegrating fabric until it was nothing more than limp ribbons, and scraps of it littered the carpet around my feet. Finally a blow struck the wire holding the painting—now an empty rectangle trailing brown bunting—to the wall. It hit the ground with a thud and fell against my legs; disgusted, unwilling to sully my hands, I kicked it away, then anchored it with one foot and lashed at it with the other until the frame cracked at the corners.

My purpose had ebbed as the painting was reduced. At first my instinct had seemed so pure and proud—to do violence against the hotel. But I was left feeling foolish, an infant throwing an impotent tantrum for an implacable adult. This was stupid; worse, it was a criminal waste of time when I should be devoting my resources to escaping the hotel or readying myself for Hilbert's arrival. Way Inn had mesmerized me like a desert rodent confronted by a predator. Having seen its inner immensities and experienced its vexing ability to revise those spaces to suit its ends, I had quite simply jettisoned any real hope of being able to outwit it or slip around its palisades. To be in the hotel was to be subject to it.

There was outside, though. Beyond the emerald-tinted window was the same view there had been from the start: the vacant lot adjoining the Way Inn, the unfinished, ready-ruined hotels and the drab fields behind in the underachieving light of a failed afternoon. On the horizon the cluster of red lights and the equipment of the airport. It was all there, right there. I didn't have to check out or call a cab or any of that—I could just walk across the fields and it wouldn't be long until I reached the airport's perimeter fence. There was no missing it. The worst that could happen was getting picked up by the police or airport security, and that was no threat at all. A warm car piloted by earthly authority.

The window was sealed—against noise, against the uncontrolled weather, against the unconditioned air, against suicide. It was thick, composed of three layers of high-performance glass, and it had small print in its corner boasting of its qualifications and fortitude and the lofty standards it met.

I took the bent-steel chair from behind the desk—the same model Dee had used to beat down Hilbert, an omen I was counting on—and tested its weight. How much force would I need to shatter the window? Would I be up to the job? It was hard to tell—but trying would be good practice for any later effort to repel Hilbert. I held the chair by the back, as she had held it, and tried to line up my shot. Part of me was excited by the prospect of this deliberate act of destruction, and wanted to properly revel in it. Another part was filled with fear—fear I might not be up to the task, and fear of what the consequences might be if I succeeded. Images of explosive decompression, of bodies sucked from disintegrating jets, flashed through my mind.

My first swing caused the chair to bounce harmlessly off the glass with a weird, flat *crack* that sent a voltaic shock of pain up my right arm. A bad move, all the wrong muscles thrown into it at the wrong time. But my body was learning. The next swing was much better—fluid, coordinated, a useful distribution of energies—but still the window didn't give. It gave, in fact, on the third impact, breaking in its entirety into a frost of tiny fragments, but staying in its frame. I kept at it, smacking away to get through the second and third layer, tiny crumbs of emerald shrapnel flying like rice at a wedding, until the exterior pane, which had bulged out like a crystal blister, popped from its moorings and fell with a muted crash to the concrete two storeys down.

A cold wind pushed into the room and animated the curtains, bringing with it a taste of rain. The taste of outside, beyond Way Inn's regimented climate. But I wasn't free yet. I was on the second floor—too far to drop without breaking bones, or worse.

I set about stripping the bed, rolling the sheets diagonally into thick cords and knotting them together at the ends. This was something I had seen done only in comics and films, and even doing it for real had a surreal air; and the fact that it produced a serviceable rope which I could use to escape injected verity into those screen and frame fantasies in an almost unwelcome way. The hotel's myriad impossibilities were hard enough to cope with, and now I discovered unsuspected realism in the realm of Road Runner. The thought made me smile as I worked, and I could see the Looney Tunes side of Way Inn itself— painted doorways that become real, the hotel's paradoxical circuits and dead ends, its infinity as a looped background, the same details racing past a character as they run, legs a-blur, on the spot.

When my makeshift rope was complete, I anchored it to one of the legs of the bed and threw the loose end out of the window. Without hesitating long enough to allow doubts to germinate, I slung my bag over my shoulder, wrapped the sheet around my hand and under my arms, and climbed onto the window ledge.

As soon as I gave up my footing on the floor, the drop to the ground looked twice as severe. Fragments of glass crunched under my feet and fell over the edge. My confidence in my plan wavered—it was a lot of faith to put in the physics of Saturday-morning cartoons.

I leaned out, moving my center of gravity into space, letting the sheet take more and more of my weight. It felt secure. The chill in the air was welcome, calming me. I planted my feet against the wall of the hotel and started to walk down.

The first unwelcome surprise was the level of strain on my arms, which felt ready to pop out of their sockets. The second was the trouble I had keeping my feet gripped to the hard, slippery cladding panels that comprised Way Inn's outer surface. Plastic, anodized zinc, high-performance laminate—whatever the substance was, I was not wearing the shoes for it. As I inched my way down, a portion of me screamed to speed up, to get it over with—but every aspect of the operation was tenuous indeed, a hair from betraying me, and the only progress I permitted myself was achingly slow.

Then the impatient part of me got its wish. I fell. In a single scrambling second the rope gave way and I dropped two or three feet. My feet lost their purchase and flailed out, and I swung on the rope like Tarzan before slamming into the window of the room beneath mine. I almost let go of the rope altogether. But the fall stopped and my tether regained its security as suddenly as it had lost it. For long moments I did nothing but hang there, feeling my heart hammering in my chest, thanking my lucky stars for its continued beating, and trying to figure out what had gone wrong. It was, I guessed, the bed—my weight had been enough to pull it across the room, giving me that sickening taste of free fall.

With some ungainly scrabbling, I reclaimed my footing and resumed my descent. The pain in my side from the impact had not eased; sharp edges rubbed against soft tissues. A cracked rib, perhaps. The bones and sinews in my hand were being steadily crushed by the sheet wrapped around it. But down I went, and within a few minutes I was standing on the ground.

A chain-link fence blocked any direct path to the hotel access road, and the vacant lot next door was sealed off by glossy hoardings. But that was the way I needed to go, running roughly parallel to the access road, toward the airport beacons. I walked toward the rear of the hotel, past wheelie bins and fire doors. The hoarding along the edge of the site soon gave way to scrappy orange plastic fencing mesh strung between rebar spikes hammered into the ground. This I could just step over. And like that I was free. I took a last look back at the Way Inn, its tinted windows mute but for the shattered one trailing knotted white sheets. A dark figure stood in that vacant frame, thrown into silhouette by the lights of the room behind him.

Had anything ever grown in the fields behind the hotels? It was tough to imagine any green springing from that hard, sterile sod. They had been ploughed into neat corduroy furrows but showed no evidence of vegetable life beyond specks of weed. Between the fields ran shallow, straight drainage ditches rather than charming hedgerows. I saw no machinery, no farm buildings, no animals, no trees. Nothing but the gray horizon and its beckoning red lights.

When my mother and I made our last trip together to see my father, farmers still razed their fields after harvest. Trains would pass through clouds of black smoke rising from a landscape being scoured by snaking ribbons of orange flame. At the end of the year, the world was ceremonially destroyed. I watched from the window seat, perhaps the only person paying attention to the scene—an unnoticed, unremarked catastrophe unfolding in plain sight. But it gave me a focus that was not my mother. She had rebuffed my childish efforts at conversation and the questions I asked about that unexpected journey. I had been fed monosyllables and silence—a silence that concealed great movements and realignments I was not to be told about, the silence generated by a woman forming resolutions. Even at that young age, I knew better than to push my luck and demand answers or entertainment. I wanted very much to think of some combination of words that might break the spell that held my mother since she had made three phone calls that morning. Innocuous phone calls, simple queries to hotels as she tried to find out where my father was staying. The third call had ended abruptly. Then we had left the house for the railway station. I never found the words that broke that spell, so instead I was left with the view. Burning fields: a renewal, but to me it resembled Hell.

My foot struck something hard, breaking my reverie. It was a smooth, pale stone a little smaller than my fist, oddly clean of the dirt it rested on. The sort of rubble I imagined a diligent farmer would have combed from his fields. But a couple of steps farther along there was another, egg-like and incongruous. Others were in view, and as I walked their number steadily increased until it was hard to move forward without stepping on them. They filled the field's furrows and were soon numerous enough to bury the soil altogether. I was left stumbling across a plain of pebbles. Was this a natural landscape or part of an agricultural process I had never encountered? How had it come about? The stone field stretched away as far as I could see to my left and right, and ahead was marked only by a shadowy growth. None of this was the product of nature, surely—indeed, the stones looked as if they had been selected for consistency and raked level.

I altered my course slightly to head toward the dark outcropping that was the only nearby feature in the stone field. Since breaking out of the hotel I hadn't seen any sign of human activity. By any logical configuration of terrain I should have encountered the old road long ago. Assuming I had been keeping a straight line roughly parallel with the motorway, as had been my intention, I would have encountered it within minutes. Thinking on it, where was the motorway? Its roar, once inescapable, had faded, and there was no orange glow to my right.

The red lights were constant, though, and some order was visible in their arrangement as I drew closer. Some regularity was cohering on the horizon itself—it was not an indistinct blur but a roofline, a suggestion of a long, low building, exactly the kind you might find near an airport.

What I reached first, though, was simpler: the outcropping, which revealed itself to be nothing more than a large, flat boulder, groomed and smooth. Still, it offered an elevation of a foot or two above the stone field, so I climbed onto it to see if that advantage offered any better insight into my surroundings. From above, I could see the small pale pebbles had been arranged in concentric rings around the boulder, radiating from it like frozen and elegant ripples. Like the patterns in a Zen meditation garden.

Exactly like that.

The long, low building filled the horizon. It was the horizon. Four storeys, off-white cladding panels, a grid of tinted windows. The red lights were on the roof of this groundscraper. They were not for navigation or for warning aircraft, they were letters.

WAY INN.

Another hotel? No. The same hotel.

I was still inside the hotel.

At once, it was obvious. What I had imagined to be the outdoors was nothing more than an immense courtyard, surrounded on all sides by Way Inn. My escape had been an illusion, a mere stroll in one of the hotel's interminable inner lacunae.

I sat on the rock and stared at the looming cliff face of the hotel, hollowed out by this discovery. Maybe there was nothing more than this—everything I knew, every place I had been, was no more than a tolerated aberration in the uniform, porous structure of Way Inn. The entirety of reality revealed as nothing more than a mote floating in a hotel courtyard. There was no way out, only ways deeper in.

A single fire door punctuated the windowless ground floor of the hotel, and it had been left ajar. An invitation, a taunt. Come back inside. Where else is there to go?

Inside the door, however, all was not quite as I expected. I was not in one of the typical ground-floor spaces, but instead a long, bare corridor with white-painted breezeblock walls and a poured concrete floor that made loud echoes of my footsteps. This sparse avenue was lit by plain fluorescent strips which buzzed and blinked, turning piecemeal sections of the path ahead momentarily dark, as if the corridor was holding itself in the realm of the real only by force of a titanic, unseen act of will. There were no doors to try, just occasional abstract paintings, and I heard the fire door slam closed behind me. For the second time, I rued not leaving a door propped open, but I doubted I could have made any lasting difference to the behavior of an aperture the hotel wanted closed. It decided where I could go and I would be deluded if I thought otherwise. My desire to escape was purely ornamental now—what propelled me forward was a grim form of curiosity, a bleak interest in what Way Inn had arranged for me.

The corridor terminated in an anonymous black door with no number on it. I tried the handle and it opened easily. On the other side was more corridor—but again, there was a variation on the familiar pattern. This portion of the hotel was only dimly lit and the impeccable minimal décor of a global chain was gone, replaced with kitschy 1950s Americana. The carpet was night blue and woven with a design of stylized yellow stars. The pattern was repeated on the wallpaper, but inverted—tiny blue pinprick stars on a yellow background. The exact color scheme was hard to make out as the only light had a reddish tinge, and was cast from a source farther down the corridor. And while the hotel had previously showed the same flawless standard of maintenance wherever I went, here it had let its standards slip. The carpet was worn through to its burlap structure in patches and the wallpaper was loosening and stained. Only the paintings looked as they did elsewhere—and I was struck by the atemporality of their design, the way they fitted into this retro environment as well as they had everywhere else.

Where had I come from to get here? I looked and saw without much surprise that the door I had used was numbered 219. In one direction, the corridor advanced into darkness; the other way was toward the arterial red glow. Toward the glow, then.

Many of the rooms I passed were open, and looking in them I saw I had missed the party of the century. Empty miniatures bottles lay thick on the floors and glass Manhattans had been built on the surfaces of the period furniture. Ashtrays overflowed with cold cigar butts and lipstick-stained cigarette ends. The sheets on the beds were twisted and splashed. Furniture was smashed and clothing, male and female, was everywhere, often torn. An airless blow-up doll was draped over one of the televisions, analogue snow showing through the translucent pink plastic of its abdomen. All the rooms had small, ancient televisions, and all were switched to empty channels, casting shivering blue static shadows across these depopulated scenes of debauchery. The air was tainted with stale tobacco smoke, sour sweat and evaporated dregs of liquor; and those odors masked a deeper waft of corruption—decay of bodies, of buildings, of minds.

After twenty or thirty meters the corridor opened up on one side, becoming a gallery or mezzanine overlooking a courtyard. I paused at the iron railing, its yellow paint measled with rust, and looked down on a defunct kidney-shaped swimming pool, its dry bottom choked with rubbish. The sky was a dull bronze and lacked a basic ingredient of sky-ness; I knew it had never been warmed by a sun. What illuminated the courtyard and sent bloody shadows into the corridor was a giant neon sign, standing like a totem pole at the open end of the U of buildings.

WAY

INN

NO

VACANCIES

Three of those words were lit, humming red; the NO was unpowered. Vacancies, of course.

I was a moth to this sign. In thrall to a compulsion I could not understand, I descended the staircase at the end of the mezzanine. The sign was a classic from the post-War golden age of the American motor hotel, designed to be seen by travellers in chrome-dazzled shark-finned cars driving along newly built interstate highways. The lettering of WAY INN was elaborate, suggestive of copperplate and California, an early branding scheme that had been abandoned long ago. Before it had been homogenized by corporate identity consultants. This was Way Inn back when it was small, local, quirky, before it became a global behemoth. Why had it preserved this relic of itself, sequestered deep in the inner hotel? Unguessable sentimentality? And why, then, let it get trashed? Was this a hideaway for Hilbert and his kind; one of the silent, secret places he alluded to?

As I walked across the courtyard, I kicked empty miniatures and beer cans into the pool. A couple of inches of coffee-black liquid lingered at the pool's lowest point, and its diving board was encrusted with brown stains. Among the bottles and cans floating in the filthy residue was a long, blond wig. The white webbing of the poolside recliners sagged on rusting frames. Pornographic magazines from four decades were strewn here and there. Party hats and strings of plastic beads. Syringes. A silent place, yes—apart from the dead sky, what made this mystery motel uncanny was the total hush that surrounded it like a moat; not the contented quiet of the countryside, but an anechoic void of terrifying nullity. All that could be heard, apart from my own shuffling, clattering steps through the litter, was the buzz of the mighty neon sign.

The sign—it was why I was here. It was what I had been brought here to see. And I was not the first. Burned-out candles ringed the metal pillar that supported the neon letters, and inscrutable patterns had been scrawled in chalk and spray paint on the concrete. What a shabby place Hilbert's utopia turned out to be—a shitty dead end where there was nothing to do but get wasted and screw, a world without limits limited to the low-grade pleasures of a motel. Not a constant cocktail party but an eternal lost weekend, raiding a bottomless minibar and sweating under a sunless dome.

And beyond the motel, nothing. A Martian desert marked by patches of black scrub. No, not scrub: bodies, dark-suited, scattered in the wasteland behind the sign. No water in the pool, nothing on TV, no highway, nowhere to go, and only one really sure way to check out.

A couple of armchairs, removed from the rooms, sat facing the sign. I sat in one and gazed up at the crackling red neon.

"Hello," I said.

The sign did nothing.

"I'm looking for a sign," I said. "Are you the sign?"

The sign went dark. But not wholly dark—three of its letters were still lit, the *y* of WAY and the *ES* at the end of VACANCIES.

YES

"Am I alive or dead?"

The YES disappeared, leaving the motel forecourt in night, its outlines only barely perceptible against the hellish bronze firmament.

"Yes or no only, huh?"

YES

"Am I dead? Did Hilbert kill me?"

The NO of NO VACANCIES lit up. No, not dead. That was good. It was a start.

"Does Hilbert want to kill me?"

YES

"Is there a way out?"

YES

"So I can get out?"

YES

"Where? How?"

The sign died.

"Yes or no, right. OK." I tried to reformulate what I wanted to ask. "Will I find the way out?"

NO

"Does Dee know the way out?"

YES

"So if I find Dee, I'll find the way out?"

YES

"Do you know where Dee is?"

YES

"It's you, isn't it? You're shielding Dee from Hilbert."

YES

I could just about see it now—at every stage the hotel had directed me toward Dee. And Hilbert's interventions had driven us apart again. I had assumed that Hilbert was working on instructions set by the hotel—but what if he wasn't? What if he was the servant who was no longer proving reliable, who could no longer hear the voice of his master, his sanity bending and fracturing under the strain of his long acquaintance with infinity? He had direct contact with his god, and it was destroying him, as it would destroy any man. All at once I was ambushed by an emotion: pity. Not pity for Hilbert, but pity for the hotel, forced to rely on such delicate, breakable creatures as we humans. A race that had been given the powers of a god, and used that power to build a chain of hotels. Maybe other, more inspired species were making towering, epic use of the Way Inn elsewhere, fashioning palaces and libraries, utopias and total artworks. Not us; we built a hotel, and limited our expressions of pride to the make of coffee brewed in the lobby.

Inadequacy took me, a sucking wave drawing the sand out from under my feet. I was in the presence of an oracle, perhaps on the slopes of Olympus itself, able to ask and be answered. And all I could think about was the immediate conundrum facing me, the question of evading Hilbert.

"Do you know the meaning of life?"

NO

Too much to ask. The hotel's brush-off didn't mean life was meaningless, merely that it didn't know the answer. And why should it? I could plumb a lesser mystery. But what was there?

•

"Can I help you at all, madam?"

"Watch my son, please."

"Are you a guest at the hotel?"

"My husband is. Watch my son, I'll be back shortly."

I am sitting on a black leather armchair that is far too large for me. My feet do not touch the ground. The man who had spoken to my mother, who wore a red waistcoat with shiny silver buttons and white shirtsleeves, leaned down to my level.

"What's your name?"

"Neil," I said.

"Would you like some juice, Neil?"

"I would like that." My mother was nowhere to be seen. The theater with the silver tray and the little disc of layered paper was acted out for me. I could ask for things and they would appear, and they would appear with panache. Although I was alone, I felt safe. After that agonizing train journey through a flame-racked world, I am warm and people are smiling at me and bringing me drinks. *This is a hotel*, I thought, and I know that I like hotels.

Big ice cubes, the biggest I've ever seen. "The Americans like their ice." Something my father said. It had been cryptic to me when he said it. Americans? We were in England. But here was a glass of big American ice cubes. There was a plastic scepter I could use to move them around.

It's an American chain of hotels, one that arrived in England in the early 1970s and has been expanding rapidly ever since. My twelve-year-old self understands at last. The memory gets a little richer, a little more detailed, as if it has access to better bandwidth. The plastic stirrer has a head shaped into the letters *WI*. I want to be able to intervene, to do the guiding that was never done.

And then my mother reappears. I don't remember if she said anything to me, but she took my hand with a firmness that neared the threshold of hurt and I was pulled from my chair and back out into the city. I don't remember which city. The juice was not even half finished—out of character for me, I had been saving it, savoring it, enjoying every freezing sip. My mother's face was wet and she quaked in an odd way, as if suppressing a laugh, but she was an epic, inconceivable distance from laughter. And I wasn't interested in what had upset her—instead I was furious, I wanted only to go back to that comfortable, solicitous place.

Later, though not much later, I understood that I had been just offstage for the terminal act of my parents' marriage. An incomprehensible psychic catastrophe had taken place in the realm of the adults and I had missed it. Like so much of childhood, all I had known on that day was random movement and unreadable motives, which to the grown-ups were transfers and dissolutions of lifetime importance. It took years to reassemble the pieces. But the frame, the hotel, was there from the start—the hotel was where adult things happened. It was the opposite of stifling, dreary childhood. It was the world beyond.

Although my mother never explained that day to me, she did, years later, try to explain her undimmed rage toward the man she had married, my father. I was expected to suckle all the explanation I needed from three words: he was unfaithful. And I couldn't: it wasn't enough. Even once I understood it on a technical level, even when I was able to infer that it wasn't a single deed but a history, a central element of his character, I couldn't endorse the severance on an emotional, visceral level. It was my mother I found myself struggling to forgive, not my father. She had ensured he would never return.

"Was my father with a woman that day?"

YES

"And my mother caught them together? In a Way Inn? In Way Inn?"

YES

And that was it, the central unanswered questions in my life given answers. Hotels were where adult things happened. Where I would no longer be bound by all the tedious restraints of childhood—its material privations, and my mother's sense of right and wrong, which had wronged me by depriving me of my father. I had rejected all that out of a desire to emulate that lost, seductive man. Even he had turned away from that life, and had been horrified by my success in becoming his image. But it was not too late to change course.

The sign crackled and WAY INN VACANCIES again burned red, obliterating the hotel's last answer to me.

"How do I find Dee?" I asked, forgetting to format my question, wanting—needing—something more than just affirmation or denial. "Can you show me?"

Nothing changed. The oracle had spoken. The moving finger writes, and, having writ, moves on. But Dee had implied that the hotel was always speaking to those guests that interested it, and the key was to listen. In the noise of everything that had happened to me, there was a signal, information that I had missed.

"You've already shown me, haven't you?" I said. "It's in front of me, isn't it? The way to Dee, the way out."

The only answer was the electric fizz of the sign against the dawnless dusk. I turned my head to look out over the desert and listened to the rhythmic chirping of a cricket.

A cricket? Was there wildlife in this monstrous place? Even insect life struck me as unlikely. Within a hundred meters of the motel, the notional "surface" of the waste crawled like magma, and the distant hills moved and churned as slow as clouds. It was a bubbling mirage, not terrain. I didn't know what had felled those of Hilbert's colleagues who had left their remains out on that unreal tundra, but I was ready to guess that beyond this bubble of dilapidated Americana lay a realm fundamentally incompatible with life of our kind. A sound that should have been soothing, the sound of sun-scorched summer parks, started to saw away at my nerves. The pseudo-cricket's song was coming from behind me, from within the hotel.

I left my seat and walked back up the steps to the second-floor gallery, following the beat of the noise. It grew steadily louder—not a cricket, but a shrill electronic alarm, coming from the dark interior. I already knew which room to look in.

Two-nineteen was locked, but my black keycard opened it. Inside, the room was exactly as I had left it—as I had left it when I exited via the window hours previously. The television was still set to the WELCOME MR. DOUBLE screen, the telephone was still in pieces on the floor, surrounded by smithereens of safety glass. The bed had, as I guessed, been pulled into the middle of the room, its corner wedged under the window; I crossed to the empty frame and looked out. The same vacant lot, the same red lights on the misty horizon, the same drab fields. Down by the edge of Way Inn's plot a small figure was clambering over the orange plastic fence and, as I watched him, he turned and saw me in the window. Opposed mirrors, multiple reflections stretching away into nothingness—mirrors in time as well as space, weird extrusions and recursions in the hotel's bubble of exceptionality. Myself, I was looking at myself.

Fearing the implications of this sighting, I shrank back from the window. Strange loops, Möbius strips, closed circuits. The alarm, continuing to bleat away, was coming from the clock radio, which had been knocked off the bedside table when the bed had been yanked across the floor. I picked up the radio and hit snooze. The digital display read 3 33. If not a time, then a number. It had been whispered and screamed at me from the start.

Once again, Way Inn had changed what lay outside room 219. And I barely blinked. I was getting used to its habits at last. We were back to the usual décor, and the layout of the MetaCenter Way Inn. Turning left, I found the lifts and stairwell in the usual place, but the stairs led only up—a poured concrete floor had replaced the descending flight. But up was what I needed.

Room 333 looked the same as all the other rooms on the third floor, and all the other rooms on all the other floors. Just as its global sameness allowed Way Inn to expand freely—it was never a surprise to see a Way Inn, and they never promised anything surprising—I saw that it made it easy for determined individuals to hide in plain sight. And Dee was certainly determined—that had also been obvious from the start.

A DO NOT DISTURB sign hung from 333's doorknob. I listened at the door and heard, I believed, the rustling of someone within. Not being able to summon any alternative ideas, I knocked.

The rustling ceased. I knocked again.

Another bout of silence, then a voice from within: "Yes?"

For a fleeting instant I considered saying "housekeeping," but to shovel more deception into this relationship would be a bad move. "It's Neil. Neil Double."

A pause. "Go away."

"I want to apologize. I really messed up. Hilbert had wheedled me into something I didn't understand. The last thing I wanted was to put you in danger."

"Go away, Neil."

"Please. You're still in danger, we both are. Hilbert is crazed. He's not serving the hotel anymore, he's on a personal crusade, and the aim is us, dead."

No answer. I waited, but the silence was stubborn.

"How do you think I found you, Dee? The hotel told me where you are. It's helping me, not Hilbert. We have to work together."

The black keycard was in my jacket pocket, and I felt its width between my fingers—that little bit of extra luxury, executive heft, pure display meant to flatter the holder. Would it open this door? Or would that merely bring Hilbert down on us? But as I considered using the keycard, the door opened.

Dee stood before me, wearing the same leather jacket and sweatpants as before, but Dangermouse had been ousted from the T-shirt by Joy Division.

"No Dangermouse?"

"Blood on it." She stared at me, her words a reminder of my treachery, and a warning of the probable consequences if I wronged her again.

"I wouldn't recommend the dry-cleaning service here."

Dee didn't reply, but stood aside to allow me through the door.

Room 333 was a mess. Not a degenerate mess like the rooms in the wasteland motel, but the habitat of a less-than-fastidious workaholic hermit. Desk and bed were thick with papers, mostly loose leaves torn from pads and covered with Dee's esoteric, geometric doodles and devices. There were other documents, too—misfolded hand-annotated maps, a couple of textbooks and paperbacks. More paper covered every wall, including the screen of the television: hundreds of printouts of photographs of the abstract paintings. Dee's tablet was slotted into a tiny clearing on the desk and attached to a keyboard and stylus pad. The paintings shifted and shuffled without a pause on its screen, having their edges matched and their vectors plotted.

As the armchair was stacked with room service trays, I sat on a free corner of the bed.

"I've seen the inner hotel, Dee," I said. "The hotel won't let me out, but it did let me *in*. I've seen the motel. I spoke to the neon sign. It answered my questions."

"I've seen the motel," Dee said, a note of injured pride in her voice, as if she was anxious to stress that she had seen it first, or irked that I had found it at all. I was privately pleased with this reaction—it was human. "There are some dark places in the inner hotel, darker even than that."

"I'm sure," I said. "Look, I don't doubt you know the inner hotel better than I do, that's why I'm here. The hotel won't let me leave. But I think it will let us leave together."

In my peripheral vision, an arabesque uncurled across the pictures stuck to the wall, and evaporated when I tried to focus on it; a fleeting impression of a larger interconnection. I found myself unable to trigger it again. Disquieted, I looked away, picking up the book my left hand had been resting on. *Gödel, Escher, Bach* by Douglas Hofstadter, battered and fringed with bookmarks like all Dee's books. It was unknown to me, but before I could flip it over to read the back, Dee snatched it out of my hands.

"Do you mind?" She started to gather up the papers around me, piling them without apparent system.

"Escher—the guy who did the endless staircases and upside-down castles? Fits right in here."

"Maurits Cornelis Escher."

"Maurice?"

She ignored me and continued to collect her papers, stuffing them into her giant shoulder bag.

"I spoke to the hotel," I repeated. "It answered my questions."

"It can be pretty chatty when it wants to be," Dee said, without warmth or very much in the way of sincerity. "I put it down to mostly having to deal with psychopaths. And aeons of loneliness."

"It said Hilbert was going to kill me," I said. "So we have that in common."

"Congratulations. What else did it say?"

"It said that you knew the way out. That if I found you, I would find the way out. And that it had been shielding you from Hilbert."

"Well, babe, I'm afraid it might be wrong about that."

This worried me—I realized that up to this point my faith in Dee's ability to extract me from the hotel had been total. Way Inn's ability to reshape reality had impressed me so greatly that I had assumed, without good reason, that its pronouncements would be infallible. But what if it was capable of error? And why shouldn't it be capable of mendacity?

"We should at least try," I said, sensing the weakness in my voice.

Dee didn't reply. Working with frantic haste, she had cleared all the papers and books from the bed into her bag, and had moved on to plucking the photos from the walls, quickly and without care. As she took the pictures from the gridded positions, again I thought I saw something in their interrelations—not a simple continuation from one image to another, but a sense of harmony. But it was gone at the moment of my noticing.

"Don't tidy up on my behalf," I said. "I'm sorry to intrude. I know it's not like you were expecting visitors."

"I'm not tidying," she said. "I'm leaving." A shake of the head, eyes closed. "Fleeing, really."

"Fleeing?" For crucial seconds the word made no sense to me, as if an archaism like *jousting* had dropped unexpectedly into the conversation. "What?"

"You're an idiot, Neil," Dee said with a kind of bitter amusement. "I like you in a way—God knows why—but you're an idiot. You wander around in the inner hotel, Hilbert's domain, his place of business, and you don't even wonder where he is? Why he hasn't pounced? You might think he's crazy but you can't imagine he's stupid. He's more than capable of biding his time. He'll wait."

"Wait? For what?"

Dee smiled—a sad, pitying smile. "Wait for you to find me. Then he has us both."

While she spoke, a chesty rattle had arisen in the air conditioning, and when she stopped it became a deep, far-dragged moan as if answering her.

"Shit."

"Major reconfiguration of hotel pseudofabric, and close," Dee said. She had cleared the walls and desk, leaving behind Blu-Tak acne and a stuffed bin, and was now topping off her bag with the few clothes in the room. "Air is forced through the system. Like a Tube train coming."

"He's coming."

This time, Dee's smile to me was a crazed grin—no fear, only exhilaration. "Oh yes, he's coming. Coming round the mountain."

The radio-alarm on the bedside table shrieked with interference, a wail like nothing in nature. breaking down into agonized chattering.

"That's not good," Dee said, real consternation appearing on her face. Glitching blocks of acid-colored digital stress spattered the screen of her tablet, the only possession she hadn't packed. "Not good, not good."

"What do we do?" I was standing.

"We go. Right now." And she was away, out of the door, grabbing her keycard from its slot as she went. It was, I saw, white. Awash with panic, saturated with it on a molecular level, I scrambled to pick up my own bag and was about to follow when I saw something jutting from the teetering room-service trays on the armchair, something I recognized: the wooden handle of a steak knife. I pulled it out from the pile, ignoring the trays as they slid to the floor in a cacophony of smashing plates and glasses. The knife was short, serrated and dirty, but it had a good, nasty point. I stuffed it into my jacket pocket and left the room.

A miracle. Dee was waiting for me in the corridor. A real miracle. She had waited. Never had she looked so beautiful to me. But her eyes, flashing with impatience, left mine and passed over my shoulder, and her expression twisted into one of terror.

I turned. Hilbert was stalking down the corridor toward us, taller than I remembered, elongated with fury. His suit flowed with black energy and the walls of the hotel caved out as he passed, as if straining to give him space. The lights stuttered and threw improbable shadows, catching angles that could not and should not be present.

All along the corridor, the abstract paintings boiled in their frames, spheres and arcs lashing across the canvases.

"Housekeeping!" Hilbert bellowed, feedback whine stripping the humanity from his consonants. He surged forward, a movement that was accompanied by an awful oceanic shifting in the ground beneath me, as if the distance between us had contracted. I had no time to consider evasion before he cannoned into me, head lowered, no finesse, a bull charge. My torso was replaced by a torso-shaped entity of pure pain and I registered being airborne. With a sickening, bitter breath the air was slammed from my body by the wall of the Way Inn and then the floor of the Way Inn.

Curled up, gasping, I found myself unable to move. My rib cage was a barrel of agony and I feared I had dislocated a shoulder. My legs were lost luggage, and something had fallen across them—one of the abstract paintings, knocked from the wall by my impact. As I tried to regain full use of them, Hilbert appeared above me, face a blur, not pausing before his attack.

I had a hold on the painting and, acting on instinct, was able to lift it to shield my throat from the elbow Hilbert had aimed at it. The painting's frame cracked apart, but Hilbert's strike was deflected onto the floor. Adrenalin fired through my body—still clutching the sides of the painting, I rolled over, onto Hilbert, the canvas covering his head and chest. He thrashed beneath this shroud and I saw sepia ovoids and curves creeping from the design onto my hands and toward my wrists. Letting go of the painting with a yelp of horror, I clumsily climbed to my feet and hunted in my pocket for the steak knife. Finding it, I knelt and stabbed through the painting into Hilbert, once, twice, three times. Blood leaped around the blows and Hilbert's legs convulsed like eels.

"Neil! NEIL!"

Dee, farther down the corridor, was urgently beckoning to me. "Come on! He won't stop! We have to go! Now!"

I sprinted toward her, striving to ignore the white-hot iron of pain that pushed into my side with each contact my feet made with the floor. My left hand was sticky with blood, fingers aching with cramp around the wooden handle of the knife. I remembered the sensation of driving the point into Hilbert—the split-second of resistance, then the fleshy give, the purr of the saw teeth against a torn edge. Seeing me stare dumbly at the reddened weapon, reading my thoughts, Dee said: "He'll be fine. You need to worry about us." Resolution flashed in her eyes.

A clatter and a thud sounded behind me. Hilbert had cast off the ruined painting and had sprung upright like an insect. He glared at us, poised and ready for another charge. Glancing at Dee for a lead on what to do, I saw her engrossed in her tablet. Two paintings were aligned on the screen, edges matched—she flicked these apart and they separated to find places in a new sequence.

Dizziness overcame me—but this was not dizziness, it was the same seasick swell I had felt earlier during Hilbert's attack. And before my unbelieving eyes, the corridor between us and Hilbert lengthened. He went from ten meters away to a hundred in a giddy second before being folded behind a corner. Another wall somehow slid into the long passage that had grown beside us, turning it into a T-junction.

My throat was tight, almost too tight to speak, and the words came in a whisper. "You did that?"

"We can't count on it working again," Dee said. "Let's go."

Both lumbered with bags, we half-strode, half-ran through the hotel—fast walking broken by bursts of jogging, to which I would always have to call a halt, wheezing and clutching my side while spots jumped in my vision. I had broken a rib, I was sure, and while my shoulder was not dislocated, it hurt abominably.

Dee led the way, of course, and at first I was too pre-occupied with the tumbling afterimages of my struggle with Hilbert to pay much heed to where we might be going. But I became aware of variations in my surround-ings, variations that were slight but deeply unnerving. Thus far, every part of Way Inn I had seen had followed a strictly orthogonal plan: the corridors were straight and intersected at right angles. In the locales we were now traversing, all these angles were somewhat *off.* We turned eighty- and hundred-degree corners and the corridors kinked and curved.

"Where are we?" I asked.

"The inner hotel," Dee said. "Deep. I didn't change Hilbert's relative position, I changed ours, projecting us into the hotel. The deeper you get, the more the environ-ment is susceptible to . . . manipulation."

"How do we get out?"

"I don't know. Not the way we came, that's gone. And this"—she waved the tablet at me, its screen still jum-bling and sorting paintings—"is barely helping. Hilbert was twisting things round as well as me. Local changes to the hotel fabric have far-reaching nonlocal effects, univer-sal effects in fact: it's like a kaleidoscope, a small shift means the whole pattern changes. The first time I tried active spatial kinesis, I was lost for a week. A week of Pringles and five-pound jars of salted nuts." She shook her head at the memory. "Like a savage."

"Minibarbaric," I said, and for the first time since I had met her, Dee laughed; she had chuckled at me, or smiled at a joke of mine or an instance of my stupidity, but this was an authentic laugh, head back, red hair blazing in the halogen spotlighting. There was no discernible natural light any more and curious shadows without origin made unsettling patterns on the walls.

We passed a light well, but it provided no illumination. The sky above it was the dull, angry, bronze dome that had sheltered the motel. We moved at tangents through angles acute and obtuse, past doors whose numbers were no longer sequential. I thought I detected an adverse camber in the floor, but I could never be certain of it.

"What happens if we are lost?" I said. "Can we get into these rooms?"

"Some, probably," Dee said. We had stalled for some time at a junction, one corridor branching into two in a sharp *Y*. Dee had photographed all the nearby paintings and was engrossed in a calculation, muttering as she worked. This was a person unaccustomed to being in company. I wanted to talk to remind her of my presence, to break into her dialogue with herself. And I was concerned she was sticking to her own ascetic standards in assessing how far we could go, how fast, and for how long. Two days of continual exertion, only thinly separated by sleep, were taxing me heavily.

"It'll be night soon."

"Not here."

"We can't go on forever—where do we sleep?"

"We have to go on as long as we can," Dee said, distracted by her tablet. "I don't know how much distance we've put between us and Hilbert, but it can't be enough, I'll tell you that."

"I'd be reassured if I knew we could get into a room, find a bed, eat something . . . "

"Not now."

"If we're going to be lost for more than a week . . . "

This broke her from her flashing screen, and she glared at me. "We will not be lost for a week," she said, cheeks flushed. "I know more now, I can figure this out, if you could just *be quiet* for *one minute*."

Don't question her abilities, I thought, that's a lesson learned. She returned to her work and I turned to the nearest door: a room door, like all the others, with the number 378. I took my keycard from my pocket and tried it in the lock.

The light turned green. When I pressed the handle, the metal moved smoothly against metal and the door opened.

"This one's open," I said, pushing the door wider and peering in. In the gloom, there were two armchairs facing a coffee table, a bed and a flat-screen telly slab. "Hey, this room's bigger than mine."

"What the hell are you doing?"

Dee was staring at me, aghast, holding her tablet so limply I feared she might drop it. A terrible quality in her voice flushed me with ice water.

"Do I have to take that fucking card away from you? You idiot. You fucking idiot." Without waiting for a reply, she lunged toward me. I had already withdrawn the key-card from the lock and was seized by a superpowered instinct to protect it from her.

"No, it's mine!" I said in a squawk, stuffing the card back into my jacket pocket. Dee stopped, hands raised and eyes wide, visibly surprised by my reaction. It had come as a surprise to me as well.

"You have raised a big, black flag over our location," she said. "Again. How many times is that? You want that damned piece of plastic, you keep it, Gollum. But you use it again in my presence and I swear I will snap it in half and insert it in you, broken edge first."

"OK, OK, I'm sorry," I said. The card radiated shame through me and I considered breaking it myself as a gesture of regret. But a tendril of desire uncurled from an unseen place within me and suffocated the idea. "How can Hilbert know where we are? Do you know where he is?"

"He's been doing this longer than I have," Dee said. "Much longer. Decades longer. Maybe since the start. He has material advantages. And a natural affinity for the work." A smile, the flash of a scalpel under the lights of the operating theater. "Like you."

Winded, a knot of agony from neck to knees, I suddenly felt the heat of possible tears, not sadness or hurt but frustration, exhaustion—our acquaintance had become a recursive loop of distrust, with me continually returned to square one. "No affinity, not from me, not any more. I just want to go."

"And yet you keep betraying our position," Dee said. Maybe this had started as a casual barb from her, but she continued to think it over, testing it for plausibility. She stepped away from me. "You're not Hilbert, but maybe you're a drone, doing what the hotel wants without knowing it. All that time in the conference rooms . . . " Another step away.

What if she's right?

"I'm not, I'm not," I said, fighting to master my inner doubt and panic. "I've made mistakes, that's all. I'm an idiot."

"You had better be."

"I promise, I am. Shouldn't we be on our way?"

Dee blinked a couple of times. "Yes. Yes. Now." She glanced at the tablet then at the three nearest paintings in succession.

"Huh."

It wasn't a sound that inspired confidence. "What?"

"Alteration," she said. "I didn't notice anything, did you?"

I looked at the painting she was staring at, to the left of the door I had unwisely opened. And as I looked it moved. A flock of cocoa spots migrated and swelled, their edges meeting. Beneath, a caramel ocean rolled.

"Oh dear," Dee said, and the quiet detachment in her voice disturbed me only the more.

A stiff breeze, scented with clean laundry and new carpets, struck through the door of the open room, produced by its aircon, which had activated with a bellow.

"I'm always the smartest person in the room and I'm always right," Dee said. "And that always *really* sucks."

In the darkness of room 378, every angle glowed. Wherever a wall met the floor, the ceiling or another wall, there appeared a needle-thin ultraviolet seam. The shape of the room stood out like a blueprint. Along these lines, the room split apart, walls sliding against walls, furniture slipping from view, the whole space stretching away, growing from a room to a gallery to a night-filled fathomless tunnel. The wall before me folded back like cardboard, the door in it slamming shut, revealing a corridor that receded to a point, a point that bored to the center of the mind, a singularity through which sanity drained until it dropped below a horizon.

"Oh dear," Dee said. "Oh dear God."

Hilbert was in the corridor. From nowhere, he had slipped himself into the emerging space. The very matter around us screamed under the outrages being perpetrated against it. He smoothed the aurora incandescence from his pinstripe lapels. The lines, the angles, in his suit and in the walls: he had come together out of the hotel itself.

"First order, explicit, nontrivial spatial kinesis," he said, walking toward us quite unhurriedly. "Do you know how that impacts on me, on Way Inn? Pronounced meta-structural curvature. Laminar flux. Random decoupling. Perception Dopplering. I wouldn't be surprised if every single guest has a nightmare tonight. And as for me"—he looked down at his shirt, which was sodden red—"executive stress takes its toll. You know how weak flesh can be."

He raised his hands—black lightning arced between his limbs and the walls, UV luminescence pulsing in the white of the pinstripes and in the muted hotel colors. An architectural spasm raced toward us, striking me as a physical force and knocking me down. A deep groan, part sound and part tremor, followed the pulse through the building.

"What do executives do," Hilbert shrieked, "but execute?"

And from nowhere he was on me, a weight holding me down—but it was not him, it was Dee, who had also been thrown to the floor and who had now rolled over to straddle me. Another attack? I had led Hilbert to her too many times, and she had decided to take me out of the picture?

"Hold on," she said. "I'm going to try something."

I would have held on if I had been given the time. Instead I had the immediate sensation of being in a plummeting lift. My innards made a bid for flight. In front of me, a wall and its painting rose from the floor, blocking Hilbert's path.

The lurch ceased. Dee stood and spun on the spot, a pirouette of joy. "Wow, wow! It worked! Vertical laminar decoupling!"

Still a little queasy, I sat up. The new path Hilbert had forced through the hotel had gone; so had one of the branches of the Y-junction we were contemplating. This was a plain stretch of corridor.

With a youthful skip, Dee checked the nearest door number. "Two-seven-eight, *two*-seven-eight. We're on Two. Fantastic. Fantastic."

"Wait," I said, climbing unsteadily to my feet. "We're on Two? We went through the floor?"

"No, the floor came too," Dee said. "This whole corridor did. Hilbert had created a cross route and I, uh, uncreated it. I uncrossed it, separating it into two corridors and moving one down. Laminar flux, he said, levels moving independently—gave me the idea. Should confuse the hell out of him."

Another shudder passed through the hotel, accompanied by a deep groan.

"Trouble?" I said. As I stood, I feared my balance might have been impaired by the punishment I had taken—either that or the floor had developed a distinct slope.

"Not Hilbert trouble," Dee said. "Maybe other trouble. He was right, we can't make these big, sudden changes to the hotel with impunity. But what I'm doing is nothing compared to his slashing and burning—I've never seen him like this, so angry, so reckless."

"What if he pursues us out of the hotel?"

"Won't happen. He won't leave the hotel. He's become dependent on it, I think. It's keeping him going."

"Hell of a bargain," I said. "You get to live for ever. But you have to spend eternity in a chain hotel on a motorway."

Dee smiled. "Not so keen now, are you?"

"No."

"Do you know why I'm still helping you?"

I shook my head.

"You've made Hilbert angry," she said. "Really angry. And that makes you OK as far as I'm concerned." She woke her tablet from power save and stabbed the screen a couple of times. "Come on. We've won some time, but not much."

Wearily, I grabbed the straps of my shoulder bag. It was heavy, much heavier than it needed to be. Maybe I could lighten it, dump some clothes, dump everything but the essentials.

I knelt and unzipped the bag. Red like innards. Thin crimson plastic crinkled.

When I had gone back to room 219 after Hilbert interrogated me, my bag had been waiting on the bed. The wardrobe had been empty. There had been no sign of the pinstripe suit—my pinstripe suit.

"Dee," I said. "Hilbert's ability to do what he does. His material advantage. Does that come from his suit?"

"Yes, I think it might, at least part of it," she said. "The suit might be pseudofabric, hotel-stuff. Why?"

I pulled the Way Inn dry-cleaning bag from my luggage and held it up for her to see. "I have a suit just like it. Can we use that?"

Eyes wide, Dee looked from the suit to me and back. "That's idiotic. Totally insane. Dangerous." She broke into a blazing paradox of a grin, equal parts devilry and innocent delight. "I love it."

As I changed into the clean pinstripe and shirt, Dee wrapped my bloodstained, torn leisure clothes in the discarded dry-cleaning plastic. They could be left here, lightening my bag. She emptied my pockets, handling the black keycard with suspicion. Once I was done dressing, I did a model's turn for Dee, stripes flickering like road markings under a speeding car.

"How do I look?"

"Like a nightmare I've been having recently," Dee said.

"How does this work, anyway? This spatial kinesis."

"Your brain tries to knit what it perceives into a seamless continuum, which we call reality. Little tricks like saccadic masking, where it shuts off visual processing when we move our eye, so we don't see motion blur. In Way Inn's representation of reality, the seams are a bit more visible, and more tractable. So . . . " She faltered, lost, hunting for the words. "So you . . . just . . . feel for them. Like finding the end of the sticky tape, but in your perception of where you are in space. I'm sorry I can't explain it better."

"You learned it," I said. "Can't you teach me?"

"It took me weeks—months—of contemplation and meditation before I had any inkling of control. That's on

top of years of study of topography and topology at doc-
toral level, and a gift for pattern recognition. It's instinct
as much as anything—overcoming millions of years of
expectations about how your environs behave."

"So what good will I be able to do?"

Dee shrugged. "You might be able to stir up some
chaos, some fog of war to give us cover. At the very least,
you've saved yourself some time. You're now dressed for
your funeral."

"Thanks," I said. "That's really comforting."

"I'm not your mum. Let's get going."

We carried on, working to no plan, letting the inner
hotel unfold and reveal itself, both hoping that an exit
would appear before Hilbert did. Our progress was slowed
by the pronounced but unpredictable slant that had developed in the floor. Never was there any visible sign that the
corridor might be listing, but at times we felt ourselves
strongly tilted to one side, and at others as if we were
climbing or descending an incline. No words passed between us about the phenomenon, but I knew Dee was
experiencing it as well as me from the caution that appeared in her steps. Combined with the irregular, and
increasingly troubling, acute and obtuse angles that had
crept into the hotel layout, I had the impression of a structure buckling under stress—or of one steadily deforming
under its own mass as we approached its core. If there was
a core. Or had I already seen the center of the labyrinth,
at the motel?

All the while, I felt the heavy wool of the suit across my
shoulders. And I asked myself if I could detect any force
or capability flowing from it to me, any new potency. But
tiredness and soreness were the only answers.

"I don't feel any different," I said to Dee after hours of silence. "No special power, nothing."

"Maybe that's for the best," Dee said. "It does corrupt."

An added layer of discomfort prickled between me and the fabric. "Do you think that's what happened to Hilbert? The suit? It corrupted him?"

"No. I think Hilbert forgot where he ended and the hotel began," Dee said. "It didn't happen overnight. He's way over the edge now. He lasted a long time, longer than all the others, but no one can hold out for ever."

"Is he the last?"

"Possibly. I don't know. The last of the first generation, maybe. The ones who went upriver, got religion, got infected with *purpose*. The evangelists. It'll be functionaries now, technocrats; not ideologues, not prophets gibbering in the desert. The new generation will know there doesn't have to be a purpose—there is no need for meaning, no need for belief, all that Way Inn wants is growth; growth for its own sake."

Her voice had risen to a pitch that was either passion or despair. It was unexpected.

"You've never met any of this new generation?" I said.

"I thought I had," Dee said, looking me up and down. "But I might have been wrong about him."

"Were you meant to be one of them? The new generation?"

"Maybe. Yes. I was a poor prospect, though. I find patterns. Meaning, possibly. The hotel is subject to mathematical harmony, like the structures of leaves and seashells. There's a kind of beauty there, even in all this"—she held out her arms and raised her head, encompassing the whole of the hotel corridor around her—"banality. Possibly because of it. Way Inn took an architecture we were already distilling down to its essentials and made it pure; cultureless, placeless, global. In that, it showed us a truth about ourselves. The other chains have copied it and it in turn has learned from them. And beyond its inner threshold it takes this form, this bloodless architectural Esperanto, and makes an infinite cathedral from it. It's beautiful, for sure. You could almost call it God."

"You could indeed."

The voice arose from the matter around us, the substance of the walls and the windows, the air itself. Particles of fiber and motes of dust rose in concert from the carpet, the lights failed and stuttered back to life, switching agitatedly between full shine and power-saving mode. The aircon wailed.

Hilbert rounded a corner that had not been there moments previously. Seeing me and the suit I wore, he shook his head and frowned. "Oh, my boy . . . Such a disappointment. You, however"—his attention snapped to Dee, and he raised an accusing finger at her—"you were trouble from the start. I said as much, whatever your freak abilities. But the hotel, you know. It's so very accommodating."

This time, I didn't need a cue from Dee—I was the first to run, seeing the expression on her face, the smirk at Hilbert's words, as I spun to flee. Or at least I tried to run, but each pace was slower and tougher than the last. The subtle slope in the floor was steepening under me, a flat dash steadily becoming an exercise in mountaineering, pitching me back toward danger.

To my rear, Dee and Hilbert continued to face off, Dee retreating step by step up the growing incline, not followed by her opponent.

"Why not call it God, why not?" Hilbert said. Around him, walls distended and carpets crackled. "These are godless times. A little faith might be just the tonic."

All the paintings in the corridor were hanging at a forty-five-degree angle, toward Hilbert. I abandoned hope of climbing away and instead began to fear slipping back down. Dee, with her trainers, was doing only slightly better.

"Have you spoken to the hotel lately, Hilbert?" This, I was bemused to realize, came from my own mouth, shouted over the din of tortured metal and glass and frantic ultrahigh frequencies. "I have. It helped me. Why would it help me evade you? Maybe you're out of favor with your god."

Hilbert diverted his glare to me. Something far from human animated his gaze, an inner furnace stoked too far. "False! False! My insight is unique!"

Dee was putting precious inches between her and the maniac. I had to keep talking, to keep him trained on me. "We mortals are nothing but rats in its walls—do you think it's truly concerned with a falling-out among rats?"

"You might be mortal," Hilbert said. "Indeed, I'm about to make a very thorough demonstration of your mortality. But I am at one with forever. I am elect, preserved for special purpose."

With a loud crack, two sections of drywall between Dee and Hilbert split apart and black electricity dripped from the fissure. In the distance, behind Hilbert, the corridor bored down into a maelstrom of darkness. Hilbert, I saw, was still able to stand upright, feet flat on the carpet, unaffected by the sinking of the floor.

"You're hurting your god, Hilbert!" Dee shouted. "Don't you see? You want us so much you're tearing your precious hotel apart!"

"We all have to make sacrifices. Management is about tough decisions."

Sacrifice—the steak knife. But it had been in the pocket of my other jacket, and must have been left behind when I dumped it. A painting tumbled past us, into the abyss. My shoes lost their purchase against the pile of the carpet and I started to scrabble, feet and hands. Raw fear, an animal terror of being cornered, clamped down on my thoughts: get out, get out get out getoutgetoutgetout*getout*.

A multiplied metallic click. Every light on every lock turned green; every door in the corridor fell open, into its room. I launched myself to one side to find a secure perch on the nearest door frame. Inside the room, furniture slid and piled up in the gloom.

Dee followed my lead and jumped for the nearest door. She and Hilbert stared at me.

"Was that you?" Dee said.

Yes, I thought, yes I think it was me, but before I could say anything, Hilbert cut in. "It doesn't change anything. Nothing at all. You get a few extra seconds. Pathetic." But the raving certainty of his previous taunts was diminished.

Paintings were falling down the near-vertical shaft of the corridor like hail. Hilbert was forced to flail his arms to bat the plummeting art away from him; then he missed, and a painting caught him squarely on the temple with a spinning corner, not far from the wound Dee had opened. He staggered backward and downward. And with this distraction, the corridor righted itself a little.

There was no end to the downpour of paintings, which also fell as splintered sections of frame and bolts of canvas, the product of collisions farther up. Farther up where? How long was this corridor, how many paintings could there be? Each was a suggestive streak of spheres and radii in a mounting racket of crashing and grinding. Hilbert was occupied full-time in deflecting the paintings as they reached him, and appeared so enraged by the bombardment that getting out of its way never occurred to him. His gaze burned like the motorway's double yellow lines, reflecting an exploding fuel tank, but it was no longer directed at us.

The bedroom I was using as an aerie was chaos. A fallen bedside table had smashed the flat-screen TV. An armchair was on its side under the overturned bed. That was what I needed: the armchair. Standing on what had been one of the walls, I worked to free the chair from the heap of furniture and then dragged it to the door. Hilbert was continuing his furious battle with the plunging paintings.

"Bombs away," I mouthed, and pushed the armchair out into the vertical corridor.

Luck was on my side. The chair struck Hilbert in the legs, a bowling ball hitting a pin and knocking it clear out of the alley. The hotel employee somersaulted in midair, all of a sudden subject to the altered gravity, and plummeted into the abyss, making bone-crunching contact with a door frame as he fell.

This impact broke whatever effect he was having over the hotel and the corridor righted itself with an immense cacophony of splintered paintings and colliding furniture. I had been crouched on the wall of a narrow hallway; as the hotel turned I, too, was thrown into the air, the door-jamb connecting with the skull behind my left ear.

Dee was standing over me, a first sight that prompted a great rush of relief. This drained away into worry when I saw the unusual expression of sympathy and concern on her face.

"What did you do?" she said.

"Hit my head," I said.

"No. To Hilbert. To the hotel."

"Nothing. I hit him with a chair." I wanted to laugh, but there was nothing in my lungs but white-hot barbed wire. Instead, I grimaced and wheezed. "So that's another thing we have in common."

I was slumped on the floor, in a doorway, half in a room and half out. Patting myself down to identify the main site of injury, I discovered a plasticated strip of cardboard lying on my chest. One end was hook-shaped. A DO NOT DISTURB sign, fallen from the door handle.

Dee smiled at the sign, then at me. "You looked very peaceful, but I thought it was best to disturb you anyway."

"Don't worry about it."

She helped me up. I had enlarged my collection of agonies, but without crippling myself. The ringing in my head, the writhing black tension in the electricity of my brain and the swimming spheres behind my eyes challenged my crumpled ribs for king of the traumas.

"Where is he?" I asked.

"Hilbert? Gone. For now. He can't be killed as long as he's inside the hotel."

"But if he leaves?"

Dee shrugged. "Are you good to get moving?"

I took an experimental step, and kicked debris. The corridor was littered with tattered paintings, their frames no more than matchwood.

"What a mess," I said. "Is the whole hotel like this?"

"No," Dee said. "From what I can tell, Hilbert was generating a localized depression in the hotel fabric, like the effect of a black hole on space-time." She shook her head at the havoc. "Violent. Reckless. He's lost it."

"He's crazy."

"He was always crazy, but the craziness came with a code. Boundaries. Limits. His own sense of fair dealing. Through-and-through perverse, but a structure all the same. That's gone. He's capable of anything."

"It works to our advantage. He's irrational, improvising, making mistakes. He didn't even see the chair I dropped."

"True."

My third step sent a spike through my knee, and I wobbled. For a moment I feared the floor had begun to tilt again. My vision doubled and blurred—the paintings beneath my feet lost their edges, their patterns melted together, coalesced . . .

No boundaries. The blurred edge.

"We can trick him," I said.

"How?"

"Can you get us back to the MetaCenter Way Inn? The first floor?"

Dee puffed out her cheeks. "Maybe. The way the hotel is shaken up, though, it could take days, or longer."

Once again, the paintings on the floor were fractured, many facedown, none contiguous. But the flowing image they had, for a neuron's flight, generated for me lingered as an after-impression, a ghost that orbited and rotated and smiled for me when my eyes were closed. A grand design, the brother or sister to what I had glimpsed on the walls in Dee's room.

"It doesn't matter," I said. "I know the way."

The DO NOT DISTURB sign was still in my hand. I hung it back on the doorknob, flipping it over after looking at the chaos past the threshold, the minibar contents dripping from the gaping fridge onto the shards of the destroyed television.

PLEASE CLEAN THIS ROOM.

We trampled ruined corporate art.

Everything had changed around us and everything was as it had always been: familiar, banal, its muted colors and composite surfaces lit with intelligence. What had changed was within me. The hotel's air, maintained at an ideal temperature, polymer-scented and laced with WiFi, spoke to me; a forest speaking to a hunter-gatherer. The paintings were only the start: meaning could be derived from the interrelation of sequences of room numbers, from the distribution of room-service trays, from the location of DO NOT DISTURB signs. Patterns everywhere, everything data to be mined and pummelled for insight.

We found a stairwell and descended to the first floor. The stairs went no farther.

Since our last encounter with Hilbert, Dee had followed me. "I can see what you're doing," she said, "but only after you do it."

"I don't think I'm doing anything," I said. "I'm just walking." Walking, yes—walking without direction or intent, letting the hotel unfold before my feet, drifting through its currents.

Dee, staring at her tablet, said nothing, but shook her head, disbelieving. I didn't know if she was shaking it at me or at the arrangements and juxtapositions that danced in her eyes.

"You were right," I said. "It's beautiful. The grand design. The harmonic structure. All I can get is a hint of it, an impression of part of the shadow of an outline . . . "

"That's all you need. Any more, you end up like our mutual friend. It's too much."

"You taught me. You showed me. I'm different, and you did it. Everything matters, everything is unique. Everything and everybody."

"What do you mean?"

"I mean, thank you."

She had not met my gaze during this exchange—perhaps embarrassed. Perhaps something else: I suspected a return of the reserve that had defined her when we were reacquainted three days ago. An unspoken thing, a mighty and significant item of knowledge that she was holding back.

"Everything OK?" I am a man. These are the only tools I have.

"Fine. Thank you. For the thank you. Let's save the congratulations for now, shall we?"

"Sure. Can you get us to the business suite in the MetaCenter Way Inn?"

"From here, no problem," Dee said. She stopped herself. "I say no problem, but there's a couple of big problems. We might still be in the inner hotel, a simulacrum of the business center coterminal with that location in the outer hotel. So even if the exit looks clear, it might just be a closed loop."

"Yup. I've gone that way already. Climbed out of a window, ended up staring at the back of my own head. What's the other problem?"

"There is no exit from the business center. It's a dead end. No way out. A perfect trap."

"Yes," I said. I had tasted the potential in the air during the battle with Hilbert, all the doors opening at once, outside and in. I wanted to taste it again. Where better to meet than the meeting rooms. The perfect environment for unfinished business.

The suites slept behind glass, lights dim, rooms silent, chairs set up like chess pieces awaiting players. What time was it? The question had lost its relevance. I had come a long way. I thought of relativity, that time slows the faster you travel, that astronauts on a light-speed spacecraft would emerge fresh-faced while decades had passed in the world they left behind. It had been late morning when I tried to check out the first time, a matter of perhaps eighteen hours ago. Eighteen hours and millions of miles and an eternity.

Lights blinked on. The aircon muttered as if stirring in a dream. Outside the Gallery Room, I stopped. Here was as good as anywhere.

"Do you trust me?" I asked Dee. I took the black keycard from my pocket and held it up, showed it to her. She looked at me and at it, eyes reflecting glass reflecting spotlights.

"The corruption that claimed Hilbert came from within him," she said, as tender an expression on her as I had ever seen. "Do you trust yourself?"

"It's two against one," I said. "Good odds."

"As long as I'm not the one."

I shook my head. "Still suspicious. What a world."

"Do it. Trust is overrated anyway. All the treachery in the world is built on a foundation of trust."

"Cynic." I put the card into the Gallery Room slot. The light turned green and the door unlocked. I pushed it open, but didn't enter. In the dark, I saw the missing painting had been replaced. The sequence was complete again.

Nothing happened.

"Never any staff on duty when you need them," Dee said.

"We could have a Nespresso."

"Maybe you should shut that door."

I did as she said. We stood in silence. With a grunt, Dee dropped her bulging bag from her shoulder. How she had carried it all this time, I didn't know—with all those books and papers, it must have been an enormous strain. But it was a life's work, I supposed: the sum of her research and discoveries. If I carried the total output of my endeavors on my back, I, too, would be reluctant to part with it.

With a twist of horror I realized that my bag did contain the measure of my time on earth: a laptop, a modestly priced suit and a spongebag. An email inbox full of e-tickets, hotel reservations and conference timetables. An experience composed of forgettable trade fairs and forgettable leisure in forgettable hotels. No memory track. Until now.

"Look," Dee said.

The Gallery Room was halfway down a corridor that led to the Vista and Garden rooms. Our presence had triggered the lights as far as the door, but the rest of the path stayed dim. As we stood and waited for Hilbert to appear, the lights we had woken one by one returned to slumber until only those in our immediate vicinity remained at full power, a little island of light. But Dee was not alerting me to this phenomenon. She was facing the other way, toward the overlook. There, the lights were coming on, one by one. But nothing was there to trigger the motion sensors.

"What's doing that?" I said. Uncertain energy sloshed within me as I wrestled with the impossibility of defending myself against an invisible assailant.

"I don't know," Dee said. "Could be . . . "

She trailed off. I stared at her. "Could be what?"

"A warning. Think like a building. How do you say, 'Something is coming'?"

"Maybe we should move," I said. I took a few steps down the corridor, toward the Vista room. No unseeable force.

"That way? Toward the—whatever?"

"This is the way." I beckoned to Dee, but she remained rooted, indecision written all over her.

Behind her, in the power-save-dim corridor, the shadows thickened into slicks and oozed from under the paintings. The way we had come was swallowed by ink. The darkness swirled and thickened—it curdled and bonded. Within it, a formation, a separation of finely spaced lines, a bar code.

"Oh God," I said. "Dee . . . "

She saw the danger at the moment it became danger. Hilbert stepped from the darkness—not simply out of the darkness but born of it, coalesced in it, the dark woven into him like the black thread of his suit. In a slight, casual movement—a man indicating a particular slice of pie chart in a PowerPoint slide—he sent Dee crashing into the wall. But this act was an aside. He was focused on me.

"Not bad, Mr. Double," he said. "Leadership qualities. Fast-track potential. I'm willing to reopen our offer, for a limited time only. The hotel needs dynamic thought leaders like yourself."

"Dee!"

I need not have worried—she was upright and swinging. Her right fist met the point where Hilbert's spine connected to his skull with freight-train force. He did not cry out or buckle; his face closed in a grimace and he reared up as if electrified. It was enough to allow Dee to slip by him and join me.

"We're stuck," she said, brandishing her tablet, a starburst of cracks spanning its dead screen. "Unless you can give me an hour or two to work out some stuff on paper. I hope you know a way out of here."

Hilbert cried out, like sound itself being torn, igniting ultrasonic frequencies and sending a shudder through the hotel. I closed my eyes, and saw churning designs, glimpses of immense and horrid panoramas, titan pillars of interlaced spheres, an abstraction, but one that repre-

sented a truth, the true form of the hotel, a fractal conti-
nuity in which our whole universe might as well be a
pebble in a courtyard.

But there was no time, thank God, to reflect on what
was revealed, or almost revealed. Hilbert had regained
that thread of composure that still held him back from
undiluted, untargeted rage. My plan snapped back into
mind—though it was less a plan than a blind throw.

I ran and Dee followed, past the glass wall of the Vista
Room, filled with the dull, orange, secondhand light of
the motorway and the secret purpose of places that have
no fixed purpose, a sense of never being used and yet always on the cusp of use.

Through the picture windows, in the amber penumbra,
the steel ribs and curved glass of the skywalk.

The first-floor reception, yet to check in its first guest.
I tore aside plastic tape and sheeting. Behind us there was
a crash, the destruction of a giant pane of the Vista's glass
wall. Bulbs flared and burned out, throwing migraine
fluoro flickers. The cast-off illumination of the corridors
disappeared and left us in security quarter-light. I kicked
aside warning signs and barriers. Polythene-wrapped
armchairs lurked in the gloom.

"Dead end!" Dee shouted, unwilling to follow but ter-
rified to stop.

Beneath my feet, the carpet was different—the same
hard-wearing, high-traffic fiber, a similar gray, but flecked
with yellow—a distinction impossible to make out in the
sodium shade.

But I had seen it before, in the MetaCenter. I knew it
was there.

We were entubed in the skywalk. It rose gently as it

crossed the motorway, and at the summit of this rise, above the central reservation, was the break: a twenty-foot drop onto concrete and crash barriers and speeding juggernauts. A yellow plastic membrane covered the hole, pulsing obscenely from the wind's movements beyond.

The tempo of the traffic was the steady, fast beat of the small hours, not the constant heavy roar of the day. But while it could be heard, it could not be seen: the lower half of the glass tube was frosted to obscure the view. The idea, perhaps, was to make the skywalk true to its name and show only the sky, so conference-goers could imagine themselves drifting through the heavens without being disturbed by the reality of the heavy-duty infrastructure that made their seminar, their espresso and their muffin possible. As long as they could ignore the constant bellowing of it, and I knew they could, with their meaningless prattle and performance laughter. I hated them, I hated them all. They had been churned into a mass by their environment; they had let it happen, becoming an industrial sludge to be processed in industrial facilities.

In the thunder of the motorway there was another gathering sound, a splitting shriek with an unmistakable note of triumph. Rushing up behind us came the darkness, limned with improbable chroma, gasping with overloaded bandwidth. Pulling it like a parachute was Hilbert, his eyes the standby diodes of Hell, his skin awash with sweat and blood, erupting with lesions, the flesh vehicle collapsing under the supernatural forces being conjured through it.

"The bottom line," he said, words hissed through dripping, fraying lips.

"Here we are, Hilbert," I said, failing to conceal my

fear. Dee kept glancing to the end of the skywalk, and I could sense her calculating the survival odds of a jump. I knew those odds were poor. "No more running. Nowhere else to go."

Come closer.

"Negotiation is a thrill, but in the end there always has to be a decision," Hilbert said, advancing, plainly savoring his approach. "No more tricks or tactics or breaks. You are no longer dictating terms. Due diligence is done, the books are open. Are you in or out?"

As I had suspected, the wild sensation of potency, of influence, that had been gathering within me since donning the pinstripe suit had dissipated with our arrival on the skywalk. It was gone. This wasn't the endlessly flexible and rewarding inner hotel, that glorious, vigorous, unquenchable labyrinth. It wasn't even the outer hotel.

I wanted to be back in the hotel. I wanted that feeling, that capability. I wanted to be back inside Way Inn. Always.

Dee was staring at me. I was, I realized, not answering—I was undecided, and she knew it. Courage was leaving her expression and with it whatever faint affection she held for me. I was losing her, and I wanted her back. More than I wanted the hotel.

"In or out?" I said. "Hilbert, I'm already out. So are you. This isn't Way Inn. We've left the hotel."

If Dee and I were above the central reservation, Hilbert had reached the inside lane, a National Express coach-width away.

He stopped, flexed his hands, looked down at them. The darkness had receded, sucking back into the hotel, leaving him behind.

"Unresponsive," Hilbert said. "Can't . . . "

Without a sound, a terrible wasting took hold of him—he thinned, his body reducing to a wire outline under his suit, then little more than a two-dimensional image. "My God," he breathed, the lines in his face multiplying and deepening, his eyes sinking into shadowed sockets, their fire extinguished, his hair graying and withering. In a second he aged six decades.

"Way to go," I said, giving my best service-industry smile.

In obvious panic, Hilbert wheeled back toward the hotel and took a couple of frail steps down the incline of the skywalk. The effort of that modest maneuver was too much for his drastically impoverished body. He crumbled; he did not fall or break apart but simply disintegrated. His suit lost cohesion along the line of every white pinstripe, separating into a mass of black ribbons that writhed around the diminishing man within, consuming what was left. Faint UV trails snaked out of the resulting heap and streamed together, neat and parallel, back to the first-floor reception, seeking corners and edges.

I ventured toward the black tangle that was all that remained of Hilbert. The ribbons were profoundly fragile, nigh weightless, already further deteriorating to graphite dust from the touch of a draft. An incinerated video tape, scorched residue needing nothing more than a stiff broom. A faint smell of acetone.

"Did you know that would happen?" Dee said. She stayed where she was, as close as possible to the yellow plastic barrier.

"No," I said, returning to her. "Not exactly. I thought tricking him out of the hotel would deprive him of his special abilities. Weaken him. Give us a straight fight. Not this."

"Liminal space," Dee said. "He didn't see the exit because there was no exit. No threshold. He didn't realize the extent to which the world has adapted itself to Way Inn."

I smoothed the jacket of my suit, an action Dee watched with odd intensity. I wanted to be jubilant, but her manner stopped me.

"So that's that then," I said, wanting to prompt some recognition from her of what we had achieved. "All over."

"Not quite."

She thrust out her arms and grabbed my shoulders. For a second I thought she was about to embrace me, but her seriousness was all wrong, threatening, and she grabbed with force.

"What—"

In a fluid, practiced movement, she stepped past me, hooked her leg behind mine and, pushing from the shoulders, knocked me to the floor. Any protest I might have made was stifled by the air again being forced from my lungs. The eruption of agony in my side was so severe I felt consciousness waver. She straddled me, pinning my arms. A hand into an inner pocket of the leather jacket.

The steak knife emerged, streaked with Hilbert's blood. She must have taken it from my jacket when I changed clothes. It was raised it over me, point down.

"What the hell are you doing?" I gasped. Somehow I freed an arm from under Dee's knee and with it grabbed her wrist, staying her hand.

"You hesitated," she said. There was no emotion in her words, it was nothing more than a plain statement of fact. "In or out, you didn't know."

"I was scared! I couldn't think straight!" She was strong, stronger than I was, and she had gravity and poise on her side. As she shifted her weight she sent paralyzing waves of pain through my chest. And at just the moment I wanted to prove my lack of temptation to Dee, to myself, I found I yearned for the power the hotel gave its servants.

"You wavered."

I wavered. My arm buckled and the blade came down. I closed my eyes.

I opened my eyes. No impact, no pain. Impossibly, she had missed. The knife had gone under my armpit, into the space between my chest and left arm, piercing only my jacket and the carpet.

Pushing down on the knife, Dee cut with it, opening a long tear in the back of my jacket. She then stood, grabbed the jacket by the tear, and pulled. More tearing, more pain from my ribs.

"It's ruined," Dee said. "Take it off. We're getting rid of it."

I sat up, cowed, and slipped the jacket off my shoulders.

"Trousers too," Dee said, working the knife into the seam that connected one of the sleeves to the jacket, amputating it. "All of it. You have a change of clothes, don't you?"

I nodded. A damp suit, but also the travelling clothes I had arrived in, the outfit I had been wearing when I first saw her in the bar. Those would do. I undid the fly and slipped off the trousers. Dee took them, stood on one leg and, holding the other leg, started sawing through the crotch with the knife.

"That's a disturbing sight," I said, dressing.

"Castration imagery got you down?" Dee said, raising an eyebrow. "It's for your own good."

"Not all that reassuring."

Once the suit was no more than shreds, Dee pierced the yellow membrane and cut a slit into it, revealing the constellation of white lights adorning the MetaCenter. She stuffed the remains of the suit through this hole, more mystery rags for the roadside. Then she turned to me and made a "hand it over" gesture.

There was no doubt what she wanted. I gave her the black keycard. Without ceremony she bent it back and forth until it snapped and flung both pieces out into the rain-streaked motorway air.

We stood in silence. Not silence, not with the song of articulated freight beneath our feet, but with no words. Then Dee took out her own keycard, the white one, broke it apart like mine, and it, too, disappeared through the hole, along with the steak knife.

"Souvenirs are for serial killers," Dee said.

The ill-mannered breeze that elbowed into the skywalk through the tear in the plastic scattered the fine black particles that marked the spot where Hilbert had ceased to be. The sky above us was primed for dawn.

Crystalline cubes of pulverized safety glass scrunched underfoot as we returned through the first-floor lobby. Panels of drywall had been crushed and heavy furniture tossed aside by Hilbert's final charge. I paused to straighten a painting.

"This had better not end up on my bill."

"Maybe we should leave another way," Dee said. "We have many exits to choose from. Where's home for you?"

By the time we reached the lobby of the Royal Docks Way Inn in East London, breakfast was being served in the restaurant. As suits queued up for their sausages, more suits waited at the front desk. Trestles were set up, scaly with laminated credentials. Flat-screens scrolled through schedules of talks and seminars in the business center.

"Well, this is my stop," I said.

"For home?"

"For a start. Then the emergency room, I think. Then I might visit my mum. How about you?"

"I might as well leave here as well. Been awhile since I've been to London. If you don't count ExCel, Earl's Court, Olympia, Heathrow, Gatwick, Stansted . . . "

"But you have somewhere to go?"

She fixed me with a mocking look. "I've got three postgraduate degrees and four years' salary in the bank. I'll be fine."

"Won't Way Inn want you back?"

"I don't think so. I think Way Inn has achieved exactly what it wanted to achieve. Two unreliable servants gone at once. You, however—it might miss a promising prospect like you, if it's capable of regret."

"No. It lost three unreliable servants at once. I think it knew that. I've changed."

"I know."

"It'd be great to see you again some time."

"Maybe I'll give you a call."

"I'd like that." Was there any more to say? All around

us was the self-satisfied human meshing of the first day of a fair: the hellos, the hugs, the shrieks and backslaps, boasting and teasing. Jokes known by their punch lines, haka of feint and dodge. In that froth of reunion, we were saying good-bye.

"Are you going to the station?" Dee asked.

"This is what I hate most of all," I said. "At the end of an event, there are all these people you half-know from spending a few days with them and you say good-bye to them. But you're all going in the same direction: check-out, bus, airport, train . . . you run into the people you've just said good-bye to, and you have to linger in their company while you wait for the shuttle to arrive or for your bags to come around the carousel. There's no fixed point where you can say a proper, real, final good-bye. You can't make a clean break, it's all smeared out."

"Liminal."

"Quite."

"And what you want is a proper, real, final good-bye?"

"A proper one, yes. From you, however, maybe not a final one."

Dee smiled. Then she hugged me, firmly and warmly, her chin cupped against my shoulder. My ribs howled complaint and I didn't care.

"Good-bye, Neil."

"Good-bye, Dee."

She released me, but was still looking over my shoulder. "Isn't that your friend?"

I knew exactly who she meant before I turned to see. Maurice had been queuing at the front desk, three bags attached to different parts of his body, brow shiny with sweat. He was leaning out of the queue, looking at us, mouth slack. When he saw my face he gave an open-mouthed smile and darted toward us with surprising speed.

"Neil! What a delightful surprise! Or is it? A surprise, I mean—of course it's a delight!"

"Hello, Maurice. Nice to see you. How have you been?"

"How have I been?" He ostentatiously examined his watch. "In the, what, twenty-four hours since we last met? Not much to report, old thing. Same old, same old. You look like you've been in the wars—she been beating you up?"

"No, we . . . " I looked to Dee, but she was gone. My heart stopped and raced at once. But she was gone, gone from my side, gone from the lobby. No lingering.

"Away like a grayhound," Maurice said, seeing my astonishment. He winked at me. "I'm beginning to take it personally."

"We had just said good-bye."

"I'm sure you'll run into her again. Always the way with these things. The usual suspects. I take it you're here for the conference?"

It was impossible to answer. All I could think of was Dee's voice, her face.

"No," I said. "No, I'm not."

Never was Dee more beautiful than when she gazed deep into the patterns and tessellations of the hotel. In those moments she lost the wariness and hardness that had built up during years alone. She lived for harmony and recursion. Not to leave something incomplete.

Maurice creased his brow. "So what are you doing here?"

I smiled at him. Nothing. That was the answer. Nothing left to do but leave.

"I'm checking out," I said.

ACKNOWLEDGMENTS

I owe my agent, Antony Topping, far more than just thanks. His advice and moral support have shaped and buttressed this book since its earliest stages. I'm grateful also to Chris Wellbelove at Greene & Heaton and Jim Rutman at Sterling Lord Literistic in New York. At Fourth Estate, Mark Richards put his faith in the book and made excellent edits; Nicholas Pearson guided it toward publication with much kindness. Thanks also to the rest of those on the publishing side at Fourth Estate and elsewhere: Stephen Guise, Michelle Kane, Tara Hiatt, Anne O'Brien, Jo Walker and, at Harper Perennial in New York, Barry Harbaugh.

James Bridle and I had several useful conversations about conferences, stock photography and network unreality. And he gave me "wet polymers." More prosaic information was gleaned from *Meetings and Incentive Travel* magazine and the Economist Intelligence Unit's 2009 report *The Austere Traveller,* some of which is quoted in Part One. My former employers Christopher Turner and Daren Newton were kind enough to grant me a three-month sabbatical, and indirectly contributed to research by putting me in a lot of hotels. James Smythe and Lee Rourke read an early draft and gave me helpful notes.

The seed of the idea probably came from Rem Koolhaas's essay "Junkspace." J. G. Ballard, the greatest writer of the twenty-first century, was here first—the swimming pool is for him.